Finding Will

Escaping the Past: Book Three

by

Suzie Peters

First Published in 2017
by GWL Publishing
an imprint of Great War Literature Publishing LLP

Produced in United Kingdom

ISBN 978-1-910603-41-3 Paperback Edition

GWL Publishing
Forum House
Sterling Road
Chichester PO19 7DN
www.gwlpublishing.co.uk

Dedication

For S.

Chapter One

Will

"I'm not happy about this." I've said it three times now and Jack's still not paying the slightest bit of attention. But then he doesn't have to; he's my boss.

"Your happiness is not my problem, Will," he says. That much has been obvious for months. "We're getting nowhere right now and we need to find out who leaked the information."

"I get that." I'm not stupid, although the way he's looking at me, it seems he thinks differently. "But you seriously want to put cameras on six of our agents? *And* you want me to hack their cell phones?"

"Yes. And it's not something I *want* to do. The hardware's being put in place as we speak. All I'm telling you to do is monitor it. By your standards, that's a walk in the park."

"*All* you're telling me to do? I know these people, and they have a right to their privacy, Jack."

He gets up, walks around his desk and stands in front of me, like I'm meant to feel threatened by him, or something. It's not working. "And the people on the streets have a right to feel safe in their own homes; they have a right to believe the men and women who are employed to protect them are doing just that – not selling their country's secrets to the highest bidder." He sounds like he's reading from a script. He puts his hands in his pockets. "You've been real quick to forget what happened," he adds. That bit didn't come from any damn script.

"No, I haven't," I snap. How could I forget? The memory of that day will haunt me until I die.

"So the lives of three of our agents don't mean anything to you?"

Now I stand up and it's his turn to feel intimidated. I'm a couple of inches taller than him, at least fifteen years younger and a lot fitter. "How dare you!" I bellow at him. "You weren't there. You didn't have to listen to the whole thing going to shit... I did."

He swallows and takes a step back. "Sorry," he mutters and goes back around to his seat. "Look, I understand that you're not happy, Will. But this is happening with or without you. And I really need it to be with you, you know that. I've got no-one else. You've been on this since the beginning." *Yeah, don't I know it.* "You're the best man we've got, so don't let me down when I need you most. Nobody inside the department can know what we're doing. That's why we're meeting here and not at the office." He looks around his study. The wall to my right is lined with photographs of him, glad-handing various dignitaries, grinning at the camera, and the one behind me is full of books that I'm fairly sure have never been touched, let alone read. Between us is an enormous oak desk, with a red leather inlay, which matches his red leather chair – personally I find it grotesque.

"I'd worked that much out for myself." I sit back down and put my head in my hands and he takes this as a sign of my acceptance of the position he's put me in.

"Now," he says, leaning forward, "I'm sending someone to help you."

"What?" I look up at him. "What do you mean?"

"Will, you can't monitor all the devices we're talking about on six subjects, twenty-four hours a day, for an indefinite period. It's not humanly possible."

"So you think you can just send someone to live at my house for an 'indefinite period' instead?" He nods his head. "Like hell you can."

"Do you have to argue about everything?"

"Why can't you just set them up remotely too?"

"There's the minor detail that you've already got an incredible set up at your house, so why waste the department's money duplicating it...

Plus there's less chance of any further leaks," he says. "If you're working together, in the same room, there'll be no comms to intercept."

"You think I can't set up secure communications between me and another agent?"

"I didn't think one of our own would sell us out, Will…" He doesn't need to finish that sentence.

I take a deep breath. "Okay, okay. Who is it?"

"A new operative."

"Oh, great – this just gets better. You're sending me a rookie?"

"A rookie with a Master's in Analytics from Northeastern."

"The same as me…?" I'm impressed.

"Yes. You'll make a good team."

"And this rookie… you expect them to stay at my house, do you? What if it's not convenient?"

"Like I said, I need watertight security on this, and it's not a big ask, Will. It's not like you don't have the space, now your brother's moving out."

I sometimes forget they know my life better than I do.

"I meant, what if it's not convenient for them?"

"It is," he replies.

"It looks like you've thought of everything."

"That's how it tends to work, yes."

"Hmm… when it works." He raises an eyebrow at me. "When can I expect this whizz-kid rookie, then?"

"I'll text you all the details when I get into the office," he says. "The flights haven't been confirmed yet."

On the plane home to Boston, I sit back and close my eyes. I'm determined not to remember that afternoon in August, even though my ears still ring with the sound of the explosion, and the screams of agents, maimed and dying… made worse because I was remote from it, listening in, watching the cameras, seeing and hearing it all unfold and unable, helpless to do anything about it. Someone had warned the terrorists we were targeting; they'd got out, and booby-trapped the house… Of the five guys who went in, three died, one lost a leg, the other had superficial cuts and burns, but he hasn't worked since and none of us are sure he ever will. Despite everything Jack says, it's not a day I'll ever forget.

Since then, on Jack's instructions, I've been working on my own at home, trying to discover who leaked the intel. Someone must have… but I've not been able to find out who, in the nearly four months since that day. This plan of his to spy on the only six people who had enough knowledge of the op to impart it to the terrorists, doesn't sit well with me. I'm going to be listening to and watching them at home and at work, with their families, their wives or husbands, their kids. It feels wrong… especially as I've got no information telling me that any of these people are responsible, which means I think we should start to look elsewhere. I've already told Jack this; I've been telling him the same thing for weeks now, but instead it seems we're doing the opposite. We're focusing everything on people I'm convinced are innocent… I just need to work out why.

Of course, one reason behind it could be the stone cold certainty I've got in the pit of my stomach that this rookie is coming to have a long hard look at me. I told Jack right from the beginning that no-one should be above suspicion; now it seems that, on this point at least, he's decided to listen. Yeah, it needs more than one person doing the surveillance, but they don't have to do it from my house; they can do it from anywhere. Whatever Jack says, secure comms can be arranged, and my equipment isn't that expensive. If it was, I couldn't have afforded to put it into my place at my own expense. I'm being set up… I've become one of the targets. Jack can't get cameras into my house, so he's doing the next best thing and putting another agent in instead.

I think I just got the nudge I needed to help me toward a decision I've been contemplating for a while now – even before the explosion and its aftermath… namely to get out. I can't keep doing this job. It's too destructive.

When we land, I make my way to the parking garage and turn my phone back on. I've got two messages. One's from Jack:

— Expect Jamie Blackwood approx. 2pm Tuesday. Jack

Well, at least it won't interrupt the weekend, and I'll need that time to prepare. I don't bother to reply to him.

The other message is from my brother, Luke.

— *Everything's moved. Dinner our place (new place), 7pm. I know you're busy. Please try. L*

I check my watch. It's four-thirty. I can easily make it. I tap out an answer to him.

— *Sure. I'll bring wine and beer. W.*

He replies immediately.

— *Good. Megan will be pleased – to see you, not so much about the wine and beer ;) L.*

I pull up outside Luke and Megan's home, alongside his new Range Rover. He drove one in Europe in the summer and, when he needed to change his car, decided this was what he wanted. I haven't had a chance to drive it myself yet, but it looks good, especially in black.

I stand and stare up at their house for a moment. Even in the dark, it's beautiful; although right now, I think every light in the house is switched on, so it's not all that dark around here. It's a wooden-clad Colonial property, with a wrap-around porch, an amazing eat-in kitchen, and four bedrooms, near Belmont. They brought me to see it a couple of weeks ago, because Luke wanted me to see that it's not too far away, to reassure me they'll still visit and I can call in anytime, and stay over if I want to. He's the most incredible brother. He's cared for me since the day our mom died and I owe him everything, including the house he now insists I now call my own. He bought it about six years ago, when his friend – well, our friend – Matt made him a partner in his firm. I then made it secure, adding the systems I wanted and the fencing and gates and, over the last few years, we've done a lot of work on the interior of the property, which we've paid for jointly. But he knows I can't afford to buy him out, so rather than sell it and force me to live elsewhere, he and Megan have moved out of the city, to get the size home they want for them and their new baby, Daisy, who's due in about three months' time.

The door opens and Luke comes down the steps to greet me.

"Will… You okay?" he asks.

I nod my head. "Sure."

"How was the flight?"

"The flight was fine… it was the meeting that sucked."

I open the back door of my Jeep and get out two bags, one of beer, one of wine, handing the beers to him. "I don't suppose you're gonna tell me about it," he says, because I'm renowned for not telling anyone about my work – for obvious reasons. We start walking toward the house

"For once, I might," I tell him and he stops and turns to me.

"Has something happened?"

"I can't tell you what's happened, but I need to talk to all of you about something that's going to happen."

"This sounds worrying," he says, and we start walking again.

"Much more so for me than for you," I mutter as I follow him up the steps and into the house.

The front door opens onto a wide hallway, with a staircase in the centre, leading up to a galleried landing. To the left is a huge living room, which I know has doors at one end leading out onto the porch, but which is currently full of boxes; to the right is the kitchen, which goes through to the dining area, set in a fully glazed sun room, and then the deck is beyond that. In the summer, this is going to be spectacular. We go through, to find Megan standing by the island unit, her hand on her now obvious bump. She comes round and gives me a kiss on the cheek.

"Hello, you," she says. She's beautiful… maybe even more beautiful now than ever. When I first met her, I'd just got back from that disastrous assignment. She was very newly pregnant with Luke's baby, but it didn't show then, and she was stunning, but now – she's positively glowing with the expectation of motherhood. I put the bag I've been carrying on the countertop and look around.

"This is lovely," I say to her.

"Isn't it? Matt and Grace are picking up dinner on their way here."

"And Todd?"

"He'll be here soon. He called about twenty minutes ago."

Luke puts the beers on the countertop and goes to stand behind Megan, bringing his arms around her and kissing her neck. She leans back into him and I look away… Luke is very openly affectionate with Megan, and I find that awkward… maybe even embarrassing. I know it's my problem, not theirs, but that doesn't make it any easier.

Matt and Grace arrive just over half an hour later, roughly ten minutes after Todd. I'm not sorry he's here – being the lone single guy would have been difficult, especially as Matt and Grace are just as doting over each other as my brother and his fiancée. Grace has become a really good friend to me since she got together with Matt; she's a really good listener and I can tell her just about anything – although there are some things that I'd never discuss with her. I'd never be able to. These are the things I've never even told Luke, so how could I possibly tell Grace?

She's nearly as pregnant as Megan, although I think she looks more so – her bump is more rounded; and while they unpack the food onto the table, the two of them discuss how Megan's going to decorate the nursery upstairs.

Todd comes over to me. "We're better off free and single," he says.

"Absolutely," I reply, because it's what's expected, and I clink my beer bottle against his.

"Yeah, right. Like you two wouldn't really love to have what we've got," Matt says, grinning at us. He's right. Now I've seen how happy he and Luke are, I'd love it – I don't understand it – but I'd love it… Still, it's not going to happen – not for me.

The girls call us over for dinner and we all sit around the table, dishing up the food onto earthenware plates, which – together with the wine glasses – seem to be the only things Luke and Megan have unpacked.

"So, Will," Luke says once we're all settled, "tell us what's going on…"

Everyone looks at me and I can feel myself redden. I hate being the center of attention. "What's this?" Grace asks.

"I went to see my boss today," I tell them, taking a bite out of my spring roll.

"Right," Luke says.

I finish chewing. "I'm sorry, guys, I can't tell you what we talked about, but the result of it is I've got someone coming to stay at the house for a while."

"What for?"

"I can't tell you that either. It's just part of an ongoing assignment. I need some help with a job I have to do."

"And how long is 'a while'?" Luke asks.

"As long as it takes."

"So basically you're telling us you've got a strange guy coming to stay with you for an indefinite period of time?"

"Yeah, that about sums it up."

He glances at Megan. "You okay with that?" he asks me. He knows I'll find it hard sharing my space.

"I wasn't really given a choice."

"What's he like?" Todd asks.

"I've got no idea – he's new to the department. I guess he's quite young, though, since this is his first assignment. Apart from that, all I know is he went to Northeastern, like me, and his name's Jamie... oh, and he's arriving at two on Tuesday."

Grace is looking at me. "Why are you telling us?" she asks. "You don't normally talk about your work. I mean, even if one of us dropped by, the very worst we'd assume is that you had a friend over."

"Or a boyfriend," Todd says, smirking. They've never seen me with a woman, so I guess it's a natural assumption to make.

I look at him for a moment, then Luke says, "And that's precisely why Will wanted to tell us, I guess... Because the cop in the corner can always be relied on to jump to the wrong conclusion."

"It's a habit I have," Todd replies, and winks at me.

"No, guys, the reason I'm telling you is that I need you all to stay away from the house." I need some time alone with this guy to see what he knows about me, what his instructions are, and what he's going to do about it. I don't tell them that part.

"How long for?" Luke asks. "Not indefinitely, surely."

"No, probably just a few days... I'll call you when you can come over." I look at him. "I know you've still got the pass codes and your key; and I wouldn't normally mind you just letting yourself in; but for the next few days, can you just… not."

"Sure." He doesn't ask for an explanation, because he knows I can't give him one.

After the meal, I excuse myself and go to the bathroom. On the way back, I take the chance to have a better look around the house, which is perfect for Luke and Megan. It's not as large as Matt and Grace's place, but Luke wouldn't want that anyway. They've bought some new furniture, which I know is being delivered tomorrow, and then they've got a lot of unpacking to do. I'm so engrossed in looking around, that I'm not paying attention to what's being said as I walk back into the kitchen.

"… But that's just what I meant," Todd's remarking. "And, in any case, there's nothing wrong with being gay, is there?"

"Who's gay?" I ask, and they all turn to look at me.

Megan stares at Luke. She looks a little startled, and he glares at Todd, then says, "I… I was just starting to tell the story of how Megan thought I was gay."

"What?" I say, starting to laugh. "When was this?"

"When we first met," he replies, smirking a little.

I look at Megan. "You seriously thought he was gay?"

"I think it's quite an easy mistake to make," Matt puts in, laughing.

"Thanks for defending me." Megan smiles at him and gets up to start clearing the dishes.

"But…" I'm lost for words. How anyone could think that Luke Myers, serial womanizer – before he met Megan, that is – could be gay, is beyond me. "Why? How?"

Luke looks at me for a moment, then grabs Megan around the hips and pulls her down onto his lap. "She didn't understand why I wasn't responding to a few women, who were throwing themselves at me…"

"So she thought you were gay?" I'm still struggling with this concept.

"Well, I was fighting my attraction to Megan at the time," he says. "But she didn't know that, so I guess it didn't make sense to her."

"And that just makes me seem so conceited… You're making it sound like I assumed you'd be attracted to me," Megan says, nuzzling his neck.

"The man's got a pulse, hasn't he?" Todd says and Luke turns to him.

"And?" he says, smiling.

"Just saying…" Todd shrugs.

"Just saying what?" Luke stands Megan up again and gets to his feet. I can't help smirking at the idea my brother could be jealous – even if only in jest. It's just not his style.

Todd stands as well. They're about the same height; they're both very useful with their fists. I'm not getting between them and from the looks of it, neither is Matt. He's sitting, holding Grace's hand, a broad grin on his face.

"Just saying, I wouldn't have fought the attraction, that's all; I'd have gone with it," Todd says and moves the chair to one side so he can make a quick getaway.

"Yes…" Megan's voice is still quiet as she puts her arms around Luke and kisses him. "But the difference is, you wouldn't have got anywhere." And everyone laughs… even me.

Jamie

"Are you going to be alright with this?" Scott asks me, for probably the tenth time. "I mean… It's Boston."

"Yes, I know that – I told you about it, remember?"

He looks at me. "I'm just concerned about you," he says defensively.

I stop packing and go over to him. He's leaning against the wall, just inside my bedroom door. "I'm sorry," I tell him. "It'll be fine."

"But you haven't been back there since…"

"I know." I put my hand on his arm. "And it'll be fine."

He shakes his head. "And if it isn't?"

"It will be. Stop worrying about me. It's not your job."

"You're my sister, of course it's my job." I'm touched. "So, how long will you be away for?"

"I have no idea." I go back across to the bed and carry on packing. "I'm sorry, but I may not be back before Christmas."

"That's okay," he says and I look up. He's grinning. "I was going to ask if Mia could come over for the holidays anyway, once her exams are over. She can't afford the fare to get back to her parents' place and I don't like the thought of her being all by herself."

"No, of course you don't." I smile at him.

"So, she can come?"

"Yes, she can come." He walks over and hugs me.

"Thanks, sis… And can I have a few of the guys around for a party… or two?"

"Scotty…" I pack some extra socks in my case… I remember Boston being really cold in December.

"Please. I promise we'll behave."

"Hmm." I hold up two sweaters – one's blue and fluffy, the other pink and more delicate. "Which one?" I ask him.

"Can't you take them both?" he says. "They're real pretty."

"I'm flying, not driving. I've got two others already, but I can't fit much more in."

"Blue, then…"

I do as he suggests. Scott has good taste.

"And the party?" he pleads.

"Alright…" I say. "But I have neighbors, so keep the noise down; and no-one – no-one, Scott – is allowed in my bedroom. Do you hear me?"

"Yes. I promise, no-one will use your bedroom. Not even to sleep in." He smirks.

"I suppose I should take a dress," I say. "If I'm there for Christmas…"

"A dress? Are you sure?" He looks at me.

"I do wear them… occasionally."

"But I didn't think you did anymore." He stops speaking. "I haven't seen you——" he mutters.

"You're right," I say. "I'll take my black pants and the pink sweater instead. It's probably safer."

"No," he says. "Take a dress, if you want to. If they can't handle it, that's their problem."

"I'm not sure any of my dresses fit anyway," I tell him. It's an excuse – but a valid one. "I'm still a little bigger than I was before…"

"So, buy a new one when you get there. They do have shops in Boston, remember?"

"I'll take the pants anyway, just in case."

"What about your exercises?" he asks. "You won't have your bike…" He nods at the exercise bike in the corner of my room.

"Maybe I'll find a local gym…" I say, packing my purple sports gear.

"You haven't used a public gym since you left the hospital… that's why you bought the bike." He's right. We both know I won't look for one, and I'm just packing the shorts and top the sake of appearances.

"Well, hopefully I won't be gone for long enough that it'll make a difference," I tell him, although the thought of how much pain I'll be in has occurred to me too.

He comes over and stands next to me. "I'll miss you," he says. "I only got here yesterday, and you're leaving tomorrow."

"Yeah, and your girlfriend is coming to stay in a few days… you won't even notice I'm not here."

He smiles. "She doesn't make pancakes like you do."

"That's only because I've been making them longer… and I use mom's recipe. If you went home occasionally, you could have mom's – they're even better."

"But then I'd never get to see Mia – or you."

And he'd argue with dad, like he usually does, but I won't bring that up now.

"I'll make some for breakfast tomorrow," I tell him. "I'm not leaving until ten."

"Hmm… that's worth getting up early for."

"You mean you wouldn't have got up early just to see me off?"

He looks at me for a moment. "Nah…" he says, grinning. "I've got a lot of sleep to catch up on."

"Well, thanks for that."

"Anytime." He sits down on my bed next to my case. "Why are you going?" he asks.

"You know I can't tell you that."

"No, what I mean is why do you have to go to Boston instead of working from your office. It's a bit dumb, if you ask me... they just gave you an office, and now they're sending you away. It doesn't make sense."

"Of course it doesn't make sense – it's the government. And I still can't tell you why. It's just the way it is."

"It's not dangerous, is it, Jamie?"

"No. I'm just gonna be sitting in a room, looking at screens all day." That's not strictly true, but he doesn't need to know the other reason I'm going, and I can't tell him anyway.

"In Boston?" he asks.

"Yes, in Boston." I don't tell him that I've spent the last four days installing cameras and listening devices at various addresses around Virginia. Scott doesn't like to think of me doing any actual field-work, so I never mention it... it's not like that's the bulk of what I do anyway. It's just on this occasion, no-one else could do it, because no-one else is allowed to know what's going on; Jack Fielding was adamant about that.

"And this guy you're going to stay with... what's he like?"

"I've got no idea – except he went to Northeastern, like me." I haven't had time to read his file yet. Jack only handed it to me an hour or so ago, together with my unofficial instructions: to find out if Will Myers has a reason to sell out his fellow agents.

"You're staying at his house, though, right?"

"Yes."

"Does he have a family?"

"I don't know. I'll find out when I get there." *Or when I read his file, assuming I get to do that before I arrive.*

"Well, if he doesn't, and he's single... and he tries anything..."

I smirk at him. "I won't call you, Scott... You'll be too busy with Mia."

He grins up at me. "Fair point," he says. "But…" A shadow crosses his face.

"I can take care of myself, you know."

"Call me?" He sounds concerned. "If you need to talk."

"Yes, I will."

"Can we go out to dinner?" he asks. "As it's your last night…?"

I really should read this file, but I guess I can do it on the plane. "Okay. But we can't be late back."

Scott enjoyed his pancakes this morning. I didn't have any. I hate flying at the best of times, but when I woke up and saw the gray clouds, I decided that eating wouldn't be a good idea. I was right. I managed to survive the flight, but only because I had nothing in my stomach. I didn't get to read the file though; I was too busy trying not to be sick.

I've picked up my rental car, a horrible bright green Chevrolet Spark, which is tiny, but sufficient for my one suitcase and me. I put some music on, plug Will Myers' address into the SatNav, and set off.

There's a fair amount of traffic, but I'm familiar with the roads, and I make good time, getting to his house at just before two. At least the SatNav says I've arrived at his house, but all I can find is a high wall, with a huge solid metal gate… This can't be it, surely?

Chapter Two

Will

I've cleaned the house, made up the bed in the guest room, stocked up with beer and food, been out and bought an extra chair for the office, and installed sensors in all the rooms. They're not cameras – that wouldn't feel right – but if this guy's going to be prying into my private business, I at least feel I have to right to know whereabouts he is when he's doing it. In terms of the job, I've got nothing to hide, and I don't intend to hold anything back from him, but it's my home. Being as he's a rookie, I very much doubt he'll be any good at this anyway; so the next few days could even be fun. Well, I would have said it was going to be fun, but something happened this morning which has kind of put a dampener on everything… I broke my mom's watch. What I mean is, it's my watch – or it was – but she gave it to me. It was the last thing she gave me before she died, it was the only thing I had left of her, and it's now in more pieces than I want to think about… So I'm not going to think about it, because that's generally how I operate. If something goes wrong, or I'm unhappy, or uncomfortable, avoidance usually works best for me. Well, actually, mentally and physically shutting down is what works best, but at times like this, that's not really practical.

I'm killing time by setting up the screens. Twenty-four cameras have been deployed. I don't have twenty-four screens, so they're split, with six of mine each showing four different views at once. This works well, because each of our 'suspects' – for want of a better word – has a screen to him, or herself. The cameras have been well placed – whoever did the installations did a good job. There's one in each person's kitchen, living room, bedroom and office and they all have speakers attached – and, for once, they all work. Last night, I stayed up and hacked their phones, and that's all set up too, so as soon as Jamie arrives, and we've dealt with the fact that he's been sent here to spy on me, but that there's nothing for him to find out about me, he and I can decide on how we want to divide the shifts and we can get down to the real work.

The buzzer sounds, bringing me back to reality. He's here. I switch over one of my spare screens to the camera outside the gate and see a disgusting green colored Chevy Spark. I guess the company wasn't running to anything too expensive in the line of rental cars, then. The window's wound down.

"Can you show your ID?" I ask. I can't see the guy's face as he leans back into the vehicle.

A hand appears, waving a badge at the camera, blocking my view of everything. I can't really see the badge clearly, but it'll do.

"Okay. Come on in." The gate slides to one side and I switch off the screen and get up, closing the office door behind me... It's force of habit, even though Luke doesn't live here any more. I make my way to the front door, double-checking on my way that everything's tidy – well, tidy enough, anyway. I didn't go overboard, in case it made him think I was trying to hide something by being a little too 'perfect'.

By the time I reach the door and open it, the green monstrosity is parked up next to my black Jeep, and the occupant has already climbed out. He's bent over, leaning back into the car, but I'd swear... I mean, I'm no expert, but I'd swear that's not a man. I'd swear that's a woman's behind pointed in my direction. Men don't fill out jeans quite like that – in fact, I don't think I've ever seen a pair of jeans look quite that good. I'm still distracted by that thought, when the owner of the behind, and the jeans, in question stands up, and turns... and I was right. It's not a man. It's very much a woman... She's got long, straight light blonde hair, a fresh tanned complexion, and is probably around five foot seven, with pale blue eyes. As well as the jeans, she's wearing black Converse, a white t-shirt and a long chunky gray cardigan, which she wraps around herself against the cold wind.

"I'm sorry," she says. Her voice is soft and a little throaty. "I dropped my ID under the seat." She comes toward me. "I'm Jamie," she continues, holding out her hand. "Jamie Blackwood." I take her hand. "And you must be Will?"

I realize I haven't actually said anything. "Yes," I mutter. "You're…" Jeez, I was about to say 'a woman'. How dumb would that sound? "Early," comes out of my mouth instead. *Because that's so much better, Will.*

"Oh… sorry," she says. "Is that a problem?"

"No." Could I make more of a fool of myself? *Definitely.*

"Good… I really don't want to have to get back in the worst colored car in the world, just to drive around the block for a while," she smiles up at me. Her pink lips part, showing perfect white teeth and her eyes light up. And suddenly, from out of nowhere, I'm hard… I'm actually consciously hard, for the first time in over a decade. I'm not counting getting hard in my sleep, or waking up with an erection, because that has nothing to do with a considered thought or reaction to an external influence… *What the hell?* I'm staring at her, and I'm aware I'm thinking about the fact that I'm hard, and what that means for me, and I'm not thinking about the fact that I haven't said anything for probably two full minutes.

"Do you have a bag?" I manage to say at last.

"Yes, I'll get it."

"No, let me. Is it in the trunk?"

"No, it wouldn't fit. It's on the back seat." I go to the rear door and open it, pulling out her sizeable case. I'm not surprised it wouldn't fit in the trunk of this tiny car. "I didn't know how long I'd be staying for," she explains, as I lift her case into the house.

"I'll show you to your room." I close the front door behind her and lead the way down the corridor to our left and into the guest room. The decor in here is neutral, unlike Luke's old room, which is completely white, and mine, which is gray… very gray. Here, we used creams for the walls – in two different shades, the bedding is a stone color, and the sofa at the end of the bed is dark blue, as is the throw which lies across the bed. I point to the door in the far corner of the room. "The shower's through there," I tell her. "I'll leave you to get settled in."

"Okay, thanks," she says, and I go – quickly – before I can make even more of an ass of myself.

I sit at my desk, staring at the screens, not even seeing the images on them. All I can think about is that Jamie isn't a guy; Jamie's a girl. A girl whose smile just made me as hard as steel... Just her smile, for Christ's sake.

I closed my eyes and my mind to girls, and to sex, and to everything associated with girls and sex, when I was fifteen years old. So that's almost fourteen years of ignoring any thought even vaguely related to anything below my waist... blown to pieces by a single smile. The problem isn't that I got an erection – I can probably handle that – it's a biological reaction after all. No, the problem is working out what to do about it... or do I mean *with* it? No, I definitely mean about it. See, I can't even think straight... This is not good news.

"Hello?" At the sound of her voice, I shoot out of my seat, nearly knocking it over, and go from the office into the kitchen.

"Hi," I say. "Sorry, I should have shown you around properly." She's standing on the threshold of the kitchen and she's taken off the cardigan... and I kind of wish she hadn't. Now she's just wearing the jeans and white t-shirt, I can see she's got an amazing body to go with that incredible smile. I make a concerted effort not to get hard again. The problem is, my cock isn't listening to me right now.

"No, it's fine. I just didn't know where you were."

"In the office," I say, staring at the floor... anything to avoid looking at her breasts straining against the material of her t-shirt, or her firm thighs encased in tight denim...

"Oh. Can I see?" She walks over

She's going to get very familiar with this room while she's here; she may as well start now. "Sure," I say and I stand to one side to let her enter.

"Wow," she says, looking back at me. "This is all yours?" I nod my head. She moves forward, leaning on the back of the new chair. "May

I?" she asks. I nod my head again. I really need to try actually speaking. She sits, looking up at the monitors. "The cameras are all working then? I was worried I might get something wrong – it's not a part of the job I'm used to doing."

"You put them in?" I pull my own chair back and sit next to her.

"Yes. I mean I was trained, obviously, but this is the first time I've done it in the field."

"I assumed Jack would get someone…"

"More experienced?" she finishes my sentence for me.

"Well, yeah, to be honest."

"He said no-one else could know." She's staring at me. "Why? Did I get it wrong?"

"No. They're perfect. I'm impressed."

"Phew!" She grins. "I'd hate to screw up on my first assignment."

"You didn't. I've been configuring everything this morning."

"So I see. I'm impressed too." She's still staring at me. I should feel uncomfortable, and I normally would, but I don't. I feel pleased that she's impressed by me… how juvenile is that? But then how juvenile is it that I just spent five minutes ogling her? Feeling her eyes on me now, it's like she's appraising me, and I can't help wondering how I appear to her.

Eventually, she looks away. "I assume we can hear through these?" Jamie pulls on one of the sets of headphones in front of us and flicks a couple of switches, but her face is blank.

I reach across her and my arm brushes against hers. I feel my cock hardening again… This could get boring, if it wasn't for the fact that I'm so intrigued by her and by my reactions to her. I turn up the volume a little. She turns to me and smiles, mouthing 'thanks'.

Then she sits and listens for a while, and I wonder how she feels about the other part of her role here: checking up on me. She may be a rookie, but now I know she installed those cameras, I no longer have any doubts about her ability to do her job. It's just as well I'm innocent, because I'm a little concerned at how easily she'd be able to find out my secrets, if I was willing to let her.

Jamie

Will's house is incredible. It's high-tech, functional, masculine, but somehow beautiful at the same time. All of that pretty much describes the man who owns the place too.

He knows what he's doing, that's for sure; his set up is the best I've seen outside of a government building. His office isn't huge, but it's modern and well equipped. In the center is a long, wide semi-circular desk, with two chairs, one for each of us. On the wall in front of us is a series of monitors, I guess around twelve of them in total, and on six of them are images displaying the surveillance video feeds. Two of the other screens show outside views of Will's house – one of a deck, and the other of the cars – and the other four are currently blank. There are three desktop computers, two laptops, and the listening equipment, all set up on the desk. He's clearly very professional; he's spent a long time getting everything ready, that much is obvious… and on top of that, he's utterly and completely gorgeous; the original tall, dark and handsome – with glasses, just to add an air of mystery and intellect. He must be just over six feet tall, very muscular, with thick dark brown hair that just skims the neck of his t-shirt, and the deepest, deep blue eyes I've ever seen. The kind of eyes you could just fall into… and I haven't wanted to fall into anything with a man for a long, long time. I need to stop this, right now, and remember I'm here to do a job, and part of that job involves finding out if he's got any secrets. And now I've met him, I'm even less comfortable about that than I was before.

I'm listening to one of the live feeds. I've flicked across two silent channels – the properties are both empty, the subjects concerned are working at their desks in their offices… and now I'm hearing a couple – a man and a woman – arguing about a paint color. He wants something called Spa Blue, and she's in favor of Friendship Yellow, evidently. *Who the hell thinks up these names?* I check the screens in front of me and see them, standing in their living room. The man's probably in his mid-thirties, with blond hair. He's got his arms folded across his chest, very defensive; his wife, or girlfriend, is pretty, and dark haired...

Will's writing notes, and eventually he puts down his pen and leans back, and I pull off the headset.

"What's going on?" he asks, staring at me. His gaze is inquisitive, like he wants to ask me a question, and can't work out how.

"Just listening in on a little domestic discussion," I reply.

"Where?"

"Subject three." He looks up at the relevant screen.

"What are they talking about?" he asks.

"Paint."

"Paint?" He smirks.

"Yes. They're decorating. He's taken the afternoon off work, as far as I can tell, for them to go and buy paint... but they're arguing about the color. Why do you ask?"

"It's just the look on your face."

"What about it?"

"You looked amused."

"So would you, if you'd just been listening to this." I smile across at him. "I feel sorry for this guy. His girlfriend..."

"That's his wife," Will interrupts.

"Okay... well, let's just say she could strip the paint off the walls with her voice alone." He chuckles. "But, she's gonna win the argument."

"How do you know that? He might be very persuasive – or bossy."

"Because she wants to paint the room yellow; and he wants it blue."

"And?"

"And I remember that room from when I planted the camera in the light fitting. The drapes are green; they'll never go with Spa Blue."

"Spa Blue?"

"Yeah... but then she wants Friendship Yellow."

"Well, they both sound awful to me." He smiles. "Did they say anything else?"

"Nothing repeatable... or relevant." We sit for a moment. "Why can't we know their real names?" I ask him.

"I do know their names," he replies. "I've prepared dossiers on each of them, with personal and background information – but no names – to help you out." He reaches forward and pulls several files toward me.

"Thanks... but why I can't I know their real names? Why are they just numbers?"

"Not my decision," he says, returning his gaze to the screens. I can tell he's not happy. *Just like me, then.* His eyes have turned an even darker blue. The intensity is astounding. "Do you want a coffee?" he asks.

"Um... sure, but why don't I come and help make it and then I'll know where everything is. You can't wait on me forever... Not that I'll be here forever, of course. I mean..." Oh, God. I'll just dig a hole and start burying myself now. He's blushing and I'm sure I am too. Except he looks cute when he blushes...

"Right," he says eventually and we both get up.

"We don't have to watch the screens all the time then?" I ask as we go into the kitchen.

"No." He gets a jug from the cabinet above the sink, and uses it to fill the reservoir of the coffee maker that's standing in the corner of the countertop. "Everything records," he says. "Whatever we miss, we can catch up on later."

I look at the back of his head, while he measures out the ground coffee into the machine and switches it on. I'm confused now. "I'm not being rude, but in that case, why am I here?" I mean, I know why I'm here, but he doesn't, so why would he agree to me coming into his home, knowing my services aren't required. It doesn't add up. "If you can record everything and watch it later, you don't really need me, do you?"

He doesn't bother to turn around, but I see his shoulders rise and fall, like he's sighing deeply and trying to hide it. "Not even I can watch the live streams and play back the recorded footage simultaneously. I do need to sleep occasionally," he says.

"Oh, yeah... of course."

"Besides," he adds, "who knows what Jack's motives are."

My head shoots up, but he's busy fetching mugs from the cabinet and milk from the refrigerator, and I wonder whether he really knows what

I've been sent to do. I can feel my palms sweating. I knew I couldn't do this… who the hell was I kidding that I was ready for this kind of assignment? I'll never be ready for this – it's too underhand; too dishonest. It's just plain wrong.

We take our coffees back into the office and he closes the door. It feels confined, but not in an altogether bad way. We're sitting right next to each other and, if I'm honest, there's a part of me that likes being this close to him.

All the screens are quiet, except one, which shows a woman cleaning a kitchen. It's quite late in the afternoon now. I guess most of our subjects are on their way home, and it being just a couple of weeks until the holidays, some of them may be catching up on Christmas shopping.

"We've only got eyes and ears on them when they're at home, or in their offices," I say after a while. "What about when they're out, or in their cars?"

"I've hacked all their cell phones," he replies. "And before you say anything, I know it's wrong." He's staring at the computer screen in front of him.

"I wasn't going to say that. Who am I to judge?"

"Yes, but you don't know these people. To you, they're just a number on a screen, one through six. To me, they're people. I've worked with them… for years, in some cases." Yeah, just like he's a real person to me, and I've got to go through his things, check him out, spy on him. It's not a good feeling.

"They're friends of yours, aren't they?" I ask, remembering to talk at last.

"Not friends, colleagues."

That's an odd thing to say. "Even so, it's bothering you, isn't it?" I ask him, because it clearly is.

"Yes. It's intrusive."

"I know. I don't like it either." There. I've said it. He might not know what I'm talking about, but at least I've said out loud that I'm not happy doing this.

"That's the problem though, isn't it?" he says. "We have to spy on people, even when we're fairly sure they've done nothing wrong…" My mouth drops open and I close it again quickly. "You see," he adds, "I don't think any of these subjects had anything to do with the leak…"

I put my cup down carefully on the table and twist in my seat to look at him. "Excuse me?"

"I don't think any of them did it," he repeats.

"Why not?"

He looks up at me at last. He seems miserable. "I've been investigating all of them – backgrounds, habits, bank accounts, families, you name it – for the last couple of months, and I can't find anything… *anything* at all that suggests it's any of these six."

"Then why are we—?"

"Because there's no-one else, I guess." He's looking into my eyes… and, for once, it feels safe to let someone get that close to me. "Jack's convinced the leak must have come from the inside – and I do agree with him on that – which means it has to be someone who worked the case. Apart from me, that only leaves these six." He nods toward the screens.

"It wasn't you, then?" I ask, hoping he won't notice my hands are trembling.

"No, it wasn't, Jamie." The sincerity in his voice is breathtaking.

He keeps staring at me just for a moment, then he looks away. He picks up the headphones in front of him, places them over his ears and flicks a switch on the panel in front of us. He might not be happy about it – I might not be happy about it – but this is our job and we've got to find out which one of these agents is responsible, before they do it again.

By six-thirty, all the subjects are back home and we're both busy listening in. I've got subjects one, two and three, the last of whom have finished discussing the paint – the wife won the argument while they were out and the decorator is starting on Monday, using the yellow. Good choice. I got bored with their conversation, and her voice, and flicked over to subject one and his girlfriend who cooked a meal together, and, while eating, have agreed that they won't go to her parents' for Christmas, because he doesn't feel he can handle her mother for the whole day. She took it well – maybe she doesn't like her mother much either. Subject two – according to the record Will's prepared – lives alone, but has a girlfriend. I can only assume he's meeting her tonight, because he's spent so long in the bathroom, it's beyond a joke, and now he's trying to decide on which shirt to wear. Just choose the white one – if she's going to rip it off you anyway, what does it matter?

Will takes off his headphones and stands up, stretching. His t-shirt rides up a little, revealing a hint of toned, muscled stomach beneath, and a little tiny part of me wants to lean over and kiss that strip of flesh. I smile to myself. I haven't felt an urge like that in years… I wonder if maybe it's finally time to lay that ghost to rest.

He stands next to me for a moment, like he's waiting for something. I look up and he's staring down at me. I pull off my headphones.

"I made a lasagna earlier," he says. "I'll go and heat it up… dinner in thirty minutes?"

"Oh… um, sounds great." I get up too. "Can I do anything?" We're right next to each other and I can feel the heat from his body warming places inside me I'd forgotten existed.

"No, you're fine. I mean, if you want to shower, or anything, then go ahead, but I can handle dinner." He moves to the door and opens it, and a draft of cold air passes into the room.

"Wow, it's cooler out there," I say.

"Yeah, I forget how warm it gets in here," he replies.

"Why don't you leave the door open then?" I ask.

"Force of habit," he replies. "When my brother Luke lived here, it was the rule. If the door was shut, he knew he had to knock, so I could turn off the screens. If the door was open, he could come in."

"But he's not here now, is he?"

"I know. Like I say, it's a habit."

And I get the sense Will's a man who likes his habits… his ways. I'd like to get to know them, maybe understand them – and him – a little better.

"That was amazing," I tell him, placing my knife and fork down on the empty plate. I'm not just being polite either. It was a really good lasagna.

"The secret's in the meat sauce," he says.

"You mean you have a secret recipe?" I ask.

"Yeah, something like that." He smiles across at me.

"Okay…" I smile back. "Well, I've got some thumbscrews in the car… I'll go get them, and torture it out of you."

He leans forward. "You could do that. Or, if you really wanna know, you could just ask." His eyes are on mine and I suddenly get the feeling we're not talking about lasagna anymore.

"And you'd tell me?"

"Yes."

I swallow. "I'm not sure how comfortable I'd feel having your secret recipe just told to me," I say.

"You'd rather torture it out of me? Or maybe sneak around to discover it?" he asks, still staring.

"No. I think I'd rather just not know. Some things are best kept secret."

"Hmm… But sometimes we just *have* to know… don't we?" he says, and his eyes soften… and I know he knows. He knows exactly why I'm here.

Chapter Three

Will

"Do we?" she asks. This cryptic discussion could get confusing, especially as I think we both know what we're really talking about.

"Have you read my file?" I ask her outright. She's so clearly unhappy with the whole idea of spying on me, I can't let it carry on any longer.

"No," she says. She's not looking at me anymore. It's like she's ashamed of herself and, not for the first time, I really hate Jack for putting someone in a position like this, especially someone like her.

"Why not? I know why you were sent here and that's the first thing you should've done."

Her head shoots up and she stares at me. "How do you know why I'm here? Jack told me you hadn't been informed..." She's biting her bottom lip, like she's worried, although it's kinda sexy... *Focus, Will.*

"Because I'm not an idiot. Jack thinks I'm the leak... To find out for sure, he needs a way in here. You're it." Her eyes widen. "So... why didn't you read my file?"

"I didn't have time. I was only briefed late yesterday, then I had to pack, the flight was awful and I couldn't read on the plane... I just haven't gotten around to it yet. I was going to do it tonight..." Her voice fades to a whisper.

"Okay. Well, read it through and feel free to ask me any questions you have in the morning."

"But..."

"But what?"

"It feels wrong," she murmurs.

"It is wrong. But it's your job. It's not your fault."

"I don't want to do this, Will."

"If you don't, Jack will just recall you and find someone else to send instead…"

"And I might feel better about that."

I want to tell her that I wouldn't, but I can't. "You've got no reason to feel bad about this," I say.

"So, why do I feel like such a traitor."

I look at her. "Because you're a good person," I say at last.

"You don't know me," she says. "How can you know that?"

I shrug. "I just do." I need to move the conversation on. "Now… As well as the file, you'll want to have a look around, I guess."

"No," she says.

"Yes. If you don't, Jack will want to know why not." I get up. "Come with me." She hesitates, then stands and I take her along the hallway, opening the first door on the right. "This was Luke's room," I say. We go inside.

"It's very… sterile," she says.

"Maybe because he's taken all his personal belongings, and the couch."

"And because it's white… I mean, apart from the carpet, everything's white."

I wonder what she'll make of my room. "He won't mind you looking around," I say, then turn and go back out into the hallway and along to my own room, which is opposite hers. I open the door and switch on the light.

"This is my room," I say, standing aside to let her enter.

She goes inside and looks around. The walls are pale gray, the carpet a shade or two darker; the bed, which is off to the left, is covered with mid-gray sheets. Basically, it's all gray. I point to the two doors in the right hand wall. "The dressing room and bathroom are through there," I say. "Feel free to look around; go through the drawers, closets… under the beds. Go wherever you need to." I turn to face her. "I've got nothing to hide, Jamie. Nothing at all. Read your file by all means, but it won't tell you everything. Only I can do that… We'll talk tomorrow."

I step around her and go out of the bedroom and down the hallway again, through the kitchen and into the office to check the room sensors. She's gone straight back into her own room already. Maybe she's decided to read the file first; then search our rooms. I shrug. I'm not in the mood for sleep anyway. I can wait.

Two hours later, she's been from her room to the kitchen and back, probably for a drink of something, but hasn't gone near either mine or Luke's bedrooms. I'm getting tired, so I leave the office, go back to the kitchen, stack the dishes into the dishwasher, set it running and go back along the hallway. Luke's door is still open, but mine has been closed and there's no light under Jamie's door, so I guess she's gone to sleep.

I go into my room and sit on the edge of the bed, wondering whether she's going to search in here tomorrow, or never; and what she found in the file.

Jamie

I stood outside Will's room, watching his retreating back until he disappeared into the office and only then did I turn and go into my own bedroom, silently closing the door.

There's no way I can go through his things. Well, not yet anyway. I need to read the file and see if there's any reason for me to pry into his private life. If I can't find anything suspicious in his record, I'm not going to look any further; and Jack can go to hell.

I sit, with my back against the propped-up pillows, open the file and start reading:

Will was born William Myers, nearly twenty-nine years ago. He has one brother, Luke, who is three years older. His mom, Annie, died – no, she killed herself – when Will was twelve years old. I drop the file onto my lap and lean back on the pillows, closing my eyes. My own privileged childhood comes to my mind, and I'm struggling to imagine his life, compared to mine. I take a deep breath and pick up the file again. His dad, who shared his name, was an alcoholic, who died twelve years ago. I put the papers to one side and sit up. Does Will drink? At dinner, he had a glass of wine – but so did I, so that doesn't mean anything. I get up, and quietly creep out of my room and down the hallway.

In the kitchen, I go through he cabinets and the refrigerator. There are beers, and a couple of bottles of wine. That's it. There's no hard liquor anywhere. There aren't any cupboards I can see in the living room, so unless he's got a very secret place to keep his alcohol, I think I can assume he doesn't have a drink problem. Besides, he doesn't act like he does…

I return to my room, close the door again and resume my seat on the bed.

He went to Northeastern, three years ahead of me, did the same course and – dammit – got better grades. He's worked in the department for four years, with not a black mark against him. In fact, he's regarded as the best there is in his field. I wonder for a moment why Jack is wasting Will's obvious talents on basic surveillance. It seems odd, but I don't know enough about the case. I flip the page.

This is the part Jack warned me about. He told me to pay very careful attention to this aspect of Will's life. I scan the page in detail. It's all about Luke, Will's brother, who became Will's legal guardian when he was fifteen. At the time, Luke was only eighteen, and Will had just moved in with him, although there's no reason given here for that. I sit forward, reading avidly. He's not done anything illegal that I can see, but according to this file, he's a womanizer. *My favorite type of guy.* Maybe he's the weakness… If he's slept with the wrong person at some time… If they've got some hold over him, perhaps? If there was anyone Will would help out, it'd be his brother… Maybe Jack was right.

I pull out my laptop and search for 'Luke Myers'. Immediately, I'm faced with a series of images. I have to double check the search and re-do it, but sure enough, the same results come back. How odd… He's like the exact opposite of Will. Where Will is dark, Luke is fair. Will has brooding, slightly sad eyes. Luke's are sparkling, devil-may-care. I have to admit, he's incredibly handsome, but there are no images of him with women. He's either alone, or pictured with another man… slightly taller than him, with short dark brown hair. They seem to laugh a lot – in nearly every picture, they're either smiling or laughing, fooling around.

I go back to the web search, and look up his company interests. He owns a twenty-five per cent share in Inspirit. Well, the file didn't mention that… I'm not a fanatical keep fit person. I exercise because I have to, but I always wear Inspirit clothing. It's the most comfortable sportswear I've ever come across. However, that's the limit of my knowledge. So, I look them up. The other shareholder is Matthew Webb. He's a multi-millionaire; the company is a huge success, with an eye-watering turnover. They've branched out into lingerie, using the brand name of Amulet, but as it's a recent innovation, I can't find out much about it. I go onto their website, just to see what kind of things they produce. If it's anything like their sportswear, it'll be good – expensive, but good. I'm not disappointed. The first picture that comes up is of the most beautiful woman I've ever seen… she's quite literally breathtaking, and she's standing in a field of sunflowers. It looks like it's early evening, judging by the light, and she's wearing a shimmering gold and silver kimono, with a matching bra, thong, garter belt and stockings. I know it wouldn't look anything like as good on me as it does on this incredible looking woman, but I immediately want to own everything she's wearing. Mainly that's because of the look on her face: she's staring just beyond the camera, slightly to the left, and, looking into her eyes, I feel like she's found the secret of true inner happiness. I sigh… I know it's only photography; I know it's all smokescreen and mirrors, but for a moment, I envy her. I guess that's the feeling they're trying to evoke, though – they want their customers to buy into the lifestyle… to want to be that woman… to have whatever it is that she's got.

I click off the window and look back at the file. I haven't found anything yet that convinces me beyond any doubt that Luke is the weak link in Will's life… the link that might make him betray his colleagues and his country, but I'll have to check him out further. I can't ignore the nagging doubt Jack planted in the back of my mind. I wish I could, but I can't.

Chapter Four

Will

"I've made breakfast," I tell her as she walks down the hallway, already dressed in just jeans and a t-shirt. I guess she got used to the office being warm yesterday. Out here though, it's cooler and her nipples are hard, peaking through the thin fabric. I drag my eyes away with some reluctance, remembering why I found it so hard to sleep last night. She's here... that's enough of a reason. "It's just scrambled eggs and toast, with bacon on the side. Is that okay?"

"It's better than okay. I'm starving."

"Good." I lay the plate in front of her as she sits down.

"Tea or coffee?" I ask.

"Coffee," she replies. "But you don't have to keep waiting on me. We should probably share the cooking, and the chores."

"Cooking, okay. Chores... we'll see. It doesn't feel right."

"What, so I can make a mess, but I can't clear it up?" she says, taking a forkful of eggs.

"Something like that."

"Not happening."

I sit opposite her and pour out the coffee.

I don't want her to feel awkward and I hate atmospheres. We need to get this over with. "Did you read the file?" I ask, pushing the cream toward her.

She puts her fork down gently, her face paling a little. This doesn't look good. "Yes," she replies.

"And?"

She takes a deep breath, then licks her lips. I really wish she hadn't done that. It makes me focus on her tongue, when I need to be concentrating on our conversation. "Tell me about your family," she says.

"What do you want to know that isn't already in the file?"

"Does anyone ever call you William?" She smiles and her eyes sparkle a little.

"Not if they expect me to answer." I don't say any more.

"Oh. Okay."

"Next question." I know she thought she was asking an easy, slightly humorous question to start out... little does she know.

"Um..." She's flustered. I don't like it. Seeing her uncomfortable because of me makes me uneasy.

"There's a lot about my life that isn't in the file, but you're gonna have to ask me about it. I'll tell you anything you want to know, but it isn't easy for me to just talk about. Ask me questions and I'll answer them..."

"Tell me about your brother," she says quietly.

"Luke?"

"Yes."

I stare at her for a long, long moment, until she looks down at her plate. "If you're thinking he's a weakness for me... that his life, or rather his past life, offers some kind of motive for me to sell out, you need to think again," I tell her.

"But, he..." She looks up at me again.

I stand slowly. "Forget it, Jamie" I say, keeping my voice calm, although I'm anything but calm on the inside. "Luke is not the man you think he is. I imagine my file says he's a serial philanderer. Well, he was, but he's also a good guy... One of the best. He always was, even when he was sleeping around. Whatever he may have been or done in the past, he's not that guy anymore. People change. He's engaged now; they're expecting a baby. He's happy; and he deserves to be." I lean forward, resting my hands on the table. "Whatever ideas you've got in your head, forget them. And leave Luke alone. Go after me, if you really think you must – I'm fair game – but leave him out of it."

I push my chair back and go into the office, closing the door quietly.

My phone is on the desk and I pick it up. I don't think, or hesitate. I bring up Luke's details and wait for the call to connect.

"Hey," he says, answering after the second ring, even though he's at work. "Everything okay?"

"Yes and no."

"Can you elaborate?"

"No."

"Great. Nothing changes."

"Sorry."

"Hey, it's fine." His voice is serious. "Are you alright?"

I don't answer him. "Can you come over?" I ask.

"Sure. When? Now?"

"No. Tonight. Bring Megan. I'll cook."

"Okay. So the coast's clear already, is it? Is there a reason for this visit?"

"Yes, but I can't tell you what it is."

"Oh. This should be fun." I can hear the smile in his voice. "Should we wear costumes – act like spies or anything?"

I laugh, just a little. "No, you idiot."

"Damn. And I was so looking forward to dressing Megan up as a Bond girl."

"A pregnant Bond girl... I think that'd be a first."

"Well, it works for me, but then I've got a great imagination." The smile in his voice has changed to a smirk. "What time do you want us?" he asks.

"Seven? Oh, and the guy who's here... it's not a guy... it's a girl."

"Oh... is that the reason you need me to come over?"

"No. I'm just warning you, that's all."

"Okay. Anything else I should be warned about?"

"No," I say. "Nothing at all." I just want him to be himself.

"See you tonight."

Because I'm used to the closed door meaning 'keep out', I'm surprised when it opens half an hour later, and Jamie walks in. She's brought us coffee, which she puts on the desk in front of me, as she sits down.

"I'm sorry," she says.

"Don't be."

"I had no right…"

"You're doing your job, that's all. And before you ask, I'm not just saying that. It's how I feel."

"Well, right now I don't much like my job."

"No. I know."

We sit quietly for a while. "You're very close, aren't you? You and Luke, I mean."

I turn to face her. "Of course we are. That's hardly surprising, really, is it? Considering what happened…"

She hesitates. "Do you mean what happened to your mom?"

"Mainly." I take a sip of coffee. "What does the file say?"

"That she committed suicide."

"And that's it?" She nods her head. "Well, that doesn't even begin to cover it."

"Can you tell me about it?" she whispers.

"I said I would… if you asked me."

"I'm asking."

"Why? Because you think I'm guilty of something?"

"No. Because I want to know. I want to understand."

"Okay." I take a deep breath. "What the file doesn't say, because I've never told anyone at work, is that it was me who found her."

"Oh my God."

I ignore her. I can't look at her, so I stare at the edge of the desk, focusing on it while I speak. It's a technique I employed when I was in therapy. I found if I focused on something else in the room, it was like I was talking to myself and no-one else… It made it easier. "She was in the bath, naked," I continue. "The water was red. I don't remember much else, except hearing myself screaming, and screaming. And then, all of a sudden, Luke was there. He hauled me out of the room, literally dragged me away. He closed the door and sat with me on the floor, cradled in his arms, rocking me like a baby. I'd lost her... At the time, I felt it was my fault, because I couldn't wake her.

"I don't know how, but he got me into my room, and stayed with me until I went to sleep – probably out of sheer exhaustion, I guess. The next thing I knew, it was morning. The bathroom was cleaned, my mom's body was gone, and Luke was there, sitting beside me... and I couldn't talk. It was like there was nothing left inside me." I close my eyes for a moment. "I stayed silent like that for about a year and a half, I guess. I lived entirely in my own world... I went to school, I came home, did my schoolwork, ate whatever Luke put in front of me; that was about it. And Luke slept on my bedroom floor the whole time. He didn't leave me. He dropped me at school each morning and picked me up each afternoon; he went and spoke to my teachers, made sure they watched me. He did everything for me... And then one day, I just asked him why we were having chicken for dinner again... We'd had it the day before, and I didn't really want it again. I don't know what made me ask, except I didn't want the damn chicken. He told me if I ate it, he'd make me spaghetti the next night. Spaghetti was my favourite, you see... And then he gave me a hug, and we just kind of got on from there, really." I look up at her face. There are tears falling down her cheeks. Seeing her like that makes me want to hold her. I've never wanted to hold a woman before, but I want to tell her it got better... because it did. Then she gets up, and goes to the door; and the moment passes.

"But he was only fifteen when your mom died," she says, looking back at me.

"Yes, I know. It took me years to realize that and to see that, while he was doing everything for me, there was no-one there to help him. I owe him everything," I tell her. "And I know you think that makes him my weak link, but there's nothing in his life for anyone to hook into... and I'll prove it to you."

"You don't need to," she sniffs.

"Yeah, I do. He's coming over tonight, with Megan, his fiancée."

"What?"

"I'll show you there's nothing behind your suspicions – or Jack's suspicions – because that's where they've come from, isn't it?" She doesn't reply but I know I'm right. "And then you can let it drop, and we can get on with doing our jobs… okay?"

She stares at me, then opens the door and goes out, closing it behind her.

Jamie

I wipe away the tears on the back of my hand and go along the hallway to my bedroom. Once inside, I lean back against the closed door, take out my phone and call Scott.

He answers on the fourth ring.

"Hey, sis… you okay?"

"Yes," I say, trying to sound normal. "I just wanted to check in with you." *And to hear your voice and make sure you're alright, because I'm so damn grateful to have you, and I don't tell you that often enough…* I don't say any of that.

"Well, I'm fine. Getting ready for Mia coming over."

"Which is more important than college work, of course." I smile.

"Of course. How's the job going?"

"It's fine," I lie, because it's anything but fine at the moment.

"Any idea when you're coming home?"

"No, not yet, but I'll let you know."

"Okay. Mom called yesterday, by the way."

"Really?" I'm surprised.

"Yeah. She said your phone's permanently turned off."

"I'm working. She could leave a message."

"You know what she's like – we have to be guilt-tripped at regular intervals. Anyway, she and Dad are going to Florida for the holidays. She was just letting us know."

"And now we do."

"Exactly."

"I'd better get back to work," I tell him.

"Okay."

"I'll call again in a couple of days."

"Take care, sis."

"You too. Love you, Scotty."

"Love you too."

He never says that normally, but I'm glad this time that he did.

I've been sitting on the edge of the bed for ages. I really should get back into the office and do my job – well, the other part of my job; the part that's slightly less onerous than spying on my host, who I'm starting to think is possibly the kindest man I've ever met. I don't think I'd be as generous to someone who came into my home, investigating me.

Will loves his brother. He has every reason to love him; and it's obviously mutual. It sounds like Luke gave up everything to care for Will; including his own grief and I can't imagine how awful it must have been for him, dealing with all of that at the age of fifteen. I remember Scott at that age; he was into computer gaming and girls, and not much else... There's no way he could have done the things Luke Myers did, or taken on that kind of responsibility.

I go through to the bathroom and wash my face, then return to the office. If nothing else, I need to pull my weight around here.

As I open the door, Will looks up.

"You okay?" he asks, pulling off his headphones.

"Yes. Sorry."

"What for?"

"All of it. Doubting you; doubting Luke."

"It's fine. Like I said, you're just doing your job."

"You don't have to prove anything to me, Will. I believe you. I was wrong to listen to Jack. I don't need to meet Luke to know you wouldn't do anything wrong – not even for him."

"Ah, but that's where you're wrong," he says, not taking his eyes from mine.

"How do you mean?" I remain by the door. He swivels his chair around, so he's facing me.

"You do need to meet Luke… precisely because he's the one person I *would* break all the rules for."

I feel my mouth drop open.

"But…"

"Luke's my brother," Will interrupts, "and in some respects, we're no different to any other brothers; we fight, we argue… we've even come to blows when we were much younger, like most boys do… But deep down, unlike a lot of siblings, we genuinely do love each other." He pauses. "You're here to investigate me, so it's only fair that I tell you… Luke's everything to me, Jamie. If he was in trouble and he needed my help, I'd do whatever it took to help him. I'd break every rule, every law and every moral code in the book. I wouldn't do anything that would cost someone their life; I wouldn't sell out my fellow agents… I'd never do that, no matter what, but I'd do pretty much anything else to help him, or anyone else I loved." He pauses. My mouth is still open and he's got me beyond confused. "But what I'm gonna prove to you tonight, and the reason you have to meet him, is, that he'd never ask me to in the first place…"

"How can you know that?"

"Because I know Luke. He'd never put me in that position."

"How can you be so sure?"

He smiles. "Luke's the most honorable man I know… out of the two of us, he's always the better man… and he never lets me down. Ever."

"So when he gets here tonight… you're going to just ask him outright if he'd ask you to sell out your colleagues to the highest bidder? How's that going to work? He'll just say 'no', won't he?" It seems like a really silly plan to me.

"Of course I'm not." He looks away for the first time. "I'm just gonna let you spend some time with him… well, him and Megan. You'll work it out for yourself."

We've spent the whole day in here, with just a short break for lunch. My leg is killing me, but I don't want Will to notice, so I'm gritting my teeth to try and get through it. Normally, I'd move around a lot more than this, and I'd have done my exercises, had a hot bath, maybe rested up a bit… I'm going to have to work something out, if this is going to be the daily routine. If I don't, I'll end up back at the doctor's office by the time I go home. I guess I might have to face the idea of finding a gym… but even the thought fills me with fear.

"I need to start cooking," Will announces at just before six o'clock. He stretches his arms above his head. "We've done enough for one day. Let it record for now and I'll catch up later."

"You sure?" I ask, desperate to get up and move my leg.

"Yes." He stands and holds my chair steady while I do the same. My leg hurts, but my foot is numb. This is not unusual… the nerve damage was extensive. But it's been a while since it's been this bad. I flex my foot at the ankle.

"What's wrong?" he asks.

"I've just been sitting awkwardly," I tell him. "I'll be fine in a minute."

"Go and lie down for a while, if you like."

"Don't you need help with the cooking?"

"No. I've got it."

He goes to the door and holds it open for me to pass through. It's chilly and dark out here. I can't help shivering. He flicks a switch and the lights come on. "I'll turn the heating up a little," he says.

"Is it okay if I go shower and change?"

"Of course it is," he says. "You don't need to ask and you don't need to dress up, either."

I feel nervous. It shows. "Sorry," I say.

"Don't be." I wasn't sure he'd know what I'm apologizing for, but looking at his face, I realize he gets it… he absolutely gets it.

"What are you cooking?" I ask, as I come back into the kitchen. I'm still in jeans – a clean pair – with the blue fluffy jumper that Scott likes. It's v-necked, but not too low cut; just enough to hint at a cleavage, but not enough to shout about it. Will turns around and looks me up and down. I'm almost certain I can see his eyes widen and darken just a little, but then he turns back to the stove. Maybe I imagined it.

"It's chicken, wrapped in bacon, with sweet potatoes and asparagus."

"It sounds and smells delicious."

"Can you put the olives on the table in the living room for me," he asks, opening the oven door. "I just need to check the chicken."

"Sure." I pick up the two dishes of olives and put them out. He's already set the table, opened the red wine and lit some candles. I'm on my way back to him, when the front door opens.

A tall woman walks in and I stop in my tracks. I've seen her before… recently and, as she smiles over at Will, then looks at me, I recognize her. She's the model from the lingerie website… except now she's about six months pregnant. She's even more beautiful in the flesh, with long, light brown curly hair, flecked with blonde streaks. Her tanned skin is flawless. I'd assumed that was some kind of photographic editing, but it's genuine; as are her piercing green eyes. She looks relaxed, glowing, and stylish in a pretty pale blue floral dress, that comes down to her mid-thigh. It's fitted and flattering to her shape, showing off her neat bump. She's wearing a slightly darker blue cardigan over the top, with a lace collar. I'm almost sure my mouth is open and I make a conscious effort to pull myself together and stop staring. She stands to one side, holding the door, as a man follows her in. I can only see his back to start with as he's dragging something, which seems to be heavy and large.

"Where do you want this?" he calls to Will.

"That depends what 'this' is…" Will replies from the kitchen.

"It's a Christmas tree," the woman says.

"You brought a Christmas tree?" Will seems surprised. He has a point… most people bring wine, or flowers when they come to dinner. A Christmas tree seems excessive.

The man in the doorway, still tugging hard, speaks again: "Well, I usually get the tree; I figured you'd probably forget, so we picked it up on the way over. Now, where do you want me to put it?"

I'm still poised on the threshold of the living room, feeling awkward, while Will goes over to the door. "Jeez, Luke, it's enormous."

"Yeah... Megan tells me that all the time," his brother replies.

"Luke!" the woman admonishes.

I snicker and they all turn to face me, Luke standing up properly for the first time. He's wearing gray jeans, a white shirt and a black leather jacket. As my eyes move up over his muscular body to his face, I suck in a breath. The pictures on the internet didn't do him justice at all. I would never normally apply the word 'beautiful' to a man, but in this case, it really is the only adjective that works. This is a beautiful man and, as a couple, these two are perfect together. "I'm sorry," Will says, "I haven't introduced everyone. Jamie, this is my brother Luke and his fiancée, Megan. Megan, Luke... This is my colleague, Jamie."

Luke drops the tree and comes over, bringing Megan with him, his arm around her waist. He holds out his hand.

"Good to meet you," he says as I take his hand.

"You too," I reply, before turning to the stunning woman by his side. "I've seen you before," I can't help but say.

"Really?" she says, surprised. "I don't remember..."

"Oh, we've never met," I tell her. "I saw your picture on the Internet."

"Oh God, really?"

"Fame at last, darling," Luke mutters, kissing her cheek.

"No, but that's really embarrassing," Megan says, putting her hands over her face.

"Why?" I ask.

"Because that means you've seen me... well... virtually naked."

"But... surely, that's to be expected if you're a lingerie model, isn't it?"

"Megan isn't really a model," Luke says, pulling her into his arms, her back to his front. "Not that you'd know it to look at those photographs." She leans back into him and he rests his hands on her bump. "Daisy agrees," he says, smiling.

"Daisy hasn't seen the pictures," Megan replies. "And hopefully, she never will. There'll be another model next year – and it won't be me."

"No... it won't." Luke's voice is a little wistful.

"I'm still..." I begin to say.

"Confused?" Megan says.

"Well, yes."

"I only took the job for the money," she says quite openly. "And I had no idea I'd be modeling lingerie."

"What did you think you'd be modeling then?"

"Sportswear. Luke's company – well, Matt's company really – they manufacture both. Only I didn't know that."

"It was the agency's fault," Luke puts in. "Look, why don't you two sit down and Megan can tell you how we met… and how I screwed up just about everything… and Will and I can find a home for this tree."

"It's staying in the hallway for now," Will says. "At least until tomorrow. I've got to find all the decorations yet."

"Unless you've moved them, they'll be in the closet…" Luke's voice fades as he goes back outside again.

Megan links her arm through mine and leads me back down the steps into the living room.

"So, you didn't know you'd be modeling lingerie?" I ask as we both sit down on opposite sofas, facing each other.

"No… and it was very awkward when I found out."

"I can imagine. I'm not sure I could have gone through with it… Not that I've got the body for it in the first place… but in the picture I saw, you looked so happy; how did you manage that if you were uncomfortable about the whole process?"

"Which picture did you see?" she asks.

"You were in a field of sunflowers. I can't even describe what you were wearing – it was kind of gold and silver… and beautiful."

"Oh, yes. It's called Rose Gold. It is lovely, isn't it? Well, the reason I looked so happy was because Luke was standing behind the camera at the time. I was looking at him."

"Was he already your boyfriend? Is that why you agreed to do the photographs?" I'm aware I'm firing questions at her, but I'm interested in learning about Will's family, and that's got nothing to do with me investigating him.

"No… well, not really. We only met when we flew out to France for the shoot. Once it became clear I had no idea what was going on, or what I was expected to wear, he would happily have let me out of my contract, but I couldn't back out – not really – I needed the money." She lowers her voice. "And if I'm honest, I was already a little in love with him."

I smirk. "Oh, I see."

"We had an amazing summer," she says, a little dreamily.

"When was this?"

"Last June," she says.

"What, the June just gone?" I glance down at her swollen stomach.

"Yes… I brought little Daisy here back from France with me." She grins, and rests her hand on her belly.

"Yeah… and then she gave me the runaround for a while," Luke adds, stepping into the room and placing a glass of white wine in front of me and a glass of what looks like sparkling water in front of Megan. "Will's just finishing the dinner. He said this would be okay for you, Jamie?" he adds, glancing down at the wine.

"Oh, yes. That's great, thanks."

"I did not give you the runaround," Megan says to him.

He takes off his jacket, throwing it over the back of the sofa, then sits next to her, placing his hand on her thigh and giving her a light squeeze. "If you're gonna tell the story, tell it properly." He looks across at me. "We met, we fell in love." He looks at Megan for a moment. It's a look most women long to see, even if it's just once in their lives. Then he turns back to me and continues, "And Megan decided for reasons of her own, that we couldn't be together. So, we split up. But then she found out she was pregnant; so we got back together again… Only then she discovered all about my wayward past." He stops and puts his arm around her. "And not surprisingly, she had second thoughts about getting involved with a guy like me, so we split up again. But… eventually – thanks to Will and Matt – she came around. And I thank God every day that she did." He leans over and kisses her gently.

"Hmm… you call that telling the story properly, do you?" Megan says and looks over at me, shaking her head. "The bits he's forgotten to tell you are that the reason we couldn't be together initially, was that my dad was a crook – a violent crook. When he found out I was pregnant and Luke was the father, he took me to Luke's office and bribed him." I glance at Luke and he closes his eyes just for a moment, like he's reliving something painful. "Then he – my dad that is – tried to get me to have an abortion."

I can't hold in the gasp that escapes my throat.

"Luke found me," Megan continues. "And I really thought we'd be okay after that…"

"Yeah, until you found out about me," he says.

"Until I *overreacted* about you," she corrects him.

"Not overreacted, no," he says. "I wouldn't put it that way. My past was hard to accept."

"Yes, but – as you, and Will, and Matt, kept telling me – you can't change the past."

"No. You can only learn from it." She rests her head on his shoulder and they both look at me. "And that," Luke says, "is the short version of how we met, and how my beautiful girl here came to be modeling lingerie."

"That's the short version?" They're incredibly open, both in what they're prepared to tell me – considering they don't know me – and in their affections for each other. They're obviously very much in love.

"Well, we could give you the long version," Luke smirks, "but Will gets easily embarrassed." I laugh.

"What's that?" Will calls from the kitchen. "Did I hear my name?"

"No," Luke says and smiles across at me, putting his forefinger to his lips.

Chapter Five

Will

"Dinner's ready," I call. They've been talking about how Megan and Luke met, which I hope has painted Luke in a reasonably good light. I just want Jamie to see that he's a good guy; that he's honest and that he'd never compromise me in the way she – or rather Jack – seems to think.

I'm putting the dishes on the table when I look up and see that Jamie's limping. She was having trouble walking earlier, when we got up in the office, but I'd have thought she'd be okay by now… it was well over an hour ago. She's holding on to the back of the sofa, and as she moves away, she's taking as much weight as she can on her left leg. I watch her take the steps, which she manages with some difficulty.

"Are you okay?" Luke asks her. He's noticed it too.

"Yes, I'm fine," Jamie replies. "I just spent too long sitting down. I'm a little stiff."

"Oh, I see." He looks up at me. He's not buying it any more than I am.

We all sit at the table, and Luke pours the wine, except for Megan, who's having water as usual.

"This looks delicious," Jamie says. She's opposite me.

"I taught him everything he knows," Luke replies from his place beside her.

"Yeah, right," I say, even though we both know it's true.

We all start eating and everyone makes appreciative comments about the food.

"Do you like to cook?" Megan asks Jamie, across the table.

"When I get the time. I'm not saying I'm any good at it, though... I have every intention of poisoning Will, if he'll let me in the kitchen."

"I'll let you," I tell her.

"But will you let me clean up when I'm done?"

"We'll see..."

"He feels uncomfortable letting me do any chores while I'm here," she explains.

"Well, it's not right, is it?" I say to Luke. "Jamie's a guest."

"Except I'm not," she says. "I'm a colleague who happens to be staying in your house."

"Which makes you a guest," Luke adds. "Sorry, I'm with Will on this one."

I automatically look at my wrist, then realize there's nothing there. "Can someone tell me the time?" I ask.

"Yeah," Luke checks his own watch. "It's nearly eight... Why? Should we be leaving already?" He grins.

"No... I've got an apple pie in the oven. It needs to come out soon."

"You made an apple pie?" Jamie asks.

"No... I got an apple pie out of the freezer. I've been a little too busy to make pastry."

"I can't think what you've been busy with," Luke says. "But then you never tell us anything."

"Because then I'd have to shoot you," I reply.

"You've been using that line for so long... At least tell me where your watch is, or is that a secret too?"

"No. I broke it... terminally."

"Oh no, Will. How?"

I feel embarrassed, so I probably look it too. "I was fixing the new chair in the office for Jamie," I explain. "And I took my watch off because I didn't want to damage it. I put it on the desk, but it must have fallen onto the floor... And..."

"You didn't run over it with your chair, did you?" Jamie asks.

"Yes." I nod my head. "I didn't know it was there, I backed up and the wheels just..."

"Oh, God. I did that with a necklace once," she says, and I don't feel so bad, just for a moment. "It was catching in my hair, so I took it off. The next thing I knew, there was the sound of crunching... Luckily it wasn't valuable, just something I'd picked up in a market. It made one helluva mess though. Your watch wasn't...?"

"Valuable? No."

"Will," Luke says quietly. "Be honest..."

"Well, it wasn't valuable."

"Not financially, no. But..." Luke stares at me. He's not going to let it go.

"Okay." I put my fork down and rest my hand on the table. "It wasn't worth much money, but..." I sigh, "but my mom gave it to me. It's had so many new straps fitted, it doesn't really resemble the original watch at all, but... She gave it to me that last Christmas before she..."

Jamie reaches over and puts her hand on mine. Her fingers are soft against my skin, and I have to focus real hard not to respond to her touch. "I'm sorry," she says. "Are you sure it can't be fixed?"

"It's in pieces," I manage to say. "I've kept them all in an envelope in the kitchen, but... well, it's toast, really."

"Do you want me to get it looked at?" Luke offers. "I can take it with me tonight..."

"No. I think it's time I moved on from a twelve year old's watch, don't you?" I say, trying to sound more convinced than I feel. "I'm gonna be twenty-nine next year."

"Well, if you change your mind..."

I nod at him. I know he'd spend whatever it takes to fix it for me. But really, I should have a more adult watch now... I'm less bothered about it than I was. I look down and see Jamie's hand is still resting on mine and I wonder if that's why I feel better.

It's a little after ten when Luke and Megan decide to leave.

Jamie and Megan are chatting quietly by the door and Luke pulls me back toward the living room.

"So, what was this about?" he asks.

"Nothing," I say.

"Hmm." He looks at me.

"Okay… nothing I can tell you about."

"Well, if you were looking for my approval, you've got it. She's nice."

"I wasn't – looking for your approval, that is – and I know she's nice. I–I like her."

"Well, that's good," he says, sounding genuinely pleased. "And you're honestly not going to tell me why we were invited over?"

"I can't."

"Okay." He doesn't question me any further and we move to the front door.

We say our goodbyes and, once they've gone, Jamie turns to me.

"You have a lovely family," she says. I look down at her. "And I know Luke would never hurt anyone."

"I know that too. But I'm glad you liked him… and I'm glad you've seen him for what he is."

"A good guy?"

"No. The better guy," I tell her. We walk back into the living room, with Jamie ahead of me and I notice her limp is even more pronounced. "And now they've gone, will you tell me what's wrong with your leg?" I ask her.

"My leg? There's nothing wrong with my leg, except for the fact that I sat for too long today." She's looking flustered again. She's a damn poor liar, which is unusual in our game.

"Okay." I'm not going to press her; not now anyway. "You head off to bed then."

"What are you going to do?"

"I'll catch up on what we've missed on the recordings for an hour or so – it's still too early for me."

"I can help, if you want…"

"No, it's fine. You rest your leg." *The one that doesn't have anything wrong with it.*

"At least let me clear up."

"No. I'll do it in the morning."

"Okay." She seems sad. Am I dismissing her? Am I being too abrupt?

"Thanks for this evening," I add quickly.

"What for? I didn't do anything."

"Well, I had a nice time," I say. I sound pathetic, but it's true.

She smiles. "So did I."

It's only taken just under an hour to quickly run through the tapes. Nothing much has happened on any of them, so I skipped through just about all of it. Not that I'm really concentrating... Since Luke and Megan left, I haven't been able to stop thinking about Jamie. The way her eyes shimmer when she smiles; the sincerity in her voice; how well she got on with Luke and Megan, like she'd known them for years... and how great I feel whenever she's close, like when she had her hand on mine earlier. Admitting to Luke that I like her was a big step for me; now I just have to work out what I want to do about that – and how to do it.

I switch everything off and head for my room. There's no light under her door, so I guess she's gone to sleep already.

I've just opened my door, when I hear a faint noise coming from behind me... from her room. I move silently across the hallway and stand right by her door, not daring to breathe. I wonder, just for a moment, if she's dreaming... It doesn't sound like it's a bad dream; not like mine can be – at least I hope not, for her sake. I wait, but there's nothing... no more noise at all and I'm about to move away, when I hear it again. It's like a muffled, loud moan, followed by a sigh, then panting. I hear the words, "Oh, yes, yes," and I still, my cock stiffening, as I appreciate what she's doing, and the meaning of those sounds. I wait a little longer and I hear a gasp, and a long groan, then a soft, gentle whimper. I don't know how, but I know it's over.

I tiptoe to my room, go inside and shut the door. I don't turn on the light, but just sit down on the bed. I haven't thought about sex for so long, but right now, I want her more than anything. I shake my head. *Don't be stupid, Will.* I'm not Luke. I can't go across the hall and make love to her; I wouldn't know where to start.

I lie down on the bed, my cock so hard it hurts, and stare into the darkness.

How the fuck am I supposed to sleep now?

Jamie

I catch my breath and let out a small whimper of pleasure, calming, coming down to earth again… My God. I haven't done that for so long, I'd almost forgotten how good it feels… and how frustrating, when there's no-one to share it with. The problem is, now I've done it once, I think there's a strong possibility I'll want to do it again… and again. And I also think that I'll find it harder and harder to conceal the fact that Will is the person I was thinking about… the man I'd like to share those moments with.

I kinda wish I'd mastered the art of coming quietly, but I never have. Still, I'm sure he didn't hear me, not all the way from the office. I wasn't *that* loud.

I turn over and snuggle down into the soft pillows, feeling contented and, within seconds, I'm fast asleep.

I wake at eight, and instantly feel guilty. I should have dragged myself out of bed ages ago. I had every intention of getting up early and making breakfast, as a fresh start between Will and I… some fresh start when I'm already running late.

I visit the bathroom quickly, run a brush through my hair and clean my teeth, then grab my robe from the end of the bed and pull it over my short pajamas, tying it up as I walk along the hallway into the kitchen. My leg is still stiff. Normally I'd cycle for half an hour to loosen the muscles, but I can't… Oh, well.

The door to the office is open and I peek inside. Sure enough, he's in here, but with headphones on, staring at the screens, he's unaware of me. He's leaning back in his chair, his feet up on the desk. I don't want him to catch me looking at him, so I return to the kitchen, start up the coffee maker and begin a search of the kitchen. In the refrigerator I find eggs, butter and milk, and in one of the cupboards, there's a big tub of flour, some baking powder and sugar. Now all I need is a bowl, a whisk and a pan.

I open a few more cabinets, and find a large bowl and a pan; the whisk is in a drawer. I'm set. Within ten minutes, I've mixed up the pancake batter and worked out how the stove functions, so the pan's heating, and I start cooking.

"Smells good." I jump out of my skin. "Sorry," Will says, coming from the office door.

"How long have you been standing there?" I ask.

"I haven't," he replies. "But I smelt something cooking."

"Pancakes."

"Hmm. With maple syrup?"

"If you have maple syrup, yes."

"Of course I have maple syrup." He goes to the cabinet and fetches it.

"I wanted to make breakfast," I tell him.

"Well, it looks like you're succeeding."

"I know, but I meant it to be a surprise. I was going to get up early. I wanted us to start afresh, after last night."

"I thought we covered this before you went to bed," he says.

"We did, but I want you to know I believe you... more to the point, I believe *in* you."

"Fine, but that wasn't the point of last night, was it?" He's staring at me. It makes me a little nervous.

"Okay. I believe in Luke." I flip the pancakes to distract myself from his penetrating deep blue eyes.

"Good. Now, can we put all of that behind us?"

"Yes. I'd like to get on with doing our jobs and forget all the other nonsense – because it is nonsense."

"I'd like that too... but I'm not doing anything until after we've eaten these pancakes."

"Well, give me a few more minutes and they'll be ready."

I turn out the ones I've been cooking onto a plate and put them in the oven to keep warm, then start the next batch, leaning on my left leg for a while.

"You okay?" he asks.

"Yes, why?"

"You looked like you were in pain."

"No, I'm fine."

"No, you're not." He comes and stands next to me. "What's wrong?" His eyes have turned to that even darker blue again.

I close my eyes and sigh. I'm surprised he hasn't noticed, being as it's visible. My robe is knee length, after all. "It's my leg," I tell him. He glances down but I guess the angle must be wrong, because he just looks back up at my face again.

"What's wrong with your leg?"

I hold onto the countertop, stand on my left leg, raise my right, just a little, bending it at the knee, and point it in his direction. "That."

He looks down again. His face doesn't alter, unlike most people's. He doesn't flinch or pull back from the ugly scarring that disfigures the whole length of my calf and shin, from knee to ankle, the skin folded and puckered, with dark red marks tracing through what was once perfect flesh. "What happened?" he asks, his voice soft, his eyes moving back up to mine once more. It's the most human reaction I've ever had.

"Patriot's Day," I tell him.

"2013?" he says. "You were there?"

I nod my head.

"Jamie, I'm so sorry," he says.

"Why? It wasn't your fault."

"Boston's my city," he says.

"It wasn't Boston's fault either. Boston was good to me. My God, the kindness I felt that day…" And the tears start welling, as they always do whenever I think about it.

"Hey," he says, and I feel his arms come around me. He pulls me into his chest and I rest my head there. I haven't been held like this in so long… "Don't cry," he whispers.

"It's hard not to. The things I saw… they—"

"I know," he says.

"I don't mean the maiming, or the blood, or the body parts, or any of that," I say. "I mean the people who just helped each other. The man who stayed with me… I don't even know his name. He knelt beside me and pulled his shirt off, wrapped it around my leg, and then he made a tourniquet from his belt to stop the bleeding. He stayed with me until the paramedics could deal with me. He talked to me for ages, distracting me from the pain… But he didn't know me. He just happened to be walking past me when it happened. And when the medics arrived, he wandered off again… He didn't even wait to get his shirt, or his belt… I'll never know who he was."

He reaches behind me and turns off the stove. "Come," he says, leading me into the living room and sitting me on one of the couches, before lowering himself down next to me. I miss his arms, but he moves and puts one around me again and I nestle into him. "You were a spectator?" he asks.

"Yes. I was there watching my boyfriend." His muscles tense a little, but then he relaxes again, pulling back slightly. "He was a serious runner. I used to run, but I couldn't have competed in a marathon, or anything like that."

"He wasn't injured though? Your boyfriend, I mean."

"No… he was fine. He'd gone through the finish line about fifteen minutes before. I was waiting for his friend to come through. If I'd gone to find Patrick, and left Nick to his own devices, I wouldn't have been there. But Nick didn't have anyone to cheer him on… Still, there's no point going down the 'if only' route." I take a deep breath, because I did that for a long time and it got me nowhere. "I was caught in the first explosion," I tell him. "When the second one went off, a lot of those who weren't injured started running, panicking. I don't blame them for that – it was terrifying. But that's what made it all the more remarkable that my rescuer stayed with me."

"No-one knew if there were more devices." Will's voice is quiet.

"I know."

"You said you used to run," he says, "does that mean you can't anymore?"

"I can now. But I lost a lot of muscle and there was significant bone and nerve damage. It took me months before I could even walk again. The not running is a choice, not a necessity. There are a few things I can't do, like kneeling. That hurts like hell and I cycle to keep the muscles strong – or at least I do when I'm at home. I have an exercise bike in my room."

He leans away from me. "Is that why you're in pain now?" he asks, looking down into my eyes.

I nod my head. "I'd go to a public gym, but I hate them… I tried one when I first came out of the hospital. It was the most intimidating place I'd ever been in… full of skinny women, staring at me, like I had no right to be there… I shouldn't let that bother me though. I shouldn't be so pathetic."

"You're not pathetic," he says and he slides his arm out from behind me and gets up. He stands above me and holds out his hand. I look up at him and he raises an eyebrow, nodding down at his hand. I take it in mine and let him pull me up.

"Are you okay to walk?" he asks.

For a brief second, I think about saying 'no', so he might carry me, but I'm far too heavy to be carried, so I nod my head instead. I've got no idea where we're going anyway. He leads me to the front of the house, then opens a door near the main entrance. He flicks on a light switch and stands to one side, letting me pass.

"Knock yourself out," he says as I enter.

My mouth is wide open as I stare at the best equipped gym I've ever seen. I don't know what most of the apparatus is, or how to use it, but in the corner is an exercise bike. It's bigger and better than mine… but who's arguing.

"Feel free to come in here anytime you like," he says. "And if you need anything adjusting, let me know."

"Thank you." I feel the tears welling again, and one drops onto my cheek.

"Why are you crying?" he asks, stepping forward and wiping it away with his thumb.

"I tend to do that when people are kind to me," I tell him. Apart from Scott, people rarely are.

"Oh." He steps back. "Was I being kind then? I thought I was just—"

I laugh through the tears. "You were," I say. "You were being very kind."

"But I don't want to make you cry…"

I shake my head, still laughing. He doesn't seem to understand good tears… I wonder why. "Not all tears are sad," I say to him.

"Oh, okay," he says. "You should've told me sooner." He leans against the doorframe. "About your leg, I mean. I could've helped."

"I know that now," I reply. "I just don't like talking about it."

"Because of the memories?" he asks.

"No… because of the pity. I hate being treated differently, so I tend to keep it to myself."

"Well, I guess we all do that." I get the feeling that, for once, I've found someone who actually understands.

He let me cycle while he finished cooking the pancakes and kept them warm until I've had a quick shower and got dressed. Thank goodness I packed lots of t-shirts. The office gets so hot… or is it just sitting next to Will all day that makes me hot? I'm not sure.

We sit in the office and eat our stacks of pancakes with blueberries and maple syrup.

"Have we got much to listen to from last night?"

"A fair amount," he says. "And there's some from this morning now too – from when we were outside talking."

I nod my head. "Okay, I might as well get started on that and you can concentrate on the live feeds." This is the first time I've done this – until now I've just watched the live footage.

He switches on a separate monitor with its own control panel. "Just watch each feed through that," he says. "You can fast-forward through a lot of it; they'll be asleep most of the time. You're really only looking for conversations. If you look at the sound output…" he points to a smaller monitor to one side, "that'll tell you when something's happening and you can stop the recording and see what they're talking about."

"Okay." He demonstrates the controls, and I get down to work.

Just over an hour later, I've gone through the recordings for subjects one and two. Subject one and his girlfriend just slept the whole time, from midnight to six am when my recording stopped and it switched to the live feed, presumably when Will first came in here this morning. And I now understand why subject two is still single. The man could turn snoring into an Olympic sport... and win a gold medal every time. I had to turn the volume down; he was deafening.

"Coffee?" I ask Will, stretching.

"Sure," he says and goes to get up, removing his own headphones.

"No... I meant I'll get it."

"Oh, okay."

As I go out to the kitchen, I wonder if – unlike me – he's been listening to something worthwhile.

I bring the coffees back a few minutes later and set them down. "Anything good?" I say to him nodding toward the screens.

"No," he replies. "Except for the fact that I think... subject five and his wife might be getting a divorce soon." I get the feeling he was about to give away the person's real name, but he managed not to, just in time.

"Really?" I sit back down. "What makes you say that?"

"She went out last night, supposedly with her girlfriends, but he's just found a text message on her phone."

"Anything of interest to us?"

"Um... no." He blushes a little.

"How can we be sure?"

"He read it out to her... It was from her lover. It was... um... explicit."

"Oh dear..."

"Yeah. He's a nice guy too."

"Then he's probably too good for her," I say.

"Probably."

I put my headphones back on and switch on the recording for subject three. Initially there's no activity at all. Then, even though the film is playing at high speed, I see the living room door open and they come in. I notice the sound monitor spike, so I slow everything down, rewind a little and listen in. They've been out to dinner; they're discussing the poor service at the restaurant and his wife's voice is worse than ever. They sit for a while, then get up and switch off the lights. They reappear in the bedroom, and I fast-forward again. I've got no desire to see them getting ready for bed. Within a few minutes, they're settled and asleep – and they stay that way. I move on to subject four. I haven't seen this one before because I don't monitor the live feed for subjects four through six. I check the file. This is a female agent, married, aged thirty-three, no kids. I turn on the recording at normal speed to start with, and swallow hard at the sight that greets me. The woman's husband – or at least I hope it's her husband, given Will's revelations about subject five's wife – is sitting on the sofa, and she's astride him, facing away from him and toward the camera. They're both naked and he's inside her. His right hand is on her right breast, tweaking her nipple and his left hand is between her legs, arousing her. Her head is thrown back and she's clearly in the throes of ecstasy as she thrusts up and down on him. Through the headphones, I can hear her moans and sighs, his words of urging. I quickly kill the volume, and glance sideways at Will, but he's concentrating on his own screens. I'm more than uncomfortable about this… and not because it's turning me on at all – it isn't. All the other scenes I've watched have been normal parts of everyday domestic life, but this… It feels wrong. It's far too intrusive.

I don't know what to do, so I nudge Will and he takes off his headphones, turning to me.

"Um… I know I can fast-forward, but do we really have to see this kind of…" I can't finish the sentence. Will looks up.

"Shit," he says. "God, I'm sorry. I should've warned you."

"You mean you're used to looking at things like this?"

"Not used to it, but it happens. You put cameras in someone's house, you're gonna see stuff." Neither of us is looking at the screen.

"I suppose I should have worked it out for myself. So, do we just ignore it then?"

"Kind of. We ignore it if we're seeing who we expect to see…" He looks up at the screen again. "So that's fine… that's her husband."

"How do I know that though? I'm not familiar with these people. Am I going to have to ask you every time I see something like this?"

"No. His picture's in the file," Will says. He takes the file from in front of me, flips it open and turns to the second page, then passes it back to me. Sure enough, there's a picture of the guy, who's currently having a great time on screen.

"Oh, okay," I say. "I didn't realize there was a second page."

"That's okay."

It isn't. It's a rookie error, but he's kind enough not to mention that. "And if it isn't who we expect it to be?" I ask.

"Then flag it up. It could give us a motive."

"Yeah, or it could just be someone having an affair."

"That too, but we need to check it out."

"I'm not sure I'm happy about this." I close the file again.

"Good," he says. "I'd be more worried if you were."

Chapter Six

Will

We've settled into a good routine over the last few days. I go into the gym early, then shower, then Jamie does her cycling while I make breakfast. She makes lunch, because it gives her a chance to move around a little, and we take it turns to cook dinner. In between, we work together. We get along well. I keep wondering if that's because I know she's got a boyfriend now, so I feel less strained being close to her. I don't have to worry about how I react to her anymore… I mean, I still react to her – a lot – because she's beautiful, and sexy, and I can't help it, but there's nothing I can do about it, so I don't fret about what I should or shouldn't be doing. I just wait for it to pass… which it does, eventually. Well, most of the time…

We've seen several more sex scenes… mainly involving Stephanie again, although the other couples have all had sex at least once or twice. With Stephanie and Mitch, on the other hand, it's a fairly permanent state of affairs, but we're handling it.

Jamie's getting coffee and I'm watching subject five again. I feel sorry for him. This is Phil Walters. His wife left after their row the other morning, and I haven't seen her appear on the screens since. He's been in to work, acting like everything's perfectly normal; then he goes home and sits, staring at the walls. He's tried calling her, leaving messages; and he's texted her. I can see the messages. He wants her back. She hasn't replied.

I feel Jamie nudge my shoulder and I take off my headphones. "They're at it again," she says, nodding in the direction of the fourth screen. I look across and sure enough there's Mitch, kneeling between Stephanie's legs in the center of their bed. I lean forward and flick the screen off on the control panel. "Should you do that?" she asks.

"I don't care," I reply.

"She's gonna wear him out, if she's not careful," Jamie says, smiling, sitting down and passing me my coffee.

"I don't notice him complaining,"

"No, I guess not. What were you watching?"

"Number five," I reply, careful not to give her Phil's name. I nearly slipped up the other day, because I wasn't concentrating. "He's missing his wife."

"How do you know that?"

"I can read the text messages he's sent her."

"Oh... That's sad."

"They are sad... he's devastated."

"Does she miss him?"

"She hasn't even replied to him."

"I said he was too good for her."

"Doesn't mean he doesn't want her back, though."

"I don't understand how he can forgive her. I know I couldn't, in his shoes. I think people should have more self respect. If a guy didn't love me enough to be honest and faithful, I wouldn't waste my time on him."

I turn my chair to face her. "I agree with you," I say, because I do. "But people make mistakes, don't they?"

"Sure, but not like that. Sleeping with someone is a conscious decision – you can't sleep with someone by mistake."

"Okay, but what about hugging, or kissing... could you forgive that?"

She thinks for a moment. "Hugging, sure, if it's just friendly – no fondling or anything. Kissing? I don't know. I think it would depend on the circumstances." I wait, hoping she'll explain. She does. "I mean, if you kiss someone in the hope of it leading to something else, then that means you're still being unfaithful, doesn't it? The thought is there..."

"So you'd never be unfaithful, then?" *Shit!* Where the hell did that come from? Is that where I've been going with this all along? Wondering if she'd betray her boyfriend… with me?

"No," she replies. "I couldn't do that."

Well, I guess that's my answer – if that was my question.

And I guess my reactions to her aren't as clear-cut as I thought they were.

It's Jamie's turn to cook and, while she does, I finish up in the office and then find the Christmas decorations. The tree has been standing in the living room, undecorated for three days now. It looks more than a little sad.

I put the box on the sofa just as she's dishing up spaghetti with meatballs in a spicy tomato sauce.

"Are we finally going to decorate it?" she asks.

"I thought we should," I reply, fetching the wine from the refrigerator.

"It's a big tree."

"We always have a big tree. It was a 'Luke' thing. He always tried to make Christmas special, even when we had no money."

"You had no money?" she says, looking around the kitchen. I know it seems hard to believe now.

"Sure." She brings the plates over and sets them on the table and we sit opposite each other. "Luke worked two jobs for quite a while, when I started college. It was tough."

"And then?" She rolls the spaghetti around her fork and pops it into her mouth… it's about the sexiest thing I've ever seen and I have to swallow hard before I can speak.

"Then Matt offered him a job… and a partnership."

"Just like that?"

"Well, one followed the other, but yeah, pretty much."

"Whoever this Matt guy is, he must have a lot of faith in Luke."

I look at her. "Loyalty's a big thing with Luke. Matt appreciates that. This is really good, by the way," I tell her, taking another forkful of spaghetti.

"Thanks," she says.

"Where did you learn to cook?" I ask.

"I taught myself, really... except pancakes. My mom taught me how to make those."

"Are you close to your parents?" I want to know about her family.

She laughs. "Hell, no." She stops and looks up at me. "Sorry," she says, "that came out wrong." I remain silent. She swirls more spaghetti on her fork, for much longer than is necessary, like she's thinking about what to say next.

"You don't have to tell me, if you don't want to," I say at last.

"No, it's fine. I've interrogated you about your family."

"Yeah, and you still don't know the half of it," I tell her.

"Well, it's only fair I share a little too," she says. "My dad was an executive for a global corporation on the West Coast... so we never saw him. He took early retirement and took up golf... so we still never saw him." She smiles, but it doesn't reach her eyes. "My mom didn't seem to mind though... She was too busy being a socialite. She lunched, she played tennis... you name it, she did it. She was pretty much a stranger around the house too."

"It sounds lonely."

"There was a cook-housekeeper... Barbara. She was more like a mother to me."

"Was?" I pick up on the past tense.

"She died a few years back."

"I'm sorry."

She looks up at me. "I flew home for her funeral. I don't think I'll cry that much when my own mother dies. There's nothing between us."

We've both finished eating. "Shall we start this tree?" I say to her, because I want to change the subject and cheer Jamie up a bit.

"Sure."

"I'll clear the dishes. You go open the box of decorations... you might have finished unraveling the lights by New Year. Luke put them away – it'll be messy."

"Great... Just what I need."

"Do you want some more wine?" I ask.

"Why not?"

I pour us both another glass and clear away while Jamie goes into the living room. "Oh my God. You weren't kidding, were you?" I look up and she's holding a mass of spaghetti-looking cables. "We'll be here all night," she says, and I laugh. I don't mind that prospect one little bit.

It's actually taken less than an hour to unravel the lights and get them on the tree. The spaghetti looked worse than it was. Now, we're strategically placing baubles. Luke bought these two years ago; they're all red and gold; in different sizes. Jamie hands me the smaller ones to put at the top, while dealing with the larger, lower ones herself.

"What do you normally do for Christmas?" I ask her.

"Not much," she says. Her voice is sad. I've done it again. I've reminded her of something that's upsetting her. *Why am I so crap at this?* "Life's been quite quiet since the... since the bombing. I used to go out partying and dancing all the time, but especially at Christmas; I loved the whole thing of getting dressed up, doing my hair, my nails, my make-up, putting on a pretty dress... But I can't now. Even if I felt comfortable wearing a dress, I've put on weight since the bombing; I don't want to be seen..." her voice fades.

"Why not? You're beautiful." The words are out before I've even thought it through. But to hell with it, she is beautiful.

She looks up at me. "I was never beautiful, not even before it happened... But thanks for saying it," she smiles.

Why doesn't she know how beautiful she is? What happened to her self-confidence? And why the hell doesn't her boyfriend tell her this? That's his job. I know if I were him, I'd be telling her every day.

She goes back to the box. "Last one," she says, handing to it to me. I place the final bauble near the top of the tree and we look at our handiwork.

"Hold on," I tell her and go across the room to turn out the table lamps, so we're in darkness, except for the hundreds of fairy lights wrapped around the nine foot tree. I come back across and stand beside Jamie. She's staring at it, her eyes sparkling.

"It's so lovely," she whispers.

"I know." I don't take my eyes from her, not even for a second.

She's been in bed for about half an hour. I've closed everything down, put the dishes into the dishwasher, and am just about to go to bed, when I hear the noises coming from her room again.

I stand outside her door, holding my breath, listening as she sighs, whimpers and moans out her pleasure. I try to imagine her naked, lying on her bed, her legs wide apart as she caresses herself. I'm so hard already, the thoughts just add to the pain of denial. I guess she's missing her boyfriend – the son-of-a-bitch who clearly doesn't even bother to make her feel beautiful, or wanted; doesn't take her out, even if it's to somewhere quiet, so she has an excuse to get dressed up and feel special about herself.

I don't wait for her to climax this time. I don't want to hear it. I go into my room and sit on the edge of my bed.

Apart from Luke, I've been alone since my mom died. I'm used to it.

But I've never felt so damn lonely in my life.

Jamie

He called me beautiful.

Okay, so he wears glasses, but I'm guessing that means he can see when he's wearing them… and he was wearing them. He was looking right at me through them… and he called me beautiful.

No-one's ever done that… ever.

I know he only said it because he feels sorry for me; because I was talking about how my life's been since the bombing… but… he still called me beautiful.

Damn. Now I'm distracted. And I was close... real close. I change position slightly and start touching myself again, wishing it was his fingers on me, or his tongue... or both. Just the thought makes me shiver, and I feel the quiver building deep inside again. I imagine his fingers inside me, his tongue flicking across my hard clitoris, while I writhe beneath him, maybe tweaking my nipples between my fingers... I touch my nipple, squeezing it... and I'm gone. I let out a little squeal of pleasure, biting my lip to try and keep the noise down.

"Please," I whisper to the darkness. "Please, Will. Please want me, just a little."

God, how desperate do I sound?

The tree still looks good in the pale early morning sunshine. Will's already turned the lights on and I pop my head around the office door before going into the gym. He's not there. Maybe he's still showering...

"Hi," his voice from behind me makes me jump and I flip around. Then my tongue turns to dust in my mouth. He's wearing nothing but shorts, which hang low on his hips, and a towel, draped around his shoulders. There's a sheen of sweat on his hard, muscled chest, and the ends of his hair are wet, and sticking to his forehead and neck. He doesn't look at me, but stares at the floor. "I overslept. Sorry if I've kept you waiting," he mutters. "The gym's all yours." He turns and walks down the hallway and I feel dismissed. It stings... more than a little.

I go into the gym and cycle for half an hour, perhaps a little faster than usual, trying to clear my head, to take my mind off him. It's not working. It's especially not working when I come out and he's in the kitchen. He's showered and is wearing jeans and a white t-shirt that clings to the muscles I've now seen first-hand. His hair is still damp from the shower. He's just as sexy in clothes as he is out of them.

He glances up at me quickly, then turns away. "Breakfast in twenty minutes?" he asks.

I nod my head, because my voice won't work anymore, and go into my room, closing the door and leaning back against it.

He's very probably the most gorgeous man I'll ever see, let alone spend time with. He's kind and generous and thoughtful. Hell, he told me I was beautiful just to make me feel better – that's how kind he is.

I'm wet just thinking about what it would be like to be with him and I feel tears welling in my eyes, because I know it'll never happen. He couldn't bear to look at me earlier. Calling me beautiful was just a platitude… I can't make him want me.

Of course I can't. I undress and go through to the bathroom. The full length mirror in here tells me why I can't make him want me. Apart from the scarring down my leg, there's the fact that the woman who was a size four is now a size ten – I've managed to get down from the size fourteen that I was, but I'm kind of stuck now. I'm not enormous, or obese, I know that – I never was, even at my biggest – but I'm not the person I was either. It bothers me. It's yet another legacy.

I turn away and shower quickly, then finger-dry my hair and dress in jeans and a t-shirt.

As I walk back down the hallway toward the kitchen, where I can smell bacon cooking, it dawns on me that it's possible he's got a girlfriend. I mean it's also perfectly reasonable that he just doesn't want me in that way, but I think I'd prefer it if there was someone else, to him finding me physically repulsive… who wouldn't?

We sit down to breakfast but my appetite's fairly non existent. I'm too preoccupied.

"Is there something wrong?" he asks out of the blue.

I look up. He's staring at me.

"No," I say. Even I'm not convinced by my answer.

"Okay," he says, then pauses. "And now would you like to give me a straight answer?"

"I just did."

"Okay… an honest answer, then."

I stare at him. Why can't he get the message that I don't want to talk right now? "I'm wondering if we're spending too much time together," I say and then wish I could take back the words and start the whole day again.

"Excuse me?" He puts his fork down.

"Well, I'm sure you've got a life… a girlfriend… I can manage here, if you want to go out." I'm floundering now; fishing for information like a teenage schoolgirl, and trying to dig my way out of the awkward hole I just stupidly put myself in.

He gets up and takes his half-eaten breakfast into the kitchen, throwing what's left into the trash. He comes back and picks up his coffee. "I don't have a girlfriend," he says. "But if you really want to spend less time with me… that's fine. I'll work out a rota, or something."

I really could bite my tongue off. He turns to leave, but I jump up, even though the pain in my leg makes me wince. "Will," I say grabbing his arm. He looks down at my hand touching his skin. "I'm sorry. I didn't mean that at all."

He looks up from my hand to my face. "Then why say it?" he whispers.

"I don't know."

We stand for at least a minute, just staring at each other, before he takes my hand and removes it from his arm. "I think you do," he says.

And he goes into the office and closes the door quietly behind him.

I clear away the breakfast things, and clean the kitchen and the living room… all excuses not to go into the office, but eventually I have to.

I open the door quietly and move to my seat. He turns toward me, taking off his headphones.

"I'm sorry," he says.

"*You're* sorry?"

"Yes. I shouldn't have kept on at you like that. You told me you were okay. It's not my place to pry into your life. If you say you're okay, I don't have the right to disbelieve you. It made you angry and you lashed out… What just happened… that was all my fault and I'm sorry."

"Will…" I say. This is all wrong. He's taking the blame for my outburst. "That's not fair. It wasn't your fault. I…"

"Leave it," he says, turning back to the console and putting his headphones back on.

I sit beside him, willing him to look at me, but he doesn't… he doesn't for the rest of the morning; and even at lunchtime, we just eat in silence.

Now it's evening and I've got a headache… in fact I've got the grandmother of all headaches and – at Will's suggestion – I've come to bed early. I'm not sorry. At least in here I can cry to myself; he can't see my tears, or ask me about them… because I'm not sure I can explain them anyway. Not without making even more of a fool of myself than I have already today.

Chapter Seven

Will

This has to go down as the shittiest day on record.

Instead of just accepting she didn't want to talk, I quizzed her to the point of making her pissed during breakfast... so pissed she actually said she wanted to spend less time with me. I mean, I know she's missing her boyfriend; I know she'd rather be at home with him than here with me, and maybe she's feeling guilty because I hugged her the other day, and I told her she's beautiful last night. Maybe I've overstepped the mark... but hearing her say it like that was like having a knife stuck in my chest.

I'd thought her having a boyfriend would make it easier, but it hasn't. All I can think about is that she wants him; she misses him and I keep wishing I was the one she's thinking about, especially when she's pleasuring herself. Coming out of the gym this morning and seeing her standing there in her tight purple shorts and top was almost more than I could take. Then remembering what I'd heard her doing last night, how she'd moaned out her pleasure, thinking about him; how she'll never be mine... Hell, with those thoughts going through my mind, I couldn't even manage to be polite. Things just went downhill from there and got steadily worse as the day went on, and now she's in bed with a bad headache, which is also my fault. I just seem to keep screwing up around her.

I need to work it out, but everything's revolving around in my head and I'm not concentrating on anything at all. I hate the atmosphere between us, but I've got no idea what to do about it or how to make it right.

I want to talk about how this feels; and there's only one person I can do that with. It's only ten o'clock and I know he won't be asleep yet. I pick up my phone and find Luke's number.

"Hey," he says, just a little out of breath.

"Am I... Sorry... am I interrupting something?" I ask, suddenly embarrassed.

"No," he says, "it's fine." And I know I am.

"I can call back."

"Will," he says. "It's fine." I guess now I've interrupted them, it's too late to undo it. "What's wrong?" I sigh. I don't know where to start. "Is it Jamie?" he asks.

"Yeah."

"What's happened?"

I don't reply, because – although I want to talk – I'm not sure what to say.

"I can sit here and try to guess," he says, " but it'll be a helluva lot quicker if you just tell me."

"I told her she's beautiful."

"Right. Well, that's good." He sounds reassuring.

"Yeah, but she's got a boyfriend."

"Oh, not so good."

"You think? And then she told me she thinks we're spending too much time together..."

"Oh... really not so good."

"She's missing her boyfriend."

"Or she's finding it hard working with you..."

"How do you mean? I'm not that difficult to work with. I'm quite—"

"Calm down, Will. I just meant that maybe she's attracted to you, but she doesn't want to be and she feels guilty because of her boyfriend."

"No. That's not it at all."

"How do you know?" he asks.

"Because she's not attracted to me. And I know she's missing her boyfriend."

"How do you know that?"

"I can't tell you."

He sighs. "Okay. But what makes you so convinced she's not attracted to you? How did she react when you told her she's beautiful?"

"She disagreed with me; she told me she's never been beautiful... It made me think her boyfriend's a bit of a shit."

"Maybe. Or maybe he's just not good with words."

"Meaning he's good with other things, I suppose?" I wish he hadn't put that thought in my head.

"I didn't say that. But she must have her reasons for being with him." I don't say anything, mainly because I don't want to think about what her reasons might be. "Look, what do you want me to do?" he asks.

"You're the expert... Tell me what I should be doing," I say outright. "Where am I going wrong?"

"That depends what you want from her," he says. "And whether she wants it too."

"She's already told me she won't be unfaithful."

"You've asked her that?" He's surprised.

"Not in so many words. We were having a general conversation about fidelity."

"Oh, I see... and she told you she could never be unfaithful?"

"Yes."

"Then, I'm sorry, man, but it doesn't really matter what you want. There's nothing you can do. If she's as into this other guy as you think she is, you don't have a chance. Sometimes these things just aren't meant to be... Sometimes it's not that you're doing anything wrong, it's just bad timing and there's nothing you can do..."

And suddenly I see red. "It'd be alright if it was you though, wouldn't it?" I shout at him. "You'd just go for it, and she'd probably fall at your feet... just like they all do..."

"Sorry?" he says. "Will, please—"

"I mean you'd just fuck her and to hell with the consequences, to hell with bad timing...because that's how you operate. All those women, for all those years, fawning over the great Luke Myers." I know it's not true;

I know I'm being unfair and unreasonable even as I'm speaking, but I can't seem to stop.

"Will, don't," he says, his voice still calm.

"Shut the fuck up, Luke," I yell. "I don't know why I thought you could help me. We've got nothing in common, have we? Hell, we don't even share the same father. Your dad was just a drunken bum who beat up on everyone else to get his own way... including me... Why the hell did I think you could help me? Why the hell did I think you'd even want to?" I hang up, because I've already said too much. I've lashed out at him before, but this time I've gone too far. I've hurt the only person in the world who really loves me and maybe, after what I've just said, there's no way back.

Jamie

I get up early and go into the gym, cycle for half an hour and then shower and get dressed.

When I come out, there's no sign of Will. I know yesterday was bad; I know we argued and I said things I regret, but I didn't expect him to sulk like this.

I go through to the office and can't help sucking in a sharp intake of breath. Will's sitting at the desk, his head in his hands. He's still wearing the same clothes as yesterday and when he looks up, his eyes are bloodshot and, if I didn't know better, I'd swear he'd been crying... surely not? What on earth can have happened?

I sit down next to him. "What's wrong?" I say. "And don't think about giving me any bullshit, and telling me everything's fine, because I'm not going to listen to it." He shakes his head. I put my hand on his shoulder and he tenses. "Tell me," I say, softly.

He doesn't move, so I turn my chair toward his and then swivel his around, so we're facing each other. "Tell me," I repeat. "Something's happened."

"I've been an asshole."

Okay… not the answer I was expecting. "To whom… or with whom?" I ask.

"You… and Luke."

"You have not been an asshole with me," I tell him. "So what's happened with Luke?"

"We argued. No… I argued. He didn't say a word."

"When was this?"

"On the phone, last night, after you'd gone to bed… God, Jamie," he says, "I was utterly vile to him… and he didn't say a word. He didn't argue, didn't fight back…"

"Did he hang up on you?" I ask.

"No. I hung up on him." He leans forward, his elbows resting on his knees. "I can't forgive myself for what I said to him," he whispers.

"Do you want to tell me about it?"

He looks up and his eyes meet mine for a second. "I hurled his father at him," he says.

"What do you mean?"

"Luke's father was an abusive, drunken piece of shit. I think I might even have compared him to Luke… I'm not sure."

"You say 'Luke's father'…"

"We don't have the same father."

I think back to the file. "So his father wasn't William Myers, then."

"No, his father *was* William Myers. I've got no idea who my father was." He leans back in the chair again and looks up at the ceiling. "My mom had an affair, which resulted in me. At the time, no-one knew about it; it only came to light after she died. Luke's father found letters between her and her lover. He burned them and wouldn't tell me or Luke the guy's name."

"I guess it was hard for him, finding out like that."

Will lowers his head, looking at me. "You'd think so, wouldn't you?" He shakes his head. "He seemed to delight in it… I guess it justified his own behavior, knowing she'd done the same thing." He sighs and twists his chair back to face the desk. "He treated me like an outcast from then on. Luke called him out on it all the time, and he protected me when the old man used to beat up on me, but once Luke left to go to college, I was on my own… It was hell."

"Is that why you moved in with Luke?" I ask. I want to hug him, but he's put up barriers that I don't think anyone could get through right now… except maybe Luke.

"Partly," he whispers.

"And is that why you hate being called William?"

He glances across at me. "Yeah. He never let me forget the irony of my having been named after him."

"So, what happened last night?"

He hesitates, like he's trying to work something out. "It was just something Luke said… I don't know why, but it got me riled."

"Then you need to speak to him," I tell him. His phone is on the desk and I nudge it toward him. "Do it now, Will, or you'll just sit here all day thinking and stewing on the whole thing."

"What if he's mad at me?"

"Then he's mad at you." I pause for a second. "But I don't think he will be." I push the phone a little closer. "Call him." I stand up. "I'll go and make breakfast and give you some privacy."

I open the door and go through. Just as I'm about to close it behind me, he calls out, "Jamie?" I stick my head back into the room.

"Yeah?"

"Thanks."

Out in the kitchen, I take some bread and eggs from the refrigerator. We'll just have scrambled eggs today; it's quick and easy. I think he might want to talk again once he's spoken with Luke and I'm happy to listen. He's troubled and, especially after being such a bitch to him yesterday, I really want to help.

I'm just breaking the first egg into the bowl, when there's a knocking on the front door. This is unusual – in fact, it's unheard of, because no-one can get in through the gate. I guess Will must have let in whoever it is while he's been on the phone to Luke, and hasn't come out to tell me because he's still talking, so I go over to the front door and open it, expecting to see a delivery man.

Standing there, looking pale and worried, his phone in his hand, is Luke. He's wearing a light gray suit, with a white shirt and a dark blue tie.

"Hi, Jamie," he says.

"Hello. Um… Why didn't you let yourself in?"

"I wasn't sure if I'd be welcome," he replies, not moving from the threshold.

"Will's about to call you, or he's been trying to call you, I'm not sure which…"

"He is?" And as we speak, his phone rings. "Oh…" he says. He checks the display, and puts the phone to his ear, saying, "Hi." I stand to one side to let him into the house. "Stop talking for a second, Will," Luke says. "Because I'm here." He pauses. "Here, at your house… I'm standing in the hall with Jamie."

The office door opens and Will stands there with his phone still held to his ear, his mouth slightly open.

"Hang up," Luke says, staring at him, and Will does.

"I'm going to check the recordings from last night," I mutter, even though I know that's probably giving away more information than I should. I walk across to the office door, which Will's still blocking. "Excuse me…" I say and he steps out into the kitchen to let me through, then I close the door behind me and hope to God I won't be picking up body parts in a few minutes' time.

Chapter Eight

Will

"I'm sorry," Luke says before I can even draw breath.

"What the hell are you sorry for?"

"Whatever it was I said that upset you." He takes a couple of steps into the kitchen and we stand at opposite ends of the room, staring at each other. "I don't know what I said, but whatever it was, I apologize."

"You've got nothing to apologize for. It was all my fault."

"No, it wasn't. I was being insensitive."

"Luke, you can't take the blame for everything that happens in my life. I'm an adult now. I have to be responsible for my own actions. In this case, being an asshole was entirely down to me."

He smiles. "You had a good teacher, though."

"Your dad?"

"No, Will. Me."

"When have you ever been an asshole?"

"Pretty much all my life… until I met Megan." I look at the floor. "Is that the problem?" he asks, taking another couple of steps closer. "Is this because you like Jamie and you can't have her?"

I nod my head.

Two more steps, and he's standing in front of me. "It hurts like a bitch, doesn't it?"

"Yeah." And his arms come around me… and I'm twelve again. And for a moment, everything's okay. He lets me go and we walk down into the living room and sit on opposite sofas. "That doesn't give me the right to take it out on you though."

"Better that you take it out on me than anyone else, especially Jamie…" he says quietly. "So, does she know how you feel?" he asks, taking off his jacket and laying it on the seat next to him, then loosening his tie.

"No. And I'm not going to tell her – and neither are you."

He holds up his hands. "No, I'm not."

"She's serious about her boyfriend. It doesn't matter how much I want her, I don't have the right to try and come between them."

"How do you know she's serious about her boyfriend? It might be casual, for all you know."

"They shared a very traumatic experience a few years ago. I can't give you the details, but going through something like that together… it's gotta bring you closer to someone. It's not something I could break… and neither would I want to."

"This traumatic experience…?"

"I can't tell you about it. Jamie told me, but she doesn't like people knowing about it."

"But she must like you, and trust you, if she told you about it," he says.

"There's a world of difference between like and love though, isn't there?"

"And you love her?" he asks.

"I don't know."

He leans forward. "I'm sorry," he says again.

"That's my line," I reply. "I'm really sorry for all the stuff I said about you and your dad."

"It doesn't matter. Besides, you didn't say anything about either of us that wasn't true."

"Did I compare you to him though? I think I might have done… I can't remember…"

"No… not really. Don't you remember what you said?"

"No. It's a bit of a blur. I just remember thinking I'd gone too far this time."

"You didn't, Will. Honestly… It's fine." He stares at me for a moment, then takes a breath. "Although I hate it when you do this…"

"I'm sorry," I mutter.

"No, Will, that's not what I mean… I hate it because it makes you feel so shitty about yourself afterwards, that's all. It really doesn't matter what you say to me, or about me, I just hate what it does to you…"

I let out a half-laugh. "Yeah… Me too."

"Next time, try and call me before you get to that point. I'll come over if you need me to."

"Hmm… I'm sure you'd appreciate me calling you in the middle of the night…"

"Are the nightmares back then?" he asks, his concern obvious.

"They're no worse than normal. I'm not sleeping that well… but I guess that's because Jamie's here…" He nods his head and I guess he thinks that's because I'm confused over how I feel about her. And in a way, it is. But it's also because being around her has awoken the worst of my memories… only I can't tell him that, because he knows nothing about it.

"Then call me," he says. "I'll come over anytime… you know that."

I look over at him and I know he means it. "I'm sorry I interrupted you and Megan last night," I say, glancing down at my hands in my lap.

"It was fine," he replies. "Neither of us minded."

"I'm sure you made it up to her."

"Well, not yet, but I will." I look up at him again to find he's smiling. "We talked instead," he says. "And then I made Megan go to sleep, because it was late; and I sat up…"

"How long for?" I know the answer already.

"All night," he replies. "I was trying to figure things out."

"So was I."

He laughs. "We could have both saved ourselves a sleepless night and had this conversation a little earlier, couldn't we?"

"No," I tell him. "I wasn't ready to talk until this morning… And even then Jamie had to persuade me to call you."

"Why?"

"Because I thought you'd be mad at me. I said some unforgivable things to you…"

"No, you didn't. Think about it, Will. Everything you said to me was true. And you didn't say anything I haven't heard before. And I'm never, ever mad at you – not really."

"Jamie said you wouldn't be."

"She's a wise woman."

I nod my head. "Yeah, she is."

"As well as beautiful," he adds, still looking at me.

"I know."

"It will pass," he says.

"Will it?"

"So they say."

"And if it doesn't?"

"I can't promise to make it better, but I'll do what I can… You know where I am…"

I make coffee and bring it back into the living room.

"I had a call from Grace last night," Luke says as I sit back down. "She asked me to pass on to you that she and Matt are having a party on Christmas Eve. Everyone's invited… including Jamie, if she's still here."

"That's kind of Grace. I don't know if Jamie will be here by then, but…"

"How's the job going?" he asks. "I know you can't give me specifics, but are you making any progress?"

"No. None at all. At this rate, Jamie might still be here at Easter."

"I take it that's a bad thing?"

"After the last couple of days… it's my worst nightmare."

Luke's just left. He's got a meeting at ten, so he had no choice, although I think he could've curled up on the sofa and crashed for a few hours. I feel so much better now we've talked, except for the lack of sleep, that is… but that's not unusual these days and I'll get over it.

I go through to the office. Jamie's got her headphones on, so I tap her on the shoulder. She flips around.

"Hi," she says, pulling off the headphones. "Everything okay?"

"Yes. Luke's just gone. Are you alright in here for a bit longer if I go and grab a shower?"

"Sure. Have some sleep too, if you want."

"No. I'll be fine."

"I don't mind, Will."

"I'm used to working all night." *And not sleeping very well since you've been here.*

"Okay." She shrugs.

"I know you're not going to ask, so I'm going to tell you… He wasn't mad with me. You were right. You can say 'I told you so', if you want to."

"I don't want to."

I smile at her. "We worked it all out."

"Good. I'm glad."

I turn to leave, but then stop and retrace my steps. "Thanks, Jamie," I say to her. "Thanks for taking the time to listen."

"Anytime," she says, her voice bright and breezy.

"I do appreciate it," I say. "I'm sorry things have been a bit strained around here the last couple of days."

"It's my fault," she replies.

"No. Goddamnit… why won't anyone let me take the blame for anything?"

"Okay… it's your fault," she says, smiling.

"Thanks."

"Now, go and shower. And then can you *please* make us some breakfast… I'm starving."

"Consider it done," I tell her and close the door on my way out.

As I step into the shower and feel the hot water cascade over me, I wish for the umpteenth time that she was free; I wish she could be mine. But I know that can't be. What Luke said was right. Sometimes the timing is just wrong. We'll only ever be friends. Still, if I can only be her friend, I'm going to be the best damn friend she ever had.

Today has been a much better day, albeit wasted, in terms of work. We've been watching these screens for a week and nothing's happened. Absolutely nothing; well, except Phil's wife has finally contacted him to say she's not coming back. He didn't go into work today. I'm not surprised. I can kind of empathize. At least in a way...

It's my turn to cook tonight. Because I'm so tired, we're just having steak and salad, and we're finishing early. I'll catch up tomorrow.

"Will?" Jamie asks as I shut down the screens.

"Yeah?"

"I hate to be a nuisance, but can I use your bathroom... or Luke's?"

"Why? Is there something wrong with yours?"

"No... I was just kind of hoping that yours or his might have a bath. My leg is still aching and it's partly because I haven't had a bath. I usually have one every day, or every other day – it just helps relax the muscles a bit. I won't be long – just half an hour or so."

I look across at her. "I'm sorry," I say. "I don't have a bath here at all."

"You mean you have three bathrooms and no bath?"

"There are four bathrooms." She looks at me, confused. "The door opposite Luke's room." I explain. "That's the house bathroom. Guests don't want to go into the bedrooms to use the bathroom."

"I see," she says.

"But there's no bath in there either. It's fine though, I'll drive you over to Luke's later, if you like. He's got two baths, so you can take your pick."

"No. It's fine."

"I really don't mind, Jamie. And neither will he, or Megan. If it helps. We'll go after dinner."

"No, really, it's okay." She stands. I can tell she's stiff and in pain.

"Let me take you," I say.

"I'd feel uncomfortable... turning up at someone else's house to use their bath."

"It's only Luke."

"I don't know him that well. And then he'd have to know why."

"I say again... it's only Luke."

"Even so. It's fine, really. I'll take a shower. The heat will help."

"I'm sorry," I repeat.

"Don't be." She goes to the door.

"Luke and I had them all ripped out," I tell her just before she goes out, "when we moved in here. I can't handle the whole idea of a bath… or even look at one really. But it never dawned on me that someone else would actually need one."

She comes back across to me. "Now I'm the one who's sorry," she says. "I should've thought about it. It makes sense you wouldn't want the reminder."

"I'm not sure it makes much difference though really. The image never goes."

"I know," she says. And I know she understands. She's seen her own version of hell. I just wish I'd been there to help her through hers, and share it with her.

Jamie's still in the shower and the salad's made. The steaks are seasoned and sitting on the countertop waiting to be cooked.

Although it's been a better day, I still feel like I'm screwing up just about everything. I'm sure there must be something I could do to make her happy; something that doesn't involve making her feel uncomfortable about being with me.

I think back through our conversations. She likes cooking, but we do that anyway; she likes cycling, but that's her therapy and hardly something we'd do for fun. She used to like getting dressed up to go out… of course!

I grab my phone and call up Grace's number.

"Hello, Will," she says. "How are you?"

"I'm good," I tell her. "I have a favor to ask though."

"Okay… go ahead and ask."

"Luke told me you and Matt are having a party on Christmas Eve…?"

"Yes. I hope he told you that you and your guest… your colleague are invited too."

"Jamie's her name... and yes he did. I'm sure he also told you Jamie isn't a guy."

"Yes, he did."

"I thought he might."

"Are you okay with that?"

"I'm coping," I tell her. *Well, I'm coping better than I was.*

"Good."

"I was wondering, Grace... Would it be possible for you to make the party a formal thing?"

"You mean evening dress? Tuxes, long dresses?"

"Yes."

"Why?"

"Hmm... would you be offended if I said I can't tell you."

"No. I'd be intrigued, but not offended."

I smile, because I know she'll be smiling too. "So?" I ask.

"Okay," she says. "If you really want me to, I'll tell everyone to get dressed up. Todd might want to kill you, but Megan and I certainly won't complain... Any excuse to get Matt into a tux and I'm happy. I'm sure Megan feels the same about Luke. Does Jamie have something to wear?"

"Yes," I say. *She will do.*

"Okay then. I'll pass the word."

"Thanks, Grace."

"You're very welcome."

Jamie

It's been a difficult couple of days, but I think we're finally over it all, and Will hasn't asked me to explain what I said about not wanting to spend so much time with him, which is good. I don't know how I'd explain the fact that I'm finding it harder and harder to be around him… that I want him, and I know he doesn't want me. I mean… who in their right mind would want me? Instead, he's taking the blame for the whole thing, which feels wrong… but what can I do?

We had a lovely dinner last night. Will was tired, but he cooked an amazing steak, and we talked about our separate times at Northeastern. It's something we share, but our memories are different, which made it interesting. And then we both went to bed early. I still can't stop thinking about how good it would be if we went to bed together, but I'm trying to come to terms with the fact that we're just friends… and Will makes a pretty good friend, too. That doesn't mean I don't still think about him all the time, and especially when I'm bringing myself to orgasm… which I seem to be doing every night, sometimes more than once… and sometimes again in the morning as well. I think I might be doing that for some time, but then he's a difficult guy to get out of your head.

It's Christmas in ten days' time and I think I want to buy Will something, but I've got no idea what. He's a technology freak, but I'm under qualified to even consider going down that road. I know I could contact Luke somehow and ask his advice, but I'd really like to try and think of something myself.

I'm cooking the lunch, still mulling over the idea and trying to find a cheese grater, when I come across an envelope in one of the kitchen drawers. It's labelled 'watch'. And I have a sudden inspiration. I forget the lunch for a moment, take the envelope, and go into my room, open my laptop and search for a watch repair shop in Boston. There are several to choose from, so I note down their addresses, and go back to the kitchen. I'm making macaroni and cheese and, once it's in the oven, I go through to Will.

"I'm thinking of going into town this afternoon," I say to him. "Would you be okay with that?"

"Sure," he says. "Do you need me to take you?"

"No. I'm sure I'll remember the way."

"Okay."

"You can manage here by yourself?"

"Yes. I'll be fine."

I smile to myself... It's inspired!

I get back at just after four. Will gave me the passcode and a key, so I let myself in.

"You were quick," he calls from the office. "I thought women liked to shop for hours."

"Not this one," I say. "I'll be through in a minute." I go along the hallway and into my room. I've just about stopped shaking now, although I'm still feeling sick, and my palms are sweating. I take the box from my bag and put it in the nightstand. They wrapped it, so all I've got to do is write the card, and it's done... his present is dealt with. I feel quietly satisfied about it. It was just about worth the stress of the afternoon. His mom's watch wasn't quite so straightforward. The man was very nice, but he said it'll never work again. The internal mechanism is too badly damaged. He's going to repair it so it'll look okay, but it'll never function as a watch. He's promised to get it ready as soon as he can... hopefully before Christmas, and it'll be delivered here.

I go through to the bathroom and wash my hands and face. The woman staring back at me in the mirror looks pale, exhausted.

Joining Will, I see straight away that something's wrong.

"What's happened?" I ask, sitting next to him. I wonder what I've missed.

He doesn't look up. "Nothing in particular," he says. "I've just been thinking."

"Right... clearly something of significance."

"Yes."

"Care to enlighten me?"

"Hmm?" He looks at the screens, then back at the files he's got spread out in front of him. "It's all this." He waves his arm expansively. "It's wrong."

"I know. Neither of us like doing it..."

"No," he interrupts. "I mean there's something wrong with it. We've been watching these guys for days and days... and none of them has said or done anything to arouse even the slightest suspicion. Nothing... not one word."

"I know."

"Which leads me back to where I started."

"You don't think it's any of them?"

"Exactly."

"Then who?"

"The one person we haven't been looking at." I look at him blankly. "Jack," he says eventually.

"Oh, be serious."

"I am being serious." He finally turns to face me and a shadow crosses his eyes. "Are you okay?" he asks.

"Yes, I'm fine... You were talking about Jack."

"Yeah. He's the only other person who knew everything about the op, but he's the only one I've never looked into. All the way through he's known every detail about my investigations and has been able to steer me in whichever direction he wanted. He pointed you at me, and Luke..."

"But that's just him doing his job."

"Is it?"

"Okay, let's say it's him... What can we do about it?"

"Start in exactly the same place I did with all the others?"

"Where's that?"

"His bank account is the most obvious..." He doesn't wait for me to answer, but turns back toward the desk and pushes all the files to one side. Then he leans over and lifts up a laptop from the floor.

"I've never seen you use that," I say to him.

"It's my own," he replies. "I know it's secure, and it's not connected to the department."

"Um... can I mention the word paranoia."

"Yes, you can mention it. I'll ignore you though." He's smiling as he starts typing.

"I'm going to make coffee," I say, getting up.

"Sounds good," he mutters, but I'm not even sure he heard what I said.

By the time I return, he's looking despondent.

"There's nothing there," he says.

"Where?" I ask, putting the cups down and sitting beside him again.

"His bank accounts – he's not loaded, but he's not poor, and there are no unusual payments in or out."

"Can you hack into his phone?" I ask.

"Starting to believe me now?" he says.

"Not necessarily, but if we're going to check, we may as well be thorough."

"Yes, I can hack his phone," he replies, and his fingers start to move across the keyboard.

"Well, while you do that, I'm going to clear up this mess you've made, and make a start on the dinner." It feels like I'm talking to myself.

"Good," he replies after a pause.

"Boiled swan okay with you?"

"Hmm. Lovely."

"Hah... I knew you weren't listening."

"I like my boiled swan served with mashed potatoes," he says, his expression not changing at all. "Is that okay?"

I can't help laughing.

"What are we really having?" he asks as I'm about to leave the room.

"Locusts on toast," I reply. He still doesn't look up, but picks up a pen from the desk and throws it at me. It only misses because I manage to duck out of the room.

I'm chopping mushrooms for the sauce to go with the chicken breasts, when Will comes out of the office and stands, leaning against the wall. He looks dazed.

"You've found something, haven't you?" I say, putting down my knife and going over to stand in front of him.

He nods his head. "There are a dozen or so messages on his phone."

"Saying what?"

"Nothing blatant, but they're too cryptic to be real; they don't make sense, and there are no replies.

"Who are they being sent to?"

"I've checked out the numbers. They're all burner phones."

I lean back on the countertop behind me. "This doesn't look good, Will."

His eyes catch mine. "I know."

"We need more though, don't we?"

"Yes."

"Would it help if we had cameras in his house?"

"Well, yes, but I don't have that kind of equipment… not here."

"I do."

Chapter Nine

Will

"What?" I can't believe it. She's brought cameras with her?

She pushes herself off the countertop and goes back to chopping mushrooms. "I didn't tell anyone at the time," she says, "but I wasn't sure I'd installed the cameras correctly. I didn't want to be responsible for this all going wrong, so I brought a couple of spares with me, just in case. I was thinking, you see, that if there was a problem, I could fly back down to Virginia and re-install them, and I'd never have to tell Jack that I'd screwed up."

I walk over to her, take the knife from her hand and turn her around to face me, resting my hands on her shoulders. "Clever girl," I say. "How many cameras have you got?"

"Just two, I'm afraid."

"That's okay. It's better than nothing." I don't let her go and she doesn't make any effort to move away. I'm glad, because I like having my hands on her, even if it is just her shoulders. "All we need to do now is find a way of getting them into Jack's house."

"That's easy," she says. "I'll go down there and do it myself."

"Like hell you will."

"What's the problem? I did the other six."

"Yes… and they didn't know what we were doing."

"And neither will Jack."

"He's guilty, Jamie. He's going to be more guarded, more suspicious of anything out of the ordinary. I'm not letting you do it."

"Have you got any better ideas?"

"Yes. I'll go. I've been to his house. It makes more sense. And I can do it this weekend. There's a message on his phone to his wife. They're going to visit her parents on Friday night through Sunday. The timing's perfect."

"You know how to fit the cameras, do you?"

It's been a while, but how hard can it be? "I've done it before. And you can remind me."

"Why don't we both go?" she suggests. "You know the layout of his house and I can fix the cameras."

What she's saying does make more sense. I'm still not happy though.

"We need someone else," I say, thinking quickly. "If we're both going to be inside his house, then I want someone on the outside, keeping watch."

"Who, though. There's no-one else in the department we can trust."

"So? We go outside the department."

"You're not thinking of involving your brother in this, are you?"

"Hell, no. We need someone who actually knows what they're doing."

"So?"

"Todd."

"And who exactly is Todd?"

"He's a cop. And a friend."

"You want to bring the cops in on this?"

"Not the cops, no... Just Todd... unofficially."

"And will he do it? Unofficially?"

"Only one way to find out," I say.

"Well, can you ask him after dinner?" she replies. "It's only about ten minutes away now."

"Okay... I've been dying to try these locusts."

"Haha."

We spend the meal – a very delicious chicken dish with a creamy mushroom sauce, and not a locust in sight – talking through Jack's messages on his phone and where we can place the cameras, being as we only have two. We've decided that he's unlikely to do anything much in the office, so we're going to focus everything on his house, and place one in his study and one in their bedroom, where he'd be more likely to talk to his wife in private – if she's involved, which she might not be.

"I meant to ask, how was your shopping trip?" I ask her as we clear away the dishes together. "Busy, I imagine?"

"Yes." That was a short reply. Something's wrong. I noticed she looked pale when she first came in, but we got sidetracked talking about Jack.

"Was it okay?" I ask. She doesn't reply. "Jamie?"

I turn from the sink and see she's still standing by the table, her hands in front of her face. She's crying... well, sobbing really. I go straight to her and pull her into my arms. I know I kind of said to myself I wouldn't do this; I said we'd be friends... but I also said I'd be the best friend she could ever have and that means I'll hold her when she's crying, because I'm sure as hell not going to just stand and watch her.

She rests her head on my chest and I stroke her hair gently while her tears soak through my t-shirt. I'm wracking my brains, trying to work out what's wrong... and then it hits me.

"Was that the first time you'd be into central Boston since it happened?" I ask her. She nods her head. "Why didn't you let me come with you?"

"Because I had errands to run."

"So?"

"Sometimes a girl needs to run errands by herself."

Oh... I see. "Well, I could have waited outside, or in the car." Does she honestly think I'd be embarrassed by something like her buying sanitary products? I guess *she* might find it awkward, though? I shrug inwardly.

She nestles into me and I hold her a little tighter. "I know," she says. "I wish I'd thought it through. I didn't think it would be that hard. It's not like I went anywhere near where it happened."

"It was probably just the atmosphere of the city."

"Yes, probably."

"So, you never went back there at the time?"

"No. People said I should. My boyfriend said it was a mistake." *Asshole*. "He thought I should face it at the time and deal with the demons…"

And there speaks a man who clearly has no idea what he's talking about. "That would be like me and baths, then…" I say to her. "I've never managed to face up to that. When I stay somewhere – like in a hotel – I have to check that the bathroom only has a shower, or I won't go there. Even at Luke's place, I always use the bathroom that's attached to the guest bedroom because it's the only one without a bath, and at Matt's, whenever I stay, they put me in the room above the garage because the bathroom there only has a shower. My mom died nearly seventeen years ago, and I still struggle. Honestly, you've done so much better than me, Jamie… it's not easy."

She leans back a little and looks up into my face. "No, it's not, is it?"

I look down at her and I'm so tempted to kiss her. If I didn't think it would ruin everything, I would. "Next time – if there is a next time – ask me. I'll take you."

She nods her head, then rests it back on my chest again and we stand like that for a long while.

It wasn't long enough, unfortunately. The need to pee eventually got the better of Jamie, but she seems better now. She's changed into pajamas, with her robe over the top and is drinking a hot chocolate, curled up on the sofa, with a blanket over her legs. She looks adorable.

"Are you going to call Todd?" she asks, as I come to sit opposite her with my coffee.

"Yes." I connect the call as I'm speaking and he picks up.

"Will," he says, "how's it going?"

"Good," I reply.

"How's the houseguest?"

"She's good too," I say.

"Whoa… did you say 'she'?"

"Yeah, I did."

"You mean it's a woman?" he says.

"Well done."

"How's that going?"

"Good."

"She's sitting there with you, isn't she?"

"Yes."

"And?" he asks.

"And what?"

"What's she like? Oh, I guess you can't tell me, if she's right there…
Okay, let me guess… Is she ugly?"

"No."

"So she's pretty?"

"No."

"Okay… now I'm confused," he says.

"Go up a notch from there."

"She's more than pretty?"

"Yes."

"So she's beautiful?"

"I'm beginning to understand why they made you a detective."

"Funny guy." He pauses, then sighs. "Oh crap. Don't tell me you're
in love too? I can't lose you as well; it's bad enough that Matt and Luke
have gone to the dark side… you can't leave me, Will."

"I'm not going to," I tell him.

"Hmm… and somehow I get the feeling you're not happy about that.
Oh… she's got a boyfriend already?"

"You got it."

"Shit… that sucks." And despite his protestations that we should
both remain single, I can feel his sympathy. It helps… just a little.

"Sure does." I look across at Jamie, sipping her hot chocolate and
watching a movie with the sound turned down. It's an old black and
white Cary Grant film; she must know it, because she keeps smiling
every so often, like she knows what's happening. I'd really like to go and
sit with her, pull her into my arms and watch the movie together. "I need
to ask a favor," I tell him, bringing myself back to reality.

"Okay."

"First, you have to tell me when's your next day off?"

"Saturday, why?"

"Great. How would you feel about helping me and Jamie out… and taking a little trip to Virginia with us? My treat."

"Jamie's the houseguest?"

"Yes."

"What do you want me to do? Take out her boyfriend, or something?"

"No," I say, although I'm tempted. "I just need you to watch the outside of a house."

"Right… and what will be going on while I'm doing this?"

"I can't really tell you that."

"Is this legal, Will?"

"I can't tell you that either."

"You have remembered I'm a cop, right? I can't actively break the law… you know that, don't you?"

"You won't be. You'll just be watching the outside of a house."

"And you? I know… you can't tell me that."

"You're a quick learner," I say.

"I've got no jurisdiction in Virginia," he says.

"You don't need any. You won't need to arrest anyone. I just need someone I can trust to keep watch, and tell me if there's any sign of anyone coming into or near the property."

"Because you'll be on the inside?" I don't reply. "I'll take that as a yes," he says, after a lengthy silence. "And where will Jamie be?" he asks.

"With me."

"Cozy."

"We'll need about a half hour, that's all."

The phone goes silent for so long I start to wonder if we've lost the connection.

"When do we leave?" he asks eventually.

I breathe out… It's a breath I hadn't known I was holding on to. "Saturday morning… early. We'll be back by the evening."

"You're buying dinner," he says.

"Naturally. We'll come by and pick you up at six."

"Six…? On my day off… You owe me one, Will."

"I know."

We end the call and Jamie looks over to me. "He's in?" she asks and I nod my head.

"What are you watching?"

"*The Awful Truth*," she replies.

"Turn the sound up, if you like." She does. "I haven't seen it before. What's it about?" I ask.

"It's complicated," she says. "Basically, Cary Grant and Irene Dunne are married, but they both suspect the other of having an affair, so they're getting divorced and, while waiting for the divorce to be finalized, they both get engaged to other people, but then realize they're still in love with each other, so they try to sabotage the other's new relationships." She looks across at me. "It's about misunderstandings, basically,"

"I see." I get up and go across to sit next to her and we watch together for a while. I'm in the corner of the sofa and, after a while, Jamie comes and leans back against me, bringing her blanket with her.

"Do you mind me doing this?" she asks.

"No," I manage to say, pulling the blanket across my lap a little to hide my erection from her.

"Thanks for today," she says.

"What did I do?"

"Holding me, earlier. It helped."

"Good." I rest one arm along the back of the sofa, the other by my side. I'd really like to hold her now, but that might be taking things too far. It's not like she's crying at the moment, so I don't have a reason... except that I want to.

We've only been sitting like this for about ten minutes, when I hear her breathing change; she's asleep. I could stay like this with her all night, but she's not mine.

I slide out from beneath her, real careful, so as not to wake her, then I lift her up and carry her to her room, opening the door and pulling back the comforter with some difficulty. I've never carried a woman before – it's kinda tricky to hold onto her and do other things at the same time. I lower her onto the bed, her head resting on the pillow, then pull up the comforter. She's still wearing her robe, but she'll be fine. If I start to undress her, she might wake up and get the wrong idea... I'd rather things stayed as they are now, than she thought I was some kind of pervert, taking advantage of her while she's asleep. I look down at her for a moment... well, maybe a little more than a moment. It's the first time I've seen her sleeping. She looks angelic, her eyes closed, her lips slightly pouting. Before I'm tempted to lean down and kiss her, I leave the room, closing the door softly behind me.

Jamie

It's been a quiet couple of days. All we've had to do is prepare the cameras and pack them. We're still watching the six suspects, but only in passing. Our main focus is on Jack; but we've got nothing to monitor, except his phone, and nothing unusual has happened on that. So, there's not much to do, really.

We've had another movie night... Another Cary Grant film – *Arsenic and Old Lace* this time – which we both found funny. I leant on Will again while we watched, and he didn't seem to mind, although I managed to stay awake until the end of the movie, and put myself to bed. I did tell him I was impressed that he carried me to my room; he made light of it... Actually he told me he'd do it again. It gave me food for thought during my orgasm that night, anyway. I allowed my imagination to run away with him carrying me to bed, stripping me naked and taking me. I had to put my hand over my mouth to dull the noise... It was intense... still lacking physical contact, but intense.

Todd is, I'm guessing around the same height as Luke, so just slightly taller than Will.

I'm currently staring at the back of his head, as he's driving the hire car from the airport to Jack's house. His hair is much shorter than Will's and a shade or two lighter; in the rear-view mirror, I can see his eyes, which are a dark chocolate brown. He's wearing jeans and a check shirt, with the sleeves rolled up, and on his right forearm, I can see a series of small Chinese letters, tattooed in black, running from elbow to wrist, in two rows. As we drive along, I can't help wondering what they mean.

When we arrive, he pulls up outside Jack's house. It's smaller than I'd expected. I don't know why, I'd assumed my boss would live in something a little more palatial than this, but it's just an ordinary looking detached house in a normal suburban street. We all remain in the car for a moment.

"Half an hour?" Todd says quietly to Will.

"Yes," Will replies. "If anyone comes near the house, call me on this number." He hands a piece of paper to Todd. "Don't program that into your phone. If you call, just wait for it to connect, let it ring twice, then hang up. I won't answer. We'll get out the back and meet you in the next street."

"How are you going to get in?" Todd asks.

"I'm not going to tell you."

"Because it's illegal?"

"I'm not going to tell you," Will repeats.

"Okay." Todd nods his head. "I hope you've got a damn good reason for doing this."

"He has," I tell him. Todd looks at me in the mirror, but doesn't reply.

"You wait here with Todd," Will says, turning in his seat and looking at me.

"What? That wasn't what we agreed."

"Just wait until I tell you it's safe to come in." He pulls out a phone, but it isn't his. Will has an iPhone… but this is like something out of the ark. It's not even a smart phone. He presses a few buttons and I feel my cell vibrate in my back pocket. "Answer it," he says. I do. "Now, stay on the line until I tell you to hang up. Bring the bag with you when you come. And remember… do everything I tell you; and nothing that I don't."

I nod my head. He's been saying the same thing for days now.

He gets out of the car and walks down the driveway, and disappears around the side of the house. I keep the phone pressed to my ear.

"How's it been, living with him?" Todd asks.

"Good," I tell him.

"Good what?" Will says in my ear, his voice little more than a whisper.

"I was talking to Todd," I say into the phone.

"Well don't. It's confusing."

"Sorry." I roll my eyes at Todd and he nods his head.

"Well, that was easy," I hear Will say after just a couple of minutes. "Jack clearly doesn't believe in too much home security."

"Can I come in yet?" I ask.

"God, you're impatient. Just hang on." I can tell he's inside now… the sound has changed; there's an echo. I wait for a few minutes, tapping my fingers on my leg. Todd reaches over and stops me, putting his hand over mine.

"Chill," he murmurs, pulling his hand away again. "He'll look after you. And I'm here. There's no need to be nervous."

I put my finger over the mouthpiece. "I'm not."

"Yeah, right."

"Okay," Will says in my ear. "You can come in."

"On my way." I hang up the phone and slide it into my pocket, then get out of the car, pulling the bag with me. "Back soon," I say to Todd.

"I'll be here," he says, checking the mirrors as I walk away.

I go down the driveway, around the back of the house, and in through the open kitchen door. I glance around, but I can't see Will. "Where are you?" I whisper.

"Here." He's right beside me.

"Shit!" I jump out of my skin. "Don't do that."

"Never walk right in like that, not without checking first," he says, coming and standing in front of me. His eyes are dark, his face serious. "You hung up the damn phone, Jamie. It's been a couple of minutes since you heard me tell you it was clear to come in. Anything could've happened."

"Like what?" He's being paranoid again.

"What if I'd been wrong? What if I'd missed something and Jack was still here, with a gun at my head? What if you walked in on that? You're not armed… You could be dead by now."

"You're not armed either," I say quietly, trying to prove a point, I guess.

"Yeah, I am." He briefly pulls up the right leg of his jeans to reveal an ankle holster, with an automatic tucked into it. "I told you… do everything I tell you, and nothing that I don't, and I *didn't* tell you to hang up your phone." He takes the bag from me and moves away. "I told you to stay on the line…"

"Sorry." I try to blink back the tears. *Grow up, Jamie.*

He turns, drops the bag and comes back to me, looking into my eyes. "No. I'm sorry," he says, his voice soft. "Just, please… don't do that again." Maybe not paranoid then; maybe he just cares.

"Okay."

"C'mon," he says and takes my hand. He pulls me through the kitchen, picking up the bag again en route to Jack's study. Once inside, he pushes the door closed. "Where's best?" he asks. I look around at the position of the desk, relative to everything else in the room.

"Do you think we can hide it in the bookshelves?" I ask him. "The angle from the light fitting is tight."

He looks up. "Yeah, it is." He studies the bookshelves for a moment. "What about here?" he says, pulling out a bound copy of *The Adventures of Huckleberry Finn*. "There's a gap between here and the end of the bookcase. Put it in there and I'll replace the book and we'll see if we can see the camera from the desk."

I do as he suggests, making sure everything's switched on before he replaces the book. Then Will goes and sits in Jack's red leather chair. "God," he says, "this is as uncomfortable as it is ugly."

"And it is very ugly." I smile across at him. "Well?"

"I can't see it. You have a look." He gets up and I take his place. He's right, there's nothing visible.

He checks his phone. "We've already been nearly fifteen minutes," he says. "Bedroom next."

We go up the stairs and, on the third attempt, find the master bedroom. It's all swags and drapes, with too many floral patterns to be called even vaguely tasteful. "This is gross," I say, as I clamber up on the footstool he's holding steady and dismantle the light fitting to put the camera in place.

"Utterly," he replies. When I'm done, Will puts his hands on my waist and lifts me down, then replaces the footstool exactly where he got it, in front of the dresser.

He checks around the room to see there's nothing out of place, then grabs my hand, and the bag from the floor.

"Let's go," he says.

We run down the stairs and through to the kitchen, leaving by the back door, which Will closes and locks. I'm about to go around the side of the house when I feel his hand on my shoulder.

"Wait," he says, taking the phone from his back pocket. He presses a couple of buttons. "It's me. All clear?" he asks and waits. "Good." He hangs up, then takes my hand again and leads me at a more regular pace down the side of the house, up the driveway toward car. He opens the back door and I get in, then I hear him put the bag in the trunk and I'm surprised when he opens the other rear door and gets in beside me.

"All good?" Todd asks, putting the car in drive and starting off.

"Yeah," Will replies, pulling out his own cell, then fishing in his other pocket. He takes out a set of earbuds and plugs them into his phone, presses a couple of buttons then hands the whole lot through to Todd. "Plug those in," he says. "The volume's turned up."

I watch while Todd takes the phone, puts one earphone into each ear and puts the phone on the seat next to him. Will clicks his fingers just behind Todd's head, but doesn't get a response. Then he turns to me.

"Who the hell trained you?" he says. "And how long did you get?"

"A couple of days... They said it was all I needed... Why? What's wrong?"

"I'm a computer geek," he continues, his head in his hands. "I haven't done any fieldwork for years, but I can't believe they sent you out to do what you did with so little training. How the hell didn't you get caught?"

"What did I do wrong?"

"Everything."

I blink back the tears again. He's being so critical. He told me the cameras were fine – but now they're not; now my work's not good enough – evidently.

He looks across at me. "I'm sorry," he says suddenly. "It's not your fault. I'm just trying to decide if sending you out half-trained is part of Jack's plan."

"How do you mean?"

"I don't know. It just feels a bit too convenient that he'd send out a rookie with no training on something like this… and also that he'd tell you to look into Luke; like he was trying to set me up, just in case I started getting too close to him."

"You think he was trying to frame you?"

"I don't know I'd go that far…" He's thinking. "Maybe. I told him right at the beginning, if he really wanted this thing done properly, he should have brought in top ranking investigators from out of state. He told me he trusted me to do the job. That was bullshit. But he should never have left it to a rookie, and a guy who's as easy to suspect as I am, because he's been in on the assignment since the beginning. It doesn't stack up."

"So… so I was only chosen because I'm rubbish at this…"

He undoes his seatbelt and moves closer. "Did I say that?"

"Well, you did say I'd done everything wrong, yes."

"Oh… I didn't mean it like that. I'm sorry. I was just scared, that's all. I couldn't live with myself if anything happened to you."

I stare at him… Did he really just say that?

More to the point, did he just mean what I hope he meant; or am I reading too much into it?

"You two done yet?" Todd asks, his voice over-loud.

Will looks at me for a moment, then turns way. He leans forward and taps Todd on the shoulder, giving him a 'thumbs-up' signal. Todd pulls out the earphones.

"Gotta love The Boss," he says, smiling, and handing the phone back to Will.

"We're not so keen on ours right now," Will replies.

"Well, I know that feeling," Todd says. "Mine's an ass."

I look from one of them to the other. "I think you two should top moaning about your jobs, give them up and go into business together," I say. "You could easily set up a security or surveillance company. You get on, you're good at what you do; and you could choose who you work for, rather than be dictated to. And, most important, you'd be the boss… well, you'd both be the boss, if you see what I mean."

Todd looks at me in the mirror and Will turns to face me.

"You might just have something there," he says.

"It's worth thinking about," Todd replies.

By the time we get to the airport, they're both smiling again. I'm not. I'm feeling more than a little used by Jack; and very confused by Will's comment. I know it probably just means he felt responsible for me on this assignment, because he's got seniority, but… well, what if it didn't? What if he meant he really cares?

That's more than worth thinking about.

Chapter Ten

Will

The cameras are working. Jack's not back until tonight though, so we've got all day to ourselves before we can expect anything exciting to happen, although we're still monitoring the other suspects, even if only in a cursory fashion.

When we dropped Todd off at his apartment after dinner last night, we agreed to talk in the New Year about Jamie's suggestion. I know we'll need some financial backing; neither of us has the kind of capital it's going to take to set up a business, and it's not something either of us can rush into, but I think it's something we'd both consider, if we can work out the details.

What's bothering me more right now is that I may have gone too far with Jamie again. I think I laid into her a bit too much about her training. I made her sound incompetent when she's not. She's just not been trained to a high enough level. That's not her fault and the more I think about it, the more I think it's all part of Jack's plan.

And I probably shouldn't have told her how I'd feel if anything happened to her… but it just kind of slipped out. I'm hoping she'll have taken that as me being the senior agent in the op, though, taking responsibility for her and the situation; not in the way I really meant it… which is pretty much exactly how I said it. If anything happened to her, and I could've prevented it, I don't know what I'd do…

After lunch, we go through to the office, and I let Jamie sit down first.

"Would you be okay on your own for a while?" I ask her, still standing by the door.

"Of course," she says.

"I just need to go out for a while."

"Okay." She doesn't ask where and I'm certainly not going to tell her.

"I'll be a couple of hours…"

"I'll be fine," she says. She's being a bit quiet today. I guess that's because I insulted her abilities yesterday. I'll have to try and explain it to her properly later… ideally without screwing up again.

I jump in the Jeep and head out, but I'm only a few minutes from the house when I call Luke. I can't do what I need to do without him.

"I need your help," I tell him as soon as he answers.

"What's happened?" he asks.

"Nothing. But there's something I've got to do… it's to do with Jamie… and I don't know how to do it…"

"Okay…" He sounds uncertain.

"And I know you're good at this kind of thing," I say, prevaricating.

"Just spit it out, Will."

"I need you to tell me what size dress Jamie would take."

He laughs. "Is that all? For a moment then, I wondered what you were going to ask me… Still, it's good to know I have my uses," he says.

"Well?" I ask, hoping he'll be able to help.

"I'd say a ten."

"Sure?"

"Yes."

"Thanks."

"Anytime." He doesn't ask any questions, and I hang up and drive into town.

It takes me a full two hours to find everything I want; mainly because I've never done any of this before, and it probably doesn't help that it's just before Christmas, and the shops are heaving. But I get there eventually.

As I'm driving home, I realize I've got another problem – although why it didn't occur to me in the store, I don't know. But I can't give her half the deal; she needs it all, or it won't work.

I call Luke again.

"Don't tell me you couldn't find anything," he says, without bothering to say hello.

"No, I did," I say, "but I've got another problem now." I don't know how to explain this one, though, because I don't want to tell him, or anyone else what I'm planning. It's kind of personal… and if I explained it to him, I'd have to tell him about how Jamie's life has changed since the bombing, which I can't do, because she doesn't want anyone to know about that. God, this is complicated.

"What's the problem?" he asks, after I've been silent for a while.

"I need underwear. The kind you make."

"Really…?" I can hear him trying not to laugh.

"Not for me, Luke. For Jamie."

"I gathered that much. Should you be doing this, Will?" he asks, more seriously. "She's got a boyfriend, remember? He probably wouldn't like it."

"It's not like that. You're gonna have to trust me. My reasons are completely respectable. Honest."

"Okay. I believe you. What do you need?"

"I have no idea. I know nothing about any of this… that's why I called you."

"When's it for, then?"

"Grace's party."

"Oh, you mean the casual Christmas Eve party, that Grace has now turned into a formal event? That party?"

"Yes, that party. Jamie's dress is black and red. Strapless, floor length."

"Sounds sexy." I don't reply. It is sexy. "Leave it with me," he says. "I'll drop some things over tomorrow on the way home from work."

"Don't let Jamie see them," I add. "She has no idea about any of this."

"Okay."

"Thanks, Luke."

We hang up and I continue the drive home. I think about Luke's words, wondering if he's right; whether I should be be buying all these things for someone else's girlfriend... but I want to. And that's only because I want to show her she can still have a good time. Her boyfriend evidently doesn't give her that, and she needs it... more importantly, she deserves it.

When I get back, the door to the office is closed, which makes things easier, so I take the box and bags along to my room, and put them in the closet in my dressing room. I'll add the lingerie when Luke brings it over tomorrow and then give it all to her on Christmas Eve before she starts getting ready for the party. I just hope it all fits... I had to guess at the shoe size, but I think I did okay. And I hope she likes it all, and doesn't think I've gone too far – again.

I need a coffee, but before I start making it, I decide to check with Jamie whether she wants one and am just about to open the office door when I hear a soft moaning noise coming from inside the room. My heart sinks. I check the clock on the kitchen wall. It's a little before five. I guess Stephanie and Mitch are busy – again – and being as she's on her own, Jamie's decided not to bother with the headphones. I'm not really in the mood for this, but I guess we don't have a choice... There's a louder moan, followed by a more guttural groan. And it becomes clear that I'm not listening to Stephanie, or anyone else on any of the monitors. The noise is too close to the door for one thing, and it's too real. It's got to be Jamie. My whole body hardens, not just my cock, and my hand stills an inch or two above the door handle, frozen, as I listen for what feels like hours to her whimper and sigh, and the occasional uttered, "Yes," her breathing becoming more labored, as the peak of her excitement approaches. I know I should walk away, but I can't. I want to hear her climax, even though it's torture, and I know it's got nothing to do with me... I can't move. My breath is caught in my throat. Then, through the barrier between us I hear, "Oh, God... Oh yes, Will, please. I need you... please... take me. Oh... Will, yes..." and her voice fades away to a whisper.

I can hear the blood rushing through my ears, my heart pumping loudly in my chest. Surely… surely I heard that wrong… She can't just have cried out my name – not at *that* moment? Can she? That's not possible. She's got a boyfriend. She misses him; she wants him, not me.

I can't begin to process what's just happened. All I know is I can't stand here any longer. She might come out through the door at any moment and find me standing here. I know I'll die of embarrassment if she does; I think she probably will too. As quietly as I can, I go over to the front door, open it and then slam it shut again.

"I'm home!" I call out, and then I go through to my room, like I've just got in.

I sit on my bed, reliving that moment; the moment when I heard my name on her lips, begging me to take her. It's something I never thought would happen. Probably not with any woman and certainly not with someone like Jamie; someone as beautiful, and kind, funny and erotic as she is… And I wish I could have seen her face; seen the want – no she said 'need' – in her eyes and known for sure that it's really meant for me and no-one else.

I don't know how I'm going to do it, but somehow I've got to discover what's going on in her head. I have to find out if she really does want me, and not her boyfriend, because if I could just be sure of that, I think it could change everything.

Jamie

Christ! He's back. That was close… I stand and straighten my clothes. I'm sure I must look a little disheveled, but I can always tell him I fell asleep and he woke me coming in. It's a feeble excuse, but it's the only one I've got.

I go out into the kitchen but he's not here.

"Will?" I call.

"Be there in a minute." I hear him reply from his room at the end of the hallway, and sure enough, within a few moments, he appears. To me, he looks even more gorgeous than ever. He's cleaning his glasses and I realize I rarely get to see him without them. It makes me wonder, just for a second, what he looks like when he's sleeping.

"Just out of interest, how blind are you?" I ask.

"Sorry, is there someone here?" he asks, looking around. "I can hear a voice, but…"

"Haha. No, seriously."

"I was being serious." He's smirking though, so I know he's not. "I can see reasonably well," he says, smiling now. "The glasses are just for show, really."

"What? Did someone tell you they make you look even sexier?" I really need to make sure I've got my head back down to earth after an orgasm before I even consider opening my mouth. I'm a danger to myself. He stops and looks at me.

"Er… no," he says, and I think he's embarrassed. But then, he's not nearly as embarrassed as he would've been if he'd come home five minutes ago and heard me crying out his name. Just the thought makes me blush.

"Shall I make the coffee?" I ask.

"If you like." He puts his glasses back on. I don't care whether he thinks so, or not… he does look damn sexy in them. I set up the coffee maker while he comes into the kitchen and stands behind me, leaning against the countertop. "Did anything happen while I was out?" he asks.

"No, it's been quiet," I tell him… *which is how I had the time to have a mind-blowing orgasm, while yelling your name at the top of my voice.*

"You can take a break for a while, if you like," he continues.

"I'm fine."

"You might as well," he says. "You could call your boyfriend; I'm sure you must be missing him."

I turn around. He's staring at me. "Um… what boyfriend?" I ask. What's he talking about?

"Your boyfriend?" he says, sounding confused. "The one you told me about."

"But I don't have a boyfriend..."

"Yes you do," he says. *I think I'd know if I did.* "You told me... he was with you at the marathon."

And the penny drops. "Oh, you mean Patrick... He *was* my boyfriend then. He isn't anymore."

Even with his glasses on, I can see his eyes widen, and darken. And his mouth opens a little, so I can see the tip of his tongue between his white teeth. It makes me want to move forward and kiss him, to see how his lips feel.

"But I thought..." he says. His voice is quiet, like he doesn't really understand.

"I probably didn't explain it very well," I tell him. "We broke up."

"I'm sorry," he says. He seems to mean it too.

"Well, it was a long time ago."

"Really?"

"Yes," I say. "He couldn't cope."

He looks at me, tilting his head to one side. "Couldn't cope with what?"

"With what happened."

"But you said he wasn't hurt."

"No, he wasn't"

"Then, I'm sorry if I'm being dense, but I don't understand."

The coffee's finished filtering and I pour it out, adding milk. "Shall we sit down?" I suggest.

"Okay." He takes his cup from me and we go through into the living room, sitting together on the sofa that looks out onto the decking.

I nestle into one corner, while he takes the one opposite, so we're kind of facing each other. I take a quick sip of coffee, then lean over and put the cup down on the table. Will's eyes are fixed on mine. "When I was injured, I couldn't walk for a long time," I tell him.

"Yes, you said the other day," he replies, placing his cup next to mine and folding his arms across his chest.

"I think it was about four months before I took my first steps; in that time, I gained around forty pounds... hospital food isn't the most healthy thing on the planet, and not being able to move meant I just piled the weight on... and I became much more introverted and dependent, and a bit depressed. I needed help with a lot of things... just everyday things, you know?" Will nods his head. "Yeah, well, he didn't. Patrick thought life should just carry on as though nothing had happened – and for him, it did. He went to work, he ran, met up with his friends, he started coming to see me less and less... and then he met someone else."

"Excuse me?"

"He met someone else."

"While you were still in the hospital?"

"Yes." I keep my head up, looking at him. I can see the muscles on Will's arms tightening. "He did at least have the decency to come and tell me to my face."

"How noble of him," he says.

"Well, I guess he didn't have to. And at least it wasn't someone I knew. It was a woman he worked with." I pull my knees up to my chest and rest my arms on them. "He explained his reasons... I needed that."

"What were they?" he asks, then shakes his head. "No, forget I said that. You don't have to tell me that. It's personal."

I focus on my hands, just for a moment. It's easier, just for this bit, if I don't look at him. "No, it's fine. He told me he didn't love me. He said I wasn't the same person I'd been before the 'accident' – that was his word, not mine... like those assholes had *accidentally* set those bombs to go off in a crowd of people, for Christ's sake. He said I was no fun anymore." I look up at him again. "It was kind of hard being fun, stuck in a hospital bed, not knowing what the future held or when I was going to get out of there, but you know... I guess he didn't get that." I take a deep breath. I'm starting to sound bitter and I don't want to. "Anyway, I stopped him at that point. I didn't need to hear that I was fat, and he didn't like the way I looked now either. I only had to see the way he looked at me to know that was his other reason."

I stop talking and focus on Will's face. His eyes are the darkest I've seen them; his lips are drawn in a thin line. He seems confused and… angry. "Have I done something wrong?" I ask him.

"God, no. Whatever made you think that?"

"You look so angry."

"I am angry. But not with you, Jamie. How could he do that to you?"

"I used to ask myself the same question… I don't anymore. He's not worth the energy, Will. People like that aren't."

"No."

"I've come across a lot of them in the last few years. That's one of the reasons I don't tell people about what happened to me. They're very quick to judge."

"Seriously?"

I nod my head. "People judge me for being overweight; for not going out a lot; even for wearing pants all the time and not skirts. It's like those skinny girls at the gym… everyone's so busy trying to conform, they never bother to think there might be a reason why someone's a little… different."

"Yeah… like maybe they just don't feel the need to look and behave like everyone else? Conforming is very overrated."

I stare at him. "I know… I do, really. Sometimes it's hard though, when you feel like everyone is judging you based on how you look, rather who you are…"

He gets up and stands over me, holding out his hand until I take it, letting him pull me to my feet and into his arms. I'm looking up at him, his eyes fixed on mine.

"Firstly, whatever Patrick, and those women at the gym made you feel, you're not overweight," he says.

"Er… I think you'll find I am."

"Jamie, just be quiet and listen for a minute." He sighs. "You're beautiful."

"I'm not, but I guess it helps that I've lost nearly twenty-five of the forty pounds I gained."

He takes a deep breath. "Can I finish?" he says. I nod my head. "You're beautiful," he repeats, patiently, "but what you are and who you are is not about how you look, or whether you're a size zero, it's about what's on the inside. I've never been around anyone who's as much fun to be with as you. Anyone who can't see that is blind. Anyone who can't see what an incredible woman you are doesn't deserve you... You're so much more than beautiful. Don't let anyone ever make you feel any different."

He kisses my forehead and lets me go, walking along the hallway to his room. I hear the door close softly behind him, and I wish he'd come back. Without his arms around me, I feel more lost than ever.

Chapter Eleven

Will

I thought my head was spinning before that conversation. Now I feel like I'm in the centre of a whirlwind. She cried my name as she climaxed. She said she needed me... *me* of all people. And, it would seem we've been talking at crossed purposes the whole time. She doesn't have a boyfriend. The stupid son-of-a-bitch couldn't see her for what she is. That's his loss. But, now I have to work out what to do. And I literally mean... *what to do.*

I've spent a the whole time she's been here either wanting her, thinking about wanting her, or thinking about trying not to want her... and all the while thinking I can't have her, making all of the above pointless. Now I know she's available... and I even know she's interested in me, I'm uncertain how to react, I'm uncertain if I can respond to her. Well, my body knows how to respond – obviously – it's been doing that since she first smiled at me. And I get the biology... I know what happens, I know what goes where. What I don't know is how I feel about being with her, and whether I can do that.

I assume she'll have certain expectations, but I'm not sure I can fulfill them. Not with my history. I think I'll be a resounding disappointment to her and maybe it'll be better if we can just stay friends... Who am I trying to kid? After hearing her cry my name like that, I desperately want to watch her come... no, I want to *make* her come. I want to know I can do that to her... for her. Whether I can do anything else, I'm not sure.

For the last fourteen years, I've avoided this situation for the very reason that I can't face it. And now I have to. Well, I don't. I could just ignore it and walk away. And then I guess hell could freeze over.

I can't sit in here all night though. I'm going to have to go out there, even if only for the sake of appearing vaguely normal – whatever normal is.

Jamie's not in the living room, and the office door is open, so I peek inside.

She's sitting at the desk, watching the monitor.

"Jack's back," she says.

"Since when?" I squeeze behind her seat and sit down next to her.

"About a half hour ago."

"Has anything happened?" I ask.

"No. He's in the shower, I think. I just hope he puts something on when he comes out." She smiles across at me. "I'm not sure I could handle that vision. His wife isn't on either screen. I'm assuming she's either cooking, or in the living room."

"Speaking of cooking; it's your turn tonight… You could go make a start, if you like. That way if Jack comes out of the shower stark naked, you won't be scarred for life."

"I was going to suggest we order something in," she says, turning her chair toward mine. "It's already quite late and I'm tired after this evening's revelations."

I swivel my chair around to face her. "I'm sorry. I didn't mean to pry." Like hell I didn't. I asked that question with the express intention of finding out about her boyfriend and how she felt about him. I didn't expect to find out he doesn't exist.

"You weren't prying. It was a misunderstanding, that's all."

"Even so…"

She reaches across and puts her hand on my arm. "It's fine, Will. But are you okay with take-out for tonight?"

"Sure. There are menus in the kitchen drawer. You decide."

"Thanks." She gets up and goes to the door. "And thanks for earlier too… the hug, and what you said."

"Don't thank me," I say, picking up my headphones. "I meant it... every word." She hovers and, because I'm scared about what'll happen next, I tell her to go find the menus and bring them back. It puts a little space between us.

After dinner, which was Chinese, Jamie decides to have a shower and go to bed early. I clear away, and check Jack's monitor. Both screens are empty. I guess it was always going to be difficult only having two cameras in their house. I hope it doesn't prove costly, in terms of proving anything against him.

I have a quick look at the other six. There's not a lot happening. Phil doesn't seem to be there. I've seen text messages passing between some of the other subjects, that he's drinking a lot, so I guess he's out somewhere getting hammered. James, the single guy, is watching TV alone in his living room. Everyone else seems to be out, except Stephanie and Mitch, who are in bed. He's got his head between her legs, which are spread wide apart and her fingers are entwined in his hair, holding him in place while she rocks her hips. I switch off the monitors and I imagine myself and Jamie in that position... I think I'd like to taste her, to discover her with my tongue and lips, and use my fingers to arouse her. Damn I'm so hard, it's painful again, and for the first time in fourteen years, I contemplate stroking myself. It's been that long... I sit back on my chair and undo the buttons on my jeans, lowering my boxers and freeing my erection. I go to touch it, but I can't and I pull my hand back. I know it'll bring all the memories back and I don't want to taint the feelings I have for Jamie with those dark thoughts. I want to keep her image pure in my head, not degrade her with my nightmare past. I'll wait... The feelings will pass. They have to.

Today, I'm still feeling just as unsure, but Jamie seems a little brighter than she was yesterday. I guess a good night's sleep has helped her. I didn't get one of those... again. I spent most of the night lying awake wondering what to do, or more to the point, how to do it... and getting nowhere.

It's been a very dull day though, in terms of what we've been watching. Jack's gone into the office, which means we can't see him, so I've spent the whole day looking at blank screens, other than when his wife has occasionally cropped up in the bedroom. She hasn't gone into his study at all. I've never met her in all the years I've known Jack and I'm surprised by how young she is. She must be at least fifteen years younger than him. They're an odd couple, in my view. Jack's probably forty-five, or a little older, and hasn't really worn well. But his wife is a good three or four inches taller than him, with long red hair and legs that go on for ever. There's a part of me that's expecting to see another man appearing on the scene at any time… but then maybe I've just become cynical after doing this job for as long as I have been.

Jamie's been monitoring the rest of our subjects and they've been just as dull. They've either been at work, or out elsewhere.

So, all in all, it's felt like a bit of a wasted effort so far.

Jamie offered to cook, being as she didn't last night, but I told her it's fine and she's gone for a shower. This is intentional on my part, as Luke texted about twenty minutes ago to say he'd be dropping by with the lingerie I asked for. I don't want her to see it, so if she's in her room, we should be fairly safe.

He arrives bang on time and I leave the dinner cooking and take him down to my room, closing the door behind us.

"This is all very secretive," he says, grinning at me and putting the bag he's brought on my bed.

"Yeah."

He looks up. "You okay?" he asks. I shake my head. "What's wrong?" He sits down. I don't. I feel the need to pace – and not look at him.

"Jamie and I talked," I tell him, keeping my voice low.

"And?"

"And I got it wrong."

"Which bit?"

"The bit where I thought she had a boyfriend…"

"She doesn't?"

"No."

"And this is a bad thing?"

"I don't know."

"Man, I'm confused," he says.

"*You're* confused?"

"Well, I'm not sure I can see what the problem is anymore," he says. He wouldn't, because I've never told him anything about what happened all those years ago. "You like her," he continues. "She seems to like you…" I'm not about to tell him that she called out my name at *that* strategic moment. That's private. "And you now know she doesn't have a boyfriend… which means she's available… so what's stopping you?"

"It's complicated."

He stands up. "Then uncomplicate it. It's fairly basic, Will." God, I wish that were true. He seems to think that's enough advice and I can't ask for more without telling him the truth. And I'm not doing that. He opens the bag on the bed and brings out about a dozen items of lingerie.

"She's really gonna need all that?" I ask him.

"No," Luke says patiently. "But I didn't know what she'd like. So I brought the bras, briefs and garter belts from three of the ranges, and there are some stockings too. I didn't bring thongs," he adds. "When I was choosing everything earlier, I was under the impression that she still had a boyfriend, and thongs felt… inappropriate. If you want them, I can bring them over."

"No. I'm sure briefs will be fine." Jamie would look great in a thong, I know she would… she'd look real sexy and the thought of that is making my head spin, but this isn't about making her look sexy, or turning me on, it's about making her feel good.

"Well… if you change your mind let me know… The sizes should all be fine," he continues. "Jamie can choose whatever she wants – or you can." He smirks at me.

"Jamie can choose," I say firmly. "This isn't about me."

He raises an eyebrow. "Fair enough."

"I'll let you have back whatever she doesn't use."

"No. She can keep it all."

"Really? Are you sure? I know how much this stuff costs."

"Yes. I'm sure."

"Thanks, Luke."

"No problem." He starts to pack everything away again in the bag. "Going back to Jamie's boyfriend… or non-existent boyfriend," he says. "What about that shared traumatic experience you were telling me about?"

"I got that wrong too." I seem to be getting a lot wrong these days.

"So there was no traumatic experience?"

"Oh yes, there was, but he left her because of it – well, the consequences of it, anyway."

"Sounds like a jerk to me."

"Yeah."

"Well, I'm glad she hasn't got a boyfriend," he says, going over to the door. "You two are good together."

We could be… I really hope we could be.

Once's Luke's gone, I check on the dinner, which is doing fine and then I go back into my room and pull out some of the lingerie again. It's so soft and delicate, and most of it is lace and see-through. I can't imagine how she'll look wearing any of it and I don't really want to. I just want her to feel comfortable and not think about having to please anyone but herself. That's the whole point of this plan.

I take some paper from the notepad I always keep in my nightstand, and a pen, and write out a quick note, putting it in the bag with the lingerie, then stow it in the dressing room with everything else.

Jack's working from home today, so there's a little more going on, although he seemed to spend most of this morning doing damn all. He's spent a lot of time this afternoon typing on his laptop, though, which is annoying, as I've got no feed into it. He could be doing anything on there and we'd never know.

Jamie nudges me and I pull off my headphones. "That's infuriating," she says.

"What is?"

She nods at my screen. "We can't see what he's doing."

"I know. That's exactly what I was just thinking."

"Is there anything we can do about it?"

"Not without getting my hands on his laptop, no."

"I can't see how we can do that."

"Neither can I."

"It might be something we'll have to think about, though," she adds, "if we don't get a break soon."

"It's only been a couple of days. Give it time."

I'm trying to sound reassuring, but I agree with her. I feel like we're up against it.

"Oh, hang on," Jamie says. "His wife's just come barging into the room." She nods at the screen again and I pull out the headphone jack so we can both hear what they're saying.

"... Well you need to do something about it," she's saying.

"What did they say this time?" Jack asks, looking up at her. She's got her back to the camera, but he's gone pale all of a sudden.

"The same as usual." That's not helpful.

Jack puts his head in his hands. "I can't cope with much more of this. I've got nothing to give them," he says.

"Then you'll have to find something. Please, Jack. I can't handle this," his wife says, sitting down opposite him.

"Really?" He glares at her. "*You* can't handle this?"

"I'm terrified," she says.

"When I think what I've done..."

Jamie and I look at each other, both willing him to say more.

"Please tell me this is recording," Jamie whispers.

"Of course," I whisper back.

"Jack," his wife says, impatiently. "They're going to get in touch again later today. What do I tell them?"

"Tell them..." He pauses. "Tell them I need a little longer. I'll come up with something to give them."

She seems to visibly sag in her seat, but then she stands and goes around to his side of the desk and pulls his head into her very ample bosom. "Thank you, darling," she says.

He doesn't reply, but when she's gone, he lets his head flop down onto the desk, his forehead resting on the keyboard of his computer.

"Did we just hear what I think we just heard?" Jamie asks.

"What do you think we just heard?"

"A confession?"

I think for a moment. "I need to replay it, just to be sure, but no, I don't think we got that."

"Seriously?"

"No. He didn't actually say he was selling agents or secrets to terrorist cells. He didn't say what he was doing, really."

"But…"

"Oh, don't get me wrong, we've got a lot. But I'm not sure we've got enough. Not yet."

"What can we do to get enough?"

"It might help if we knew who the wife's been talking to."

"Can you hack into her phone? Maybe they've been contacting her that way." I nod my head and start working on it. "What do we know about her?" Jamie asks.

"Nothing," I reply.

"Shall I see what I can dig up?"

"Go for it."

"What's her name?"

"According to his phone, it's Kimberley."

"Yeah… she looks like a Kimberley. And she's probably one of those Kimberleys who doesn't have a last name."

I laugh. "Are you trying to say you think she's a pointless person?" I ask.

"I'm sure she's very nice… although what she sees in Jack is beyond me."

"I'm with you on that."

It takes me a while but I eventually find that there's absolutely nothing on her phone, other than messages to other women who only seem to have a first name, which makes Jamie laugh out loud. These are arranging lunches, meetings for coffee and at the gym, or the tennis club, or the beauty salon. There really doesn't seem to be a point to her life at all. There aren't even that many messages between her and Jack, other than the odd one when he's telling her he's going to be late home from work, or asking where they're supposed to be meeting for dinner. I'm starting to think Jack's life is fairly pointless too.

She definitely said someone was contacting her, so I guess she must have a burner phone just for that purpose. "This is getting us nowhere," I say at last, stretching my arms above my head.

"Don't be too sure about that," Jamie says, looking over at me, a big smile on her face.

"Why? What have you found?"

"I'm not sure. It might not mean anything at all."

"But, judging from that smile on your face, you think it does?"

"Well, it explains her name, at any rate."

"Sorry?"

"It might even explain what she's doing with Jack."

"Okay, stop speaking in riddles and tell me what you've discovered. I can tell you're dying to."

"Before they married, Jack's beloved Kimberley was a hooker," she says.

My stomach flips and I start to sweat. I can't stay in the room a second longer. I leap up, knocking my chair over and bolt out through the door. The living room is in semi-darkness, but I go straight down the hallway, into my bedroom, and just manage to make it into the bathroom before I throw up.

Jamie

I didn't expect that reaction.

I thought it was a useful discovery, but Will just went really pale, put his hand over his mouth like he wanted to be sick and ran out of the room. Maybe he is feeling sick… it's possible, although he's been fine all day. It's been about ten minutes now… Perhaps I should go check on him and see if he's okay.

I leave the office and close the door. He's not in the living room. I'm surprised by how dark it's getting outside. I had no idea it was this late. I check my watch. It's nearly five o'clock. I can see we'll be ordering take-out again tonight. I assume he must be in his room, so I go along the hallway. His bedroom door isn't closed, so I peek inside. He's sitting on the edge of the bed, with his back to me.

"Is everything okay?" I ask. He starts at the sound of my voice, but doesn't reply. "Will?" I go into the room and walk over to him. He's just staring at the wall in front of him, his hands clasped in his lap. He looks dazed, although I know he can hear me. "What's wrong?" I ask. "Are you unwell?" He still doesn't respond and I'm starting to get concerned. He's completely immobile.

I sit next to him and wait, because I don't know what else to do. We're like two statues sitting on the edge of his bed. I don't feel like I should move, because he's so still. It almost feels like I'm not breathing… I am, but only in very shallow breaths, because to take a deep breath would disturb the silence.

After what feels like forever – and it must be some time because it's now completely dark outside, although there's a bright moon, so I can see him – I can't take any more and twist slightly on the bed. My muscles ache from sitting in the same position for so long and I wince.

"Talk to me," I whisper to him. "Tell me what's wrong."

"I can't."

Well, he's at least talking.

"Are you unwell?" I ask again and he shakes his head, just slightly from side to side. "Is it something I did?"

He turns his head toward me. "No," he says, almost sounding surprised by my question.

"Something I said then?"

He turns his face back to the wall again. Okay, so it was something I said. I think back over our conversation just before he ran out of the office. The last thing I said to him was that Kimberley Fielding was a prostitute before she married Jack. Well, my exact word was 'hooker', not prostitute. We'd been talking perfectly normally up until then. So, that's got to be it. For an awful, awful moment, I wonder if he knows her – if he's used her services, and maybe hadn't recognized her until I reminded him of her former profession. It's not a thought I'm very happy about, but I can't think why else he'd react that way.

I reach across and place my hand over his, in his lap. He's freezing. I take a deep breath.

"Is this something to do with Kimberley being a prostitute?" I ask. He tenses beside me and tries to pull away. "Will…" I say, "whatever it is, you can tell me."

He turns his face toward mine. He looks tortured… there's no other word for it. "No, I can't."

I swallow down my own pride and fears. "Do you know her… professionally?" I ask.

He jumps off the bed, going over toward the bathroom door. "What? No!" he cries. "How could you think that?"

I get up and go to him, but he's backing away from me. "It's okay. I'm sorry… I'm sorry," I say and, even as I'm saying the words he crumples before me. His legs give way and he falls to his knees, his hands in front of his face. He's crying; I know he is because his shoulders are heaving… but he's utterly silent.

I go and kneel in front of him, balancing on my left leg, my right one bent up so it's more comfortable, and pull him into my arms and – thank God – he lets me. He rests his head on my shoulder and his arms around my waist and I hold onto him until it passes. Whatever it is, whatever's troubling him… it runs deep.

"Sorry," he mutters eventually and pulls back a little.

"Don't be."

He kneels back and looks at the small piece of floor between us, then goes to stand. I grab his hand and pull him back down. "No, Will," I say. "Whatever's wrong, you need to talk about it."

"I haven't talked about it for fourteen years," he says. "I'm not going to start now."

"Not even to Luke?"

"No." I'm surprised. I guess it shows. "I've never told anyone."

"I think you should." I lean back a little. "If you don't want to tell me, that's fine. Maybe you should tell Luke… or someone else, but you need to talk about it."

He stares at me in the near darkness. I can see his glasses more than his eyes, and myself reflected in them. It's making me uneasy. I reach up and carefully remove them, leaning over and putting them on the nightstand.

"That's better," I say.

"Why?" he asks.

"I can see you now," I tell him.

"And that's a good thing?"

"Yes. That's a good thing." He looks at me. "Do you want me to call Luke?" I ask. "I'm sure he'd come over…"

"No." He takes my hand and holds onto it.

"You need to—"

"If I'm gonna tell anyone, I'll tell you."

I hesitate. "Okay," I say, wondering if I'm ready for this, and he sits down in front of me, his knees bent, his arms resting on them, but still holding my hand between both of his. I sit too, cross legged, ignoring the twinges in my calf, and getting as close as I can to him.

He doesn't look at me, but stares at our entwined hands, and then he starts to talk.

"You know about my mom," he begins, his voice really quiet. "And I told you Luke's dad drank…" He pauses, but I don't say anything. I just want to let him talk. "He also screwed around – a lot. And he did all of it much, much more once she'd died, especially after he found those letters between my mom and the guy who was my dad. He'd come home drunk and yell foul things at me about her… I was only twelve or thirteen then, I didn't really understand what he was saying. One time, he started hitting me, real hard. Luke came in and distracted him, took his attention away from me, and he went for Luke… and then Luke hit him so hard, he knocked him out." He sighs. "After that, he only picked on me when Luke wasn't around.

"Then, when I was fifteen, Luke wanted to go to college. He pretended he didn't; he said he'd stay with me and get a job, but I knew that wasn't what he wanted at all, so I talked him into going. I told him I'd be fine. I'd started training and I'd bulked out a bit by then. I thought I could stand up to the old man, and I probably could've done, if it'd just been him…"

I swallow hard, blinking back the tears that are on the threshold of falling. "It was about six weeks after Luke had left, his dad brought home a couple of hookers, and two of his so-called friends from the pub. They were all so drunk, I could hear them from half-way down the street. I pulled the covers over my head and hoped they'd all pass out downstairs." He pauses again, for a bit longer this time, then says quietly, "They didn't."

"They came crashing into my room, all five of them. Two women and three fat old guys, Luke's dad being one of them. He started taunting me about being the bastard of a whore, and needing to learn a few things about being a man and then he pulled the covers off me." I feel my blood turn cold and I bring up my other hand, covering his with it, so all four of our hands are now entwined. "They stank," he says, like he's reliving the memory in a certain order and the smell is the next thing that's come back to him. "Booze and cigarettes… and a kind of general disgusting filth. I had a desk in the corner of my room, and one of the other guys bent one of the hookers over that and lifted her skirt and was… well… you know." I nod my head, even though he's not looking at me. "Luke's dad pulled me up and sat me on the bed, then he and his other friend stood either side of me, holding my head in place and telling me to watch what this guy was doing to the hooker. I closed my eyes, because I didn't want to see what was happening, but he hit me a couple of times. It just seemed easier to at least look vaguely in their direction."

I can feel my breathing becoming tighter, as I re-live that moment with him, although I can't begin to imagine the horror of it. "Then," he says, really quietly, "the other hooker came and knelt down in front of me." Oh God… Surely not… "She pulled down the front of my shorts and started…" He swallows hard. "She started trying to suck me, while Luke's dad and the other guy held me down on the bed," he says, getting the words out fast. "But she was so damn ugly, and she stank so much, I couldn't get hard." He shudders. "She tried all kinds of tricks… but nothing worked. Eventually, she gave up with me and Luke's dad and the other guy took turns with her." He sighs again. "I kept trying to get away, to leave the room, or even just bury my head in the pillows, but they wouldn't let me. One or other of the guys would just come over and hit me, or kick me. The hookers called me names… horrible names… It went on for an hour, maybe two, until they all passed out in my room. I packed my things and snuck out and called Luke, begging him to come get me."

"But you didn't tell him what they'd done?" I ask, speaking at last.

"No, I just said his dad had beaten me up. I had enough bruises to make it look true."

"And you never went back?"

"No. I sat down on the porch steps and waited. Luke and his friend Matt arrived a couple of hours later and they took me back to their place. I stayed with them for the rest of their time at college. Luke got me into a new school, and pretty much gave up having a social life for a while – he certainly gave up having a sex life until I was better… I had nightmares… well, sometimes I still do. But Luke thinks they're always about my mom… you know, about finding her body in the bath. They're not. Well, not always. Sometimes I'm back in that room and I can't get out… and it just goes on and on."

There's one thing that confuses me. "You didn't react badly to seeing those colleagues of yours having sex on the monitor," I say. "I think I found that more disturbing than you did."

"No. I'm much better than I was. The first time that happened, I freaked out, but I was on my own here, so no-one saw it. I'm quite detached about things like that now. It's part of the job, nothing more, nothing less. I just can't…" He stops.

"You can't what?" I say when it becomes clear he's not going to continue.

"I can't apply that detachment to my personal life."

"How do you mean?"

I can feel him stiffen. "I can't… What I mean is, since it happened, I haven't been able to…" He stops again. Whatever it is is clearly very hard for him to say.

"Are you trying to tell me you can't get an erection?" I ask.

He gives a slight laugh. "No... I can do that without any problem," he says. "But I've never used it."

"Never used it?"

"I've never been with a woman," he says. "Christ, I don't even touch myself. Everything to do with sex is tainted by those memories. And there's nothing I can do about it." He pulls his hands free of mine and, in one swift move, gets to his feet and goes toward the door.

Chapter Twelve

Will

"Stop," she calls from behind me. I keep going. "Please, Will." Something in her voice makes me stop, but I don't turn around. Away from the window, it's completely dark, but I feel her come around to stand in front of me. She's not touching me, but she is blocking the door. "Please don't walk away," she says.

"I shouldn't have told you."

"Why not?"

"Because it's…"

"Embarrassing?"

"Well, yes, and it's not your problem."

"Neither is my leg, or my lack of confidence, or Patrick being an asshole your problem, but I still told you, and you listened. That's what people do, when they care." She cares? And she knows I care too… Is that what she's saying? She reaches for my hand and turns me, leading me back into the room.

"Sit down," she says when we reach the bed, and I do, and she sits next to me and I feel the heat from her body. It proves one point… I can definitely get an erection – but I knew that already. It's what follows that's the problem.

Her next question throws me completely. "Are you hungry?" she asks.

"Sorry?"

"Are you hungry?"

I think for a moment. "I guess. Why?"

"Because we should eat something."

"Okay," I say. It feels almost like I haven't just told her my darkest secret, and we've just been talking about the case, or Christmas shopping, or something equally mundane.

"I'll go order something," she says, and leaves the room.

The kitchen light coming on creates shadows in the bedroom. I don't like them, so I turn on the lamp beside the bed. It's less gloomy now. A few minutes later, Jamie returns and comes to sit beside me. "It'll be here in twenty minutes," she says. "I just ordered the same things we had the other night. Is that okay?"

"Sure."

She nestles into me and it feels right to put my arm around her. "Are you okay?" she asks, looking up at me.

"I don't know. I never expected to tell anyone all of that. I thought I'd take it to my grave."

"What? And never have a physical relationship in between? Not with anyone?"

I shrug. "No, probably not."

"That's no way to live, Will."

"Priests do it... so do monks."

"You're neither of those," she says.

"No."

"And you've really never even touched yourself? Not ever?"

"Well... not since it happened."

"Oh yes," she says. "You were fifteen, weren't you...?"

"Yeah." I look away.

When the food arrives, we spread it out on my bed and sit cross-legged, eating it out of the cartons. We don't talk about my revelations. We don't talk about the case. We talk about likes and dislikes – music, food, movies. It turns out we both like old black and white movies, especially James Stewart and Cary Grant although Jamie also likes Bette Davis, who I'm not so keen on. We have no musical tastes in common whatsoever. Like Todd, I'm into Bruce Springsteen, and anything rock, really. Jamie likes softer, more 'girlie' music, as I call it. We argue for nearly half an hour over the virtues of Genesis with Peter Gabriel, versus Genesis with Phil Collins. It's easy to guess which one of us went for which of those. As for food, I knew we'd have a lot in common, because we've been cooking and eating together for a couple of weeks now and neither of us has made anything the other hasn't liked.

Once we've cleared away, Jamie comes back into my room and we sit together on my bed, with the pillows propped up behind us. I turn to her.

"Thanks for this," I say.

"What? Eating Chinese food on your bed and telling you your taste in music sucks."

"Yeah, that, and listening."

She shifts across the bed and rests her head on my chest. I feel myself stiffen.

"Jamie," I say quietly, "It doesn't matter what I want... I can't just forget everything that happened... not after..."

"Shhh," she says. "I'm tired. Turn out the light."

I do as she says, and feel her hand come across and rest on my stomach. I pull her closer and move us both down the bed a little. We're still fully clothed, but I guess that makes it safer, and maybe she's worked that out – maybe she's realized I'll feel more comfortable like this than if we get undressed at all.

"I know it's hard," she whispers. She does? How can she tell in the dark? "But you need to try and put the past behind you." Oh, she wasn't talking about that. I forget my erection for a moment and try to concentrate on what she's said.

"I wish I could. I wish it was that easy," I say to her.

"Nothing worth having is easy," she says. "But just remember, Luke's dad, his so-called friends, those women... none of them matter. They're not important enough to have an opinion about you. The people who matter, the people who love you, they're the ones who you've kept in your life... Luke, and your friends... the rest is history."

"Are you going to apply that to yourself?" I ask.

"Which bit?"

"All of it, really. But especially the bit about other people's opinions not mattering… All those people who judge you, or who you think are judging you. Their opinions don't matter either."

"I know," she whispers. "It's a bit different though."

"How?"

"Mine's a little more recent, and I'm still being judged – at least it feels like it. The people who said those things about you… they're in your past, Will."

"The words are still fresh," I say. "The memories are still there."

"I know they are, but maybe they won't be quite so bad, now you've told someone."

"Maybe." I hope she's right. She snuggles into me, bringing her arm around even tighter.

"And perhaps you should think about trying to make some memories of your own, to block out the bad ones…"

"I wish I knew how."

"You'll work it out," she says, her voice sounding a little sleepy. "When you're ready."

I hope so.

"Goodnight," she whispers.

"You wanna sleep in here?" I ask, before I even think about the words.

She sits up a little. "I don't have to, not if you don't want me to."

I pull her back down again, holding her close. "I want you to… as long as you understand… I'm not… I'm not ready to—"

"I understand," she says and rests her head back on my chest.

I come to feeling unusually hot… in fact, just unusual. Apart from anything else, I'm absolutely certain I've slept all night, for the first time in ages, but that's not all that's different. My arms and legs are being restricted in some way and, to start with, I assume I've gotten myself tangled in the comforter. Except that's not right, because I'm on top of the comforter. I force myself to wake up properly and it's then that I become aware of Jamie. She's lying on her front, her body partially covering mine. I can feel her breasts pressed into my chest, her arm across my thighs. We're kind of tangled and I'm as hard as steel. If she were to move her arm up about two inches, she'd find out how much of an erection I can get.

Her breasts feel soft against me, but even through the materials of her t-shirt and my shirt, I can feel her nipples pressing into me. That's not helping. Neither is the sight of her ass, encased in her tight jeans. Her face is turned toward me and she looks so beautiful, her lips slightly pouting again. Does she always look like that when she's sleeping? I need to get out of here.

I manage to slide out from under her. She stirs a little as I lie her down again, but she goes back to sleep, and I head straight for the bathroom, locking the door.

I strip off, and step into the shower, turning the temperature to cold, and standing underneath it for several minutes. I've never tried this before – I've never needed to – but it works. I'm distracted enough by the cold water to take my mind off everything that's going through my mind. And that's fine, until I turn the water to hot and start washing my hair, and body and thinking about her hands touching me, caressing me… I try to wipe the thought. I can't risk it. If we tried something and the dark thoughts returned, it would ruin everything, maybe forever. I don't want that.

But would they? Would the memories come back if it was Jamie? She's nothing like those whores. She couldn't be more different. Surely I wouldn't be reminded of them… not if I was with her. I've heard that need, that desire in her. Surely we can make this work, can't we?

I just wish I knew how… Should I ask her how we go about this? She's the woman I want to be with; the only woman I've ever wanted. I've told her the worst, so how hard can it be to ask her to help me with this?

I turn off the shower and wrap a towel around my hips, then go out into the bedroom.

"Jamie?" I say tentatively, looking up at the bed as I come back into the room.

Damn… She's gone.

Jamie

When I wake up, I can hear a shower running. I'm a little disoriented and I look around the room. It's all gray. The walls, floor, ceiling, even the bedding. Of course, I'm in Will's bed. And he's not. I can't deny that I'm disappointed, but then this isn't about me.

He's probably snuck off to the shower, because he's feeling embarrassed about our conversation last night, or the fact that we slept together.

I turn over and lie on my back for a while, thinking. I guess it might be better if he didn't find me here. I deliberately stayed with him last night because I felt it would be better if he wasn't alone. I thought he needed to know I was here; he needed to know I care and I want to help in any way I can, but I think today he might need a little privacy; a little time to himself to think things through. He won't want me waiting out here for him. It'll make him think I have expectations. I don't.

I get up off the bed and go through to my own room, close the door and strip off, then head into the shower and turn it on, standing underneath the hot water for a long time.

His story is horrifying and shocking, and just thinking about it makes my stomach churn. Again, I'm forced to think of Scott at that age. I was twenty when he was fifteen, and I was at college, but we still saw a lot of each other and I can't imagine him going through an experience like that and coming out even vaguely sane.

By rights, Will should be much more screwed up than he is. When I asked if he could still get an erection, I fully expected him to say 'no'. My relief when he said he could had nothing to do with my own desire for him, and everything to do with the fact that at least his experiences haven't damaged him to that extent. He still functions, even if he has a mental blockage when it comes to the physical side of things. And I guess that's easy to understand too. An experience like his would probably be enough to put you off.

The trust he's placed in me, telling me his story, is staggering. I feel honored and a little humbled by his belief in me. I'd like to think it means something, even if I'm not sure what that 'something' is.

There was one thing he said last night, which I didn't comment on, but which keeps rolling around my head, going nowhere. When I was snuggling into him, and he was telling me that he couldn't do anything with me, he said 'it doesn't matter what I want'. Part of me hopes that means he wants me; but there's another part that keeps telling me he could also have been talking in general terms – it doesn't matter how much he wants to have sex with someone, he can't… the 'someone' doesn't have to be me, it could be anyone.

I also think that, for him, it wouldn't be just about having sex. I think he needs a lot more than that. I think he needs a relationship; he needs commitment; he needs to feel loved. I sigh. That makes two of us then.

I slowly wash my hair, and then my body, taking my time but not touching myself. I'm not in the mood today. I know why. It's got nothing to do with Will's story. I want my next orgasm to be with him. I want his hands on me. My own feel like a poor substitute now.

I step out of the shower and wrap a towel around my hair and another around myself, tucking it in above my breasts, then I go out into my bedroom.

In the middle of the bed, there's a piece of paper, folded in half, with my name written on it. I open it and read:

> *'Jamie,*
> *I'm just going out for a couple of hours.*
> *I'll be back later.*
> *If you need me, call.*
> *Will.'*

He's written his cell number underneath.

Did I do something wrong? I was happy to give him some space… I didn't expect him to leave the house to get it.

Should I have waited for him in his room?

Or has telling me his secret changed everything?

Can he not face me anymore, now I know?

Has this spoiled our chances of being together?

I sit down on the edge of the bed, clutching the piece of paper in my hand, and let the tears flow.

Chapter Thirteen

Will

I rarely visit Luke's office, so it's not surprising that his secretary doesn't recognize me.

"He's in a meeting at the moment," she says when I ask to see him.

"I'll wait," I tell her.

"Can I have your name?"

"Will."

"Will...?" She wants my last name.

"Myers. I'm Luke's brother," I explain.

She stares at me for a moment. *Yeah, I know we don't look alike... There's a reason for that.* She gets up from her desk, goes to his door, knocks once and enters.

I go across to the window and look down at the city below. I couldn't work somewhere like this. I know I work in a sterile gray box, but I don't like distractions – well, except for Jamie, of course, but that's something new, which I'm still getting used to. If I worked here, I know I'd spend my whole life looking out the window... There's too much going on.

"Will?" I spin around when I hear Luke's voice. His secretary is sitting at her desk, looking back and forth between him and me.

"You didn't have to interrupt your meeting," I tell him.

"It's only Matt," he says. "C'mon in."

He stands aside and I go into his office. Matt's sitting on one of two chairs in front of Luke's desk, but he gets up as I enter.

"Hey, Will," he says. "How's things?"

"Good," I lie. "I didn't mean to interrupt you guys."

"That's okay. It's nice to see you here."

Luke comes back into the room. I think he must've been speaking with his secretary. "Is something wrong?" he asks, coming over to me.

I don't reply. I just look at him, hoping he'll understand.

"Okay," he says quietly, then turns to Matt. "We're pretty well finished here, aren't we?"

"Yeah, sure," Matt says, and gathers up some papers from the desk. He looks at Luke, raising an eyebrow and I notice Luke shake his head. Matt walks past me on his way out. "See you Christmas Eve," he says, patting me on my arm.

"Yes, thanks…" I reply a little vaguely. He closes the door softly behind him.

"Tell me what's wrong," Luke says, sitting in the chair behind his desk. I take the seat Matt's just vacated, but I don't look at Luke. Instead I stare at the back of his laptop, the Apple logo glowing gently. It's a reasonable distraction. "Will?" he urges. "Is it Jamie?"

"No."

"It's you then."

I nod my head.

"Talk to me."

"She said that too, last night."

He looks confused. "Jamie, you mean?" I nod my head. "And did you? Talk to her?" he asks.

"Yes."

"Well, that's good. What did you tell her?"

"The whole story. Everything that's happened to me. I needed to explain to her."

"You mean about mom's death and my dad, and that he's not your dad, and how he treated you?" he asks.

"Yes… And the rest of it."

He leans forward, his elbows on the desk. "Um… What 'rest of it'? There is no 'rest of it'. Is there, Will?"

"Yeah, there is. There's the one thing I've never told you... or anyone else for that matter, except Jamie now. Not even the therapist ever knew about this."

He sits back again and I glance up at him. His face is white. "What are you talking about, Will?" he whispers.

Somehow, it's easier to say it all the second time around, and I can use words and language with Luke that I couldn't with Jamie; I'd have been too embarrassed with her, but with Luke, I can just say it how it was. He lets me talk, without interrupting, just like she did and when I've finished telling the story, he comes around to my side of the desk and stands in front of me, leaning against it, his legs crossed at the ankles. His face is dark, angry. I don't think I've ever seen him look like this before, not even when his dad used to beat up on me. When he speaks though, his voice is still soft... still Luke.

"Are you telling me that piece of shit tried to get his hookers to fuck you... and when you couldn't, they taunted you, beat you, abused you... and then he and his buddies fucked them in front of you?"

"That just about covers it, yes."

"And this was that night? The night you called me to come get you?"

"Yes."

"Why the hell didn't you tell me, Will?"

"I didn't want to admit it."

"Admit what? What had you done wrong? You were fifteen years old... you were still a child."

"They made me feel ashamed that I couldn't get... you know... hard."

He stills. "And that's why you've never told anyone?" I nod my head and swallow hard.

"And it's why I've never been with a woman... why I've never had sex."

A short silence descends, until he says softly, "Never? Not once?"

"No."

I look at him now. He's running his fingers through his hair. The anger has left his face completely. Instead he just looks sad. "How could

140

I have been so blind? I should've seen," he says, his voice barely audible. "I should've noticed."

"Noticed what?"

"You. You never had a single girlfriend. Now I think about it, you never did. I should have paid more attention. Over the years, I've kind of imagined you must have been with a few women, but now I really think about it… you haven't."

"No."

"If only you'd told me about it at the time, Will…"

"What? What would you have done?"

"Probably killed the son-of-a-bitch," he replies.

"Exactly. And how would that have helped either of us? You'd have ended up in jail and I'd have been stuck in care."

He calms a little. "Okay… so that wouldn't have helped at all, but I could have helped you, if you'd told me sooner."

"How?"

"By explaining to you that their opinion… that their words, their actions, what they did… it was all wrong, and none of it was your fault."

"Jamie said something like that too."

"How come you had this conversation with Jamie? Did something happen between you guys?"

"No. It was to do with work…"

"So you can't tell me?"

"No, I can't. Sorry." I pause for a moment. "The thing is… the reason I'm here is, I want something to happen between Jamie and me."

"Yeah… I kinda got that much already, just seeing you with her."

"But I don't know how."

"Surely you understand how it all works, don't you? Hell, I remember explaining it to you myself when you were a kid—"

"I don't mean that. I understand the mechanics of it. I just don't have a clue how to actually make it happen; how to be with a woman, the emotional part of it; how to make her feel good."

He sighs and leans back a little. "Jeez, Will. I can't give you instructions—"

"Well, if *you* can't, I don't know who can…"

141

"Okay… thanks for that."

"Sorry." I look down at my hands.

"What I mean is, all women are different. There is no great instruction manual that fits all of them."

"So how have you always known what to do?"

"I guess I've just worked it out as I've gone along…"

"Oh great… I'm screwed then."

"Well no, the basic idea is the other way around, really," he smiles down at me and I can't help but smile back. I can always rely on Luke to find the humor, even when I don't think there is any. "I don't know Jamie," he says, "and I have no idea what she'll like, or not like. And that has to be your guide. It's all an instinct."

"An instinct I don't have."

"You will do… when the time is right, trust me, the instinct will be there. And trust yourself that wanting her will be enough to make it right. And then stop worrying about it. Jamie's a good person; she helped you when you told her your story, right?"

"Yeah, she slept with me last night."

"Sorry? In that case, why are we even here talking about this?" he asks.

"I mean *slept*, Luke. I think she just wanted to keep me company, rather than leave me on my own. She stayed the night with me… but we kept our clothes on."

"Oh, I see. But that's just what I'm saying… she's a good person. She helped you last night, she stayed with you; she was there for you. She'll help you with this. A lot of it's about communication."

"So I should ask her what she wants?"

"Well, yes and no… There's a fine line between continually asking a woman what they want and what they like, and how it feels for them, and if it's working… and just going for it regardless. Nothing annoys them more than a guy who keeps asking – it interrupts the flow. But at the same time, you need to make sure you're giving her what she needs, not just thinking about what you want out of it."

"And how the hell do I know if I'm doing that, if I don't ask her?"

"Watch and listen."

"Okay." I study him for a minute.

"Not me, Will… her."

"Oh…"

"Women give away all kinds of things with the noises they make, and the expressions on their faces and in their eyes. You'll get to pick up on that; try and keep eye contact if you can – at least to start with – and listen to every single sound she makes. God, I can't believe I'm having this conversation with you." he says, laughing a little. "Essentially, moaning, groaning, sighing, even screaming is good – especially if it's your name she's screaming. Anything that sounds like pain means you got it wrong and you should try something different, and stony silence is a definite problem."

"And that's it?"

"That's about all I can tell you, yes, except you should always – and I mean *always* – be a gentleman. Be kind… be gentle. Put her first… The rest is down to the two of you to work out. Like I say, it's different for different people. Let her guide you."

"So you're telling me that with all the women you had, you did all that, but it was different every single time?"

He looks at me. "No, that's not what I'm saying at all," he says, coming and sitting next to me. "We're talking about two completely contrasting things here, Will." He pauses. "There's an emotional commitment involved in what you're asking about. You wanted to know how to make love to Jamie, right?" I nod my head. "And that's what I've been telling you. That's where the consideration, the kindness, the caring, the being gentle and being a gentleman comes in… The rest," he says, "what I used to do… it's just fucking."

"There's a difference?"

"Yes. Fucking is cold and emotionless by comparison. There's nothing to it. It's just physical."

"Sounds horrible."

He laughs. "It's not horrible, not at all… but making love is so much better." He looks at me. "Still, hopefully you'll never get to find out the difference. At least if it works out for you guys, anyway."

"So before... with all the others... you didn't care if they got anything out of it?"

"Yeah, I did, kind of – but that was more to do with my ego than their pleasure. And I didn't lose any sleep over it. I told you, I was an asshole before I met Megan."

I stand and he follows me. "I've taken up a lot of your time," I say. "Thanks."

"Did it help?" he asks.

"I don't know. I think so. I've got a lot to think about."

"Don't. Don't overthink it. Just go with your instinct, Will. It'll work out. And I'm sorry."

"What for?"

"For not noticing sooner."

"I didn't want you to notice. I hid it well."

"Yeah. Don't do that again, okay? How many times do I have to tell you... I'm here. You can always talk to me."

"I know. Thanks."

I go over to the door. "Will?" he calls after me. I turn to face him. "Yes."

"There's just one thing…"

"What's that?"

"If you ever repeat any of that conversation to Megan, or anyone else for that matter… I will come after you… I will find you… and I will kill you." He's grinning at me. "Now, get out of here."

All the way home, I think about what Luke said. The one thing that keeps going through my mind is his words about the sounds women make. I've heard Jamie several times now, and I want to hear those sounds again – but I want them to be with me next time. I know that better than anything after talking to Luke. I want to pleasure her, and show her how I feel about her. All I have to do is work out how… and hope the need she spoke of is still there, and I haven't killed it with the revelations about my past.

When I get back the house is quiet. The office door is open and I peer inside. Jamie's sitting in her chair, with her headphones on. I check the screen she's watching. Jack's in his study, but he's typing on his laptop, so I don't think she can be listening to anything important.

She looks as beautiful as ever. She's wearing jeans, and a dark blue and red check shirt, with the sleeves rolled up. I stand and watch her, taking her in.

'Go with your instinct,' Luke said. Well, at the moment, my instinct, my gut, is telling me to kiss her. I've wanted to, deep down, since she smiled at me that first afternoon. I take the couple of steps to bring me behind her chair, then put my hands gently on her shoulders. She startles a little, then tilts her head back and looks up at me, pulls off her headphones and smiles.

"Hello," she says, and with that one word, I'm already hard, but I have the back of her chair between my erection and her; she doesn't need to know what she does to me... not yet anyway. I don't say a word in reply, but stare into her eyes as I lean down and brush my lips across hers. They're soft, tender, inviting. She moans gently and, as her mouth opens, my tongue finds it way to hers, and we explore each other, the intensity building real fast. She brings her hands up and places them over mine and I deepen the kiss, delving further into her mouth, tasting her. She's sweet, like chocolate... and mint. I hear her sigh and a breath hitch in her throat and I pull away slowly. Her cheeks are flushed, her eyes shining and, with her mouth still sightly open she looks too tempting for words.

I want to believe that expression means I got the kiss right, but I can't be sure.

Jamie

He's been gone all morning, to the point where I was starting to get worried, especially after what happened last night, but it seems I had nothing to worry about.

As he breaks the kiss, I stare up into his eyes, not really able to believe what's just happened; that the man I've been longing for and dreaming about, fantasizing about for days on end, has finally kissed me… and what a kiss! I've never been kissed to the point of breathlessness before, and I think I'd like to be kissed like that again… quite soon… in fact, right now… thank you very much.

I turn the chair and stand up to face him. "That was… unexpected," I tell him.

"Good unexpected?" He's really not sure?

"Yes… good unexpected." I move closer and rest my hands on his chest. "Very, very good unexpected," I whisper, looking up at him.

He suddenly looks a little shy; pleased with himself, but shy, and he puts his arms around me, his hands flat on my back, and pulls me in close, kissing me again, like he's been able to read my mind and knows I wanted more. His tongue is soft, yet demanding in my mouth and I match it with my own, seeking his. A gentle growl from the back of his throat echoes into me and I can't help but sigh back at him, like we're having a kissing conversation. Slowly, I move my hands from his chest up around his neck and into his hair, tangling them there, and he changes the angle of his head, tilting it, so he can delve deeper. His hands tighten on my back and he pulls me in a little closer, so I can feel his long, hard erection against my hip. It's gratifying to know I do that to him, that the want and need I'm feeling isn't one way. My nipples stiffen against his chest and there's pool of wetness gathering at the top of my thighs. Yeah, I want him… badly, but I can't do or say anything to progress things. This has to go at his pace, however slow he needs that to be.

We're both breathless by the time he pulls away, and moves back. He seems a little embarrassed by his body's reaction to me and turns away.

"Would you like a coffee?" he asks.

"Um… sure." It wasn't quite the response I'd hoped for, after a kiss like that, but he needs time to get used to how this works, I guess. He squeezes past me, not making eye contact, and goes out into the kitchen.

I stand with my hands in my pockets for a while, wondering if I should go after him, or ignore what just happened. If I go after him, he might start thinking we have to dissect and analyze every thought and feeling; and that's counter-productive, when we should just be following our instincts, going with what feels natural and right. But if I don't say something, he might never kiss me again, just out of sheer awkwardness, and fear of the way his body responds when we do. I'm still standing, undecided when he walks back in, with a cup in each hand.

He puts them both down on the table and then looks at me and puts his hands in his pockets, mirroring my stance.

"I liked that," I tell him. "What you did… I really liked it." I want him to know it was good.

"You did?"

"Yes." I smile up at him. "I liked all of it."

"I'm sorry I got…" He can't seem to finish the sentence.

I wait a couple of seconds, then try to do it for him. "Aroused?" I suggest.

He nods his head and I take a step forward so I'm standing right in front of him, but I don't touch him, or even take my hands from my pockets. "Please don't apologize. I especially liked that," I whisper. "I liked that kissing me had that effect on you. That makes me feel good." A frown creases his brow. "But I understand if you're not ready to act on it yet, and that's okay. Take as much time as you need, Will. I can wait." He goes to speak, but I take my right hand from my pocket and place my fingers flat over his lips. "Shh, you don't need to say anything," I tell him quietly.

He reaches up and, with his eyes fixed on mine, he takes hold of my hand, and one by one, he kisses my fingers, then slowly slides the tip of each one into his mouth and I watch, mesmerized, my lips parting. The look in his eyes, the dark promise behind them, and what he's doing with his mouth is so hot, and yet I'm sure he doesn't even know it.

He holds my forefinger in his lips, sucking it gently before just nipping it slightly between his teeth, then he lets go and I have to grip the back of the chair, just to stay upright.

"Oh, God," I whimper, because I can't help myself

"Are you okay?" he asks, reaching out for me with both hands.

"Um… yes." I stare up at him. "That was…"

"What?"

"Really sexy… and very, very arousing."

"Oh." He takes a half step back, letting me go again.

"And I liked it," I tell him quickly. "A lot… And none of that means we have to do anything more, not if you don't want to. We can take this at whatever speed suits you."

"I'm sorry," he says.

"Why are you sorry?"

He pauses, looking down at the floor between us. "Because I didn't realize that would arouse you. I just did it because I wanted to… but it's hardly fair to do things that turn you on when I can't do anything about it."

"Am I complaining?" I ask.

"Well, no."

"Precisely."

He raises his head and looks at me. God, the intensity in his eyes… "I do want you, Jamie. I really do… I want you so much… I'm just not ready."

"And I told you, I'm okay with that." I close the gap between us and stand still, just a few inches from him, letting him choose whether or not to touch me. He does. He pulls me into his arms and holds me.

"Thank you," he murmurs into my hair, and I snake my hands around his waist. And standing here like this… it feels like the best place there's ever been.

We sit and drink coffee in silence for a while.

"Has much happened this morning?" he asks eventually.

"No, absolutely nothing. Jack came into his study about an hour before you got back, and spent the whole time on his laptop. Other than that, I haven't seen either of them."

Another silence descends. I don't like it. I don't like the thought that our new-found intimacy is making us feel awkward together. I reach down and roll up the sleeve of my shirt, which must have unraveled itself while Will and I were kissing.

"Your friend Todd," I say, turning to Will, wanting to find something to talk to him about, other than work and kissing, and where kissing might lead.

"What about him?"

"He's got a tattoo on his arm."

"Yes."

"It's in Chinese."

"And you want to know what it means?" He turns and looks at me and, thank God, he's smiling. "You'll have to try asking him. We all have and he's never told any of us."

"That's mysterious."

"It's probably nothing at all," he says. "Just Todd trying to be enigmatic. Either that or it's his favorite take-out order, and he's had it tattooed so he can't forget it." He grins and leans forward, so he's closer to me. "You can ask him on Christmas Eve, if you like."

"I can? How come?"

"We're going to a party."

"We are?"

He nods his head. "Matt and Grace are having a party at their place. We're invited."

"With who else?" I'm suddenly nervous.

"Just Luke and Megan, and Todd. Matt and Grace are the only ones you won't have met. It'll be fine." He's sensed my concern about being in a crowd of people straight away.

"So… it's just an informal dinner, is it?"

"No." He hesitates for a moment. "It's a formal thing. Long dresses, tuxes… you know the deal."

It's like suddenly the room's gone cold and yet my hands are sweating. I wipe them down the sides of my jeans.

"But… I can't, Will. I mean, I've got nothing here to wear for something like that. Well, I've got nothing at home either… nothing that fits anyway. And I can't face the shops just three days before Christmas, not with my leg like it is right now. No-one's gonna miss me if I'm not there. You go on your own. I'll stay here." I know I sound pathetic.

He's staring at me. "No," he says.

"But I can't go."

"Why not?"

"I just told you. I've got nothing to wear."

"Is that the only reason?"

"Well… mostly."

"What's the rest of it?" he asks, grabbing the arm of my chair and moving it a little closer to his.

I start fiddling with my fingers in my lap, until he places his hand over mine. "Tell me," he says, echoing my words to him from last night.

"Megan's beautiful," I tell him.

"Yes she is," he replies.

"And I'm sure Grace is too."

"Yes."

"And I'll feel out of place."

"Why? Because you don't think you are?" I don't reply. "Look at me," he says, and I do. His eyes are focused on mine. "You're the most beautiful woman I've ever seen," he says. "And you're wrong… If you don't go, *I'll* miss you. So you're going."

"But…"

"You've got nothing to wear?" He gets up and goes round behind my chair and out of the room, then returns a few minutes later, carrying a large, black, flattish box, with a silver ribbon around it, and two bags.

"You can't open these yet," he says. "Not until it's time to get ready for the party. But you have to trust me… you've got something to wear."

He places the packages on the desk in front of me. "You bought me a dress?" I ask him.

"Wait and see," he replies, smiling and sitting back down again.

"Is this where you've been all morning?"

He looks up. "No," he says. "I went out and bought these things at the weekend… on Sunday afternoon."

Sunday afternoon… I think back. It was when he got back on Sunday that we talked about Patrick and I told him I wasn't seeing him anymore. Up until then, he thought I had a boyfriend – a long-standing boyfriend. So, when he went out and bought all this… whatever it is… for me, he had no idea we could ever get together, or be anything, other than friends.

I get up and move to stand in front of him, placing my feet between his, then I turn to one side. "I know this might make you a little uncomfortable," I tell him. He looks up at me, and tilts his head to one side, because he doesn't seem to know what I'm going to do... so I just sit on his lap. He hesitates for a second, then brings his arms around me and I curl into him, pulling my legs up. "Thank you," I say into his chest.

"You haven't seen it yet," he says.

"I'm sure I'll like it, whatever it is." I'm excited to see it already, and it's been a long time since I've felt like that. I lean up and kiss his cheek. "I think it's the nicest thing anyone's ever done for me."

He shifts slightly in his chair.

"Sorry... Am I too heavy for you?" I ask, going to get down again. He tightens his grip a little.

"No... of course you're not. But, you were right. I am uncomfortable."

"Okay. I'm sorry... I'll move."

"No. I don't want you to. Not yet."

"But if me being here makes you feel uncomfortable..."

"Not that kind of uncomfortable," he whispers and I clearly look confused. "Jamie," he explains, "you're sitting on my lap; you're beautiful, you're sexy, and I want you. You figure it it out."

And he leans down and kisses me.

Chapter Fourteen

Will

I'd planned on keeping the dress until just before the party, but seeing that crestfallen look on her face was too much. I couldn't make her wait another two days, worrying about it, or threatening not to go. As if I'd let her not go with me. That's been the whole point of all the preparation.

Her lips are soft and gentle on mine. I really like kissing her; and it's good to know she likes it too; and that she's not phased by what she does to me. I'd expected... well, I don't know what I'd expected really. Outrage, maybe? Embarrassment? But she likes that I'm aroused by her, and that's good, because there's not a lot I can do about it. Just being in the same room with her turns me on. Having her sitting on my lap, like this, is driving me insane. But it's a good kind of insane.

I'm still not sure what to do about it, how to take things further than where we are now, but I like that we're both okay with being turned on by each other. Now I know there's no pressure, I'm feeling more relaxed about it – much more than I thought I would be.

There's something different about this kiss. Her lips and tongue still feel the same, still delving around mine and she's moaning into my mouth. Her body still feels fantastic, pressed against me. I'm still hard... it takes me a minute to work out that it's the taste that's different. She's not chocolate and mint this time; there's a saltiness. And her lips are wetter. *Shit...* she's crying. I pull away.

"What's wrong?" Crying while kissing can't be good. Luke didn't mention it, but it can't be good.

"Nothing," she says.

"I must've done something. Tell me... What have I done?"

"Oh, Will. You haven't done anything... except be the sweetest, kindest man I've ever met."

Now I'm really confused. "Then why are you crying?"

"*Because* you're the sweetest, kindest man I've ever met. They're good tears," she says.

"So you're not unhappy, or hurt?"

"No. I'm the opposite of both of those."

I breathe out. "Okay." That's alright then. "I thought I'd done something wrong," I tell her.

"You've done everything right," she replies, and places her hands on my cheeks. "So right," she whispers, and places her lips over mine again.

It's only when I hear her stomach grumbling that I realize we haven't eaten yet. It's nearly two o'clock as well. I didn't have breakfast; I'm not sure Jamie did either, and neither of us has had lunch. She's resting her head on my chest, still sitting on my lap.

"We should eat," I tell her.

"You noticed I'm hungry then..."

"It was hard to miss."

I glance up at the screen. Jack's still typing. "We're not missing anything here. We'll go make something together."

"There's some cold chicken. We could have a salad?"

"Okay."

I lift her off my lap and onto her feet, then stand and take her hand, leading her into the kitchen.

It doesn't take long to throw together a salad and we take our bowls back into the office. Jack's on the phone, and I quickly pull on my headphones, hoping we haven't missed anything, although we've got it all recorded.

Jamie's looking at me expectantly and I pull back one side of my headphones.

"It's nothing," I tell her. "I think he's talking to his mother. They're discussing plans for Christmas."

She starts eating her salad. "We're not getting very far with this, are we?"

"No." It's disheartening. I really thought we were onto something, but since the conversation between Jack and Kimberley, nothing's happened.

"What else can we do?"

"We really need more surveillance. I need access to his laptop, and we need more cameras… at his home and the office. There must be another cell phone too, a burner they're using to contact Jack's wife."

"But we can't do all that… We don't have the equipment, or the manpower."

I take a forkful of chicken and lettuce and chew for a minute. "We could probably manage without the manpower, but we can't check out the equipment without Jack knowing and asking questions… There is one thing we can do, though."

"What?"

"We can take what we've got to Sean Donaldson."

"Jack's boss?"

"Yes."

"Have we got enough evidence to do that?" she asks.

"No. But I can't think of a way of getting more… not by ourselves."

"Do you think he'll listen?"

"I'm not sure. He and Jack go back a long way."

"And if he doesn't listen?"

"Then I might well be out of a job. I've already broken quite a few rules to get what we've got."

"Then I've broken them with you."

"Yeah, but I'm the senior agent, Jamie. You can always claim you were acting on my instructions."

"I couldn't do that."

"You could. And you should. I'd want you to. You're forgetting, I don't really want this job anymore."

"Neither do I."

I look across at her. "What do you think? Shall I call him?"

She shrugs. "What have we got to lose?"

"Our jobs, our livelihoods, our homes…"

She puts her fork down in her bowl and turns to me, looking into my eyes. "Nothing important then."

I lean over and kiss her gently. "No, nothing important."

There's no time like the present. Once we've finished eating, Jamie clears away and makes us both a coffee and I look up Sean's contact details and dial his number, while Jamie sits beside me. She's nervous – I can tell because she's fidgeting with her fingers, so I hold her hands in my free one, while waiting for the call to connect.

"Hello?" Sean picks up eventually.

"Sean," I say. "It's Will Myers, from the Boston office."

"Oh… We've met before, haven't we?"

"Yes. We met when you came down here in August… after…"

"Yes, I remember. Bad business that."

"Yes, sir."

He waits for a moment. "How can I help you, Will?" he asks.

"I need to speak with you, sir, about the investigation into what happened that day."

"Jack's handling that, isn't he?"

"Well, Jack gave it to me to look into, and report back to him."

"Then why are you calling me?"

I swallow and take a breath. "Because it's Jack I need to talk to you about, sir."

The line goes silent and I wait for what seems like a long time. "Carry on," he says eventually.

"Jack sent Jamie Blackwood down here to help me with monitoring the six agents who participated in the op, who all had access to the information and could reasonably have been assumed to have passed it on to the terrorist cell," I tell him, then I glance at Jamie. "She was also given instructions by Jack to investigate me."

"Well, that's legitimate, isn't it? You were involved in the op too."

"Yes, sir."

"I take it Miss Blackwood hasn't found anything on you?"

"No, sir. There's nothing to find." He doesn't reply, so I carry on. "We monitored the subjects, as instructed, even though I'd already told Jack that my earlier investigations gave me no reason to believe any of them were guilty."

"And?" he asks.

"And nothing, sir. They've all just been living normal lives. Not doing anything out of the ordinary."

"Right…" He's waiting.

"I decided that the only other person who knew everything, who had the same opportunities as these other subjects – and myself – was Jack. And yet no-one has looked into him."

"So you think we should?" he asks.

I clear my throat. "I already have." Again there's a long silence.

"And?" His voice is very quiet.

"I don't have much, except a conversation between Jack and his wife. Someone's blackmailing them."

"What about?"

"Her background," I tell him.

"What's her background got to do with anything?"

I take another deep breath. "Before they were married, Mrs Fielding was a prostitute."

"You are kidding me."

"No, sir."

"Why the hell didn't we know about this?" He's mad… he's really mad.

"I don't know that, sir."

I can hear him sighing on the end of the line. "Okay," he says, "so, she was a hooker. How do you know she's being blackmailed?"

"I put cameras into his home, sir." Jamie nudges me and points to herself, but I shake my head.

"You did what?" I don't reply. I know he heard me. "Where did you get the equipment?"

"I had the cameras here." Jamie nudges me again, but I ignore her this time.

"And you unilaterally decided to break into his home and plant these devices, did you?"

"Yes, sir."

"With no help at all… Not from Miss Blackwood, or anyone else?"

"No, sir."

There's another long silence. "You'd better have gotten something concrete out of this, or I'll throw the fucking book at you, Myers," he says. "The very least I expect from my agents is loyalty."

"Loyalty's a two way street. And as far as I'm concerned, you can throw whatever you like at me. But check out what I've got first."

"Okay. Send me everything you have. I'll call you back." He hangs up.

I put my phone down on the desk and turn to Jamie.

"Why did you do that?" she asks. "Why take all the blame? We both made the decision to go after Jack. We both went down there."

"They can hang me out to dry, if they want, but I won't let them do anything to you." I run the back of my fingers down her cheek and she closes her eyes, leaning into my touch. "We broke more than a few rules doing this, Jamie… we broke the law. I can't let them near you – or Todd. This is all on me."

She opens her eyes again. "Does that mean you could go to jail?"

"No." I'm lying. Jail time is a real possibility, but I'm not going to tell Jamie that. "They can't let that happen," I continue. "They can't afford the publicity."

"Then why say you acted alone?"

"To protect you."

"You don't have to."

"Yeah, I do." I reach across and pull her closer, kissing her. "I do," I say into her mouth. Then I break away and sit back. "I've gotta send these files over to Sean."

"And then what?"

"And then he'll look at them and call us back."

"How long will that take?"

"Depends on what he makes of it all."

He clearly made quite a lot of it. He calls back within the hour. We're standing in the kitchen when my phone rings.

"I'm going to fly up there on Monday," he says, not bothering with a hello.

"The day after Christmas?"

"Yes."

"Okay."

"Where shall I meet you?" he asks.

"You can come here, if you want."

"No... somewhere out in the open would be better. Somewhere I know there aren't any cameras. Where no-one's listening in..."

"Are you saying you don't trust me?" I ask him.

"I'm saying I'm starting to question my own judgment," he replies. "Tell me where to meet you."

"There are some benches, by the frog pond in Boston Common. I'll meet you there."

"Okay. I'll be landing around eleven, so we'll say twelve-thirty." He's already booked his flight then.

"Still want to throw the book at me?" I ask.

"No. What you did was fucking unethical *and* illegal, but you're a lucky son-of-a-bitch. It looks like you were right." He hangs up.

"And that makes everything okay," I mutter to myself, putting my phone down on the countertop.

"What happened?" Jamie asks. She's been nervous as hell since my earlier call to Sean, terrified someone was going to come and drag me away in cuffs, never to be seen again.

"He's coming up on Monday."

"And you're meeting him at Boston Common... I got that. What did he say about throwing the book at you?"

"It's fine. I'm in the clear."

"Are you just telling me that so I'll feel better?"

I put a hand on both of her cheeks, and look deep into her eyes. "No. He said it's okay, because we were right."

"Oh, so it's 'we' again now, is it? Because *we're* safe, you're happy to include me?"

I nod my head. "You did just as much work as I did."

"But you'd have taken all the blame if we'd been wrong?"

"Well, yeah. But I knew we weren't wrong."

She puts her arms around my waist and holds me. "Don't ever take a risk like that again," she says.

"I wasn't."

"Oh, really?"

"Okay, I was, but it was a calculated risk."

She leans back a little and looks up at me. "Get one thing straight," she says. "And remember it… It's not just you anymore, okay?"

What does that mean? "I don't know…" I start to say.

"You can't make decisions like that by yourself," she explains, and her voice catches. "I care about you, Will. I care about what happens to you… and to us. Okay?" She's upset, but also verging on angry, I think.

"Okay," I tell her. "I'm sorry." I hold onto her. "I care about you too, you know."

"I think I got that." She breathes out a long breath and snuggles into me.

Jamie

I calmed down eventually yesterday, but I was angry with him… Well, angry and upset and kind of humbled that he'd do that for me. But mostly, I think I was scared. I was really scared. Once I realized how serious it could be; that he could go to jail for what we'd done, fear overcame everything and, in my relief, it came out as anger.

I think he understood what I meant. He must have done. We spent the whole evening on the couch together and he kept telling me how sorry he was… and kissing me. It was almost worth going through that traumatic afternoon, just for an evening of his kisses.

At bedtime, I kind of hoped we might end up sleeping in his room again. Sleeping would have been enough; but he kissed me goodnight and opened my bedroom door, letting me know he's not ready for that yet. I guess it's one thing to sleep together because you just need someone to hang onto; it's something else entirely when you know you both want more.

Still, I've told him – and myself – that I'll wait… and I will.

We monitored Jack yesterday, but he went into the office for most of the day, so there was nothing much going on and we've stopped watching the others completely now, and their monitors are all switched off, which is a relief for both of us, I think. Not only was it boring, but prying into their private lives was unpleasant and left us both with a nasty taste in our mouths.

Today, being Christmas Eve, Jack and his wife left early to go visit with his parents for the holidays. They won't be back until Tuesday, so we've got nothing to do until then, except prepare for Will's meeting with Sean on Monday. And there's not even much to do for that.

We're sitting on the couch, after lunch. Will's in the corner and I'm resting between his legs, leaning back on his chest, with his arms tight around me.

"Tell me about your friends," I say to him.

"You'll meet them tonight."

"I know. That's why I want to know about them."

"You know most of them already."

"I know Luke and Megan. I've met Todd. I don't *know* him, and I've never met Matt or Grace."

"What do you want to know?"

"How did you all meet?"

"I know everyone through Luke. Matt and he shared an apartment at college. Todd and Matt met at a gym a couple of years later."

"Are they all the same age?"

"Matt and Luke are. Todd's a year older."

"And Matt owns the company Luke works for? Or do they own it together? I didn't really understand that."

"Matt started the company straight out of college…"

"Manufacturing sportswear?"

"Yeah. Then he brought Luke in a couple of years later, and a while after that, he gave him a share in the business. They started the lingerie side two, maybe three years ago. I don't keep track."

"And how did Matt and Grace meet?"

He turns a little, so I'm lying on the couch and he's propped up on his elbow next to me. "Grace is British," he says, looking down at me. "Matt took her on to design the company's website. They fell in love."

"You make it sound simple."

"Well, there was more to it than that."

"Such as?"

"Grace had a stalker, who we all thought was her husband."

"Wait a minute… she had a husband?"

"Well, no. He was dead."

"Will, you're not explaining this very well."

He chuckles. "No, I'm not." He moves down the sofa, lying next to me and pulling me into him. "Grace had been married," he begins. "Her husband died the day Matt was due to meet with her to discuss the new website."

"Oh no, how awful."

"Normally, yes. But Grace's husband was an asshole. He… well… he used to beat her. Badly. And he had a mistress… several mistresses, actually, but one in particular, who was pregnant, with his child."

"Okay, I'm not sorry he died now."

"Neither was Grace. But a few months later, someone started sending her nasty text messages. It went on for ages and, when she started seeing Matt, he found out about it and asked me and Todd to look into it. It looked, to start with, like it might be her husband."

"How? He was dead."

"He was also a doctor… a fairly eminent surgeon… perfectly capable of faking his own death. Todd didn't really go with my theory. He was right."

"So the guy was dead?"

"Yes."

"Then who was the stalker?"

"An ex-girlfriend of Matt's."

"You're kidding."

"No. I wish I was. He only dated her for a few weeks, but she didn't like him ending it and turned up at his apartment with a knife. Todd arrested her and she went to jail for a while… It should've been longer," he explains.

"And she was the one who was sending the messages?"

"Yes. And then when Matt brought Grace back here and they moved in together, she turned up at their place. She'd tricked Matt into leaving by telling him Luke had been in a car crash. She'd upgraded from a knife to a gun this time though."

"Oh my God… what happened?"

"I wasn't there. Luke went… with Todd, but she shot Matt. Then Todd shot her. She didn't make it. Matt did – obviously."

"And Grace?"

"She was unharmed." I take a deep breath. "It was a distressing time for both of them," he adds.

"For all of you," I tell him.

He shrugs. "I guess."

"And Todd?" I ask. "What's his story?"

"He's been a cop all the time I've known him."

"Here in Boston?"

"Yes."

"And does he have a girlfriend?"

"Not at the moment, no."

I take a deep breath. "You're all very close, aren't you?"

"Yeah. Luke and Matt are the glue, really. Everything kind of hangs off them. You'll see them together tonight. You'll see what I mean then."

I hope so.

Will switches on the TV and flicks through the channels. *It's a Wonderful Life* has just started. It's the perfect Christmas Eve movie and we settle down and watch it. I love this film. It's one of my all time favorites...

James Stewart is just congratulating Clarence on getting his wings, when I move to get up, brushing away a couple of tears. This movie always does that to me.

"Where are you going?" Will asks. "And why are you crying?" He grabs hold of me and pulls me back down next to him.

"To start getting ready for tonight." I sniff. "And it's the movie. I always cry at the end."

"It's only four o'clock," he says.

"Yes, which means I've only got two hours."

"Oh... this is the whole getting ready thing, then?" I nod my head, smiling. I've been looking forward to this ever since he gave me the box and the bags and told me I could open them today. "And the tears? Good tears?" he asks.

"Yes."

"Okay." He lets me go again. "See you in a couple of hours, I guess."

I get up, but lean down and kiss him. "Thank you," I say, then I go through to my bedroom and close the door. I haven't felt like this for years; it's that frisson of excitement, knowing an evening out, all dressed up, awaits.

An hour and a half later, I'm showered, I've moisturized, I've done my makeup and my hair is nearly finished. Will's never seen me with my hair up. I take a deep breath. I hope he likes it. Putting the last clip in place, I step back from the mirror. Not bad... not bad at all.

I've waited until now to open the packages. It's like waiting for birthdays or Christmas... half the pleasure is in the anticipation. Sitting on the edge of the bed, I open the box first, and pull back the delicate tissue paper. And my breath catches in my throat. I stand and pull out the most beautiful dress I've ever seen. It's black lace, strapless, with a sweetheart neckline, and it appears that parts of it are see-through, but they're not because it's got a flesh-colored lining. And around the neckline, across the bodice, and down the long, flowing skirt, are red embroidered roses. I turn it around. The pattern of flowers is repeated on the back. I can't stop staring at it. I check the size, just in case... Size ten. It's perfect. How did he know?

An awful thought occurs to me. I've got no suitable shoes, or underwear to go with this. I guess I can make do with my underwear – no-one but me will ever know – but shoes? I can hardly wear Converse with this.

I lay the dress on the bed and open the first of the two bags. Inside there are two boxes. The first contains a black clutch bag. It's plain black satin, very simple and elegant. In the second, there is a pair of black Jimmy Choo strappy sandals, with heels that are a good four inches high. It's been a long, long time since I've worn anything like this. I'm not sure how long I'll be able to keep them on for, but I'll certainly try. They're gorgeous... Again, I check the size, and again, they're exactly right.

This leaves me one bag. I pull it open and peer inside and then tip out the contents on the bed. I'm staring down at a pile of sexy, lacy lingerie, the like of which I've never worn before. Some of it is black, but a couple of things are what I guess would be termed 'nude'. A piece of paper is lying on top. It must've been inside the bag. It's folded in half with my name written on it. I open it and read:

'Jamie,

I didn't want to make this choice for you.

Whatever you don't wear tonight, you can keep – courtesy of Luke, not me.

Choose whatever you want to wear... for yourself, and no-one else.

Because tonight's all about you.

Will'

I perch on the edge of the bed, and the tears flow down my cheeks, a sob accompanying them. How can he be so kind? Luke obviously helped, but the idea was his, I know that. All these things... he's spent a lot of money and put a lot of thought into it. And it's all for me. I sob again. Then I hear a knocking on my door.

"Jamie?"

"Yes?" I clear my throat.

"Are you okay?"

"Yes."

"Are they good tears?" he asks. I smile. He knows – he gets it.

"Yes," I call out to him.

"Do you need anything?"

He's given me all this and he's still offering more? Actually, I could do with a hug, but it'll wait. "No, I'm fine. I'll be out in a few minutes."

"Okay."

I look at the time. I haven't got long.

I go through to the bathroom and check my make-up. Hmm, it's going to need work...

A few minutes of repairs and I'm good to go again. Now, I just have to choose the underwear. I rifle through the selection. All the bras have removable straps, so I choose a black one, and check the size... 36C... Once again – how did he know? I try it on. It's so comfortable and a perfect fit. The cup is made of the finest, softest lace I've ever felt; it's completely see-through, with scalloped edging and embroidered flowers with crystals in the center of each. There are matching briefs and a garter belt, with lace-topped black stockings. I put it all on and stand in front of the full-length mirror. I haven't looked, or felt this sexy in my whole life. Time's moving on though, and I unzip the dress and step into it, pulling it up and fastening it. It does up at the side, thank goodness, or I'd need Will's help. Then I sit on the bed, put on the shoes, buckle them and stand, once more, before the mirror... Just a quick re-touch to my lipstick and hair. I'm ready.

I feel good about myself; really good. I even feel beautiful... and Will did that... for me.

Chapter Fifteen

Will

She wasn't supposed to cry. It was supposed to make her happy; to make her feel beautiful, good about herself; valued; appreciated for what she is now, not what she used to be.

I've been pacing the living room floor for the last half hour, waiting for her to come out, worrying that I got it wrong – again. I hope the tears were because she likes it all, not because I've reminded her of anything bad. She said they were good tears, so…

I hear her door opening and I can feel myself holding my breath, the sweat forming on my palms. What if she hates it? What if none of it fits…

She appears in front of me… and my voice won't work. She's stolen it, together with my breath, and my sanity… and my heart, which she's been slowly claiming, piece by piece since the day she arrived. And now, looking at her, I know my heart is hers, entirely.

I'm staring, and I think my mouth is open and there's not a damn thing I can do about it. There's an expectant look on her face and I know I'm supposed to say something; do something… I just need my mouth, my voice, my body and my heart to start functioning again. *C'mon Will… for Christ's sake.*

"You're exquisite," I tell her, although I know my voice sounds a little croaky, and I know there aren't enough words to describe her, or how I feel about her.

The dress hangs perfectly, hugging her figure, showing off her breasts and her waist, and giving the impression – the hint – of nudity, although it's all illusion; the lining behind the lace provides that effect, but the impression is seductive... and so damned sexy. She's smiling at me. Her eyes are shimmering in the lights from the Christmas tree behind me and, with her hair up and her shoulders exposed, she looks spectacular. "You really are the most beautiful woman I've ever seen, Jamie," I say, and her smile broadens still further. I walk across to her and take her hands, then kiss her cheek.

"Thank you," she whispers. "You've done so much for me..."

I press my finger to her lips. "I need to ask you a question," I say. She looks at me. "Do you mind getting your Christmas present a day early?"

"This isn't my Christmas present?" she asks, a little incredulous.

"No. That's not the present." I pull the mid-sized square box from my pocket. "This is your present. The rest is just something I wanted to do for you. This..." I tap the box. "This is for Christmas. But, if you want to wear it tonight, you'll have to accept having it a day early." I pass it to her. She looks up at me and slowly starts to open it. As she does, I snap it closed again and her sparkling eyes dart up to mine. "There's one condition though," I tell her.

"What's that?"

"You can't cry. We're already running a little late. There isn't time for you to re-do your makeup again."

"I'll try," she says, smiling, and I let go of the box.

She opens it and gasps, then looks at me again.

"No, Will," she says. "I can't... It's too much."

"Do you like it?"

"Of course I do."

"Then it's not too much." I take the necklace from the box and move around behind her. Her hair's up, and just before I fasten it, I trace a line of kisses from her shoulder, up her neck to her ear. She shivers and a tiny moan escapes her mouth. Then I fasten the necklace and let it hang, before I come around in front of her again. I wasn't wrong. As soon as I saw it, I knew it was perfect for her. It's in the shape of a rose, in full bloom, the petals alternating, either matte white gold, or tiny studded diamonds. I drag my eyes away from it to her face. She leans forward, her eyes on mine, and kisses me gently and I pull her into me, feeling her bare back and shoulders as I deepen the kiss. She opens to me, her tongue finding mine and her arms come around my neck, her fingers twisting in my hair.

"I don't know what to say," she murmurs, when she finally pulls away, breathless.

"Just tell me you're happy."

"I'm happy," she smiles.

"Good." I take her hand. "Then we need to go."

Jamie

As if the dress, the underwear, the shoes and the bag weren't enough, he's also given me the most beautiful necklace. The rose shape mirrors the embroidery on the dress, and the diamonds shine and sparkle in the light. I've never owned anything like this before – let alone been given it by a man who's gotten so far under my skin, he's become a part of me.

His eyes when he saw me were a mirror of my own when I first glimpsed him in a tux. Having lived and breathed in jeans and casual tops for the last couple of weeks, it came as a shock to see him in the smart black jacket, pants, white shirt and black bow-tie. I've seen men in tuxes before – often – but I've never seen a man wear a tux quite like this.

The half-hour drive is over quickly and I'm more nervous than I expected as Will helps me out of his Jeep. I didn't think to bring a jacket or anything else to wear and I'm freezing, but he's parked as close to the steps of Matt and Grace's house as he can. He rings the doorbell and, within seconds, a woman answers. I'd expected her to be beautiful, and pregnant, because that's what Will had told me... I hadn't expected her to live up to her name as well, not within a second of meeting me for the first time.

"Jamie…" she says, opening the door wider to let us in. "You look beautiful, and that dress… it's just stunning. Come in out of the cold… welcome to our home."

Behind her, a man appears. He's also wearing a tux and he carries it just as well as Will. He's very tall, with dark hair and gray eyes, and he puts an arm around Grace, before leaning forward slightly.

"I'm Matt," he says. "You must be Jamie."

"Yes."

"And this is Grace," Will adds. I turn to the woman who opened the door. She's about my height, with brown hair, that she's wearing in an elegant, loose bun at the nape of her neck. Her dress is black, with a cross-over neckline and capped sleeves. The bodice, from the top of her bump up, is made of black scallop-edged lace, with a background of dusky pink lining. It's stylish and sophisticated.

"It's so lovely to meet you," she says and I notice her British accent.

"Thank you for inviting me."

"How could we not invite you?" she says. "Now, come on through and meet everyone else, although I think you already know them all, actually."

She steers me gently from the hallway into the large living room, where Megan and Luke are sitting on one couch, and Todd on another, either side of a roaring log fire. In the corner is a huge Christmas tree, decorated with white lights and glass ornaments. Grace is definitely a woman with style. Luke and Todd stand as soon as they see me and Luke helps Megan get to her feet, then they all move forward.

Each of the men looks stunning in their suits… although my eyes are still drawn to Will, who hasn't taken his from me. Todd and Luke both kiss me on my cheek, and then I turn to Megan. She's worn her hair long, cascading over her shoulders in soft ringlets, and her dress is silver-grey, all-over lace, with a blue background, and a dark blue sash across the top of her bump.

"It's good to see you again," she says, coming over to me. "You look so good in that dress."

"Thank you. Not as good as you do though."

"Oh, Grace and I had such fun choosing these," she replies, laughing a little. "It's not often pregnant women get to be this elegant, is it? So we thought we'd go all out."

"I know," Grace says, joining us, "I'm so used to maternity jeans, or leggings and baggy tops, it's really quite nice to be wearing a skirt for a change."

"When are you both due?" I ask.

"I'm due at the beginning of March," Megan says. "Grace is a few weeks later."

"It wasn't planned that we'd have our babies so close together," Grace replies, laughing.

"In my case, it wasn't planned at all," Megan jokes.

"Still, it must be nice having someone to share it all with though," I say.

"Oh, yes. It is." Grace gives Megan a look and they both smile. "Matt?" Grace calls over her shoulder.

"Yes, baby?" He breaks away from the group of men and walks toward us.

"Can you fix some drinks?" she asks.

"Of course I can." He brings his arms around her from behind, kisses her neck and turns to me. "What can I get you, Jamie?" he asks.

"White wine?"

"Sure."

"I'm okay with my water," Megan says.

"And I'll have another orange juice, please," Grace tells him.

"Coming right up."

He goes away and the men all follow him out of he room.

"Don't they look amazing in their suits?" Megan says. "I've been teasing Luke about it all evening."

"Teasing? How?" I ask.

"As to which one of them looks best."

"And?"

"Who do you think?" she asks.

"Will, of course," I reply.

They look at each other and at the same time, they both reply:

"Luke," and "Matt," both loyal to their respective partners.

"But," says Grace, "Todd looks pretty good too."

"I heard that," Matt's voice filters into the room before he enters, bringing my glass of wine and Grace her orange juice. He hands them to us.

"I did say you looked best," Grace says, turning to him. "But I can't leave him out."

"No, really… you can," Matt replies. "He can take it." He grins down at her.

"He can take what?" Luke says, coming back into the room, with a beer in his hand.

"Not you, Todd," Matt says.

"What about me?" Todd joins us.

"My wife was just telling Jamie and Megan that she thinks you scrub up okay."

"Was she now?" Todd grins at Grace.

"Don't get excited," she says.

"Yeah… you don't scrub up nearly as well as me, evidently," Matt adds.

"She's only saying that because she has to live with you."

"She doesn't *have* to," Grace says.

"Oh? Doesn't she?" Matt turns to her, smiling.

"No… she *chooses* to."

"Oh, excuse me while I go vomit somewhere," Todd says. "Anyway, I'm intrigued… why are we all dressed up like this anyway? We don't normally bother when it's just us."

"Because you all look so lovely," Grace says. "And, anyway, don't you enjoy getting dressed up?"

"Not especially, not after the day I've had."

"Well, I thought it would make a change," Grace answers.

"And that's always a good thing, is it?" Todd asks.

"In this instance, yes. So stop moaning."

I can't help enjoying the easy-going conversation and I glance across at Will, who's standing to one side. He's smiling, watching me, and I smile back.

"Now," Grace says, "I just need to check the dinner. We'll be eating in a few minutes."

"What are we having?" Todd inquires.

"I've done a traditional British Christmas dinner," she replies.

"Yeah… basically, it's Thanksgiving all over again," Matt adds.

"You can always sleep in the guest room, you know," Grace tells him, a grin spreading across her face.

"You'd never get through a whole night without me…" he teases, grabbing her and pulling her into him.

"Would you like to test that?" she teases back, trying and failing to break free of him.

"No." He kisses her just briefly on the lips, and his face turns serious just for a moment. "Never," he adds.

"No, neither would I," Grace replies and he releases her. She moves toward the door.

"Can I help at all?" I call after her.

"No, Jamie, thanks," she replies. "It's all just about done. You make yourself at home." We all sit down on the couches: Will and I on one, Luke and Megan on the other, cuddled together, with Todd on the chair in between and Matt perched on the arm of the sofa, next to Luke.

"How's work going?" Luke asks Todd.

"Busy," he replies. "I'm working tomorrow."

"Christmas Day?" Megan says.

"Yeah, although I probably won't do a full day."

"Why do you have to work Christmas Day?" I ask him.

"I'm on a murder case," he says. "A double murder case…"

"But surely there's not a lot you can investigate on Christmas Day?" Matt asks.

"It only happened yesterday. There's still all the evidence to go over, interviews to look through, forensics… I could go on, but I'm having a night off. Although I never thought I'd spend my first night off in a week trussed up like a turkey." He runs his finger around his collar.

"The turkey's for dinner," Matt says.

"I feel like I am right now," Todd replies.

"It can be arranged," Luke adds, "if you don't stop whining."

I notice Will doesn't join in their banter, but watches them all with affection, sipping his beer, and glancing at me every so often.

Grace pokes her head around the door. "Dinner's ready," she says, and we all go through the hallway and into the formal dining room, which has been laid with silver cutlery, fine china, crystal glasses and candles… lots of candles. There's another Christmas tree in the corner of this room, and while this also has white lights, the ornaments in here are all miniature wooden toys, like soldiers, trains and teddy bears.

As we walk in, I can't help but gasp and smile. It's magical, like something out of a fairy tale.

It's easy to find where we're supposed to sit around the circular table, as each place has a parcel set between the cutlery, with our name on it. I'm between Will and Todd.

Grace comes in from the kitchen, through double doors at the other end of the room and starts setting out the food, with Matt's help, and once we're all seated, she tells us to open our gifts.

"Matt and I spent last weekend in London," Grace explains. "And we went to a particular store to choose these gifts. Matt bought the ones for the ladies," she adds. "So don't blame me."

The three of us open them pretty much together. They're all similar, but different. Each is a thick silver cuff, with an enameled design around the outside, based on a peacock feather. Mine is red, Grace's is dark blue and Megan's is deep pink. On the clasp, is a stamp which says, 'Liberty – London'.

"Matt," Grace whispers. "They're beautiful."

"Thank you, so much," I say, and Megan echoes my gratitude. I look from Matt to Grace, dumbfounded. These people don't even know me…

"You're very welcome," Matt says, smiling.

"Now, gentlemen," Grace says, "your turn."

The men all open their gifts too. Each of them has a wallet, in black leather, with the same peacock feather design embossed on it.

"We even got the same design?" Matt says, looking across the table at his wife.

She nods her head. "Looks like it."

"Thank you, darling," he says.

"Thank you, Grace, Matt." Luke and Todd both say.

Will stands and goes around the table, leaning down and whispering something in Grace's ear.

"Oh, you're welcome, Will," she says, patting his hand. "It's nothing."

He comes back around and sits down next to me, taking my hand and giving it a gentle squeeze. I glance across at him and he smiles.

"Let's eat," Grace says.

The food is great. A British Christmas dinner isn't really the same as Thanksgiving at all. Grace cooked a turkey, and there was cranberry sauce. There were also roast potatoes and parsnips, carrots, Brussels sprouts with chestnuts, and bread sauce. Even Luke and Todd, who keep saying they despise Brussels sprouts with a passion, taste Grace's and then come back for more. She tells us she sautéed them gently in butter, with garlic and then added the chestnuts at the end. They're delicious.

Although we're all full, Grace brings out a flaming Christmas pudding, and a chocolate-coffee cheesecake for dessert.

I've never had Christmas pudding and Matt encourages me to try it. Grace picked up the ingredients during their trip to London and, I have to say, I like it a lot. He then, with a grin on his face, encourages me to try the cheesecake.

"Really? I'm so full, this dress is going to burst."

"Try just a taste," Matt urges.

"Oh, okay."

Grace cuts a slither and puts it onto a plate, passing it over to me. I put it into my mouth and chew. The textures are great… but the taste… it's weird.

"I don't understand," I say, once I've swallowed.

"Very few people do," Matt replies.

"It's not sweet, is it?" Grace says.

"No. It's not unpleasant… it's just unexpected."

"It's Matt's favorite." Grace explains.

174

"And Matt hates sweet things," Luke adds.

"Yeah, so Grace created this dessert and then seduced me with it."

"I did not seduce you with it."

"Um… yeah, you did."

"I fed it to you. That's not seducing."

"Seduction's in the eyes of the beholder," Matt says. "And I was seduced."

Grace smiles across at him. "I can't help that."

"Was that before, or after you started wooing Grace with song lyrics?" Luke asks, grinning.

"After," Matt says.

"I'm sorry?" I ask. "Wooing with song lyrics? This I have to hear." I glance at Will, raising an eyebrow, but he just smiles, shaking his head.

"Remind me to fire you, Myers," Matt says.

"You've tried that before," Luke says and winks across the table at his friend, then turns to me. "Before Grace and Matt started seeing each other properly… even after they were dating, I think, they communicated via text and e-mail a lot, because he was here and Grace was in London."

"Okay…" I say.

"And, when they couldn't think what to say to each other—"

"More like how to say it," Matt puts in.

"They used song lyrics," Luke finishes.

"I see."

"And they used them as ringtones too," Luke adds. "And considering the number of texts that went backward and forwards… it nearly drove me crazy."

"Yeah… and then you fell in love too," Matt says. "And you got it."

"Okay. I got it," Luke says. "But I didn't need song lyrics."

"We didn't *need* them," Grace replies, then looks at Matt. "Well, except maybe Joe Cocker."

"Definitely Joe Cocker," Matt says, looking at her.

It's a sweet moment, and Will squeezes my hand again.

Chapter Sixteen

Will

While Grace is fetching the coffee and Matt and I are clearing the table, Jamie excuses herself and goes to the bathroom.

Todd's still fiddling with his collar.

"Undo the damn thing if you're that uncomfortable. No-one minds," I say to him, coming back into the dining room from the kitchen.

"I don't mind wearing a tux normally, but I've had a bitch of a day... I could have done with just hanging out. I just don't get why Grace made us get dressed up in the first place," he replies.

"She didn't," I tell him. "So leave her alone."

Grace is right behind me. "It's fine, Will," she says.

"No it isn't." I turn to Todd. "Stop giving Grace a hard time about it; it wasn't her idea. She made the evening formal because I asked her to, okay?"

"Why?" he asks.

"I can't tell you."

"Well, I refuse to believe this has anything to do with your work..." he says.

"Of course it hasn't," Luke joins in. "I'm sure Will's got his reasons." He looks across at me as I sit down again.

"It'd just be nice to know what they are."

Matt comes back in, carrying the coffee things on a tray, and puts them on the table in front of Grace.

"What does it matter?" she asks. "Will called me and asked me if tonight could be formal. And I think it's been lovely getting dressed up, and seeing you all in your tuxes. I've enjoyed wearing a pretty dress, and I'm sure Megan and Jamie have too. And I'm not interested in Will's motives."

"I am." The quiet voice from the doorway makes us all turn. *Shit.* How much of that did she hear? Clearly enough to make her want to know what my motives are. She's staring at me and it's like there's no-one else in the room but us. I feel like she can see inside me and, from the hurt look in her eyes, she doesn't like what she's seeing. "Why, Will?" she asks me, and even from here, I can see the tears welling, waiting to overflow. "Why?" I still don't reply and she takes a couple of steps forward. "Are you ashamed of me?" she asks, her voice a little louder. "I mean of how I normally look?"

"No," I say, standing up. "You know I'm not." No-one else says a word. "I could never be ashamed of you."

"Were you worried about what I'd wear, then? If you left me to my own devices, I mean… Were you scared I'd wear a shorter dress, or a skirt, and your friends, your brother, would see what I look like?" She chokes back a sob and I take a step toward her, but she holds up a hand to halt me. "Is that why you asked Grace to make tonight formal, so I'd have to wear something long? Is that why you spent so much money on all of this?" she waves her hand in front of herself, indicating the dress. "So I'd come out to play, like a good girl, but be safely hidden away at the same time?" The tears start falling and even I know these are not good tears… they're not even vaguely good tears.

I ignore everyone else and go across the room to her, to hold her, but as soon as my hands touch her, she pushes me away, and I let her shove me backwards. Something tells me it would be wrong to resist, or try again, so I stand in front of her, waiting.

"How could you do this?" she says.

"Do what? What is it you think I've done?" I ask.

"Told your friends about me, so they'd agree to this charade?"

"I haven't told them anything."

"Not even Luke? He helped you, didn't he?"

"Yes, he did. He got the underwear for me, and he told me what dress size to buy, because I didn't have a clue, but I didn't tell him why, and he didn't ask." I reach out for her again, but she takes a step back. "I can't tell them about you, Jamie, because you have to decide who knows and who doesn't, not me." I don't need to turn around to know that the five people at the table are all staring at us, or maybe they're not... Maybe they're looking at the table, or around the room, embarrassed. Who knows? Right now, I don't care. I only care that the woman I just realized I'm in love with is falling apart in front of me, and it's my fault.

"Then why do it?" she asks, sobbing. "I don't understand why you got me all dressed up... why you got everyone all dressed up."

I take a deep breath. "I asked Grace to make the evening formal, because I wanted to spoil you. I wanted to treat you like a lady, Jamie, not just a work-mate who sits around watching monitors with me all day long. You said you used to like to go out dancing and to parties." I hesitate. "I can't give you dancing – well, not tonight, anyway – but I just wanted to show you that you've go no reason to hide away, because you're beautiful, whatever Patrick told you and whatever you might think. Obviously I got it wrong. Maybe I should've bought you a different dress, but I didn't know how you'd feel about that. I didn't know if you'd feel inhibited about wearing something shorter... whether that would make you want to hide away... and I didn't want you to hide away. I wanted you here, with me. And in any case, I saw that dress, and I knew it was perfect for you. And it is. You look perfect, Jamie, so I didn't need to look at anything else, however long or short." I move forward again. She doesn't back off this time. "I'm sorry, Jamie. I know I got it wrong, and I'm sorry. I just wanted you to have a good time. My sole intention for tonight, from the moment I asked Grace to make it formal, to right now, was that you should be able to get dressed up, like you said you used to, and that you should feel good about yourself, and have a great night out... with people who care about you... with friends."

She's staring at me and I don't know which way to turn. I've got five pairs of eyes drilling into my back, and Jamie's piercing mine. I can't read hers... but I've got an awful feeling I've really screwed up this time.

Jamie

What have I done?

I stare at him and he doesn't need to say or do anything more. I know he's telling the truth and I've just ruined everything.

"I'm so sorry, Will," I whisper. I'm shaking my head, and before I can say anything else, he grabs me and pulls me into his arms and holds me.

"Forgive me…" he murmurs into my hair.

"No…" I reach up and rest my hands on his shoulders. "You have to forgive me. I should never have doubted you."

He leans back a fraction, our eyes lock and then his mouth is on mine, his hands moving up to the bare skin of my back and shoulders, caressing me there. He takes a step closer, so our bodies fuse and his lips press hard against mine, his tongue delving deeper into my mouth. I sigh into him and a quiet rumble from deep in his throat echoes back at me. We're joined for ages, until he breaks the kiss, resting his forehead on mine.

"If I got it wrong…" he whispers.

"You didn't. I did. I'm sorry. Please forgive me."

"Nothing to forgive." He gently kisses my forehead, then lowers his arms and takes my hand, turning us around.

There's no-one in the room but us. The table is deserted, with the tray of coffee things still set out in front of the place where Grace had been sitting. We didn't even hear them leave.

"They'll be in the kitchen," Will says, nodding to the double doors at the other end of the room. "It's the only place they can have gone."

He's right. They'd have had to come right past us to go out of the door beside where we're standing, which leads into the hallway.

"Can we just sneak off home?" I whisper.

"No."

"But I'm so embarrassed."

"Don't be. They're our friends."

I look up at him. "They're *your* friends."

He shakes his head. "And that makes them *our* friends." He turns back to face me again. "When I spoke to Sean the other day and you got mad at me—"

"I got scared for you."

"Okay. When you got scared for me, you said it wasn't just me anymore, you said you cared about us. You made whatever we've got into an 'us', Jamie. I like that... a lot." He raises my fingers to his lips and kisses them, one by one. "So... if we're an 'us', then my friends are *our* friends."

"But they don't know me."

"Then let them get to know you. You don't have to tell them anything you don't want to; they won't judge you either way. They're good people."

"I know they are." He just stares at me. "Okay," I say, and he leads me through into the kitchen.

Grace and Megan are sitting at an island unit; Todd, Matt and Luke are leaning against the countertop around the kitchen.

Grace is the first to notice us as we come in through the doors.

"Jamie, Will," she says and they all turn.

"I'm so sorry," I look around at their faces, and all I see is concern. Luke is staring at Will and I notice him nod his head, before he looks down at me. "I behaved so badly," I continue.

"Shush," Grace says, getting to her feet and coming over. "That's nonsense. It was a misunderstanding, that's all."

"No. I behaved really badly." I glance up at Will. "And I'd like to explain, if that's okay. I'm not making excuses for the way I acted in there; there aren't any. But I would like to explain why I said the things I did..."

"You don't have to," Grace replies. "Not if you don't want to."

"I want to."

"You sure?" Will asks. I nod my head.

I grip his hand. "Can you help me?" I say to him.

"Of course I can. What do you need me to do?"

"Start the story?"

"Okay," he says, "but shall we all go sit somewhere more comfortable first."

"I think that's a very good idea," Grace replies. "And Matt can bring the coffee through as well."

We all go into the living room, with Matt bringing up the rear, carrying the tray, which he places on the low table between the two sofas.

Will sits me next to him on one couch, with Todd on my other side. Luke and Megan sit opposite. Grace takes the chair and Matt sits on the arm of it, beside her.

Will holds my hand, placing it in his lap. "I wanted to make tonight special for Jamie," he says, "because she doesn't go out very much, not socially anyway. She used to, but over the last few years, her life's changed a lot." He stops and looks down at me, nodding his head.

"I was watching the marathon, in Boston," I tell them, "when the bombs went off."

"You were there?" Todd asks.

"She was injured." Will looks at him over the top of my head.

I scoot forward on the couch and raise my skirt up to my knee. Even through the thin black stockings, you can still see the scarring. None of them gasp or recoil, they just look at it, and then return their eyes to my face. I lower my skirt again. "Jamie couldn't walk for some time, and even now, if she doesn't exercise, and take regular hot baths, she finds it painful," Will continues.

"So, how's she been getting on at your place?" Luke asks, his brow furrowing.

"Will's been letting me use his gym," I explain.

"But the baths? He doesn't have any... We ripped them all out." He looks at me.

"Yes, I know. He explained."

"And you didn't think to bring her to our place?" Luke says, turning to Will. He almost sounds cross.

"Yes, he did. He offered," I tell him. "He suggested it straight away, but I didn't want to trouble anyone. That was my choice. Don't blame Will..."

"Okay," he says, calming down, "as long as he's looking after you."

"He is. He couldn't be doing any more." Luke smiles across at Will now.

"It wouldn't be any trouble, you know," Megan says. "You could have driven over anytime you wanted."

"I didn't want anyone knowing," I say. "I've had some difficult reactions over the years."

"Really?" Matt says. "Like what?"

"Like her boyfriend," Will says. "The guy she was there watching run on the day… He decided he didn't like sitting around waiting for her to get better, learning to walk again. He didn't like the fact that she's gained a little weight because she was stuck in a hospital bed. And he didn't like the fact that she'd changed from the person she'd been before. So he found someone else."

Now, they all gasp, collectively. "I'm better off without him. I know that," I say. "But some of the things he said; some of the things other people said and the judgments people made, they've been harder to get over."

"This ex of yours," Todd says, leaning into me a little. "He lives in Boston, right?"

"As far as I know, yes."

He smiles. "Good. Give me his name. I can make his life a living hell, you know that, don't you?"

I laugh. It feels good to laugh. "I'll bear that in mind."

"He's serious," Luke says. "He can really make the guy suffer. You should take him up on his offer."

"He'd do it, too," Matt adds.

"Hey, that's what friends are for," Todd says, and I feel Will squeeze my hand.

"So," he says, continuing the story, "when Jamie told me what happened, and that she used to like to get dressed up and go out dancing, I thought this was a good opportunity to let her do that again… but on a smaller, more intimate scale. I got it a bit wrong, but…"

"No you didn't." I turn to him. "You didn't get it wrong at all."

"If you guys are gonna start kissing again, we'll leave now," Matt says, grinning.

"Well, I think you're very brave to have told us," Grace says. "I know it's not easy."

I turn to face her and she smiles at me. It's a very understanding smile and I remember Will telling me about her first husband and how he and Todd helped with the stalker. I guess she had to reveal her past to them, in order for them to help her out. I smile back and she gives me a nod of her head.

"Shall we have this coffee before it gets cold?" Matt says and he gets up, then kneels down by the table and starts pouring out the coffee and handing out the cups. As Todd's handed his, he turns to me.

"I was there, you know…"

I look at him. "At the marathon? Really?"

"Yes. I was at work that day… It was my last week in uniform." He looks down at his cup. "I'd always enjoyed the marathon, but I was glad afterwards that I'd never have to patrol another one… ever again." He lets out a sigh.

"Were you… close…?" I ask.

"I was about a couple of hundred yards away, I guess. And when the bombs went off, I just ran… kinda like every other cop on the street that day." Everyone's looking at him. I guess they already know his story. "I got to the second bomb site… it was hell. Or the closest thing to hell I ever want to see."

"Yes, it was."

"The things I saw," he continues, closing his eyes for a moment. "I had flashbacks for a while, and nightmares, although it's okay now… And nothing happened to me. I didn't go through anything like what you did. I just did my job…"

"I doubt that very much. From what I remember, every person there went above and beyond," I tell him.

"Well, things like that do tend to bring out the finest in the finest," he says. "There were some brave guys out there that day. They kept their heads when it was needed."

I glance across at Luke, then at Matt and, from the expression on their faces, I begin to wonder whether they have ever heard him speak of what happened, or his involvement in it. Maybe this is the first time he's mentioned it in front of them.

"It was a bad day," he says, shaking his head, "with bad consequences for a lot of people. Good people, like you, whose lives changed forever."

"Oh… I don't know," I say to him. "I feel quite lucky really. So many people lost limbs, or loved ones." I turn and look at Will. "And I've gained so much."

Chapter Seventeen

Will

I hold her gaze, and I know I need to tell her. I need her to know how much she means to me. I can't tell her I love her; not yet, and not here, in front of everyone. But I still want her to know.

I twist to face her, her hands in mine. "Do you remember, when you first arrived, I told you about Luke…?"

"Yes," she says.

"Do you remember what I said?"

"Which bit?" she asks, glancing across at him, confused. I think she's concerned that I might tell them why she was sent to my house… and that my friends, and Luke especially, won't think too kindly of her for spying on me.

"The bit where I told you he means everything to me."

"Oh… Yes."

I lean in a little closer. "It's not just Luke I feel like that about… not anymore."

Her lips curve upwards, and her eyes sparkle, and then she rests her head on my shoulder. I put my arm around her and pull her close.

"Was that meant to make sense to the rest of us?" Luke asks.

"No." I smile across at him.

"I really hate it when you do that," he says.

"Well, you'll be pleased to hear, I might not be doing it for much longer."

"What?"

"I'm pretty sure I'm gonna quit."

Everyone turns to face me. I look at Todd. "We – that is Todd and I – had a long discussion on our way back from Virginia—"

"When were you guys in Virginia?" Luke interrupts.

"Last Saturday," I reply. "But I can't tell you about that either."

"Will…" Luke sounds frustrated.

Todd leans forward. "I don't have a problem telling them about it… No-one swore me to secrecy. It was nothing major," he says, turning to Luke. "I just kept watch in the car, while your little brother broke into a house." I flip my head around to him. "What?" he says to me. "You think I didn't know what you were doing, just because you didn't tell me? You were good." He smiles. "I didn't even notice there was an alarm until just before you and Jamie came out."

"Yeah… and that's why I was the one doing the breaking in; and you were the guy sitting in the car. The alarm was easy…"

"Well, I don't have your secret service training, do I?" He grins.

Luke's staring at me. "You broke into a house?" he asks.

"Technically, yes. But only in the sense that I didn't have the owner's permission to be there. I didn't actually *break* anything."

"See, I said he was good." Todd's still grinning.

"You're a cop, for Christ's sakes. Why didn't you stop him?" Luke turns his attention to Todd for a moment.

"I knew Will wouldn't be doing it without a good reason."

"I wouldn't," I say. "I can't tell you much, but the guy whose house it was… he'd sold information which cost the lives of several agents. It was an op we were running in the summer. A building exploded… with our guys on the inside…"

"And it didn't make the news?" Matt asks.

"Yeah, it did… but it was reported as a gas leak."

"And where the hell were you when this building exploded?" Luke's paler now.

"I was… nearby."

"Shit." Todd's serious again now. "You didn't tell me any of that."

"I didn't tell you anything, remember?"

"Have you caught him? The guy who sold you out?"

"Not yet, but I've started the ball rolling."

"Good. Need any more help?" he asks. "I'm busy, but…"

"No. I'm handing the whole case over on Monday, to someone a lot further up the food chain."

"And there's no comeback on you for breaking into the guy's house?" he asks.

"There might have been, if I'd got it wrong…"

"What kind of comeback?" Luke asks. He still looks pale.

"Maybe some jail time. There's no getting away from the fact that I broke the law, Luke."

"So did I," Jamie puts in. "But your brother told them it was all him, and no-one else was involved. He also told me he *wouldn't* have to go to jail." She's staring at me.

I turn to her. "I can't be sure what they'd have done. The publicity wouldn't have been good, because I sure as hell wouldn't have gone quietly. They might have been prepared to just let it rest."

"So you lied to me…"

"Only to protect you," I say. "You were scared. I didn't want to make it worse."

"Um… What about me?" Todd says. "I seem to remember being there too."

"No…" Jamie says quietly. "According to Will, you and I were nothing to do with it."

"Aren't you forgetting something?" Todd says.

"What?" I turn to him.

"We flew to Virginia… there will be records of the flight, credit card receipts for three tickets with our names on, restaurant checks… There are cameras at the airports… need I go on? It's good of you to try and cover for us, but…"

I take a deep breath. "No… there won't."

"No, there won't what?" Todd asks.

"There won't be any records."

"Why not?" He looks confused.

"Because I made sure there weren't any."

"And how did you do that?" he asks.

I settle back into the couch. "Well… I bought the tickets with cash, which I withdrew from two separate bank accounts to make the amounts less traceable. All the food we bought in Virginia, I paid for with cash too."

"Okay," he says, "so no credit card receipts, but my ticket was in my name… I'm sure yours and Jamie's were too… and the airline will have a record of that."

"Well, they did…"

"What do you mean?"

"I mean that, after we got back, I hacked their systems. The records now show that I flew to Virginia alone… and sitting either side of me were David Preston and Gale Bowyer."

"You… changed the record?"

"Yes."

"What about the car we rented? I did that in my name, with my license, because I was doing the driving… You can't have changed that…"

"Sorry… that was David Preston again. His license is on record as having rented that car for the day and returned it in the evening before catching the flight back to Logan. You weren't there, Todd."

"Who exactly is this David Preston guy?" he asks. "I'd like to meet him…"

I lean closer to Todd. "Um… He doesn't exist," I whisper.

"Oh…" He hesitates. "But what about the cameras at the airports? Surely they'll have picked us up when we arrived, or departed."

"It's real weird… They had a mysterious power outage. And, oddly, they lost several random sections of recordings from that weekend, and a couple of days either side."

"Don't tell me, each one of them was when we were at the airport?"

"Might have been." I shrug. "And, before you ask, I used a burner phone while we were there, which I threw in the river the next day when I went shopping for Jamie's dress… and, if you remember, I told you not to store the number on your cell. There wouldn't even have been a trace of any communication between you and me, if you'd needed to call… which you didn't."

He looks at me, thinking things through. "Wait a second," he says. "You sent me a text a couple of days before we went, with the flight details."

I look down at my hands. "Yeah… sorry about that."

"Why are you sorry?" he asks.

"I hacked your phone after we got back."

"What the…?"

"That text doesn't exist anymore – and neither does your reply to me."

"You hacked my phone?" I'm not sure if he's angry.

"Yes… I'm sorry."

"Hey… don't be. I'm impressed." *That's a relief.*

I look up at him. "You're nearly as bad as Matt, though," I tell him. "You need to change your passcode." I shake my head. "Still, at least you didn't use your own date of birth."

"How did you know?"

I let out a sigh. "Christ, Todd… it's basic stuff. It wasn't your birthdate, so I tried your mom's…"

"But how did you know my mom's date of birth?"

"Um… she's on Facebook…"

Matt lets out a laugh.

"So we really weren't there?" Todd says quietly.

"No, you weren't. It was too much of a risk to let either of you be seen to be there."

"But you didn't alter the record to protect yourself?" Megan asks.

"No… someone had to be there. It would have looked like a set up if I'd taken us all out of the records."

"But you could've gone to jail…" Luke is still shocked.

"It was a possibility. Like I said, if I'd been wrong, they might have wanted to hang me out to dry… or they might have decided it was best to just keep quiet, and avoid potentially damaging media attention. I took a risk, because I was fairly sure I was right… so it was a calculated risk, and it was *my* risk. None of it's traceable back to Jamie or Todd. I've

189

made damn sure of that." They're all staring at me. "What? This is my job, guys... I know I don't talk about it, but it's what I do."

"You're good," Todd says quietly. "You're real good." I don't have an answer to that. "Thanks, man," he adds.

"Don't thank me. I asked you to be there in the first place... I wasn't about to let you get in trouble for helping me out."

"I don't understand why they'd have put you in prison," Grace says. "You were trying to do the right thing."

"Doing the right thing doesn't count for much in my line of work," I say to her. "Which is one of the reasons I want out."

"What will you do?" Luke asks. "If you leave, I mean."

"Todd and I are thinking about starting our own business together. That was what we talked about on our way back from Virginia. It was Jamie's suggestion. We're looking at security and surveillance... We'll take on corporate and government work, but I really don't want to get involved in domestic investigations... they're too messy."

"You're going to leave the police force?" Grace asks Todd.

"When I've finished with this murder case, yeah. I want to see this one out because it's... it's real nasty. But you know how much I hate my job, Grace." He turns to face her. "Well, my boss, anyway..."

"Yes, I do."

"We're gonna talk about it, aren't we?" He looks at me.

"In the New Year." I nod back at him. "Between us, we'll try and and come up with a business plan... maybe go and see the bank."

"Don't go to the bank... Come and see me," Matt says, looking from me to Todd. "When you're ready... once you've had your discussions."

I look at Todd, then at Matt. "Um... why?"

He smiles. "We can talk about it," he says. "If the numbers stack up, I'd like to invest."

"You'd do that?" I say to him.

"After what I've heard tonight, yes I would."

"I don't understand..."

"You don't?" I shake my head. "Todd's right, Will... you're good. I think, because you never talk about your work, we've none of us realized how good you are... But it's more than that. You're like your brother... you're loyal. You do the right thing and, outside of this room, that's a rare thing. I don't like the thought of you two being in debt to the bank."

"You'd rather we were in debt to you?" Todd says, laughing.

"You won't be in debt to me," he says. "Either of you. Ever... Put your figures together, then come see me."

As we're saying goodnight on the steps, I realize Jamie didn't bring a coat or scarf, or anything, so I take off my jacket and put it around her shoulders before helping her into the Jeep. Matt and Grace go indoors out of the cold, Todd drives off, waving to everyone and Luke takes Megan to his Range Rover, helping her into the passenger seat, before he comes back over to me. I undo my tie, letting it hang, and loosen my top button. It's cold, but I don't care.

"Is everything okay?" he asks, nodding toward Jamie in the car.

"I hope so," I tell him.

"Jamie looked beautiful tonight. That was one helluva dress. You did good."

I shrug. "I tried."

He pats my shoulder. "It was kind," he says. "What happened was just a misunderstanding, like Grace said. Jamie gets that now." He keeps his hand where it is, giving my shoulder a squeeze. "I never understood what you do until tonight, but having that little insight into your life... well, I felt proud of you," he says. He lets his hand fall back to his side then adds, "But if you ever pull a stunt like that again, I'll do you a serious injury."

"Jamie's already threatened me."

"Good... What the fuck were you thinking?"

"I wanted to do the right thing, for once. I can't let this guy get away with it, Luke. It's all wrong. I watched it all go to shit. I heard them dying... and a man I've worked with for years was responsible for that."

"Shit," he whispers, staring at me.

"Anyway, once I'd done what I had to do... well, it was just about protecting Jamie, and Todd."

"I get that," he says. "But from now on, if you could avoid breaking the law… and getting too close to exploding buildings, I'd be real grateful. I'd kinda like for Daisy to get to know her uncle."

We stare at each other for a moment. He seems reluctant to go.

"You know what you said?" he asks eventually.

"Which bit? We've done a lot of talking tonight."

"What you were saying to Jamie… when you said I mean everything to you."

"Oh… Yeah."

"Was that for real?"

"Of course."

He smiles. "Goes both ways. You know that, don't you?"

"You've got Megan now, and the baby coming," I reply. "I understand that."

"Do you? Do you really…? You're right, I've got Megan, and the baby… and they're my whole world. But does loving Jamie make you care any less about me?" he asks.

"No, of course not."

He looks at me. "There you go then. I can care about them, and you at the same time too."

"How did you know I love Jamie?" I ask him, realizing what he's just said. "I only worked it out properly for myself tonight."

He starts to walk away, but turns back. "Really? I've known for quite a while now," he says, smiling.

"I'm so sorry," Jamie says almost as soon as I get into the car. "Please forgive me."

"Didn't we cover this already?" I start the engine and reverse out of Matt and Grace's driveway.

"Yes, we did. But do you forgive me?"

"Yes… well, no. What I mean is there's nothing to forgive. I probably should have explained what I was doing… what this evening was about."

"You wanted to surprise me," she says.

"Yes."

"But I thought you were taking pity on me."

I take a right onto the main road. "I kind of was," I tell her. "But not in the way you were thinking. I thought you seemed sad, and I just wanted you to have a good time."

"I did." She twists in her seat, so she's facing me. "I really like your friends."

"*Our* friends, Jamie. And they really like you too." I change lanes. "But am I forgiven?" I ask her.

"What for?"

"The work thing... telling you I wouldn't go to jail."

"I get why you did it... and I'm grateful. Just remember what I said..."

"I do."

"Then repeat it to me."

"It's not just about me anymore, it's about us."

"Exactly."

"But – in fairness to myself – when I set out to cover our traces in Virginia, I didn't know that was how you felt."

"Well, you do now."

She leans back into the seat, pulling my jacket around her, and watches me drive... all the way home.

I let her into the house and turn on the lights. It's nearly one in the morning, but I don't feel tired enough to sleep yet.

"I'll be back in a minute," she says, and goes along to her room.

I go through into the living room and across to the window, where I bend to switch on the Christmas tree lights and stand up again, turning back around, just as Jamie comes into the room. She's still got my jacket around her shoulders; it's enormous on her, and she looks real cute. She's carrying a small square parcel in her hands, which she brings over to me.

"It's Christmas Day," she says. "I wanted to give you this."

"For Christmas?" I look at her. She nods, and hands me the parcel. "You want me to open it now?" I ask.

"Yes."

There's a small card attached, which I turn over and read.

'Will,

Happy Christmas,

With love,

Jamie x'

I look up at her. *With love?* I stop myself from reading too much into that and peel off the wrapping to reveal a black box, with an Apple logo on top. Inside, is a sleek, black Apple Watch. I look up at her.

"It's… It's incredible… Thank you. You didn't have to…"

"You said you wanted a grown-up watch…"

"I know. But you didn't have to buy it for me."

"I wanted to."

I close the gap between us. "Thank you," I say, and lean down to kiss her. She takes the box from my hands and drops it onto the couch beside us. Then I pull my jacket off her shoulders and toss it on the floor, running my hands along her shoulders and down her back, pulling her closer. "You taste good," I whisper into her mouth.

"So do you," she says, and I kiss her again, biting gently on her bottom lip. She groans loudly, and I slowly bring my right hand around, placing it over her breast.

"Oh, God…" she murmurs, breaking the kiss and throwing her head back. Her neck is exposed, so I lean down, tracing kisses along her soft skin, cupping her firm breast in my hand. "Oh… that's good," she whispers. She brings her head forward again and I stand upright, staring into her eyes.

"I want to see you," I rasp out and I reach around the side of her, for the zipper on her dress, holding my hand there until she nods her head, then I lower it all the way to her hip. The bodice of the dress falls away from her and slides down, pooling on the floor at her feet, and I take a half step back, letting my eyes travel down her body. The lace underwear conceals nothing. I can see her dark nipples, hard and extended, her rounded hips, covered with the soft lacy garter belt, attached to black stockings… and my breath hitches in my throat… through the lace panel at the front of the panties, I can see she's shaved bare. "God, Jamie," I whisper. "You're beautiful." I move in close again

194

and place my hands around her waist, feeling her smooth skin against my fingers, as I pull her close, letting her feel my hard arousal through my pants.

"Will," she breathes, but I swallow her words into my mouth, before kissing my way slowly down her body, exploring the tops of her breasts, above the lace, brushing my lips across them, one at a time. I reach around behind her and undo the clasp of the bra, then pull the straps from her shoulders and release her, dropping the bra to the floor, with her dress, and leaning down to kiss and gently bite her nipples. She's breathing hard now, and holds my head in place, while I take her nipple into my mouth. She hisses out a long, "Yes," between her teeth. I pull away and move lower, kneeling in front of her, until I'm faced with her panties and the secrets they barely conceal. I hook my thumbs in the sides and look up into her face, waiting. I know Luke said not to keep asking, but I really hope Jamie understands how out of my depth I am. I have to ask… because I don't have a clue. She nods her head once more – she seems to get it, thank God – and a smile touches her lips, as I slowly lower the lace briefs to the floor, then, still kneeling, I hold her hand.

"Step out," I whisper, and she does, and I pull, the dress, bra and panties to one side, so she's standing in her heels on the wooden floor, her legs slightly apart. Then I lean back and look up at her. She's still wearing the the black stockings and garter belt, and my cock is painfully hard against my zipper. Her shaved mound is right in front of me and I bend forward, placing a kiss on her soft skin. She moans, and I run my tongue along the length of her delicate fold. I'm still holding her hand and she squeezes my fingers tight. There's a slight quivering in her thighs.

"Sit down," I say quietly, nodding to the sofa behind her and she takes a step and lowers herself onto the seat, lying back into it. I move forward and, not taking my eyes from hers, I part her legs, my hands on her knees. Then I run my hands slowly up her thighs, my lips following until they reach the apex, and I use my fingers to spread her wide, exposing her to my tongue. I circle around her clitoris, flicking and licking at her core, tasting her honey-sweet nectar. She arches into me, uttering a strangled cry of pleasure with every stroke. I increase the pressure and pace a little, and at the same time, I insert first one, then two fingers into her. She's wet, and tight, clamping onto me, her hips bucking into my face as I create circular motions, inside her, which seem to drive her wild.

Her hand comes down on the back of my head and I go a little deeper, just as she screams out my name, her muscles clenching around my fingers, her thighs bracing against me.

Her moans, sighs and screams fill the room and I feel her juices coating my fingers, running down onto my hand. This is so much more than I'd expected.

As she starts to calm, I slow my movements, then look up at her, gently removing my fingers from her.

"Jesus, Will," she murmurs softly. Her expression is glazed. I can't tell whether this is good or bad. Her breathing is still ragged, her breasts heaving. I lick my lips… I taste of her. It's intoxicating. She's looking down at me, and at that moment, her eyes widen and she bites her lip. I'm dying here… I need to know…

"It's never been like that," she whispers. But is that good, or bad? "I've never felt pleasure that intense before. Ever."

And I feel the relief wash over me.

Jamie

I'm still floating, somewhere far above cloud nine.

I've had my share of orgasms – all at my own hand, I'll admit. Patrick wasn't the most considerate of lovers, and he's the only man I've been with, until tonight. But I've never, ever felt anything like that. I don't even know what happened. It started deep inside me, right at the center of my body, then spread, really slowly, taking over me, right to the tips of my toes and the ends of my hair. My skin is still tingling now… and it ended minutes ago.

How do I get back down to earth after that?

I had to tell him how good it was. He needed to know how he made me feel, and that I've never had that before. He's smiling up at me now, and I want to touch him. I want to return the favor in some way, and show him how it can be for him too.

I sit forward on the couch and put my hands on his shoulders, bending my head to his and joining our lips. He tastes of me… I like it. It's arousing and I groan into his mouth. I feel his fingers rubbing my nipples, squeezing and pinching them. God, this is good… a tingling bolt of electricity passes straight from my breasts, down to the pit of my stomach, pooling there and I instinctively part my legs a little. Will leans in further, pushing me back against the sofa again.

I was meant to be giving, not taking more from him. I insinuate my hand between us, undoing his shirt buttons, and running my fingers down his chest to the top of his pants.

He pulls back, looking down at me, then gets to his feet, his eyes, dark and intense. He holds out his hand to me and I take it, letting him pull me up to my feet and into his arms. His chest has a dappling of soft hair, and feels hot against my naked breasts. I like the feeling of his skin against mine.

His hands come around behind me, clasping my buttocks, pulling me onto him, his erection hard against my hip. I want him. I want him now.

I return my attention to his pants, undoing the button, but he grabs my hand and leads me down the hallway toward our bedrooms. Outside my door, he pushes me gently back against the wall, placing one hand on my hip, the other on the side of my face, his fingers in my hair. Then he kisses me again. It's a frantic, wild kiss, his tongue deep in my mouth. I can feel the arousal building deep inside me again. I need his touch, his tongue, his fingers… I want all of him.

He pulls away and stands back.

"I'm sorry," he says quietly, and turns away. He crosses the hallway and opens the door to his room, going inside and closing it softly behind him.

I stand, looking for ages at the space where he was just standing, then I look at the closed door.

What happened? What did I do wrong? I must have done something for him to stop so abruptly, like that.

I know I told him I'd wait, but I thought... I thought he wanted more too. Or was it just me?

I shiver, and realize I'm standing in nothing more than a garter belt, stockings and high heels. Without the heat of Will's body, I'm cold. I bring my arms up across my breasts, clasping my shoulders, covering myself.

I look back down the hallway. All the lights are still on. I go back along into the living room. My dress, his tux... my underwear... they're all scattered on the floor. I glance at the box containing his watch, discarded on the sofa in the heat of the moment. I grab it and place it on the coffee table, where he'll find it, then I pick up our clothes. I drape his jacket on the back of the sofa and carry my dress and underwear to my bedroom. I pause outside his door, wondering...

That was the best time I've ever had. I thought he liked it too.

I guess not.

Chapter Eighteen

Will

I kick off my shoes, then shrug off my shirt and throw it across the room, followed by my shoes, pants, boxers and socks, then I sit on the edge of the bed, naked and hard. If I wait, it'll go... I just need it to go...

It's not going to though, because all I can think about is how she felt when she climaxed on my tongue; her slick, wet juices flowing out of her onto my hand; her thrashing screams and moans; the way her hips bucked into me wildly.

How am I supposed to calm down if I can't stop thinking about that?

Or her words when she told me how good it had been and that glazed, satisfied look on her face when she looked down at me, still crouched between her legs, tasting her sweetness on my lips.

I lie back on the bed, staring at the ceiling.

God, I wish I could just go across the hallway and make love to her; take her in my arms, lie down with her, enter her, and make her mine completely. I want that more than anything... but I can't. I still can't. It's like there's a barrier – a blockage. I can't even explain it properly. I like the idea of it, the thought of it, the image of it... The doing of it – that's a whole different matter.

I really thought I was going to be able to, as well. When she undid my shirt and I felt her breasts against my chest... I thought I could. I really did. But then, outside her room, while I was kissing her, that thought just vanished, and the fear came back. I didn't want to try, in case it went wrong and tainted everything.

I sit up. She looked real disappointed… I mean *real* disappointed. I suppose I kind of led her on, really. Bringing her down the hallway, like I was gonna take her to bed – which I thought I was – and then walking away like that. It was hardly fair, was it? I hope she realizes it was no reflection on her though. I hope she knows how much I want her. I lower my head into my hands. *How the hell would she know that, Will?* Even I don't understand why I did what I did… How can I expect Jamie to get it?

I jump up off the bed, go into my dressing room and grab a pair of shorts from the shelf, pulling them on. I don't care if my erection is obvious. She knows how turned on I was… am.

I open my bedroom door. It's dark out here. She must've gone back and switched off the lights. I wonder if she put a robe on first, or wandered around the house in her garter belt and stockings. That thought makes my cock twitch. *Great.* I can think like that now. Why the hell can't I keep my head in the zone when it matters most?

The light is still on in Jamie's room, but I'd knock on her door even if it wasn't. I go across the hall and tap gently. Within a couple of seconds, she opens the door and stands on the threshold wearing her pale pink silk robe, with nothing on her feet, so I guess she's naked underneath, evidenced by her hard nipples protruding through the thin material. My eyes journey upward. She's removed her make-up and taken her hair down… and her eyes are sad. And I want, more than anything, to hold her.

"Can we talk?" I ask her.

She glances down at my shorts.

"Talk?" she asks.

"Yeah, talk."

She pulls the robe a little closer around her and stands to one side.

"No." I say. "Come into my room."

She looks at me, then flicks off the light switch beside the door, leaving her room in darkness. I stand to one side and let her out into the hallway and she walks across and to my room. I follow, closing my bedroom door behind me.

She's standing in the middle of the room and, as I pass her, I take her hand, bringing her with me to the bed and lying her down beside me. Her gown falls open slightly and neither of us make any attempt to close it.

"I'm sorry," I say, raising myself on one elbow so I can look down at her.

"What happened?" she murmurs. "I don't understand."

"If I'm being honest, neither do I."

"Why didn't you want me?" she asks.

Not want her? Hell... "I want you, Jamie." I run my forefinger from her neck, down between her breasts, resting my hand there. She shudders out a breath. "I want you so much."

"Then why...?"

"I don't know... fear, I guess."

"Fear of what?" She blinks up at me, placing her hand over mine. "If you're worried..." she pauses. "If you're worried it'll be over a bit too quick," she says, "that's okay. It doesn't matter. It's your first time. I understand."

"I'm not afraid of that. I'm not saying it won't happen – it probably will, but I know that's not important... not really. There'll be plenty more times to get it right." At least I hope there will.

"Then what are you afraid of?" she asks.

"My mind's a mess," I tell her. "You remember the fairy lights; that tangle of cables?" She nods her head, looking a little confused. "It's kinda like that in here." I tap the side of my head. "I guess I'm scared that I'll lose my focus at a vital moment; that the bad memories will come back and taint everything... and that I won't be able to make love to you – or even think about making love to you – without being reminded of it." Now I've said it, it kinda makes sense. I think. "I need to be certain I can stay focused before I try," I tell her. "It's no reflection on you. I promise. It's just all the shit that's still in here." I tap my head again. "I'm sorry."

She turns onto her side, so we're facing each other. "Can I ask you something?" she says.

"Sure."

"What were you thinking about? When you were licking me, kissing me, touching me… when your fingers were inside me… when you were making me come… What was going through your mind?"

I think for a moment. "Firstly what a lucky son-of-a-bitch I was to get to see you naked – well nearly naked. Seeing you in those shoes, the stockings…" I feel my mouth go dry. "I think that image will stay with me for a long, long time."

"And then?" she prompts, her eyes sparkling.

"And then, I was thinking how great you felt, how sweet you tasted, how wet you were, how tight you were on my fingers. I was focused on pleasuring you, giving you what you needed. And how I loved hearing your voice, all the different sounds you make."

"So, nothing to do with the whores Luke's dad brought into your room, then?" she asks, breathing a little faster.

"No," I say slowly. She's right. "My mind was filled with you, Jamie. Just you."

She stares at me. "I know it was," she says. "You couldn't have done what you did, in the way you did – making me feel that good – if I hadn't been the center of your world for those moments."

Those moments? *You're the center of my world all the time, baby.* She brings her hand up and rests it on my chest.

"I said I'd wait," she says. "And I will. I won't pressure you."

"And I won't make you wait too long. I just need to sort my head out." She smiles at me and goes to sit up.

"Stay with me," I say. "Sleep in here tonight… Please?"

She lies back down. "If you want me to."

"I want you to. I sleep better when you're here."

"Do you want me to go and put something on?" she says.

I shake my head. "No. I want you just as you are. Well, minus this." I touch her silky robe.

She smiles up at me, then looks down at my shorts.

"What do you want me to do about these?" I ask her.

"Whatever makes you most comfortable. If you'd prefer to keep them on, that's fine. If you take them off, I promise I won't touch you – not unless you decide you want me to."

I hesitate, but only for a couple of seconds, before getting up and pulling off my shorts, then stepping out of them. I'm surprised that I don't feel more vulnerable being exposed like this in front of Jamie, but I'm okay with it, and I glance down at her, lying on the bed. She's staring straight at my cock and, I can't help but smile at the wide-eyed look on her face.

"Oh…" she says, standing and taking off her robe so she's naked, just a few inches away from me. "I so wish I hadn't made that promise to wait." She plants a kiss in the center of my chest, nuzzling into me for a second, then grins up into my eyes, turns and pulls back the comforter, climbing into bed. I get in after her and she snuggles down next to me, her head on my chest, her arm across my stomach. I pull the covers back up over us.

"Do you think it'll go down eventually?" she asks, looking down the bed to my still-obvious erection, and I can hear the smile in her voice.

"Probably not, no. Not with you lying naked in my arms. I have enough trouble with it when you're on the other side of the hallway."

She giggles and I switch off the lights.

"Goodnight," she says.

I kiss the top of her head. "Goodnight, baby."

Jamie

When I wake up, Will's still asleep. I've got my back to his front, his arms around me and I can feel his erection pressing into me. I guess he was right. It didn't go down… or if it did, it's back again. I smile, and avoid the temptation to wiggle my behind back into him.

Now I've seen him naked, the desire is even greater than it was before, but I have to let him do this at his pace, or I could spoil everything. And I really don't want to do that.

I slide out from his arms and visit the bathroom, then go out to the kitchen and make us both a cup of coffee, bringing them back in with me. I stand, just for a moment, watching him sleep. It's good to see him looking so untroubled and peaceful. I put his cup on the nightstand beside the bed and carry mine around to my side of the bed, climbing back in and under the covers. The movement disturbs him and he wakes.

"You went somewhere?" he asks, his voice sleepy. I've never seen him like this. He's even more lovable than normal. *Lovable…* I smile across at him and he smiles back. I'm so in love with him. I wonder if I should tell him. But what if it scares him off? What if he's not ready for that? He's staring at me… probably because I haven't replied to his question yet.

"I made coffee," I tell him.

"Oh… good." He looks at his cup on the nightstand. "Thanks."

"You're welcome."

He leans over and kisses me, gently on my lips. "Good morning," he whispers.

"Good morning."

He sits up a little, looking down at me. "Did you put anything on when you made the coffee? Or did you wander around the house naked?" he asks.

"Why? Is me being naked a problem?"

He smirks. "Not for me, no. But Luke has a key…"

"Oh God." I clasp my hand to my mouth. "I totally forgot."

He pulls me into him for a hug. "It's okay," he says. "He wouldn't be coming over today anyway. We're going there…"

"I'll remember for next time, though." He leans back a little. "If there is a next time, that is. I mean, I'm not assuming—" His kiss cuts me off.

"There'll be a next time," he says. "And I'll speak to him. I'll tell him to call, or use the doorbell, rather than just walking in." He runs his fingers down my back and I shiver at his touch. "I like you walking around naked; and I want you to feel at home here."

"You do?"

"Yes." He turns me onto my back, lying beside me, and traces light circular movements with the very tips of his fingers from my neck, across my breasts, stopping to gently pinch my nipples between his thumb and forefinger, before progressing downward until he reaches the apex of my open thighs. He stills, looking at me, just like he did last night, waiting for my approval.

"You don't have to ask," I tell him.

"But I'm not completely sure about what I'm doing," he murmurs. "I don't know if I'm doing the right things... And besides, I can't just take," he says.

"But you're not... you're giving." His fingers slide in between my already slick folds, finding my clitoris, and I arch off the bed. "And... oh, God, yes... trust me... Hmm, yes, just there... you're doing the right things... oh, yes." He strokes me, caressing and circling, varying the speed and intensity until I'm panting, desperate for release. "Please, Will," I breathe. He applies just a little more pressure and I tip over the edge into ecstasy, writhing wildly. His lips cover mine, swallowing my cries, until I begin to calm.

Once I'm still, he leans back a little, his hand still resting between my legs. His eyes are alight.

"You're very good at that," I whisper. He blushes, and I reach over and place my hand on his cheek. "I mean it," I tell him. "You really are." He smiles, a shy smile.

"I like watching you," he says eventually.

"Good, because I have to tell you, you can do that to me as often as you like." I smile up at him, and as he leans down and kisses me, his fingers start to move again.

We cook breakfast together. I make pancakes while Will chops some fruit and prepares fresh orange juice and coffee. I'm just turning the second batch of pancakes in the pan, when he comes up behind me, puts his arms around my waist and kisses my neck.

"You okay?" I ask him.

"Yeah... I'm more than okay. I don't think I've ever been this happy."

I turn in his arms to face him. "Good."

"I like where we are," he says, then runs the back of his finger down my cheek. "I know you want more… so do I. And I know we'll get there… soon. But right now I'm really happy with where we're at." He brushes his lips across mine.

"Me too," I whisper. And I open my mouth to tell him I'm in love with him, just as he reaches behind me to pull the pan off the heat.

"Burnt pancakes," he laughs and bends to kiss me. "Worth it, though."

After breakfast, we showered and dressed separately. That was a kind of mutual agreement, really. I'm not sure I could have kept my hands off him in the confined space of a shower; and I think Will knew that, so being separate made him more comfortable. While I was dressing in my room, I called Scott to wish him a happy Christmas. He and Mia have a quiet day planned… truth be told, I don't think they've got any intention of getting out of bed. We didn't talk for long… I had the feeling he had better things to do.

"I'm surprised Megan and Luke didn't want to have Christmas Day on their own," I say to Will as we set off to visit them for the day.

"When the plans were originally made, it was just before they moved out, and we were expecting I'd be on my own for the day," he explains. "I did call him, once it became clear you'd still be here. I offered that we'd stay here and they could have their first and last Christmas alone, but he was adamant we should go. Why? Would you rather stay at home?" He glances across at me as he changes lane.

"No, I like your brother, and Megan." I reach over and place my hand on his leg. "But, if you're offering more of what we did this morning…"

"We can do that again when we get back," he smiles. "As many times as you like."

I leave my hand where it is for the rest of the journey.

We're all in the kitchen, standing around the island unit.

"You've finished unpacking then," Will says, helping himself to a couple of potato chips from the bowls in front of us.

"Just about. The rest of the boxes are upstairs in one of the guest rooms," Megan replies. "But they may never get unpacked. Your brother keeps keeps telling me he'll do them, because he doesn't want me lifting anything heavy…"

"Quite right too," I say.

"Well, it would be… except he never actually unpacks them."

"That's because you keep distracting me," Luke says, winking at her. "Spending time with you, or unpacking boxes – it's hardly a fair contest." He grins, then takes her hand in his. "Shall we tell them now?" Megan gives a slight nod of her head.

"Tell us what?" Will says.

"We wanted you guys to know before everyone else," Luke says, "Megan and I have set a date for the wedding."

"Really? That's great."

"It'll be after the baby's born," Luke says. "Megan doesn't want to get married while she's so obviously pregnant."

"The timing's not been great," she says, "but there's nothing I can do about that now."

Luke puts an arm around her shoulder. "And that's my fault," he says, kissing her cheek. "I know I should've been more careful, but it'll come out right in the end, I promise."

"So, what's the date?" Will says.

"We wanted to ask if you mind…" Luke replies.

"Mind what?"

"If we kind of kidnap your birthday?"

Will stares at him. "I'd be… I'd be honored," he says.

"Which makes it when?" I ask. I read the file, but I can't remember when Will's birthday is.

"April 30th," Luke replies.

"It's not even two full months after Daisy's due, but hopefully it'll give me time to lose most of the baby weight," Megan adds. "It's a good incentive."

207

"You haven't told the others?" Will asks. "Not even Matt?"

"No," Luke replies. "Like I said, we wanted you two to know first."

Luke's talking to us, and about us like we're a couple – with permanence in our relationship. I turn to Will. He takes my hand and kisses my palm, then holds it against his chest.

"Thanks," he says to his brother, then pulls me into him and I snake my arms up around his neck as he gently lowers his lips to mine.

Maybe Luke's onto something.

Chapter Nineteen

Will

We've finished lunch, which Luke cooked to perfection – as usual – and we've cleared away, and Megan and Jamie head up to the nursery, to talk paint colors and fabrics. As they start up the stairs, Luke pulls me back into the living room.

"Let them go," he says. "They'll be ages. Megan bought some baby clothes last week. They're the first things she's bought for Daisy and she's been dying to show them off… Anyway, there's something I need to talk to you about." We each take a sofa. "Are you sure you don't mind us having the wedding on your birthday?" he asks me.

"Absolutely."

He looks at me. "Megan didn't want to wait until the summer; and I wanted it to be a special day – obviously. And when I thought about it, it just felt right. But if you don't want us to…"

"Luke. I'm fine with it. I'm thrilled. Stop worrying."

"Okay." He breathes out. "That wasn't what I wanted to talk to you about though," he continues.

"Oh?"

"I wanted to ask if you'll be my best man."

"Me?"

"Yes."

"Not Matt?" I can't hide my surprise.

"No. You."

"But Matt's your best friend."

"Yes, he is."

"Then it should be him."

"No." He leans forward. "I know Matt would be there for me and I know he'd do a great job of it. But when I stand up there and promise my life to Megan, there's no-one else I want at my side, except you."

I swallow down the lump in my throat. "I'd be proud to be your best man," I say.

"Good." He leans back on the sofa and exhales a long breath, and I wonder for a moment if he was nervous about asking me.

"While we're asking each other things, I've got something I need to ask you," I say.

"What's that?" He looks across at me.

"It's a favor really."

"Then ask it."

"I was wondering if you'd mind calling, before you come around to the house… Or even just using the doorbell, instead of your key." He looks confused. "It's Jamie," I add. And still he looks bewildered. "This morning," I explain, "she got out of bed and went to make us coffee… and she didn't bother to put anything on. So, if you'd decided to come round… I mean, I know you wouldn't have today, because we were coming here… but…"

He starts laughing. "No problem," he says, calming down. "I was thinking I should stop acting like I still live there. It's your home now, not mine." He pauses. "So everything worked out after last night, then?" There's a twinkle in his eyes.

"In a way, yes."

"Well, you said she got out of bed… so I'm guessing she slept with you?"

"*Slept*, yes."

"Oh. Just slept? Nothing else?"

I hesitate. I don't want to tell him too much, because it's personal – it's between Jamie and me. But I value his perspective. "We've done stuff," I say.

"Stuff?" His mouth twitches upwards. "What the hell is 'stuff'?"

"I'm not giving you details," I say. "You told me to always be a gentleman. That means I can't tell you what we do together. I'll talk about me, but not Jamie."

"Okay." He looks kind of pleased... and I feel like maybe I got something right. "The 'stuff'," he says, smiling, "it's going okay, is it?"

"I guess..."

He tilts his head to one side. "You mean you don't know?"

"Jamie likes it, so yeah, I guess it's going okay."

"And you don't? Like it, I mean."

"I like what I'm doing to her."

"And how about what she's doing to you?"

"She isn't doing anything to me."

"Why not? Doesn't she want to?"

"It's me that doesn't want to." I think about it for a moment. "No, that's not true... it's not that I don't want to..."

"Then what is it?" He gets up walks around the coffee table and comes to sit next to me. "Talk to me, Will," he says.

"I've still got this mental blockage. I'm scared it's all going to come rushing back – you know, the bad memories... and that it'll taint whatever I've got with Jamie... maybe forever."

He leans back on the sofa, and so do I. "Okay," he says eventually. "In the past, when you've thought about sex, or being with a woman, have you always ended up thinking about what my dad did to you?"

I look across at him. "I've never really thought about sex, or women... not until I met Jamie."

He twists to face me. "But surely, I mean, you must have. Over the years... you must have..."

"What?"

"You must have jerked off."

"No." I turn away from him.

"Shit, man," he says. "Not ever?"

"Not since I was fifteen; before that night, I did. Afterwards... no. It's there, the whole time, Luke. The thoughts... the memories, they don't go."

"You get hard though, right? I mean, you can get an erection?"

"Yes."

"Thank fuck for that." He smiles across at me. "I thought for one awful minute, I'd missed something else." He pauses for a moment. "It's in your head, Will," he says.

"Yeah... I know that much. The problem is, how do I get it out of my head?"

"You really want my advice?" I nod my head and he sighs. "Stop letting him run your life."

"What, so just pretend like it never happened? How the hell am I supposed to do that?" He wasn't there; he has no idea of the images in my head.

"I didn't say that," he says patiently. "Okay, just think about it this way for a minute... You love Jamie, don't you?" I nod my head again. "And you want to be with her?"

"Yes."

"Then don't throw that away because of what that asshole did to you. Don't let him win, Will. Don't give him the satisfaction of beating you this one last time. You can't forget it, but you can try and beat it – beat him. Think about what you've done so far with Jamie, and how good it felt... then think about how much better it could be. Try it. Let her in, Will. She's worth it. Love's worth it. Okay... so it might not work out the first time, but if it doesn't, just keep trying until it does." He nudges into me with his shoulder. "But I think it'll work just fine and I guarantee you, you won't look back." He gets up and goes toward the door, grinning. "And you probably won't want to stop, either."

Jamie

I sigh, coming back down from the heights of yet another orgasm, and Will looks up at me from between my legs. He runs his tongue along his lips, savoring my taste and I smile down at him.

"You're so sweet," he murmurs, moving up my body, kissing me as he goes, until he's directly above me, then lies down next to me.

I turn toward him in his arms. If I'm being honest, I'm really struggling to keep my hands to myself. I want to touch him and taste him too. But I've said I'll wait, so even mentioning it feels like I'm pushing. The frustration is getting to me though.

"You're not happy, are you?" he says.

"Yes, of course I am. How could I not be happy after what you just did."

"That's not what I meant," he replies.

"Then I don't understand."

"You've got a look in your eyes," he says.

"And?"

"There's something sad behind them. If I've put that there, I want to know how... why..."

I decide to tell him the truth. "I'm not sad, I'm frustrated," I tell him.

"You are? Am I not doing it right? I thought..."

"It's not about what you're doing to me," I tell him quickly. "That's perfect. It's about what I want to do to you... and what we can do for each other."

"Is this about wanting more?" he asks.

"Yes."

"So you're not fed up with me?"

I break free of his arms and sit up next to him. "God, no, Will. It's just I want you so much, I'm finding it difficult to be with you and not touch you... that's all. But that's my prob—"

He takes my hand and slowly moves it toward his erection, but I pull back.

"No," I say. "It's okay. I *can* wait."

"And what if I can't?"

"Are you saying you want to make love?" I ask him, looking down into his face.

"I'm not sure I can do that yet. But I'd like you to touch me... if that's alright with you."

I smile – because I can't help it – and I hold out my hand to him again, moving a little closer. He looks at me, confused. "You guide me," I tell him. "Your pace."

He smiles up at me and takes my hand in his, wrapping my fingers around his length. He's warm to touch; warm, hard, swollen. I keep my hand still for a while, beneath his. I glance up at his face, but his eyes are closed.

"Look at me," I tell him. I don't want his memories intruding. He opens his eyes and they meet mine. They're the darkest blue I've seen yet. "Do you want me to move my hand?" I ask. He takes his away and nods his head, just once… and, very slowly, I slide my hand down to the base of his cock, resting it there for a moment, before raising it to the tip, twisting my wrist slightly as I do. Will exhales. "Keep looking at me," I tell him, moving my hand down again.

"Christ, Jamie," he whispers.

I'd really like to watch my hand working on him, moving up and down his long, hard shaft, forming a regular rhythm, but I don't want to take my eyes from his. He needs to feel the connection between us. After a while, the expression on his face changes. He seems pained and I wonder if we're doing the right thing, whether it's too soon, and something's triggered a memory.

"Stop!" he calls out suddenly, and I do, removing my hand from him. He closes his eyes, shuddering out a breath and I lie down next to him, propped up on one elbow and putting my arm across his chest.

"It's okay," I tell him. "Don't think about it. I'm here."

He looks up at me. "I know," he says, looking perplexed.

"I'm sorry… We should have waited. That brought it all back, didn't it?"

"No," he says, still seemingly baffled.

"Then why…?"

He turns to face me, pulling me closer. "I don't want to come," he says. "Not yet."

I can't help but chuckle. "Then when?"

He kisses me gently. "Inside you," he whispers into my mouth. "I want my first time to be inside you."

We sleep in late, only waking at nine o'clock. Will has to meet Sean Donaldson at twelve-thirty, so he pulls on sweats and a t-shirt and I put on one of his shirts, rolling up the sleeves and we have a quick breakfast.

As I clear away the dishes, Will comes up behind me, putting his arms around my waist. "Shower with me?" he says, kissing my neck.

I lean back into him. "Do you want me to?"

"Yes."

"You're not just asking because you know it's what I want?"

"No. I want it too."

He takes my hand and pulls me out of the kitchen and along the hallway, into his bedroom. He pulls down his sweats, then drags his t-shirt over his head, dropping it to the floor. Slowly, he undoes the buttons on the shirt I'm wearing, keeping his eyes on mine.

"Come," he says, once I'm naked, and takes my hand, leading me into his shower room. Like his bedroom, it's dark in here. The tiles are dark gray, although one wall is entirely mirrored, which adds some relief. The walk-in shower is huge, with enough room for both of us and he stands me beneath the waterfall shower head and turns on the water.

"Shit! That's hot!" I yelp and he quickly adjusts the heat.

"Better?" he asks, grinning.

I nod my head, and he leans down and kisses me. "Sorry," he says. "When I'm not having cold showers to try and stop thinking about you, I like the water to be scalding hot."

"There's scalding… and there's third degree burns."

He smirks, and reaches behind me for the soap, lathering up his hands, and rubbing them over my body, starting at my shoulders and working down… lower and lower. "Does that help?" he asks.

"Hmm." I seem to have lost the power of speech, as he tweaks my nipples between his fingers.

I hold my hands out for the soap and he passes it to me. Once I've got a good foam in my hands, I move them between us, taking his shaft and massaging back and forth along his length.

"God, Jamie," he hisses between his teeth. "That's good." He moves back a little, letting me go and watches as I stroke him, his eyes widening and his mouth dropping open. He leans back on the tiles. "That's really good," he whispers.

I keep up the motion, the pressure and the pace, until he's panting hard.

"Oh… yeah," he mutters. "I can't take much more."

"You want me to stop?" I ask him, holding still.

"Yes and no." He grins.

I move my hands away and let the soap wash from his hard cock, and my hands.

"There's something else I want to try," I tell him. "But I can't do it in here." I wish I could. I'd love to do what I've got in mind in here… but I can't kneel down. Even crouching is uncomfortable. Still, I'm not going to let that stop me.

He looks intrigued. "Okay…" He turns off the water and grabs a couple of towels from the shelf. He wraps me in one, then puts the other around his hips. "Where do we need to go?" he asks.

"Your bed?"

He takes my hand and leads me through to the bedroom.

"I need you to lie down," I tell him.

"Which way?"

"On your back." He does as I say, lying in the middle of the bed, with his head on the pillows, and I lie beside him, pulling the towel away to reveal his throbbing erection.

"Do you trust me?" I ask, looking into his eyes.

He stares at me for a moment, then nods his head.

I move further down the bed, keeping my eyes fixed on his, and I take his cock in my hand, working up and down his length again. I move my head closer, so he knows what I'm going to do, and then I kiss the end of his cock, swirling my tongue around the tip. His eyes darken. I wait until he nods, just as he did for me that first time, then I take him into my mouth, sucking him, my tongue coiling over and around him as I take him deep down my throat.

I feel his hand come up behind my head, fisting my hair, holding it out of the way of my face as he pushes into me, flexing his hips. I release my grip on him, resting my hand on his thigh and, still watching him, I begin to move my head back and forth.

"Oh, God, Jamie... that's... that's so..." he growls between gritted teeth. "Jamie..." There's a warning edge to his voice and I pull back, letting his cock pop free of my mouth.

"Do you want to come?" I ask him.

"Yes."

I smile and take him in my mouth again. "No," he says. "Stop."

I do as he says, and look up at him. "I'm sorry." I move up the bed, so we're lying next to each other. "I thought..."

"I'd love to come in your mouth," he whispers. "But I still want my first time to be inside you..."

Without taking his eyes from mine, he reaches down between my legs and starts to circle his fingers around my clitoris, but I grab his hand, pulling it away.

"What's wrong?" he asks.

"Nothing, but I want my next orgasm to be when we're making love," I tell him.

He leans down and kisses me, his tongue clashing with mine, deep and hard. Neither of us says anything. I hope that means we don't need to.

Chapter Twenty

Will

If I can let her take me in her mouth, surely I can make love to her? The whore tried to suck me… That's the image that's haunted me most all these years; her yellowed teeth grinning at me and her chapped lips around my flaccid dick… That's the thought that's stayed uppermost in my mind. Watching Jamie's mouth on me this morning was the hottest thing I've ever seen. I didn't – I couldn't – think about anything except what she was doing. So… if I can do that, I can make love to her. I'm sure I can.

I'm walking to Boston Common to meet with Sean Donaldson; and making love to Jamie is all I've thought about all the way here.

It's cold, but not too cold, and there are a few people out walking, but no-one sitting on the benches. It's not the weather for sitting around. I take the third bench along, and watch a young couple holding hands as they stroll along the path. They're smiling at each other and he leans down and kisses her cheek. They look happy. I smile to myself… *I've got that. I've got it with my girl at home.* That thought feels good.

"Will Myers?" I turn.

"Yes." The man in front of me is wearing a navy blue cashmere top coat, his black pants and shiny black shoes visible beneath. He has gray hair, and wears metal-rimmed glasses, through which his light brown eyes seem to be appraising me.

He removes a black leather glove and holds his hand out to me. I stand and shake his hand, and then we both sit. He looks around us, as though he's checking we're not being observed and I suppress a smile. I'm suddenly reminded of a 1960s spy movie. I've never liked them very much anyway.

"I've gone over your recordings, and your notes," he says, getting straight to the point.

"And?"

"Well, you're talking to me, rather than looking at the inside of a cell."

"Funny," I say. "Look, if you're trying to intimidate me, it won't work."

He stares ahead. "It damn well should. You should have come to me sooner. Not gone rogue, doing your own thing."

"And you'd have listened, would you, if I had nothing concrete? He's a friend of yours... we both know that. Besides, until I discovered they were being blackmailed and it related to his wife's former occupation, I didn't really expect to find anything."

"In which case, I'm perfectly entitled to want to throw the book at you for doing what you did. I repeat, you should have come to me first. There are ways of going about these things."

"Yeah... but doing it my way, if I hadn't found anything, you'd never have known I'd been there in the first place. I'd have gone back in and removed the devices, and you'd have have been none the wiser. I took a chance, based on a hunch that I knew no-one else would listen to in the first place... So what?" He glances at me before resuming his stare across the pond. "Threaten me all you want, there's nothing you can do to me. You know and I know that I'm right. We also both know that if you try and do anything to me, I can do more harm to you and the department than you even want to think about," I tell him. "But we're not here to talk about me; you're missing the point."

"No I'm not. Jack's as guilty as sin."

"Right. But the question is, what are you going to do about it?"

"I've been thinking about that," he says slowly. "He needs something to give whoever it is who's blackmailing his wife."

"Clearly."

"So, we'll give him something."

"You're going to set up a fake op." It's not a question.

"You're quick."

"You're patronizing."

He turns and looks at me for a little longer this time. "I'm allowed to be. I'm your boss."

"For the moment."

He raises an eyebrow, but ignores me. "You should never have been carrying out this investigation, you know that, don't you?"

"Yes. I told Jack right at the beginning he should have brought in someone from outside the department, or – better still – from out of state."

"And what did he say?"

"He said he trusted me to do it."

"And then sent Jamie Blackwood in to investigate you?"

"Yes. But I knew that was what she was there for. Besides, him using me on the case is just evidence of his guilt really, isn't it…?"

"How so?"

"If he'd wanted the leak investigated properly, he'd have done what I suggested. This way, he could manipulate everything. He controlled who I investigated and to what extent. He had no intention of letting me get anywhere near him. Bringing in someone from the outside would have meant handing everything over to them, including his own interests."

"And you're seriously telling me Jamie Blackwood had no idea what you were doing? She didn't come down to Virginia with you?"

"No, she didn't. Check the airline records if you don't believe me." I offer, calmly.

"I already have."

I sit in silence for a moment, staring at him.

"Then why are you asking?"

I know the answer to that question: he's looking for a reaction. I don't move a muscle.

"You're off the case," he says abruptly.

"I expected that."

"And I want Jamie back in the office the day after tomorrow. I can use her to help set up the fake op. I need someone who's up to speed with Jack's involvement, and she wasn't involved with last August's debacle. I'll bring in people from out of state to work with her."

"The day after tomorrow?" I say, my voice little more than a whisper.

"Yes." He turns to me. "From what I've read about you, I'd have thought you'd appreciate that. You'll get your house back to yourself."

He stands. The meeting's over. He looks down at me. "I need to know for sure I can trust you before I send you anything else to work on. You'll be kept on full pay, of course, until…"

"You're *suspending* me?"

"Call it extended leave," he says.

I lower my eyes and stare across the common. "Fuck you."

"Somehow I thought you'd say that." He turns and walks away.

The day after tomorrow… that means she has to fly home tomorrow. I get up and start walking home… then quicken my pace and, before long, I'm running. I have to get back to her.

"Jamie!" I shout as soon as I've let myself in.

"Yes?" She's lying in the living room, watching TV. She sits up, looking at me over the back of the sofa. "What's wrong?" she asks. "What happened?"

I go to her, crouching down beside her. The movie on the TV is distracting, so I hit the mute button on the remote, glancing at the screen. It looks like she's been watching *The Shop Around The Corner*.

"Talk to me, Will," she says.

"I met him," I tell her, still catching my breath.

"I gathered that."

"They're going to set up a fake op, to give Jack something to tell whoever's blackmailing Kimberley."

"Okay."

I swallow hard and take a deep breath. "And Sean wants you back in the office the day after tomorrow, to help with that."

"The… the day after tomorrow?" Her voice falters. "But…"

"I know."

"That means I have to go…"

"Tomorrow, yes."

"No. I can't," she says, throwing her arms around my neck. "I can't leave, not yet."

Jamie

He holds me close, his hands rubbing up and down my back. "Shh," he says into my hair. "Don't cry, baby."

I lean back a little and he wipes my tears away with his thumbs, looking into my eyes. "I don't want to go," I say.

"I don't want you to go."

"Then I'll stay." He shifts and perches on the edge of the sofa, next to me.

"Do you need this job?" he asks.

"Well, yes. I need it to pay for my house, bills, food…" My car's really old, so it's paid for, although I've been thinking about upgrading it… it's so unreliable. My parents might be rich and they helped with the down-payment on my house, but my dad made his money for himself and he believes Scott and I should do the same. If things got really bad, I know I could go to them, but I don't want to.

"Then you have to go back," he says. "They've suspended me for being involved in this."

"They've *what*? They can't do that."

"They already have."

"Then fight them."

"Why? I don't want the damn job anyway. This has just helped me make my mind up."

"But can you afford to resign?"

"I'm not going to… not yet. They're suspending me on full pay for now… so let them. I'll stay quiet while I work out what to do with Todd and the new business idea; and I'll resign when I'm good and ready. They've made enough use of me over the years…"

I smile. "Good for you."

"But, if they can do that to me, it means you have to go back. If you don't, they'll probably just fire you. You haven't got my track record. You've only been working for them for a few months. You're a lot less trouble to get rid of."

He's right, I know he is, but that doesn't make it any easier.

"How can I go, though?" I stare up at him and feel the tears brimming again. "We've only just… and we haven't…"

"We can… if you want," he says.

"What? Now?" He nods his head. "You want to?"

"Yes. More than anything."

"And you're not just saying that because I have to go home?"

"No. On my way to meet with Sean, all I could think about was what we did this morning… well, what you did to me anyway… and how much I want to do more too. I want to make love to you, Jamie." He stands, holding his hand out to me. "Please. Let's not waste any more time."

I take his hand and let him lead me to his bedroom.

As we stand on the threshold, he leans down and kisses me, then suddenly steps back.

"Shit!" he says. "Condoms… I don't have any. I never thought I'd need them."

"I'm on birth control," I tell him softly. "We're fine." I smile up at him.

He nods, grinning, then opens the door and lets me through.

We're lying naked on his bed, and he's next to me, his fingers teasing and caressing me.

"I don't know how well this will go," he says. "I don't want to disappoint you."

I reach up and place my hand on his cheek. "You couldn't."

He smirks. "I think I probably could," he says and starts to spiral his fingers around my clitoris, gently arousing me, varying the intensity and pressure, until I'm on the brink.

"Please, don't make me wait any longer," I whisper. "I need you."

He changes position, kneeling between my legs, then spreads them wide, his hands on my knees, exposing me.

I fully expect this to be over quickly, and I want to climax with him, so I move my hand down to where his has just been. Then I look up at his face. He's watching me intently, kneeling back a little.

"Don't stop," I tell him.

"I just want to watch you… just for a minute."

I rub myself, gently to start with, then harder, faster, keeping myself close to the edge and my eyes on his. "Please," I say to him. "Please." I arch my back off the bed.

He leans over me, rubbing the head of his cock against my entrance, and then he's inside me, stretching me. He inches slowly forward until the whole of his length is buried in me. Then he stills.

"That feels so good," he whispers. "So. Damn. Good." He looks down at me, his eyes blazing.

I'm close already… I'm really, really close. The feeling of him filling me is taking me beyond the edge. He starts to move, pulling out almost all the way, pausing, and then plunging deep inside me again. Just that one stroke is more than I can take and I spiral into a mind-shattering orgasm, screaming his name. He stills as I clamp around his shaft, my inner muscles pulling him into me. The waves of pleasure wash over me and, as I calm, I look up at him. How can it be this good? It's just not possible that something can be this good – and that I have to give it up tomorrow.

He's completely still for a moment, but then, very slowly, he inches out of me again, before he thrusts in… and out, building a slow, steady rhythm. Soon, I can feel the familiar tremor start to build and tremble through my body yet again.

"Please, Will," I mutter. "Now… please. I want us to come together."

He rams into me hard, one last time, and I struggle to keep my eyes open through the intensity of watching him throw back his head and howl out my name, as he releases inside me, over and over, heightening my orgasm even further, as he claims me.

"Oh God… Will, I love you. I love you so much," I scream, and I'm overwhelmed once more.

Chapter Twenty-One

Will

I collapse on top of her, completely spent, and yet aware that something momentous just happened. It's hard to breathe, my head is fuzzy and my chest feels like it's exploding, but I know that was the most incredible experience of my entire life. Vaguely regaining consciousness, I'm mindful that I could well be crushing Jamie so, keeping us joined, I turn us onto our sides, facing each other. Jamie's legs are wrapped around me and my arms around her.

She looks at me, smiling a little sheepishly.

"And I love you," I tell her quietly.

"You heard me say that?" she whispers.

"Of course. When the woman I'm in love with tells me she loves me too, I'm gonna pay attention, even if I was on the verge of losing my mind at the time."

She laughs. "I wasn't sure whether to say anything… if it was too soon."

"I've been thinking it for days," I tell her. "Well, pretty much since you arrived, really."

"Since I arrived?" She kisses me gently on the lips.

"Yes. You smiled at me. That was all it took."

"Seriously?"

"Yes, seriously."

She snuggles in even closer. "Can I let you into a secret?" she asks, blinking up at me. I nod my head, a little uncertain what to expect. "I've fantasized about this since I first got here."

I have to be honest with her. "I think I knew that," I say. She leans back in my arms, her cheeks reddening.

"How? I mean…" She starts to glance around. "You don't have cameras in the rooms, do you?"

I laugh. "No." I pull her back close again. "I heard you."

"You did?"

"Yes. Only to start with, I assumed you were thinking about your boyfriend. I got very jealous… and then very confused when I heard you calling out my name."

She buries her head in my chest. "Oh God. I can't believe you heard that."

"It's the main reason I asked about Patrick. I wanted to know why you were thinking about me, if you were still with him."

"Because I wasn't with him," she mumbles.

"I know that now," I tell her. I reach between us and raise her face to mine, my finger beneath her chin. "I like that you wanted me in your fantasies," I say, my lips just an inch from hers. "I like it a lot."

"I prefer the reality," she replies and, as our lips meet, my cock stiffens inside her.

She must be able to feel it, because she breaks the kiss and looks at me. "You want more?" she asks, smiling.

"I've got a lot of time to make up for." I smirk.

"And you're planning on doing it all in one day, are you?"

I roll her onto her back, stare down at her beautiful face and slowly start moving inside her again. "Do you want me to stop?" I ask.

She brings her legs up a little, so I can go even deeper. "No," she whispers. "Never, ever stop."

We decided to eat early; mainly so we can go back to bed again. We haven't bothered to dress, but have just put on bathrobes and I'm cooking lasagna, because I know she likes it, while Jamie packs and books her ticket home.

"What are you doing for New Year?" I ask once she's finished on the Internet.

"Nothing that I know of. I guess it depends on the case, really."

I put the lasagna in the oven to cook and join her in the living room, bringing two glasses of wine with me. "Can I come and see you?" I ask. "Spend a couple of days with you?"

"Of course you can." She's grinning. "I'd love to have you come and stay with me."

I lean over and kiss her. "Good. Shall I come up on New Year's Eve? It's a Saturday, so I can catch an early morning flight."

"That sounds good."

"And we can spend the whole weekend together?"

"Definitely."

"And maybe, if the case is going okay, you can come back here for the weekend after?"

"I'd like that." She smiles.

I reach over and pull her closer. "We can make this work," I whisper into her hair. "I know we can."

She twists and puts her arms around my neck, then I move us, so we're lying down, Jamie on top of me, her head on my chest. Our robes fall open, and she feels good naked against me. There's still a sadness in her eyes though, that I don't like. "The distance doesn't matter, you know that, don't you? You're only a couple of hours away. There are flights pretty much every hour."

"I know," she says, not raising her head. "It's just, I've just gotten used to us being together."

"We'll still be together."

"I know… but it won't be the same."

I feel a wetness pooling on my chest. "Hey… Are you crying?" I lift her so I can see her face. There are tears flowing down her cheeks. "Please don't," I say. "It'll be okay. We'll still see each other – as often as we can." As I'm saying the words, they sound hollow, even to me… Are we just gonna get weekends from now on? Is that enough, when we've become so close?

More tears are brimming in her eyes. "I love you," she whispers.

"I love you too."

When we go to bed, it's still quite early – before ten anyway. Jamie's flight is at eleven, so she's leaving at eight-thirty to get to the airport and drop off the rental car.

We lie still, just holding each other for a while. We've hardly spoken since before dinner. I know she's concerned about us being apart, but there's nothing I can do about it for the moment, except… I turn to her.

"Are you still thinking about tomorrow?" I ask

"Yes… Well, and the day after that… and the day after that. And every day until New Year's Eve, when I'll see you again."

"And what are you thinking?" I ask.

"How much I love you; how much I'm going to miss you… and us, and what we do with each other."

"In that case, can I ask you something?" I say.

"Sure."

"Can I watch you?"

"Watch me what?"

"Touch yourself. Like you did before, like you did when you fantasized about me. I want to see what you look like. I want to have that memory. Then, I want you to watch me. And when we're not together, we can still talk and we'll both be able to picture each other. I'll be able to imagine your fingers, your breasts, your face, how your body reacts to your touch."

She sits up a little, leaning on one arm, looking down at me. "Are you suggesting we have phone sex when we're apart?" she whispers, smiling.

"Yes. I guess so. If you want to."

"It's not something I've ever done before."

"Well, neither have I – obviously. I just thought…"

"I think it's a good idea," she says, leaning over and placing a kiss on my chest. "I'm going to miss you so much. I want to have that connection with you still."

"Me too. I don't think I can wait until New Year's Eve."

She grins. "Neither can I." I reach up and pull her down to me, kissing her deeply, my tongue finding hers with ease, my hands roaming over her naked body, feeling her soft skin against mine.

I roll her onto her back, our mouths still connected, then I break the kiss and kneel up next to her. She stares into my eyes and, very slowly moves her hand down between her legs, parting them wide. I watch, entranced as she starts to rub herself, slowly to begin with, and then with increasing speed and pressure, her back arching off the bed. Every so often, she inserts a finger or two inside her entrance, before returning her attention to her tight hard nub. At no time does she take her eyes from mine, but after a while, she uses her other hand to squeeze and tweak her breasts and nipples. I'm so turned on, it's all I can do not to stroke my cock... I've got to wait so she can watch me, but seeing her do this is so erotic, I'm struggling to stay in control. It doesn't take long before her breathing alters, her moans and cries become louder and then, she screams my name, bucking and writhing on the bed, begging for more.

It takes her a while to calm, but when she does, I've changed position slightly, so I'm lying on the bed, raised up on one elbow and I'm already fisting my cock, gently running my hand up and down its length.

"Oh God," she whispers, sitting up and staring into my eyes.

"Hush, baby," I say. "Watch." And she lets her eyes drop to my hand. I haven't done this since I was fifteen, and it's not something you forget how to do. But having Jamie watch me makes it even more exciting than I remember. I stroke myself, over and over, watching her reaction, the way her eyes widen and she bites her bottom lip. All I can think about is her mouth on me, her tongue swirling around the tip of my cock and being buried deep inside her... With those images in my head, it doesn't take long before I explode, breathless, coating my hand and myself.

"God, that was hot," she whispers, lying down beside me.

I kiss her forehead. "Just let me get cleaned up," I say. "This isn't anywhere near as much fun as being inside you..."

"But it'll do?"

"If I can't have you... yes." I go to the bathroom, clean up and come back to her, lying down and pulling her close.

"You looked incredible," I tell her, running my fingers down her back. She shudders to my touch.

"So did you."

"Can I call you tomorrow evening?" I ask. "I won't be able to wait much longer than that…" I grin at her.

"Of course you can. I won't know what to say, though. It'll be odd, being in my room, on my own, with you here…"

"We'll work it out," I tell her. "At least it's something we've neither of us done before. If we get it wrong, we won't be any the wiser."

She sits up and looks down at me. "Did you want to do this because you're worried that I might think about Patrick when we're not together?" she asks. Did I? I don't think so.

"No, but I am aware you're more experienced than I am… not that that's hard. And I know I might not compare well. I've still got a lot to learn."

"Oh, Will." She runs her hand across my chest. "It's not about making comparisons… And anyway, I'm not *that* experienced. There was only Patrick before you… and, to be honest, it was never great with him. Being Patrick, he was only interested in pleasing himself. I never had an orgasm with him…"

"What? Not once?" I'm shocked, and maybe a little pleased with myself that she's had so many with me.

"No. He never gave me any time, or attention. I used to do it myself, once he'd gone to sleep."

"And he didn't notice?"

"No."

"Was the guy deaf?" I can't help but smirk.

She slaps me playfully on the arm. "I used to go into the bathroom. I'd lean up against the wall, or the basin…"

"Now, that's a sight I'd like to see."

"Well, maybe at New Year's I'll re-enact it for you." She leans over and traces a line of kisses, starting in the centre of my chest and working slowly downwards. By the time she reaches my cock, I'm hard again.

It's early when I wake up, just after dawn and I lie, watching Jamie beside me. She's lying on her back and makes slight moaning noises in her sleep and, even in the couple of times we've slept together, I've gotten used to them. I've gotten used to her. Christ, what am I going to do without her?

I don't wake her until I have to, and when I do, she smiles up at me, until she remembers she's leaving, and her eyes fill with tears again.

"No," I tell her. "No more crying. It's only going to be for a few days." I'm putting a brave face on it for her sake.

She nods her head, swallowing hard and blinking a few times. "Okay."

"We've got an hour and a half," I tell her. "Shower or breakfast first?"

"Shower. I won't have breakfast – I'm not the best flyer."

"Oh… okay." I get up and lead her into the bathroom. I guess that means we can have longer in the shower.

Taking her from behind, her hands flat on the tiled wall, while the water cascades over us, I'm deeper inside her than I've been before. Her screams, my groans, echo off the walls and when we're done, we hold onto each other for as long as we can. It's nowhere near long enough.

Jamie

We're out of the shower, I'm packed and ready to go and we're in the kitchen, having one last coffee together.

"I'll call you tonight," he reminds me.

"I'm looking forward to it already," I say, trying to smile.

"Me too." He puts his cup down on the countertop and takes the two steps to close the gap between us and holds me in his arms. "Be naked," he whispers.

"I will. And tomorrow night?" I grin at him.

He pulls me closer still. "I'll be happy to call tomorrow as well," he says. "But it'll be late. I'm going out to dinner… well, everyone's coming here first, and then we're all going to an Italian restaurant around the corner."

"Sounds lovely," I say, wistfully.

"You were meant to be there too," he replies. "Matt arranged it all last week. The table's booked for seven people." He pulls me into his arms. "It won't be the same without you. I don't know what time I'll be back, though… do you still want me to call?"

"Yes. I'll wait up."

"Sure?"

"Yes."

He leans down and, just as our lips are about to touch, the door buzzer sounds. We both sigh, frustrated, and Will pulls away and goes to the intercom, pressing the button to activate the camera and speak to whoever's outside.

From where I am, I can't see the screen, but I can hear Will agreeing to let them in. I wonder for a moment if it's Luke, and as much as I like him, I hope not. I want us to have these last few minutes together on our own.

"It's a courier," Will says.

"Is it work?" I ask.

"Not for me," he replies. "I'm suspended, remember?" He goes over to the door and opens it, taking the package from the man on the other side and signing for it.

"Well…" he says, coming back across to me, "I guess it could be work, after all. It's for you. No-one else knows you're here, do they?" He holds out the parcel to me and I immediately know what it is. How could I have forgotten about this? I suppose I must've been a little pre-occupied in the last few days.

"Oh. I guess so," I say, trying to sound nonchalant. "I'll go put it with the rest of my things in my room. And I'd better bring them out, hadn't I?"

"Do you want some help?" he asks.

"No. I'm fine." I need to leave this package behind for him, and I don't want him to find it until after I've gone.

In my room, I gather up my things and switch my phone on to check for messages. I haven't done this since Christmas Day… and while I'm waiting for it to start up, I look around, trying to find a good place to hide this package. I guess I can just leave it on the bed, tucked under the comforter… It won't be obvious, and Will's bound to come in here to change the bedding and he'll find it then.

My phone beeps a few times. I've got messages. I scroll through the numbers. There's one from my mother, which I ignore, and two from Scott, from this morning – really early. That's most unlike him. Besides, he knows my phone is off, so if he's calling, it must be important. I call him straight away.

"Hi," I say to him as soon as he picks up, sitting down on the edge of the bed for a minute.

"Hey, sis," he says. He sounds exhausted.

"What's wrong, Scott? You called… something's wrong."

"Yeah… well, kinda. I didn't want to worry you, Jamie. I just thought I should let you know, I've got to go away for a few days."

"Really? Where are you going?" I'm surprised.

"I'm taking Mia back to her folks' place in Phoenix."

"But I thought she couldn't afford the fare."

"I'm paying for the fares," he says. I don't question him, because I can sense there's more. "Her grandmother's in the hospital. She was taken ill yesterday evening. We're leaving at lunchtime."

"Lunchtime?"

"Yeah… is that a problem?" he asks.

"No… it's just that I'm coming home today."

"Oh." He sounds as disappointed as I feel.

"I won't get home until about one, maybe just before."

"And I'm leaving at twelve."

"So we'll miss each other," I say.

"Yeah."

I take a deep breath. "It would have been good to go out for lunch, or dinner. We need to catch up…"

"I won't be gone for long."

"I know… but I miss you." I really don't want to be alone right now. I need Will, and being away from him is going to be so hard; I'm not sure I can do it. Scott would have been good company for me.

"I miss you too," he replies.

I look at my watch… time's moving on. I've got to leave in fifteen minutes. "I've got to go," I tell him. "I need to get to the airport."

"Okay," he says. "Safe trip."

"You too. Stay in touch… Love you."

"Love you too, sis."

I end the call and look up to see Will standing in the doorway. He looks… weird. His eyes are dark, and shadowed.

"Will? What's the matter?" I ask him.

"Who was that?" he asks, his voice strained. "Who were you talking to? Or, more to the point, who were you saying 'I love you' to?"

Oh, hell. I get up and go over to him. I reach for his hand, but he pulls away from me.

"Will…" I say quietly. "Please… come and sit down… let me explain."

"I don't need to sit down. I just wanna know, who the hell you were saying 'I love you' to…" He raises his voice a little. This isn't good.

"My brother." I keep my voice soft

"Your brother? I didn't know you had a brother…"

"No."

"Why?"

"Why what?"

"Why don't I know about your brother?"

"He's just never come up, I suppose."

He looks at me. I need to explain… and keep calm, because, from the look in his eyes, I can tell Will's not handling this. He's not handling this at all.

"His name's Scott. He's five years younger than me and he's studying electrical engineering at Virginia Tech. He called to let me know he's flying to Phoenix with his girlfriend because her grandmother's in the hospital… That's all there is to it, Will… I promise."

He takes a long, deep breath. "I'm sorry," he whispers. "I... I heard you saying that... and I thought..."

I take his hands in mine and he lets me this time. "I know," I say quietly. "I'm sorry too. I should've told you about Scott before. It's not like he's a secret, or anything... it's genuinely just that we never got around to talking about him. I'm not keeping anything from you, Will... honestly."

"I know. I'm sorry."

"You don't have to be sorry."

He pulls me into a hug, holding me tight. "I... I thought there was someone else," he murmurs into my hair.

I lean back in his arms. "Of course there isn't. I love you, Will Myers. Don't forget that."

"I love you too," he says.

"Good." He leans down and kisses me really tenderly. "Have you got everything?" he asks, breaking the kiss eventually.

"Except the dress." I nod to the closet, where the dress he gave me for the party is still hanging up on the door.

"Aren't you going to take it with you?" He seems hurt.

"I can't fit it in my case. I... I thought I'd leave it here for now, if that's okay."

He smiles. "Sure." He hesitates for a moment. "I guess you can take it back when you've got less luggage."

"Or... I can just leave it here for the next time I need a party dress."

"Or that." His smile becomes a grin. "I kinda like the idea of you leaving your things here," he adds.

"Me too." He kisses me again, until it's time for me to leave.

Will can't even drive me to the airport, as I have to return the hire car. So, we say goodbye outside his house. He holds me, leaning up against the car, for a long, long time until eventually, I have to go.

"I'll see you on New Year's Eve," he says.

"I can't wait."

He leans down and kisses me, hard. His tongue swirls around mine, deep in my mouth, his hands in my hair. When he pulls back, we're both breathless. "I love you," he whispers. "And I miss you already."

"Me too."

He loads my case onto the back seat, closes the door and helps me in behind the wheel.

"Take care," he murmurs, through the open window.

"I will. I love you." I'm really struggling to hold back the tears.

"Don't cry," he says. "Please don't."

"I won't." *Not yet anyway.*

"And I'm sorry," he whispers. "About your brother… about misunderstanding."

"Don't be, Will… It's really fine."

I start the engine and, with one last, long kiss, I pull away through the open gate and onto the street. I don't look in the mirror. I don't want to see him standing there; I don't want to think about everything I'm leaving behind.

The drive to the airport is short, which is just as well, as I'm in a daze. I'm half blinded by tears and I'm so in love with him, I can't think straight. I never expected to come back to Boston and fall in love, I never expected to even be happy here. But I did, and I am. Leaving here… leaving him is the hardest thing I've ever had to do. And I've done some pretty hard things in my time. I know it's only a few days until we'll see each other again, but I really don't want to go.

Chapter Twenty-Two

Will

"How was your day?" she asks me. I've got her on speaker, with the phone beside me on the bed and I hate the fact that she's not here. I hate the fact that she's miles away and I can't touch her...

"Horrible," I reply honestly. "How was yours?"

"The same."

"Had your brother already gone when you got back?"

"Yes." I can hear the sadness in her voice. "It's real lonely here."

"Hey," I whisper. "I'm here."

"No you're not... you're there." She gulps down a sob.

"Don't cry, Jamie." It wasn't meant to be like this. "What did you do this afternoon?" I can't hug her, so the least I can do is change the subject.

"I went grocery shopping. Scott and Mia had left pretty much nothing in the house... bless them." I can hear a slight smile... or at least I think I can. "Still, the place was at least clean and tidy, which I'm guessing was down to Mia, not Scott."

"He's not a tidy person, then?" I ask.

"He's twenty-one..."

"And?" I don't get the connection.

"Were you tidy at twenty-one?"

"Yeah, I think so. Luke was kinda strict about that. He didn't have time to clear up after me, and I slept on the couch in his and Matt's living room for years... so I had to be tidy."

She pauses for a moment before replying, "I guess not having your own space made growing up even harder."

"Not really." It didn't. My memories and nightmares made it hard. Living with Matt and Luke was a breeze. "Okay… so I never got to do all the usual teenage stuff, but Matt and Luke included me in pretty much everything they did – well everything that was legal for a kid of my age."

She lets out a half-laugh. "Maybe you can teach Scott a thing or two. He's a good kid, but…" She doesn't finish her sentence.

"Well, if you think it'll help."

"Can't hurt." She sighs. "What did you do today?" she asks, trying to sound brighter. I'm not that easily fooled.

"I dismantled some of the equipment in the office."

"Really? Isn't that your normal set-up, then?"

"Not all of it. The wall-mounted screens are permanent, but the desktops were just for this op. I usually work on laptops, so I've packed all the desktops away and put them back into storage. They're just taking up space."

"Wow… you really do like to be tidy."

"Well, I don't like clutter."

"What *do* you like?" Her voice drops down a note or two.

"You," I whisper. "I like you a lot. Especially if you're naked…"

"You asked me to be… so I am."

My cock stiffens. "Oh, God…" I murmur, stroking myself just gently.

"Are you touching yourself?" she asks.

"Yeah," I whisper. "You?"

"Oh, yeah…" Her voice is a little breathless all of a sudden.

"Tell me what you're doing…" I grip the base of my cock to stem my rising excitement, knowing what she'll be doing, picturing it in my head.

"I'm… I'm…" She pauses. "Oh God, Will, this is really embarrassing," she says, "and it's kinda hard holding the phone and touching myself at the same time."

"Then put the phone on speaker… that's what I've done."

"Okay." There's a moment's pause and then I hear her again, although her voice is really distant. "How's that?" she says, or at least I think that's what she says.

"Um… where did you put the phone, Jamie? Kentucky?"

"Oh… hang on…" There's a shuffling noise, then she comes through more clearly. "Sorry, it fell down between the pillows." She huffs. "This isn't working, Will. It's too… mechanical." She sounds frustrated, and a little upset.

"It's okay," I tell her. "We can just talk, if that's what you want."

"No… that isn't what I want. I want you. I want to feel your hands, your fingers, your tongue… I want you inside me, Will."

"Keep talking like that and I'm gonna come, Jamie."

"Are you still…?"

"I'm still touching myself, yeah."

"Then you tell me what you're doing," she whispers.

"Okay…" I think about it for a moment. "Although I'd rather tell you about all the things I want to do to you," I say quietly, rubbing my cock real slow.

"Such as?"

"Such as running my hands over your perfect skin, and touching your breasts," I murmur, keeping up steady strokes along my length. "And sucking your hard nipples, biting them gently between my teeth."

"Oh… yes," she breathes.

"Touch yourself, Jamie," I say to her.

"I already am."

"Good. Imagine it's my fingers on you, circling around you. Imagine my tongue brushing over you, licking you, tasting your special sweetness…"

"Oh, God, Will… yes."

"And picture me kneeling between your legs… imagine how it feels when my cock enters you. Remember that feeling…"

"Of being stretched… oh… God… yes… being filled by you…" she murmurs.

"That's it, baby." I'm close to coming, so I slow down and wait for her, although I don't think she's far behind me. "Feel me taking you, long and hard, my whole length buried deep inside you. You feel amazing on my cock, baby… so wet. We fit together perfectly."

"Don't stop… Will, I'm gonna come…" Her breathing changes, she's panting. And then I hear her cry out my name, real loud. Two more strokes of my cock and I explode over my hand, and the bed, in an almighty orgasm that wracks through my body. Jamie's still screaming out her ecstasy, even as I calm. I wait until she's quieter.

"You okay?" I ask quietly.

"Please…" she whispers. "Please take me."

"I will… soon, baby. I promise." I hear a sob. "Hey… don't cry."

"I can't help it… I miss you."

"I miss you too."

Jamie

Last night's call was much harder than I'd thought it would be. We'd built it up as something fun and exciting… and it turned out to be embarrassing, awkward… and really upsetting. Will got us both there, but I was pretty useless at it to start with, and I couldn't help crying when it was over. It was so hard not having him with me to hold onto, to share it all with and it took him nearly half an hour to calm me down again. I know he found it just as difficult as I did, that he couldn't hold me in his arms and make it all better again.

He phoned me again this morning… not to have more long-distance sex, but to make sure I'm okay after what happened. I'm not okay, but hearing his voice makes everything a little better. We're still going to talk tonight, but I'm not sure we'll try the phone sex thing again. Just talking to him seems to soothe my fractured nerves… maybe that'll be enough to last us until New Year's Eve.

He told me that he's going to clear up the guest room today, and change the bedding... he said he's stretching the chores out, so they'll last until New Year, filling the time. I guess he'll find the package I left behind for him, under the comforter. If I'm honest, the thought of his reaction is making me a little nervous too... just to add to the tension of the day.

I've got to go to work this morning and I'm not looking forward to it. I've never worked at the office before. I've never met Sean Donaldson, and I've never met the person from out of state who's going to be heading up the case... Will was encouraging on the phone, reminding me that I've got the edge on everyone else, being as I know all the background on the case. He's sent me copies of all his notes, and we talked through as much of it as we could. I felt better for having his advice. His friends are right... he's really good at this.

Having the house to myself does have some advantages. Even allowing for Will's phone call, I'm up, showered, dressed and ready to leave in plenty of time. I want to get in early, to create a good impression with Sean Donaldson, who – according to Will – might be hard to please, but who I shouldn't let brow-beat me. I wish I had Will's self-assurance when it comes to things like that...

My car's been sitting on the driveway for weeks now. I'm not sure if Scott drove it at all, but it doesn't look like it... there are even a few cobwebs around the side mirrors, which I wipe away, before getting in and putting my bag on the passenger seat. God, it feels damp in here. I turn over the engine and nothing happens... absolutely nothing... not even a sound. The battery is completely flat. *Why today, of all days?*

I'm mechanically useless when it comes to cars, but this has happened to me before – twice – and the last time, I was told it'd probably be a good idea to replace the battery... and I started to wonder about changing the car instead. Only then I was sent to Boston and I forgot all about it.

I rest my head on the steering wheel and, although I feel pathetic for doing so, I call Will.

"Hey," he says, answering on the second ring. "You okay?" We only spoke about half an hour ago, so his question isn't that surprising.

"No," I whimper.

"What's wrong?" I can hear the concern in his voice.

"My car won't start." I sound really feeble.

"Your car won't start?" I'm sure I can hear a smile in his voice.

"Yes."

"What's wrong with it?" he asks.

"I think the battery's flat. Nothing happens when I turn the key... and I had trouble with it a couple of times before."

"And you didn't replace the battery?"

"No..."

He sighs. "Okay," he says. "Where are you now?"

"I'm sitting in the car, in front of my house... feeling sorry for myself."

"Oh dear." Now he is smiling... I can hear it. "How far do you live from the office?" he asks.

"About five miles... why?" I hope he's not gonna suggest I walk there.

"Then call a cab; get to work... and deal with the car later."

"Why didn't I think of that?"

"I guess because you're nervous... and a little wound up about today?"

He understands me so well. "You're right... I am."

"It's okay, baby" he says, softly. "You're gonna be fine... Now, get out of the car, go back inside and call a cab..."

"Okay." I do as he says.

"And send me a text when you get to work."

"I will... and thanks."

"Anytime... I love you."

"I love you too."

"Sorry I'm late," I say to Sean, who's sitting behind his large oak desk. He gets to his feet, as does the man who's sitting in the chair nearest to me.

"This is Gavin Jacobson," Sean says as I close the door. "He's from the Chicago office."

"Hi," Gavin says, offering his hand, which I shake. "Nice to meet you at last. I've just been hearing all about you, and your exploits in Boston."

God, I hope not. "Really?" I say out loud, feeling even more flustered.

"Yes," he says. "I've read the reports. Excellent work."

"Most of which wasn't mine," I tell him. "Will Myers—"

"The least said about that the better," Sean interrupts, sitting back down again. He shifts some paperwork on his desk, then looks up at me through his metal-framed glasses. "Now we're all here, we can go through everything."

Gavin offers me his seat and fetches another from beside the wall, bringing it alongside mine. He's tall, probably a couple of inches taller than Will, with dark brown hair, green eyes and a handsome face, that lights up when he smiles, which he's doing at the moment. I guess he's around thirty... maybe thirty-five, and as he sits down beside me, placing his hands on his thighs, I notice he's wearing a wedding band.

"Do you want to fill us in, Jamie," Sean suggests. "We'll ask questions at the end."

I nod my head and start going through the documents, falteringly to start with, but I gain confidence as I work my way through Will's file. The familiarity of his words helps me explain to them what we've found, and the implications.

"That all sounds very... efficient," Sean says, reluctantly.

"Sounds like damn good work to me," Gavin adds. He looks at Sean. "If you decide not to reinstate Will Myers, let me know. I'll welcome him onto my team." Sean lowers his eyes for a moment, but ignores Gavin's comment and starts to brief us both on his idea for the fake operation that we're supposed to set up as a trap for Jack. Once he's finished, he looks at Gavin, ignoring me completely now. I guess I've served my purpose as far as Sean's concerned.

"What do you think?" he asks.

"Well," Gavin replies, "I don't know about Jamie, but I think you're making it much more complicated than it needs to be. How do you see it?" He turns to me.

"I..." I can't believe he's asking my opinion. I look up at Sean, who's glaring at me, daring me to disagree with him. I wonder what Will would do and I smirk inwardly, because I know exactly how he'd respond to Sean. It wouldn't be pretty. "I agree with Gavin," I say, my voice sounding a lot stronger than I'd expected. Sean's lips form into a thin line, but he says nothing. He's going to give me enough rope to hang myself... clearly. "It's too elaborate. We don't have enough time to set up something like that," I say, leaning forward a little, gathering momentum, imagining Will behind me, encouraging me. "Jack needs something he can give these guys in the next few days, not the next few weeks or months. He won't wait long enough for this to be set up. And besides..." I pause.

"What?" Gavin asks. I look at him.

"Well... this seems ever so similar to the operation the department ran in the summer. I mean... I know I wasn't here, but from what I've heard, there are a lot of similarities between that op and the one Sean's suggesting. I'm not sure Jack will fall for it." I stop talking, take a breath and sit back, waiting for Sean to yell at me.

"I completely agree," Gavin says, not giving Sean a chance to respond. "I think Jamie has summed it up perfectly." He's still facing me. "Would you agree that Jack's fairly desperate?" he asks.

I nod my head. "Yes. He certainly came across that way."

He shrugs. "Then I don't think we need to go to the extent of setting up anything fake at all," he says. "I think we can just feed him some information, and watch him closely to see what he does with it."

Sean looks defeated. He'd have fought me off, without any problem; but Gavin's a senior investigator... "I'm not so sure," he says, seeming to want to persevere with his idea.

Gavin shifts in his seat. "Okay," he replies. "Why don't Jamie and I put our heads together. We'll see if we can come up with something that might convince Jack to take the bait... something small and quick to put together. We'll bring it back to you by tomorrow lunchtime, and if you don't agree, we'll start working on your idea... although I still think we'll have to pare it down and change it a little, so it doesn't have as many similarities to the August op... Jamie's right. He's gonna see right through that." He looks from Sean to me and back again. "How does that sound as a plan?"

I shrug. "It works for me," I say.

"Very well." Sean is still reluctant. "I suppose we'll only be losing a day."

Gavin gets up. "You're assuming our idea won't run," he says. "And I'm assuming it will... so we won't be losing anything at all."

They've allocated Gavin an office just down the hall from Sean's, so we grab a coffee and sit either side of the desk.

"We need to make this work," he says quietly, taking off his jacket and turning to drape it over the back of the chair. "Sean's idea is crap." I laugh... I can't help it. He looks up at me. "Well, it is."

"I'm not disagreeing."

"Good... so... any suggestions?"

We spend the next half-hour bouncing scenarios off each other, before my phone beeps, and it's only then I recall I forgot to text Will to let him know I'd got to work. Sure enough the message is from him.

— *Hi. Let me know you're okay. Getting worried here. W x*

"Sorry," I say to Gavin. "I just need to reply to this."

"That's fine," he replies. "I need another coffee anyway. Do you want one?"

"Sure. Thanks." I hand him my cup as he passes out through the door.

I send a text back to Will:

— *Sorry. Cab was late. Had to go straight into meeting. Didn't mean to worry you. I'm fine. Love you. xx*

His reply is immediate:

— *Okay. As long as you're safe. I'll call you tonight as planned. Love you too. W xx*

I'm still smiling when Gavin comes back in.

"Everything okay?" he asks.

"Yes, thanks."

His jacket is hanging on the back of his chair and he reaches into the inside pocket and pulls out his cell. "While we're taking a break," he says, "are you okay if I just call my wife?"

"Sure... Do you want me to leave you alone for a minute?"

"No…" He shakes his head. "It's fine. I just want to check in with Laura. Our daughter was sick overnight."

"Oh dear…"

"I had to fly here yesterday afternoon, so Laura's on her own… and she's three months pregnant. It's not great; she's got really bad morning sickness and she's not sleeping well anyway, and she was up most of the night with Becky… that's our daughter… and I'm talking too much, aren't I?"

I smile across at him. "It's fine. You're worried about them."

"Yeah, I am." He presses a few buttons on his phone and holds it to his ear, while I sit closer to the desk and start going through the papers we've scattered across it's surface, with various ideas jotted down on them.

"Hey, honey," Gavin's voice is soft. "How's things?" He waits, listening. "Okay… well that sounds a little better. Are you gonna take her to the doctor?" He waits again. "Alright. Yeah, that's probably best." He leans back in his chair. "How have you been this morning?" he asks. There's another pause. "Oh, baby," he says, his voice so full of concern. "Has it stopped yet…? Try having some toast, and get some sleep while Becky's resting." He pauses. "I don't know yet," he says. "I'm hoping to be able to keep it short, but whatever happens I'll be home for New Years… I know… I know it's really bad timing." He waits. "Maybe we should call your mom… get her to come and help you?" He laughs. "Okay… so it's not *that* bad then?" I can't help smiling as I straighten some more papers. "I'd better go," he says. "I'll call you tonight from the hotel, but text or call if you need me, okay? I mean, I know there's not a lot I can do from here, but call me anyway." There's another pause, then he lowers his voice. "I love you too, baby," he says. I sit back and try to pretend I'm not there, as he ends the call and puts the phone back in his jacket pocket.

He looks over at me. "Sorry about that," he says.

"No, it's fine… Is… is everything okay?" I'm not sure I should ask, but I want to know… and he seems concerned.

"Laura's still suffering, but Becky's a little better," he replies.

"How old is she… your daughter, I mean?"

"She'll be three in February," he says, and turns in his seat, reaching back into his jacket and pulling out his wallet this time. He opens it and shows me a photograph of a stunning woman with dark blonde hair, and deep violet eyes, who's staring at the camera, and holding onto a toddler, who's got slightly darker hair, but the same incredible shade of eyes... and the cheekiest smile.

"They're beautiful," I say as he closes the wallet.

"I know..." he replies, grinning. "I'm one helluva lucky guy." He puts the wallet back in his jacket. "You married?" he asks me.

"No," I reply. "But I'm... well... I'm with someone."

"Oh?" he says.

"Yeah... Will Myers."

Gavin smiles. "I wondered," he says.

"You did?"

"Yeah..."

"How?" I ask.

"Oh... You just got a kind of look in your eyes when you were talking about him, that's all... Besides, I know how easy it is to fall for someone when you're thrown together like you two were."

"Really?"

"Yeah. Laura and I met in similar circumstances. She's not an agent, she's a psychologist and she was brought in on a case I was working. She knocked on my office door, I took one look at her and I knew."

"Funnily enough, that's kinda what Will said."

"Then he's your man." Gavin smiles. "Now... let's get back to work. The sooner we get this done, the sooner I can get home to my girls."

Chapter Twenty-Three

Will

I was going to spend some of today clearing up the guest room, changing the bedding, cleaning the bathroom… but when I went in there this morning, the room still had a scent of Jamie about it. I kinda liked that and I'm not ready to lose it yet. Maybe in a day or two… or after I get back from hers in the New Year, when I'm more used to this long-distance relationship thing and I'm not missing her every single second of the day.

So, I left the door open, letting her scent permeate the house a little more, and I've been cleaning the kitchen instead… well, cleaning the kitchen and worrying about her, because she said she'd text when she got to work and I didn't hear a thing from her.

I waited until eleven-thirty, and worry got the better of me.

But she's fine… so I'm fine.

I've finished the cleaning by lunchtime… and now I'm kinda stuck for what to do. I'd thought that, if I spread my chores out over the few days I have to fill before I go visit Jamie, it would fill the time and make it easier to be here without her, but it's not working.

This is weird for me. I've lived a solitary life for years and it's never bothered me in the least, but I'm so damn lonely right now I can't think what to do and I'm wandering around the house like a lost puppy, which is – frankly – pathetic.

I guess the difference is that, for the last fourteen years, I've had work of some kind to keep me occupied. School work, college work, or agency work... there's always been something – until now.

I go back into the guest room... and her scent overwhelms me again. God, I miss her so much. And then it dawns on me. I've got no work to do... There's nothing to keep me here for the next few days. So, why am I waiting for New Years? Why don't I just go and visit her now? Obviously she'll have to into the office, but I can stay at her place, work on the figures for my meeting with Todd, and we can be together in the evenings... Besides, with her car playing up, I can give her a ride into work each morning, and pick her up afterwards. I can cook for us... It's perfect.

Well, it's perfect, except for the minor detail that I've got no idea where she lives. But that's only a very, very minor detail...

I go down the hallway, through the spotlessly clean kitchen and into the office, where I start up my personal laptop and hack into the department's personnel files. I know it's illegal, but no-one's ever going to know I was here. It doesn't take more than a few minutes to bring up her details and copy her address to my contacts list. Then I purchase a ticket on the four o'clock flight.

While I'm copying Jamie's address from my contacts list onto my phone, I notice the reminder for tonight's dinner... *Damn.* Still, no-one's gonna mind if I don't show up... Except, we're all supposed to be meeting here... I stare at the phone for a moment, then call up Luke's details and connect the call.

"Hi," he says.

"Hello."

"What's up?" he asks.

"How do you know something's up?"

"The tone of your voice."

"Hell... you should come work for the agency," I say to him. "You're good."

"Nah," he replies. "It only works with you. I know you too well."

"Hmm."

"So... what's up?"

"I need to bail on tonight's dinner," I tell him.

"Oh? Why?"

"Because I need to go to Virginia to see Jamie."

"Why is she in Virginia?"

I remember that he doesn't even know she's gone home.

"Because that's where she lives," I explain. "I handed my information over to our boss and he recalled her to the office."

"Oh… and you're not coping too well with that?"

"No… I'm not."

There's a moment's pause.

"And would that be because you guys finally worked things out?" he asks.

"Maybe…"

"Hallelujah!" he laughs.

"Yeah… okay. The thing is, I miss her."

"I get that. But can you just take off to Virginia, Will? I mean, don't you have work of your own to do?" he asks.

"No… They suspended me."

"They what?"

"I'm untrustworthy, evidently."

"For fucks sake, Will. You did the right thing."

"Not according to my boss, I didn't."

"They haven't changed their minds about locking you up, or anything, have they?"

I smile. "No."

"When did this happen?" he asks.

"Jamie left yesterday morning."

"You should've called me."

"I didn't think it would be this bad."

"You didn't? You don't remember what I was like without Megan?" I recall how Luke stayed in his room, didn't shower, or get dressed, or even eat for the first couple of days…

"Yeah… I suppose I should've thought…"

"So what have you been doing?"

"Wandering around the house… and cleaning."

"Man… it's *that* bad?" He's smiling, I know he is.

"Yeah… which is why I'm gonna fly down there. We planned for me to visit her over New Year anyway, but I figured I might as well go now. I've got nothing to keep me here for the next few days… except tonight's dinner."

"Hell, don't worry about that. I'll call around. We can easily meet at Todd's place. He's not too far from the restaurant."

"You don't think anyone will mind?"

"Not when I tell them why, no."

"Okay. And, I'm due to meet with Todd on Monday, so can you tell him I'll still be back for that?"

"Sure. When are you leaving?"

I check my watch. "In an hour or so… I'm booked on the four o'clock flight. I'll need to hire a car when I get there, so I should be at Jamie's place by just after six, I guess."

"Okay. And you'll be back for Monday?"

"Yeah. I'll come back Sunday night. Todd and I have arranged to meet early Monday morning, before he goes to work."

"Well… have a good time," Luke says. "And Happy New Year… because I doubt I'm gonna hear from you much in the next few days."

"You won't be hearing from me at all… I'll have far more interesting things to do."

"I knew it. I knew you wouldn't be able to stop… not once you'd started." He's laughing again.

"Does it get boring?" I ask him.

"What, sex?"

"No… being right all the time…"

Jamie

"I think we've got at least three ideas that'll work," Gavin says, leaning back and stretching.

"You think?" I shuffle the papers in front of us.

"Yeah." He looks at the clock on the wall. It's nearly five-thirty. "I think we should call it a night," he adds, "and come back to this tomorrow morning. I only want to present one idea to Sean, so we need to decide which one's gonna fly the best, then work it up and get it ready to present to him at lunchtime."

"Okay." I lean down and pick up my purse, opening it and finding my car keys… and then remember that I don't have my car. "Damn," I mutter.

"What's wrong?" he asks, pulling his jacket on.

"Oh… it's nothing. I'm just gonna need to call a cab, that's all."

"Why? Don't you have a car here?"

"No… it decided not to start this morning."

"Oh. Well, I've got a rental car. I can give you a ride, if you like?"

I look up at him. "Really? It's not too far out of your way?"

"Well, I don't know where you live, but I can't imagine so. I'm staying at the Hilton in Falls Church."

"Well… that's handy. I live just outside Falls Church. About five minutes' drive from the Hilton, I guess."

"Then I can easily drop you home," he says, coming around the desk. "I'll even have a look at your car, if you want. Although I can't guarantee I can do anything."

"Neither can I." He opens the door and lets me pass through. "I think it might be beyond saving."

"Oh dear."

The ride home is uneventful. It's not even very busy on the roads, but then it rarely is at this time of year.

I give Gavin directions to my house and it doesn't take long before he pulls up outside, parking across the driveway.

"Do you want me to take a look at the offending vehicle?" he asks.

"It's up to you," I reply. "If you think you can get it working…"

"Like I said, I offer no guarantees, but I'll see what I can do." He switches off the engine and climbs out. I get out too, and follow him up the driveway. "Hell… this is old," he says, looking at my car.

"I prefer to call it a classic," I say to him. "Let me go and turn on the outside lights. You'll be able to see better.

"I think antique is a better word than classic," he calls after me. "Do you have your keys?"

I throw them over to him to him and he unlocks the car, climbing in and trying to start the engine. I go indoors and flick the switch that floods the front of the house with brilliant light. To my relief, as I come back outside, the car doesn't even turn over. As much as I'd love to have my car running again, I'd have felt such an idiot if it had started first time.

"Your battery's flat," he says.

"Yeah… I know." I'm not sure I want to confess that it's happened before. He'll think I'm a complete fool.

"I'll pop the hood and have a look," he offers, "but I don't think there's much I can do. You're gonna need a new battery."

"I thought as much."

He reaches under the dash and pulls the lever which opens the hood, then he climbs out and walks around the front of the car. The hood creaks as he lifts it. "I think that noise tells you everything you need to know." He smirks at me.

"That I might be better off with a new car, rather than a new battery?"

"Maybe…" He leans over and starts inspecting the engine compartment. He fiddles with a few things, tweaks some cables and connections, then gets back into the car and tries to start it again. This time, it makes a heaving sound, and then dies. He tries again, but there's nothing. "I think it's dead," he says. "We could dig a hole and bury it, if you like."

I laugh. "Would you like a coffee?" I offer. It seems the least I can do when he's tried to get my car going for me... and brought me home.

"I won't, thanks," he says, "but I could do with washing my hands. I got a little dirty under that hood."

"Sure. Come on in."

I lead the way indoors and show him to the bathroom. He comes back out in a couple of minutes.

"Thanks for the ride," I say to him as he goes back outside, with me following.

"It's no problem," he replies. We get to his car and he turns back to me. "I'll see you tomorrow," he says.

"Yeah."

"Do you want me to come by in the morning and pick you up?" he offers.

"No... I'll get a cab, it's fine. I might even hire a car until I can get a new one."

"Okay... if you're sure."

"I am, thanks." He opens the door to his car.

"I hope your wife's feeling better," I say, standing beside him.

"Thanks. The sickness tends to ease off in the evenings, so providing Becky's a little better, she should be okay." He pauses. "I just wanna get home to them, really."

"I know that feeling."

He looks at my house. "Um... This *is* your home."

"It doesn't feel like it anymore."

"Oh... I see. Home is where Will is... is that right?"

I nod my head. "And he's in Boston."

He puts his hand on my shoulder. "We'll pitch this idea to Sean," he says. "We'll make it work, and then we can both get back to where we want to be."

I smile up at him. "Sounds good to me," I say.

Chapter Twenty-Four

Will

The flight's on time and I land at just after five o'clock.

I hire a car at the airport, which takes a little longer than it should have done, plug her address into the SatNav and head out there, following the directions. While I'm driving, I think about how surprised she's gonna be to see me. I can't help getting hard when I think about all the things I want to do with her. I want to hold her in my arms... and I want to taste her, and make love to her, real slow. And I want to make her come... over and over. It's gonna be a very long night.

The street where she lives is smart, tidy. The houses are neat and well cared for. I'm not surprised. This is just the kind of place I imagined she'd live. I'm driving slowly down the road, checking the house numbers, when I notice a property a little way ahead that's lit up like Christmas. Someone's got some seriously powerful exterior lights... A guy appears at the doorway and turns, talking to someone who's still inside. He walks down the steps, and the other person follows... and I stop the car, pulling over to the side of the road. It's Jamie. Who the fuck is the guy that just came out of her house?

My heart is beating so loudly I can hear it in my ears. They walk slowly down the driveway and stop by a car that's parked at the bottom.

They talk, standing close together and then... he puts his hand on her shoulder, looking down into her eyes. What. The. Fuck. My instinct is to get out of the car and go over there and punch the guy... but that's not who I am... is it? I'm gripping the steering wheel so tight, my knuckles are white... and they hurt. I don't know, maybe that's exactly who I am...

She's with another guy? How is this even possible?

She's smiling at him now. I know that smile. It's the one that made me hard for the first time in years... the one that made me fall in love with her. I know the look that'll be in her eyes as well... I know how they sparkle.

I don't need to see anymore. I don't want to either. I turn the car around and drive away.

It's eight-thirty. I was supposed to be with Jamie now, maybe having dinner in her kitchen, or her dining room – I don't even know what her house looks like... but he does. Or maybe we'd have skipped dinner and gone straight to bed. Her bed... which again, I've never seen, although he probably has. He's probably had her in her bed this evening. He'll have done all the things I wanted to do... *He'll* have felt her, tasted her, made love to her. *He'll* have made her come, felt that body writhing beneath his.

He'll have done all that, because I'm not there. As far as she knows, I'm in Boston... except I'm not, I'm on the flight *back* to Boston, sitting next to a suited businessman, who seems to think I'm interested in his plans for the New Year... I couldn't care less. My New Year has just been blown away. Hell, my whole fucking life has just been blown away.

I get home at just after ten. The house is the emptiest it's ever been. There's literally nothing here for me. I sit in the living room, in the dark, staring out at the deck and the wall beyond.

I created this space, closed myself in so the world would leave me alone... I guess I got what I wanted... because I'm the loneliest I've ever been.

Jamie

Today turned out to be easier than I thought in the end – mainly because I didn't have to spend too much of it with Sean Donaldson – although I was more confident with him than I thought I would be… and that was all thanks to Will. Still, it was hard work. Gavin and I spent hours, running plans back and forth, coming up with loopholes and having to start again. Gavin's right though. I think we've got enough ideas together to present something good to Sean tomorrow. Assuming he's not a complete idiot and doesn't insist we stick with his dumb suggestion, we should be able to get started on feeding dummy information to Jack fairly quickly, and then watch him to see what happens. I can update Will on all of this later, and run our plans past him too. That might not be strictly ethical, being as he's been suspended, but he may have some advice or ideas he can add… and if that speeds things up and means I can spend more time with him, who cares about ethics?

Once Gavin left, I decided to go online and book a hire car. It's being delivered at seven-thirty tomorrow morning. It's not ideal, but I figure I can go out with Will at at the weekend and look for a new car – and in the meantime at least the hire car will be cheaper than using cabs every day.

I did find a frozen lasagna in my deep freeze, but I couldn't face it – well, it was never going to be as good as Will's – so I ordered in Thai and sat in front of the television, eating it. The movie wasn't great, so once I'd finished the take-out, I came in here to bed, and I've been reading ever since, waiting for Will to call.

As I finish the latest chapter and turn the page, I check the clock. It's nearly midnight. I know he said he'd be later tonight, but I didn't realize he meant this late… I'm getting kinda tired now and my eyelids keep closing, no matter how hard I try to keep them open.

I guess, even if he's still at the restaurant, I can call him. He can always take the call outside, or speak to me in front of his friends… He kissed me in front of them on Christmas Eve, so talking to me shouldn't be a problem.

I call up his details and wait for the call to connect. It rings four times and then his voicemail cuts in. I guess there's a lot of noise in the restaurant, maybe, and he can't hear the phone. I listen to the message… it's good to hear his voice, even if it is just recorded.

"Hi," I say quietly. "I guess you're still busy. It's late, and I've got an early start, because I've got a hire car being delivered at seven-thirty, so I'm gonna go to sleep now. We can catch up in the morning. Hope you've had a good evening. Say 'hi' to everyone for me. Goodnight… Love you." The end of my message sounds kinda empty, when there's no-one to say 'love you' back.

Well… it's another Chevy Spark. Still at least it's not green this time. It's silver, which is much more acceptable. As a car, it's fine… it was just the color of the one I had in Boston that was the problem. I sign all the paperwork and go back inside the house, checking the time on my watch. I take a gulp of coffee. I've got fifteen minutes before I have to leave for work. Will hasn't called, but I guess he's sleeping in after such a late night… Still, I want to talk to him and I'm sure he won't mind me waking him.

The phone rings twice before he picks up, although he doesn't say anything.

"Hello?" I say, hearing the uncertainty in my voice.

"Hi." Wow. He sounds so distant… something's definitely not right.

"What's wrong?" I ask him.

"Nothing," he replies.

"That's nonsense, Will. Something's obviously wrong… and I can't help if I don't know what it is." He doesn't reply and the silence hangs between us. "I called you last night," I say eventually.

"I know. I was here…" He was?

"Then why didn't you pick up?"

"Because I didn't want to talk."

"Will… what's wrong?" I ask again.

"Everything," he replies. Well, I guess that's different from 'nothing'.

"Can you elaborate on that?"

"At the moment... no, I don't think I can. I'm sorry, Jamie. I don't wanna talk right now."

I'm about to ask him why, when I realize he's already ended the call.

I stare at the phone... well, I don't, because I can't see it properly. Everything's a blur, because my eyes are overflowing with tears. Something's happened... something or someone has hurt him. I need to find out what.

I go to the bathroom and grab some tissue to wipe my eyes, then I sit on the couch and calmly type out a text message:

— Will, don't shut me out. Please tell me what's happened, so I can help you work this out. Call me anytime. I'm here for you. I love you. J xx

I can't wait for his reply. I've got to get to work. I throw my phone in my purse and head out the door, hoping he won't wait too long to call me.

Chapter Twenty-Five

Will

I read her text through again… and again.

Don't shut her out? She's the one who had another guy with her last night. She's the one who's cheating… not me. She thinks she can help? How can she? There's nothing she can do to help… except explain why.

I pick up my phone and type out a reply.

— It's not me doing the shutting out, Jamie. I flew to Virginia yesterday to surprise you. I drove by your house and saw you outside… with him. If you really want to help me… tell me why you're seeing someone behind my back. And when you've done that, please will you just leave me alone.

I read it through and press send, then head for the shower, feeling like shit… but then I haven't slept. I didn't even bother trying. I just lay on the couch all night, because my bed reminds me of Jamie… and I can't handle those memories right now.

When I come out, a towel wrapped around my hips, I sit on the edge of the bed, staring at my phone. Part of me wants to check, to see if she's replied. The other part keeps telling me I don't care… except I do… I do fucking care. And that's why this hurts so much.

I pick up the phone. There's no text message, but there's a voicemail. I call it up and listen.

"Will," she says, and I can hear her crying… What the hell has she got to cry about? "I've just parked the car and I'm going into work. Sorry it took me a while to get back to you, but I couldn't read your message while I was driving." She pauses. "I don't know what you thought you saw, but there's nothing going on. The man outside my house… his name's Gavin Jacobson." Like I care what his name is. "He's from the Chicago office," she says, and I feel an icy shiver run down my spine. "He gave me a ride home and checked over my car for me… and then he went into the house to get cleaned up. That's all. I promise you, Will… absolutely nothing happened between us. I'd never cheat on you." She sobs again. Oh God… what have I done to her? "Check Gavin out, if you don't believe me… I-I love *you* Will, and I'd never do anything to hurt you. Please, please… just call me." I hear another sob as the call ends.

I don't bother dressing, but go through to the office and start up my laptop. Gavin Jacobson, she said and she told me to check him out… so I'm going to.

Ten minutes later, I'm sitting in the living room, with my head in my hands. I've more than fucked up this time. I've accused her of seeing another guy, when he's just another agent, working on the case with her. On top of that, he's married. He's got a young daughter. Okay, I know that doesn't mean he wouldn't cheat, but Jamie… with a married man? No. She'd never do that. Never.

I've only got one option. I've got to call her, explain what I saw, how much it hurt, how it made me feel, and beg her to forgive me. And hope she'll understand. And I've got to do it now.

Jamie

I'm finding it really hard to focus… and I'm fairly certain Gavin has noticed.

He hasn't said anything, but he keeps staring at me. I've got to say, he's very patient, considering the number of times I've asked him to repeat himself.

We've decided on the information we're going to feed to Jack, and Gavin's typing out a report for Sean. I guess I should be doing this, but even Gavin's worked out I'll probably make too many mistakes for it to be legible.

"I'll take this along to Sean," Gavin says eventually, closing the lid on his laptop. "I don't think you need to sit in on the meeting… unless you want to?"

"Sorry… um. No, that's fine. I'll clear up here," I tell him. We've scattered papers over the floor as well as the desk today.

"Fine," he says, getting up and going to the door. He stops just before opening it, and turns around. "Tell me to butt out if you like, but is everything okay?" he asks.

"Yes… Everything's fine."

"Hmm. You're a really shitty liar." He opens the door and the tears start again. Will didn't think I'm such a shitty liar. He thinks I'm having an affair, so he must think I'm pretty good at it.

I delve into my purse for a Kleenex, but there aren't any, so I go along to the Ladies' room and grab some tissue from there, before returning to Gavin's office, just as my phone starts ringing.

I pull it from my purse and my breath catches in my throat. It's Will. I connect the call immediately.

"Hello?" I whisper.

"Jamie?" He says… and I know he's back. His voice is just like it should be and the relief is so great, I have to sit down, flopping into my chair.

"Yes," I say quietly.

"I'm so sorry," he says. "Can you forgive me for doubting you?"

"Yes…" I sob.

"Oh… please don't cry," he whispers, and I hear a crack in his voice. We need to be together, not hundreds of miles apart.

"Tell me," I mutter. "Tell me what happened?"

I hear him take a breath. "I was so lonely here by myself," he says. "I was just wandering around the house... feeling really lost without you. And then I realized it didn't need to be like that. I didn't need to be here. I could be with you. I knew you'd have to go to work, but I thought I could work on my figures for Todd during the day and... and we could be together in the evenings."

"I see."

"So, I called Luke, re-arranged the plans for last night, booked a flight, packed a bag and came for a visit... Except... when I was driving up to your house, I saw you coming out with another guy."

"Gavin."

"Yeah... but I didn't know he was another agent, did I?"

"Who did you think he was?" I already know the answer to that, but I want him to admit it.

"I'm sorry," he says. "I assumed you had someone else."

"What on earth would make you think that, Will?"

"You're beautiful, Jamie. I don't really know why you love me... especially when I treat you like this... and I guess I assumed another guy would find you just as beautiful as I do..."

"And that I'd just jump into bed with him?"

"Well... yeah."

"Thanks." That hurt a bit.

"I'm sorry," he says quickly.

"You keep saying that."

"Because I mean it."

"I know you do."

"I got it wrong, baby... So wrong."

"Yes. You did. I love you way too much to ever cheat on you... surely you know that?"

"Can you forgive me?" he asks. He sounds so desperate.

"Well, I'd rather forgive you to your face," I say, a smile forming on my lips. If he's free to come up here, then... well, why not?

There's a pause. "Can I come and see you?" he asks.

"Yes, please... the sooner the better."

I hear him laugh. God, that's better. "Okay," he says. "I'll book a flight for this evening."

"This must be costing you a fortune air fares."

"I don't care."

"What time will you get here?" I'm already excited at the thought of seeing him.

"Well, there's no point me arriving much before you finish work… so I'll catch the same flight as yesterday, which gets me to your place around six, or just after."

"Okay."

"And can I take you out for dinner?"

"No."

"Sorry? I thought… Jamie?" Oh dear… he sounds upset again.

"Wait," I say quickly. "I don't want to go out. We can cook, or we'll order in. But before we do either of those, I think you need to apologize to me properly… at home… in my bed."

"Oh… I see." He's smiling again now. I know he is. "I really am sorry."

"Shh." I say. "You can show me just how sorry you are later. I'm just glad you came to your senses, and called me…"

"Well, finding out the guy's married helped. It made me realize—"

I feel my tongue dry. "I'm… I'm sorry…" I interrupt him. "What did you say?"

"Gavin," Will explains. "He's married."

"Yes, I know he is… but what difference does that make?"

"It makes all the difference."

Is he serious? "It does?"

"Of course it does."

I can hardly speak. "W-Why?"

"Isn't it obvious?"

"Not to me."

"Well, him being married makes him off limits… doesn't it?"

All my excitement vanishes, along with the joy I'd been feeling that we were back on track again. We're not… we're so far off track, I think we might have completely lost our way. "He's off limits because he's married?" I say quietly.

"Yeah… of course he is. I know you'd never go with a married guy."

That's it. That's really it. "But you think I'd cheat with someone who's single… is that what you're saying?"

"I… I…"

"Don't bother, Will. I understand exactly what you're saying. You checked him out, didn't you?"

"Well, you told me to."

"Yeah… but I didn't think you actually would…"

"Then why suggest it?"

"To show you there was nothing going on… for crying out loud."

"I don't understand."

"Clearly."

"What's wrong?" he asks.

"Everything's wrong. You don't trust me at all, do you? You think if Gavin was single, I'd be in bed with him… and the only reason I'm not is because he's already taken… And that's the extent of your trust in me."

"That's not—"

"Yes it is, Will. That's exactly what you meant and don't you dare insult my intelligence by trying to deny it." I take a breath, trying to calm down. It doesn't work. "Can't you understand? If you can't trust me… if you can't believe in me, then what's the point in any of this? We really don't have any future at all…" My voice cracks on a sob and I end the call before he hears me break down.

Chapter Twenty-Six

Will

I've been sitting here for half an hour trying to work it out.

She *told* me to check him out. She gave me his name and the fact that he came from the Chicago office and she told me to check him out. And that's what I did… and yet, somehow that was the wrong thing to do… I don't get it.

My phone rings and I pick up.

"Jamie?"

"No… it's Todd."

"Oh."

"You okay?" he asks.

"Yeah… I'm fine."

"No, you're not."

"Really, I'm fine."

"Then why did you think I was Jamie."

"Because she's gone home."

"Yeah, I know. Luke told us last night. He also told us you were going to visit her. I assumed you'd be there… The fact that you thought I was her suggests you're not there, and you're still here…?"

"Yeah, I'm here."

"So, what happened."

"Nothing."

He pauses. "Okay… so you don't want to talk about it."

I don't reply.

"Look, I was just calling you to say something's come up and I'm not gonna be able to make our meeting on Monday. Can we reschedule for Tuesday at the same time?"

"Sure."

There's another pause. "Do you want me to come over?" he asks. "Or I can call Luke?"

"No, I'm fine," I tell him again, maybe a little too forcefully.

"Okay," he says quietly. "I'll see you Tuesday."

"Yeah."

I drop the phone on the couch. I'm still so confused. If she didn't want me to check the guy out, why did she tell me to? It doesn't make any sense... None of it makes sense...

I'm not dressed yet, the damp towel is still draped around my hips, so I get up and start walking toward the bedroom, when the phone rings again. I run back and grab it.

"Jamie?" I say again.

"No." It's Luke.

"Todd called you then?"

"Yeah. What's wrong?" he asks.

"Who says anything's wrong?"

"Todd... and me, now I've spoken to you."

"Really, I'm okay."

"Todd says you're still in Boston... so what happened?"

"Nothing happened."

"Will, stop bullshitting me."

"Jamie broke up with me," I tell him, in a voice that doesn't even sound like my own.

"I'm coming over," he says and hangs up.

I drop the phone on the couch again and go through to the bedroom and into the dressing room, grabbing some boxers, jeans and t-shirt.

Once I'm dressed, I go back into the lounge and sit down, staring out the window, but not seeing anything.

I don't understand what's happening... why would she tell me to do something, and then break up with me, because I did it? Where did I go wrong?

My mind's such a muddle, I'm only aware that Luke's arrived when he's standing in front of me, having let himself in.

"Hey," he says and I look up at him.

"Oh... Hi."

He comes and sits down beside me. "Tell me what happened," he says quietly.

"I don't really know," I reply, staring at the bookcase now, as a distraction.

"Well... you were going to visit her, so start there."

I take a deep breath. "I hired a car at the airport," I begin. "And I drove out to her house."

"Okay."

"And when I got there, she was with another guy."

"Sorry? What do you mean 'with another guy'?"

"They were standing on her driveway, talking and he touched her."

"How?" he asks. "Where did he touch her."

"On the shoulder. It was kinda intimate, I guess."

"Was it?" I can feel his eyes on me, even though I'm not facing him.

"It looked that way to me, yeah."

"Okay," he says gently. "So then what happened?"

"I drove away and came straight home."

"You didn't talk to her?" he asks.

"No, not then."

"But you talked to her later?"

"I was supposed to call her last night, but I didn't. So she called me and left a message."

"You didn't pick up the call?"

"No. I didn't want to talk to her last night."

"Okay..."

"And then this morning, she called me again."

"And?"

"And I was... a little abrupt with her, I guess."

"Will..." He sounds disappointed. "What did you say?"

I turn and look at him. "I just told her I didn't wanna talk to her." He's staring at me. "Well... I didn't."

"Okay... So then what happened?" he asks.

"Well, she sent me a text, asking what was wrong, asking how she could help."

"Did you reply?"

I nod my head.

"Can I see?" he asks. I guess it'll be quicker than explaining. I unlock my phone and hand it to him. He sits forward and opens my message app and reads, scrolling back and forth between the two messages.

"Nobody broke up with anybody here, Will," he says.

"No, I know... that came later."

"Oh." He keeps hold of my phone, twisting it in his hands. "What happened?"

"She called me. I was in the shower, but she left a message, explaining who the guy was... that he's working with her on the case, that he'd given her a ride home because her car broke down... and she told me to check out his file, if I didn't believe her."

"Right... but I don't understand how you've broken up."

"Neither do I..."

He takes a deep breath. "Did you call her back? he asks.

"Yeah... After I'd checked the guy out."

"Oh, Will..." He runs his fingers through his hair. "You didn't."

"Of course I did. She told me to." Am I the only one who doesn't get this?

"She... she told you to..." he echoes, his voice barely audible. He stares at me.

"What?" I say.

"When a woman says something like that to you, they're basically telling you to believe them... or else. They're not telling you to actually check the guy out." He pauses. "It's about trust, Will. She was telling you the information was available... not that you should actually go and look at it."

"Seriously?"

"Yeah... seriously. Think about what you just said."

"Which bit?"

"You said Jamie told you to check his file, if you didn't believe her… You checked his file, which means you didn't believe her."

"No…"

"Yes." He's nodding his head. "So, I'm guessing you told her you'd looked at his file?"

"Yeah… and that I was okay with it, because he's married."

"For fuck's sake, Will." He drops back onto the couch, staring up at the ceiling.

"What now?" I get up and turn around, staring down at him. "That's the bit that got Jamie really riled too… only I don't get it."

"You don't?"

"No. I know she'd never go with a married guy."

"Please, please tell me you didn't say that to her."

"Yeah… I did," I whisper. "Why?"

He sits forward again, looking up at me. "Because that will be the reason she broke up with you."

"I don't understand…"

"What you were telling her was that you don't trust her at all. You trusted him, because he's married, but you don't trust her."

"But that's not what I meant…" My voice fades.

"Really?" he asks, raising an eyebrow.

"Well, I guess I felt safer, knowing he's married."

He lets out a long breath. "Let me ask you something," he says. "If Jamie was alone with Todd, would you trust them that nothing would happen? He's not married, so how would you feel about that?"

"I'd be fine with it. Todd would never try anything with Jamie…"

He stares at me, long and hard. "And that's your problem," he says. "That's not how it works. You're putting all the emphasis on the guy not to try anything with Jamie. You trust Todd, so even though he's single, he's okay… other than that, you're okay with married guys… and then it all gets a bit muddy. Has it occurred to you that Jamie wouldn't cheat anyway, no matter who the guy was… because she loves you and no-one else. So, to her, it doesn't matter whether she's working with a married guy or not?"

I look at him. I remember Jamie saying something like that… "I've fucked up, haven't I?"

He nods his head. "Yeah…"

I slump down onto the couch again. "It kinda makes sense now," I say.

"What does?"

"Her breaking up with me."

"Do you blame her?" he asks.

"No. I deserved it."

He leans over. "You deserved to be yelled at," he says. "I don't know that you deserved for her to end it with you… Are you absolutely sure she did?"

"Er… yeah."

"Tell me what she said."

"She… she said, if I couldn't trust her, and believe in her, then there was no point… we don't have a future." I turn to face him. "She was really upset."

"Well, that's not surprising." He leans into me. "You hurt her. But sometimes, when you love someone, you end up doing that, even when you don't mean to."

"I didn't mean to. I hate the idea of hurting her."

"I get that." He says. "Look, I'll make us some coffee," he says and gets up, wandering off into the kitchen.

He comes back a couple of minutes later with two cups, and my phone, still in his hand. "Sorry," he says, "I took that with me by mistake."

"S'okay." I take it from him and put it down on the table.

"Are you still gonna go and visit her for New Year?" he asks, sitting down next to me again.

"I was gonna go up there today… this evening, but I really don't think that's a good idea."

"No, neither do I. I think it's best to give Jamie some time… Doesn't mean you can't go for New Year though."

I'm not so sure. "Why would I? I mean, what's the point? We're through…"

"You don't wanna see if there's a way back?"

"I don't think there is."

"You told me not to give up over Megan… so I'm telling you the same… At least think about it. Give her a few days to cool down…"

"If only it was that easy."

"No-one said love was easy." He smiles at me… I can't smile back.

Jamie

I'm still too upset to even think straight, which meant I wasn't much use yesterday after I'd spoken to Will. He obviously didn't fly down… which may have been a good thing, because the way I felt last night, I think I'd just have yelled at him. But having all of this going on, unresolved in my head, also meant I got very little sleep, so today I'm being even less help.

He doesn't trust me at all, it would seem. Evidently, it's only okay that Gavin was in my house with me, because Gavin's married. He's safe for me to be around, because a wedding band gives him protection from me… Okay, maybe that's going a bit far, but that's how it feels… and the more I think about it, the more I go from being upset to being downright mad.

Now I've had a little time to go over things, I realize that what we need right now is to talk it through… well, I need some sleep, and then we need to talk it through. We need to get his trust issues out in the open once and for all. I need to explain to Will how his words made me feel, and he needs to tell me why he reacted like that… and, once we've done that, we can hopefully put this behind us and move on. Because I may be mad with him… I maybe even still want to yell at him a little… but I still love so much, and I want him more than anything… Except he's in Boston and I'm here… and I guess I'm not going to be seeing him now until New Year's Eve, which is the day after tomorrow… and that feels like a lifetime away at the moment. I don't want to do any of this over the phone, or by text... I want him to explain how he feels to my face, so I can see his eyes and know what he's really thinking. And then I want him to hold me in his arms... and you can't do any of that over the damn phone.

Sean went with our plan... his decision swayed, evidently, by the fact that there's significantly less cost involved in what we've got in mind, than there is in setting up an entire fake op.

Now we've just got to create the illusion...

"I could do with Will working on this," Gavin says, completely out of the blue, holding his head in his hands and staring at his computer screen. "This really isn't my strength, and I'm not sure I'm making any of this completely untraceable."

"No?" I can't think what else to say.

"No." He glances up at me. "Do you think Sean could be persuaded to re-instate him?" he asks.

"I doubt it," I mumble, not looking up from my screen, where I'm creating false e-mail accounts.

"Do you think Will would come back if he did?" Gavin continues. "Speaking to Sean, it doesn't seem like they parted on very good terms."

"They didn't."

"So me going to Sean and trying to persuade him to let Will come and help us... that probably wouldn't work?"

"Probably not."

He stops typing. "Jamie?" he says. "You're being real quiet... Are you okay?"

Shit... I can feel tears pricking behind my eyes. I can't cry here... not in front of him. "Sorry," I get up and leave the room, walking quickly to the Ladies room, where I go into the first stall, sit on the closed toilet seat and sob into a handful of tissues for a good ten minutes.

Luckily no-one comes in to hear my outburst and, after a while, I calm down and leave the stall, going to the basin and looking at my reflection in the mirror above it. God, I look a mess. A lack of sleep has left me with dark circles beneath my eyes, which aren't helped by the blotchy tear-stained cheeks below, or the swollen red eyelids. There's no way of disguising this… except maybe for wearing a bag over my head, which is a little impractical.

I splash some water over my face, but that doesn't help in the slightest and, drying off on a paper towel, I shrug my shoulders and go back along the corridor to Gavin's office.

He looks up as I enter, but says nothing, his fingers tapping on the keyboard of his laptop.

After a good half-hour of silence, he gets up and comes around my side of the desk.

"Coffee?" he asks.

I nod.

"You okay?"

I shake my head.

"Wanna talk?"

I shake again.

"Okay."

He leaves the room, returning a few minutes later with two cups of coffee and a plate, on which is a double chocolate muffin, with frosting, which he puts down in front of me, alongside the coffee.

He sits opposite me and I look at him over the top of our computer screens. "It's chocolate," he says, shrugging his shoulders. "It usually works for Laura." And he goes back to his typing.

We managed to muddle through the rest of the day without mentioning our personal lives and I'm more than relieved to get home. All I want tonight is a hot bath to soothe my leg, a glass of wine and a book. And Will… I want Will. I can't phone him though. Whatever we've got to say to each other is going to have to wait until Saturday morning, when he gets here. If he calls in the meantime, I'll speak to him. Of course I will; I'm not going to be petty… I love him.

I'm not hungry at the moment, so I go through to the bathroom, and start running a bath. My water runs quite slowly – it always has, so I go back out into the kitchen and pour myself a glass of red wine from the bottle I opened yesterday.

I'm just going back through into the living room, when the front doorbell rings. Although it's not late, it's dark outside and that always makes me wary when I'm here on my own. I go up to the front door, standing a couple of feet away and call out, "Who's there?"

"It's me," says a vaguely familiar voice on the other side.

"Who's me?"

"Sorry," the voice replies. "It's Luke."

I step forward and unlatch the door, pulling it open.

He's standing on the top step, wearing a dark gray suit, a white button-down shirt with no tie, and the top two buttons undone. He looks tired.

"Hi," I say.

"Hello." He looks at me. "Can I come in?"

"Sure. Sorry." I stand back and make way for him to enter.

He comes past me and into the living room, looking around.

"Nice place," he says.

"Thanks." I close the door. "I was just… shit!" I thrust my wine glass into his hand.

"Jamie?" he says. I start running through the house toward the bathroom.

"Bath!" I cry out, skidding to a halt and frantically turning off the taps. The water's just starting to overflow onto the floor.

"Let some of the water out," Luke's voice says from behind me.

I do as he suggests, then stand and turn. He's holding out his hand.

"There's water on the floor," he says. "Take my hand, in case you slip."

I put my hand in his and he helps me back out of the room.

"Do you have towels?" he asks.

"Yes." I go into my bedroom, and return with an armful of towels.

"Here, you take this." He gives me the wine and takes the towels, going into the bathroom and spreading them out on the wet floor. "There," he says, coming back out again. "That should soak up the worst." We go back into the living room.

"Thanks," I say to him. "I'm sorry about that."

"That's okay."

"I was running a bath."

"Yeah... I got that."

"Would you like a glass of wine?" I ask him.

"I think I'd kill for one," he says, smiling.

"Well, you keep this one," I reply, giving him mine again. "I haven't touched it yet... and I'll get another one for myself."

He takes a sip as I go back into the kitchen, returning a couple of minutes later.

We stand for a moment, staring at each other.

"I imagine you're wondering why I flew down here?" he asks.

"The thought had crossed my mind."

"It's about Will."

"That thought had crossed my mind too." He smiles. "Shall we sit?" I suggest, nodding in the direction of my cream colored couch over by the window.

"Sure," he replies and we go over, sitting down at opposite ends.

Another awkward silence descends.

"I guess I need to start this conversation," he says quietly.

"Well, being as I don't really know why you're here... it might be best."

He looks across at me. "You don't know why I'm here?" he repeats.

"Not really." I shrug.

"So, you don't recall having a fight with Will?"

"Yeah... of course I do. But I'm not sure why you're here."

"Call me an ambassador," he says.

"A what?"

"An ambassador... a representative."

I must look as confused as I feel.

"Coming to test the waters?" he adds. "Although judging from your bathroom, that may not be the best way of putting that." He smiles.

"I don't understand... I'm sorry, Luke. I'm tired and I really don't have clue what you're talking about."

He leans forward and puts his wine glass down on the coffee table, letting out a long sigh.

"You guys had a fight, yeah?" he says.

"Yes... He saw me with Gavin, from work, and assumed I was having an affair with him."

"I know. And then you told him who the guy was, and that he could check him out, if he wanted to."

"And he did!"

"Yeah... he didn't understand that you didn't mean that as an actual invitation."

"Oh."

"That's Will, you see," he explains. "He can sometimes take things a bit too literally."

"But why does he need you to come and test the waters? I don't really understand what you mean by that."

"I'm here to see if you'd be prepared to take him back."

What? "Um... I wasn't aware I'd let him go."

"You mean you didn't break up with him?" He seems incredulous.

"Well, I wasn't aware I had, no. I told him he needed to learn to trust me, or we don't have a future together. But I didn't mean we were through, Luke."

He leans back on the couch, looking up at the ceiling. "I feel like I've been looking at ceilings a lot the last couple of days," he says, then leans forward and turns to look at me. "He thinks you broke up with him," he says.

"He does?"

"Yeah." He sighs.

"Oh, no." I sit up straight. "That's not what I meant at all. I wanted him to think about what he was saying... I wanted him to realize how hurtful he was being."

"He does now... The thing is, when you said you had no future, he thought you meant you were through."

"But I didn't."

"Like I say, Will takes things literally."

"I just want to sit down and talk it through with him... but how can I do that if he's going to react like this to everything I say?"

"He's never had anything like this before... It's all completely new to him. He'll get used to it..."

"And in the meantime? What do I do?"

He stares at me. "If you wanna be with him…"

"I do… I do want to be with him… I just need to know how…" I interrupt, and he smiles – a big broad smile.

"You'll have to try and be patient with him. 'Cause I guarantee you, he's gonna screw up. Hell, I'm still screwing up all the time, and I've got a whole lifetime's more experience than Will. He's different, Jamie."

"I—I know."

"Do you?"

"He's sensitive," I say quietly. "More sensitive than most guys, I guess."

"Oh, it's way more than that." He takes a gulp of wine and puts the glass back down on the table again. "You might consider yourself damaged on the outside, but he's damaged on the inside. Sometimes those kinds of wounds never heal. I can spend time with you and help you to understand him, and what happened to him, but if you're serious about making this work, a lot of it'll be down to you. You'll have to be tolerant of his difficulties and especially of how he blames himself so easily for everything, because that's one of his most self-destructive traits. Think about any time things have gone wrong. He'll always be the one saying sorry, and taking responsibility. Sometimes it might be his fault, like now – this situation over Gavin – but a lot of the time, it isn't and he'll still take the blame and feel guilty. He may never tell you this, so I'm going to… The reason for that is because my dad literally beat it into him that everything was his fault. And I mean *everything*. There are times when it's like he's still the twelve year old kid, who just lost his mom, and lost his way at the same time. He doesn't always know what to make of life. Other times, his abilities and calmness astound me. I'm sorry… I'm making him sound like hard work, and he isn't. He's my brother, and I love him. He's troubled by his past, and there are some elements of what happened to him that will probably always haunt him, but I know you were making things better for him, more so than I ever could. Will is an amazing guy to have in your life, Jamie… he's worth taking the time over, and the good stuff far outweighs the bad. Every. Damn. Time. I'll always be there to help you… both of you. And if there's anything you can't handle, or if he falls apart on you, you just have to call…"

I stare at him, tears forming in my eyes.

"He's lucky to have you," I whisper.

"Spend a little more time with him, Jamie," he replies. "You'll find out real fast it's the other way around."

Chapter Twenty-Seven

Will

After Luke left yesterday, I spent the rest of the day moping around doing absolutely nothing. That's real unusual for me. In fact, I can't recall the last time I did nothing for an entire day.

Today is Friday... which means tomorrow is New Year's Eve...

And I think I've decided I'm still gonna go and visit Jamie. I know she broke up with me. I know she probably won't want to see me and I know I probably should have called her before now to apologize for what I said and did... but I need to see her face-to-face and tell her how sorry I am... show her how sorry I am, and ask her to forgive me and beg her to let me back into her life. Because I'm lost without her.

I'm back to trying to keep busy, killing time before tomorrow... so I've decided to change the bedding in the guest room. As I come into the room, Jamie's scent in here has faded now, which I hope isn't an omen of things to come...

I'd forgotten about the dress though... and seeing it hanging there reminds me of how she looked that night. Was that really less than a week ago? I guess so... Before the party, there was her anticipation, her delight in the things I'd bought for her, and the knowledge, that hit me there and then, that I was in love with her. After the party... that was when I got to see her naked, to touch her and taste her for the first time... To demonstrate my love for her, in actions, if not in words... The words came later.

I go over to the bed and pull back the comforter, and there, up by the pillows, is a packet. It's the one that was delivered on the morning she left. What's it doing here, hidden beneath the covers? I pick it up. There's a card attached and I turn it over. It's addressed to me and I read it. It says:

'*Will,*

Time passes,

Memories fade,

Love endures.

Your Jamie x'

This is for me? I'm confused. What is this and why didn't she tell me it was here? The card… the words, they're beautiful, like her. I prize open the box and turn to sit down on the edge of the bed, but I stumble and end up on the floor. I can't breathe. I can't blink, because if I do, the tears that are welling in my eyes are going to cascade down my cheeks.

It's my watch. It's the watch my mom gave me when I was twelve, just a few weeks before she died… before she killed herself. I can still remember the look on her face, her smile, the happiness in her eyes, when I opened this that Christmas morning and threw my arms around her neck.

Tucked underneath it, is a piece of paper. I pull it out and unfold it.

'*Dear Will,*' it reads, in Jamie's handwriting, '*I took this to get it repaired for you as a Christmas present. The man in the repair shop said he couldn't get it to work again, but he could make it look the same; so I bought you the Apple Watch as a replacement. I know this isn't ideal, because it won't tell the time, but nothing's perfect, is it? Besides, I hope just being able to look at it will remind you of the good times you had with your mom, just like being able to hold you reminds me of how much I've gained by being with you, how much your love means to me and how much I will always, always love you. Jamie xx*'

I make the mistake of blinking, as the words blur, and the tears overflow. I wipe them away with the back of my hand and study the note again. She's too good for me… far too good. How can I go to her? How can I ask her to take me back? I'm never gonna be worthy of a woman who can do something like this. Never.

My phone rings late in the afternoon. I didn't change the bedding in the end… I didn't do anything… all day… again.

I pick up the call. It's Luke.

"Hi," he says. "How are you?"

"Okay."

"Bullshit."

"Yeah."

"You doing anything tonight?" he asks.

"Um… No."

"Wanna come over here?"

"Thanks… but no."

"You sure?"

"Yeah. I'm not very good company."

"Okay." I'm surprised he didn't try harder to persuade me to go out, but I guess he can tell it's not going to work, no matter how hard he tries. I don't tell him about my plan to go visit Jamie tomorrow… after opening her present, I'm not sure I'll go anymore. I still can't decide…

"Don't mope," he says, interrupting my thoughts. "It'll work out. I promise."

"I wish."

"I promise," he repeats.

He's never made me a promise he hasn't kept… but there's a first time for everything.

I've been sitting in the living room for the last two hours, just thinking. It's a dangerous thing to do… because all I think about is Jamie and how much I miss her. It's not just her physical presence I miss. I do miss holding her and kissing her and being inside her, but I also miss just knowing she's around, knowing I can go to her talk to her and she'll understand me, because she does understand me, almost as well as Luke does. I miss the smell of her, too, especially now it's fading from the house. I miss the noises she makes in her sleep... and when we're making love...

It's weird, but even though I think about her all the time, I haven't been hard – not once – since she left. It's like that part of me has died again.

I keep going over where I went wrong. It's easy... I judged too fast, thought too slow and acted like the twelve year old I sometimes can be. The boy who lost his mom and has been lost ever since. Not that that's any excuse for the way I treated Jamie. She deserves better – better than me anyway. I guess at least she knows that now.

I check my watch. It's nine-thirty-five. I rest my hand over the top of the watch face. She gave this to me. It was a great present, but perhaps not as great as getting my mom's watch repaired. That's in its box on my nightstand, with the note from Jamie tucked inside. I've read it over a couple of times... okay, more than a couple... just to remind myself what a complete idiot I am to have thrown away something so good...

I glance across at the refrigerator. I didn't bother eating tonight, but I know there's a bottle of white wine in there... and I'm tempted to open it. I've thought about it on and off since Jamie left. I'm not a big drinker, but I think I'd like to get drunk... really drunk... maybe that'd help me forget her... just for a few hours.

I get up and go into the kitchen, and I'm just reaching into the cabinet for a wine glass when I hear the key turning in the front door. That can only be Luke. I close the cabinet again and go into the hall, and stop in my tracks, my heart stopping with me.

It is Luke... and standing beside him is Jamie. He's carrying a small holdall, which he puts down on the floor just inside the door. Jamie's looking at me, kinda wary, uncertain. What's going on?

Luke looks from one of us to the other and then his gaze rests on me.

"Invite the lady in, Will," he says.

"S-sorry," I stutter, and stand back, letting Jamie into the living room. I follow her. "Take a seat," I offer and she does, sitting on the couch that faces toward the window. "Can I get you a drink?" I ask.

"A glass of wine would be lovely," she says... my nerves sparkle at the sound of her voice.

"I'll get it," Luke offers and goes into the kitchen.

I sit down at the other end of the sofa from Jamie and Luke returns a minute or so later with two glasses of wine, which he puts in front of us. He stands to one side.

"I'm not gonna hang around," he says. "You guys need to talk and, apart from anything else, I've got a pregnant wife at home, who's starting to forget what I look like." I don't understand what he's talking about. He starts walking toward the door and I get up and follow him.

"What's going on?" I ask him.

"Jamie will explain," he says. We've reached the door and he turns to face me.

"I don't understand," I say to him. "You called me earlier and invited me to your place…"

"Yeah… well that was a bit devious, I'll admit." He looks down at the floor just for a moment, then back up at me. "I never expected you to agree to coming over, I just needed to be sure you'd be here. I'd arranged to pick Jamie up from the airport and bring her over. It wouldn't have gone too well if you'd been out."

"Where would I have been, apart from here?" I ask him.

"I don't know… you might have decided to go and see Todd, or something."

I nod my head. It's unlikely, but I guess…

"And why is Megan starting to forget what you look like?" I ask him as he opens the door.

"Because I wasn't home last night either." He checks his watch. "I need to go," he says. "And you guys need to talk."

"Where were you last night?"

"Virginia." My mouth opens. "Jamie will explain everything," he says. He goes out, then stops and turns back. I've moved away from the door already. "Call me if you need me," he says and when I look up at him, I realize he's not talking to me. He's staring at Jamie. Before I can ask him what he means, he's gone.

I turn back to her, going over and sitting down on the couch beside her again.

"What was that about?" I ask.

She leans forward, picks up her wine glass and takes a long sip, then puts it down again. "Your brother came to see me," she explains.

"I kinda gathered that, but I… I don't understand."

"He came to test the waters… on your behalf."

"But… I didn't even know he was coming to see you."

"I know you didn't," she says. I can't help staring at her. It's so good to see her sitting here. She looks exactly the same as she always did, in jeans, a t-shirt and a cardigan, with her hair loose around her shoulders.

"Why was he testing the waters?"

"Because he… well, he told me you thought we'd broken up… and he wanted to know how I'd feel about taking you back."

"And… and what did you tell him?" I can feel the sweat forming on my hands and I look away. I'm almost too scared to hear her answer and a part of me wants to tell her not to reply… just in case.

"I told him the truth," she says.

"Which is?"

She waits… and waits, until the silence stretches out for so long, I feel I have to look up at her. She's smiling. She's actually smiling… and, once again, I'm hard. Jamie smiles, and I'm hard. I guess some things never change. "I didn't break up with you, Will," she says. My stomach does a kind of somersault that flips up into my chest. "That wasn't what I meant when I said those words."

"It wasn't?" I ask her.

She moves along the couch, just a little. "No," she says, shaking her head.

"Then what did you mean?"

"I meant you needed to work out how to trust me, and we needed talk that through… so we *could* have a future, because that's what I want with you."

"Then why didn't you say that?"

"I did. I was just trying to get you to see that without trust, there is no future…"

Which is kinda what she said, I guess… I'm confused. "But…"

"But that doesn't mean we can't move forward, Will. It just means we need to talk, and you need to learn to trust me… to believe in me, and know that I'll never hurt you. Because I won't."

"But, I thought…"

"I know you did. Well, I didn't, but I knew it after Luke explained how you'd reacted. I'm sorry. I should have thought more carefully what I was saying; made myself clearer… I didn't mean to hurt you… or confuse you."

"Why are you saying sorry to me? I'm the one who got it all wrong…"

"No, you didn't, Will. It was just a misunderstanding…"

"So… we're not over?" I whisper, the meaning of her words finally sinking in.

"Not unless you want us to be, no."

"No," I say quickly. "That's not what I want… that's the last thing I want." I move along the couch so we're right next to each other. "The last couple of days have been hell, Jamie."

"Then why didn't you call me? I'd have picked up… you know I would."

"Because I thought you were mad at me… because I thought we were through."

She nods her head. "So, this is kinda like when you fought with Luke," she says, thinking. "You didn't want to call him, because you thought he'd be mad at you…"

"I guess, yeah."

"Okay." She reaches over and takes my hands in hers. How can I have forgotten how good her skin feels in just a couple of days? "When people fight, sometimes they say things they don't mean… and sometimes they say things that hurt the people they love the most. But that doesn't mean they don't still love them. It doesn't mean they don't wanna be with them anymore… It just means they've had a fight."

"I know… but sometimes I can be… well, unforgivably rude."

"Only in your eyes, Will."

I stare at her. It's so good to just look at her… but I really want to hold her.

"Can we put this behind us?" she murmurs. "Because I've missed you so much… and I don't wanna keep missing you. I want you back."

"You do?"

She leans into me. "Of course I do. I love you." She rests her head on my shoulder.

287

"I love you too," I say, and I turn and sit her on my lap, moving back on the couch and pulling her with me. I hold the back of her head and kiss her, real deep, my tongue delving into her mouth, finding hers, entwined together. It feels like it's the first time all over again and when I look down into her eyes, I know she feels the same. I feel her hands running up my arms, around my neck and into my hair, knotting there. God, she feels good. She squirms on my lap and I run a hand down her back. She moans into my mouth and leans forward, pressing her breasts into my chest.

I pull back, just a little. "Please... stop, for a second," I mutter, breathing heavily.

"What's wrong?" she asks.

"I can't do this."

"Oh..." She looks disappointed.

I smile at her. "You're gonna make me come," I tell her. "It's been a few days... and I want you... a lot."

"I want you too."

"Then can we move this to the bedroom?" I ask her.

"I thought you'd never ask."

I sit forward, then stand, with her in my arms.

"Careful, Will," she says.

"Why?" I ask, starting toward the bedroom.

"You'll hurt yourself, lifting me like that. Put me down..."

I stop on the steps up to the kitchen. "Hell, no. I'm not putting you down until I get you into the bedroom... and stop implying you're heavy. You're not." She smiles and rests her head on my chest – where it belongs.

We carry on down the hallway and reach my bedroom door, which I open and carry her inside, putting her down in the middle of the floor. I don't bother with the lights; there's enough moonlight shining through the windows for me to see her... and she's beautiful.

"I'm so glad you're back," I say, pulling her cardigan from her shoulders and letting it fall to the floor.

"Me too," she says. "I've missed you so much." She runs her hands up my arms and I undo the button on her jeans and pull down the zipper.

"I've missed you too, baby." I smile at her, then lean down and kiss her gently. When I pull back, she's breathless, wanting more. I kneel down and undo her shoes and lower her jeans and panties to the floor, my breath catching in my throat as I see her again.

"God, you look good." I lean forward just a little and kiss her intimately, sliding my tongue down her slick folds. "You taste good too," I murmur. I hold her hand while she steps out of her shoes and clothes. Then I stand again and pull her t-shirt over her head and cup her breasts, rubbing my thumbs over her hard, taut nipples through the thin white lace, before reaching around behind her and undoing her bra, releasing her into my grasp. She lets her head fall back as I take first one and then the other nipple into my mouth, gently biting them between my teeth.

I stand up fully again and, holding her face in my hands, I kiss her, walking her backwards until we reach the bed, where I lower her gently and stand above her, staring down.

"You're incredible," I say, and I yank off my t-shirt, then pull off my jeans and boxers, my erection standing proud as I lay down beside her. "This is the first time I've been hard since our phone call," I tell her.

"Seriously?" She looks shocked.

"Yes." I nod my head. "When you were staying here, I just had to think about you and I'd get an erection. It was almost embarrassing how often it'd happen. After I thought you broke up with me, it didn't matter what went on in my head, or how much I thought of you, it was like the connection was lost. Losing you was like losing a part of myself and I couldn't get it back again."

She reaches up and touches my face gently with her fingertips. "We can never lose that connection, Will," she says. "Not really."

"Not if we're together. I know that now." I want her to stay... I want her here with me forever. I move my hand down her body feeling her soft skin, until I'm between her legs, parting her, feeling her wetness. She spreads her legs further, welcoming my touch. I start to circle around her clitoris, slowly, gently, teasing her. "Don't leave again," I whisper.

"I... I have to go back to work," she murmurs softly, trying to catch her breath as I increase the pressure just a little.

"Do you?" I ask.

"You know I do."

"But do you?" I mean... does she?

She's silent for a moment. "I don't know." She pauses again. Then her back arches off the bed as I insert a finger gently inside her. "Oh God," she breathes. "I can't think straight when you're doing that to me."

I smile, although she can't see me through her closed eyes. "I'll just keep on doing it then, and you'll have to stay." I increase the pressure a little more. I can tell she's close. "Stay with me," I urge.

"What about... what about... Oh God... I can't think... What about catching Jack... And there's my house," she says, seemingly trying to concentrate on our conversation.

"Sell it. Rent it out..."

"But... what about Scott..." What about him? She said he was at college... "Oh, please, Will..." I slow the pace and bring her back from the brink. "Scott sometimes stays there with me during vacations," she explains, more coherently.

"Then speak to him. See what he wants to do. He can always come here instead." I pick up the pace again, and the pressure, circling faster and harder.

"Oh, yes... yes." I know she's not saying yes to staying... she's about to... And even as I think it, she explodes, arching her back and pushing up into me, forcing my finger deeper inside her, riding the waves of pleasure. I wait until she's calmed, until her eyes are starting to open again and I know she'll hear what I'm saying.

"I love you, baby," I whisper gently. "I'll do whatever it takes. Just please, don't ever leave again. Stay with me... we'll find a way to make it work."

Jamie

If only it was that easy. "I'd give anything to be able to stay," I tell him, as my breathing returns to normal.

"Then stay."

I turn toward him so we're facing each other, our legs entwined, his hard erection pressing into my hip and his arms tight around me. I know he thinks it'd be easy to just leave my job, but he was the one who convinced me to go back, because they'd fire me if I didn't. Besides, we're actually getting somewhere with our efforts to catch Jack... or we would be if either Gavin or I had Will's abilities.

"It's not that simple," I murmur.

"Why?" He raises himself up on one elbow.

"Normally, I wouldn't have a problem. You know I didn't really want to go back, and I'd resign in a heartbeat to be with you... but Gavin persuaded Sean to ditch his dumb plan to trap Jack... and we've been working on something a lot simpler..."

"But...? I can hear a but." He's smiling at me.

"But we're not very good at certain elements of it, and Sean won't let us bring anyone in from outside... We need someone like you, working with us... someone with your technical capabilities, but he won't sanction it. He says the plan's simple enough for us to be able to handle it. It's like he's agreed to our idea, but he's making it almost impossible for us to carry it out..."

He looks down at me. "Tell me what is it you can't handle?" he asks.

"Essentially, it's making the information we're going to feed Jack completely untraceable... We're not absolutely sure it is."

He nods and shrugs at the same time. "Okay."

"Gavin wanted to ask Sean to reinstate you."

"He won't do that. He'd never admit to being wrong. That's probably why he won't sanction bringing in someone to help you... it's not his plan... if it was, he'd throw everything he had at it. Sean's petty like that."

"Great. So…" I'm not sure I should be asking him this. Gavin only put it forward as a suggestion… "Earlier on, before he left for Chicago for the weekend, Gavin came up with the idea that you could do some unofficial work… for him, not Sean, to help us out. I know it's not practical and it's highly irregular…"

"It is… but there are more important things than being practical and playing by the rules, Jamie."

I look up at him. "If you did this and Sean found out…"

"He wouldn't find out. Let's face it, he only found out we'd been to Jack's house because we told him." He leans down and kisses me gently. "I guess this means you're going back then?"

"I have to, Will… at least for now. At least until we've caught Jack."

"When… When will you go?"

"Sunday night. I have to be in the office on Monday."

"Okay. Then I'm coming with you."

"But… don't you have a meeting with Todd?" I ask him.

"He's moved it to Tuesday. I can reschedule it for the weekend… and I can stay with you for the week… if you'll let me, and we can come back here on Friday night to meet with Todd… And, in the meantime, I can help with the case against Jack."

"How? I mean, won't you need to be here, in your office, to do that?" I think about all his equipment… There's no way he can move all of that into my house.

"No," he replies. "Assuming I've understood what you're trying to do – which I'm guessing is just to feed him dummy information and see what he does with it – I'll just need my laptop… my personal one. You can do the rest, if I tell you how."

"And you'd be okay about working unofficially… with Gavin?"

He nods his head. "I'll make you a deal," he says.

"Okay."

"I'll come back with you… I'll help out, assuming Gavin really wants me to, and we'll stay at your place until Jack's been caught… And then we'll both resign and you'll come back here… and live with me."

Live with him? Did he just ask me to live with him? I guess he did. I can't help but smile at the simplicity of how he did that, like he was asking me what I wanted for dinner, not to completely change our relationship. "What about my house?" I ask him. "And Scott? And what would I do for a living?"

"You could work with me… in the new business. If you want to. We work well together, Jamie. And I like being with you… Well, I love being with you."

"Me too… but won't Todd mind?"

"No… And in any case, he's not ready to come on board yet. We're looking at figures still, but he's already told me the case he's working on – the one he wants to see out – it's proving more complicated than he thought. It could be weeks, or even months before he can resign."

"Oh… I see. And my house? And Scott?"

"Like I said… sell the house. Or you can rent it out, if you want to keep hold of it. And I meant what I said, Scott can come here during his vacations, if he wants."

"You'd do that?"

"Of course I would."

"But you value your space, your privacy… I told you… he's messy. And he's twenty-one, and noisy. He shares a house with a friend of his… they don't really have rules."

He kisses me gently. "It's fine, Jamie. If that's what it takes to have you here, living with me; I'll do anything." He takes a really deep breath. "I'll even have a bath put in."

I gasp. I can't help it. "No, Will. You don't have to."

"If you're gonna be living here, then I think I do." He swallows hard. "I'm not saying I'm strong enough to have it in our bathroom." *Our bathroom…* He's moved me in already, and that makes me smile. "I don't think I could look at it every day. But we've got three others to choose from…"

I reach up and touch his cheek gently with my fingertips. "Thank you."

"You don't have to thank me."

"Yeah... I do." He leans down and kisses me gently, letting his tongue dance with mine. "Can we talk about all this tomorrow?" I murmur, breaking the kiss.

"As long as you agree in principle... to moving in..." He sounds worried.

"Yes... if I can work out what to do about my house."

"And if you can, you'll move in here? You'll live with me?" he reiterates.

"Yes."

"Good." He kisses me again. "I'm sorry, you must be tired... We'll talk through everything else in the morning."

"I'm not especially tired..." I tell him. "But we've spent a lot of time talking... and I can think of plenty of other things I'd like to be doing right now." I pull him down for a deep, long kiss, and he rolls us over, so he's on his back, with me on top of him. "I want you..." I murmur into his mouth.

"Then take me," he offers, flexing his hips up into me.

"I... I can't." I lean up a little and look down at him.

"Why? What's wrong."

"I can't kneel, Will. I can't straddle you. It hurts my leg too much. So, I–I can't take you. I'm sorry"

He rolls us over again, so I'm on my back now, and he's raised above me. "No, I'm sorry, baby," he says, his voice filled with concern. "I should've thought."

I run my hands up his arms, resting them on his biceps. "No..." I can feel tears welling in my eyes.

"Are there any other things you can't do?" he asks. "Any other things that are uncomfortable for you?"

"To be honest, I don't really know. You're the only person I've had sex with since the bombing..."

"We'll work it out," he whispers, leaning down. "I'm pretty much making this up as I go along anyway."

"You're amazing," I tell him, truthfully.

"No... that's you. You're the amazing one. And if you can't take me, then how about if I take you instead?"

I nod my head, smiling. "I'd like that... a lot."

I wake in the early hours. We're side by side, facing each other… and we're still joined. He's hard inside me and, as I move, his cock shifts and I feel a flare of arousal within me.

"You feel good," he murmurs.

"So do you, but I didn't mean to wake you," I whisper.

"I don't care." He starts to move, slowly, in and out of me, each stroke heightening the pleasure, making me moan loudly with every movement. He brings his hand around behind me, cupping my ass and pulling me closer onto him, increasing the pace and taking me harder. I'm getting close.

"Will…" I mutter. "Please…"

"Come for me, baby."

His words push me over the edge and I feel the first wave of my orgasm shatter over me, consuming me. He groans out as he fills me, pushing me higher, further into that beautiful abyss, where my body hovers, held on the precipice, seemingly forever… until another wave overwhelms me and I scream his name, over and over into the darkness.

We're sitting in the living room. We had a very long, sensuous shower together and now I'm lying between Will's legs, leaning back on his chest, and I twist to look up at him.

"I never got around to asking you," I say, "how did you know where I live? I know you came to visit… and saw Gavin, but how did you know where to come?"

He looks a little sheepish and I turn over properly so I can look at him. "I hacked the personnel files," he says, his voice barely audible.

"You did what?"

"I wanted to see you…" He stares at me for a moment. "Are you mad at me again?" he asks.

"No, of course not." I put my arms around him and hug him. After a few minutes, he sits up, taking me with him, in an uncomfortable heap.

"Wait a second," he says, scratching his head. "I know how I found out where you live, but how did Luke know your address?"

"I have no idea. I'm not listed, so I assumed you must have told him."

"No." He shakes his head. "He didn't call you?"

"No. He didn't have my number. He gave me his last night, in case I needed to call him, but he didn't have mine."

"Why did he think you might need to call him?"

I'm not sure how to put this, but I guess the truth is as good a way as any. "He was worried about you... well, you and me. He just wanted me to know he was there if either of us needed him... that's all."

"I told you before... he's always there when I need him." He puts his arm around me. "I guess that extends to you now."

"Yeah," I reply, "he did kinda say that."

He smiles, then leans down and kisses me. "I still don't understand how he got hold of your address," he says.

"Neither do I... does it matter?"

"Not really." Except I can see it does. He sits still for a minute and I can see he's thinking. He shakes his head, then gets up and goes to the kitchen, grabbing his phone from the countertop. He presses a couple of buttons, then holds it to his ear.

"Hi," he says. "Yeah... we're fine." There's a pause. "Everything's fine, Luke. I promise." He looks at me. "I'm not gonna tell you that," he says, smirking a little. He comes over and sits back down again. "Stop it." He's grinning now. "Look... I called for a reason. I wanna know how you got Jamie's address." He waits a little while. "You did?" He seems surprised. "How the hell did you know the passcode?" Again, there's a pause. "But surely you can't have guessed that..." He listens. "I know I did, but I didn't think you were actually listening... Damn... I'm gonna have to change it now." He smiles. "No, I don't mind," he says. "It worked, didn't it?" He pulls me into a hug, leaning back into the couch. "Oh... just so you know, I'll be going back to Virginia with Jamie tomorrow night." He waits for a moment. "I'm gonna re-arrange my meeting with Todd for next weekend, so I'll be back on Friday." He hesitates, just for a moment. "But that'll be just for the weekend... and then I'm gonna go back to Virginia for a while... until the case Jamie's working on has finished." He looks down at me. "I don't know," he says. "Weeks, not months, I would've thought." He kisses my forehead. "Of course I'll stay in touch. We'll come back for weekends... and we can come see you... I won't let this impact on the wedding plans... And I'm

not on assignment, so my phone will be switched on. You can call me."
He shifts in his seat as he listens. "Well, it seems I can't live without her,
so this is the best solution, until the case is over and Jamie can move
here." There's another pause. "Yeah... she's gonna move in." He
chuckles. "Be quiet... I'm gonna go now," he says. "Well, I've got a lot
of catching up to do." He pauses, his face becoming more serious.
"Thanks, Luke... for everything," he murmurs.

They end the call, he puts his phone down on the sofa beside him and
turns to me.

"Well?" I ask. "How did he get my address?"

"He got it from my phone." I raise my eyebrows. "I'd put it on there
before coming to see you," he explains. "And, when Luke came to see
me... after I thought we'd broken up... he kept hold of it while he went
to make us a coffee. And he got the address then... I wasn't paying a lot
of attention at the time."

"And the passcode? I imagine yours is fairly secure."

"Well, I thought it was," he says, smiling.

"But he got around it?"

"Yeah." He seems impressed.

"How?" I ask.

"Well, I'd told him a few weeks ago, about using a word as a passcode
and converting it into numbers."

"Oh, I see... you mean using the letters of the alphabet, so one is 'A',
two is 'B', and so on?" I ask him.

He looks at me. "No," he says. "I mean using the numbers on a phone
keypad."

"Oh... okay. So what was your word?"

"Luke, so five-eight-five-three."

"But that's only four numbers, don't you need six?"

"Yeah. It's best to use a shorter word, then add random numbers to
get you up to six."

"Completely random?"

"Well, they can be... or you can make them numbers that are
personal, but they shouldn't be connected to the word. So I wouldn't
have used Luke and his year of birth..."

"And you explained all this to him?"

"Yeah… But I didn't think he was actually listening. He'd just got a new phone not long before he and Megan moved out of here, and he was going to use Megan's date of birth as the passcode… I saw him entering it and explained how insecure it is." He rolls his eyes.

"So what were your two random numbers?" I ask him.

"Six and three."

"Which are?"

"The year our mom was born. Nineteen sixty-three," he explains.

I nod my head and we sit still for a moment.

"I still don't understand," I say, "how Luke knew that would be your passcode."

He turns to look at me. "Because he knows me. I'd told him the word had to be something really important, something you wouldn't forget."

I snuggle into him. "So, what are you going to change it to?" I ask.

"I'm not," he replies.

"But you said…"

"I know. But I'm not going to."

"But won't he try…?"

"No probably not. He's got no reason to try and get onto my phone. But even if he does, he'll assume I've changed it… probably to something that starts five-two-six-four-three. It'll drive him insane trying to work it out." He chuckles.

I twist, so I can see him, my confusion clearly obvious. "Five-two… what?"

"J-A-M-I-E" he says, and kisses me.

Will's in the kitchen, making lunch and I'm on the phone to Scott, who's just called me. Firstly he tells me his good news, which is that Mia's grandmother is a little better and the doctors think she'll make a full recovery. I'm pleased for her and her family.

I tell him I'm at Will's, and that I'm going to resign from the agency once I've finished the case I'm working on… and that I'm going to move to Boston.

"Good for you, sis," he says. I can tell he's pleased for me.

"I need to talk to you about the house," I say.

"What about it?"

"Well… I'm gonna have to sell it, or rent it out." I feel guilty already.

"I think you should sell it," he says firmly.

"But…"

"If you're gonna give me some crap about feeling responsible for me, just… don't. I'm twenty-one, Jamie – nearly twenty-two. I'm not your responsibility…" He pauses. "Besides, Mia and I have been talking while we've been in Phoenix…"

"And?"

"And we've decided she's gonna give up her room and move in with me until graduation. And then we'll see about getting a place together…"

"Really?" I don't know why I'm surprised – Mia spent most nights at Scott's place anyway. This makes a lot more sense.

"Yeah. She really doesn't get on with one of the girls who's moved into her house this year. She's fairly sure this girl's on drugs… and there are way too many guys going backward and forward… and you know I never liked her living in that neighborhood… and… well, I do like the idea of her living with me…"

"How does Conor feel about this?" I ask him. I wonder if it's occurred to him that his housemate might object.

"He's fine with it," he says. "Jessica moved in with him last summer… so he can hardly complain."

"Won't it be a little cramped, with the four of you living there?"

"Yeah… but we'll cope."

"I'm sure you will." I can't help smiling. "So, when are you coming home?" I ask him.

"Tuesday, I think," he replies. "Will you be there?"

"Yes. Can we get together? All of us…?"

"Sure."

"I'll buy dinner…" Will suggests.

"Will says he'll buy dinner," I tell Scott.

"Sounds good. I'd like to meet him. I think I should check him out… make sure he's suitable to date my sister."

"Oh, do you now?"

"I'll be nice, don't worry."

"You'd better be. He's bigger than you," I tease.

Scott laughs. "Yeah, but I'm younger than him. I can run faster."

"I doubt that; he works out."

"Okay... I get it. Be nice to the boyfriend." He pauses for a moment. "You're happy, aren't you, sis?" he asks, serious all of a sudden.

"Yes, I am. Very happy." I glance up at Will and he smiles at me.

"Good," Scott says. "I'm pleased for you..."

"Thanks, little brother."

"See you Tuesday."

"Love you, Scotty."

"Love you too." He hangs up, and Will checks on the lunch and then comes over to me.

"Okay?" he asks.

I nod my head.

"It's gonna be fine," I tell him.

"Good." He sits beside me. "I've just remembered," he says, putting his arm around me, "I need to thank you for getting my mom's watch fixed. That was so kind of you... I didn't find it until yesterday morning."

"Really? What took you so long?"

"I was spreading out the chores, like I told you... and I liked the way the house smelt of you. I was trying to keep that going for as long as possible, but by yesterday, it had started to fade... I was just gonna start changing the bedding, and I was thinking about whether I should come visit you today, like we'd planned... and I found the package, under the comforter. It was a beautiful thing to do, Jamie. And your note... I... well, I ended up on the floor, crying..."

I gasp and turn to him.

"No, Will... Oh no." I put my arms around him and hold him tight. "I didn't want that."

"I know you didn't." He pulls me closer still. "It made me have second thoughts about coming to see you, though."

"Why?" I pull away from him, just a little, so I can see his face.

"Because I knew I could never hope to deserve you."

"Excuse me?"

"How could I hope to be worthy of someone who could do something like that?" he says. Is he serious?

"Will… You've given me so much," I say to him.

"I have?"

How can he not know?

"Yes. You've given me back my confidence, my belief in myself. You've made me so much stronger than I was when I came here. I may have fixed your mom's watch… but you fixed me."

He looks confused. "H-how?"

"By making me feel special."

"Oh… you mean the dress… the party?" he asks.

"No… I mean, you make me feel special all the time. Every. Single. Day. Just by loving me for who I am… with all my imperfections."

"You don't have any imperfections." He leans down and kisses me.

"I think you'll find I do," I murmur, when he finally pulls back again. "And I'm sorry the repairman couldn't fix the watch completely."

"Don't be," he says. "Do you know? I think think it's better this way. I think it'll help remind us that everyone is a little broken, a little damaged and scarred; we can all malfunction and screw up, and get it wrong from time to time… We don't have to be perfect by other people's standards, baby…" He kisses me again, more gently. "Because we're perfect for each other."

Epilogue

∽

Jamie

I love this bridesmaid's dress, and judging from the look on Will's face as he stands next to Luke, he's pretty impressed with it too. It's floor-length and champagne colored, and has a lace off-the-shoulder bodice, which is embellished with embroidered flowers in pale pink and green, coupled with delicate beading. It's cut quite low at the front, and even lower in the back. Matt, who's standing just beyond Will, can't take his eyes from Grace either. She may have been cursing Megan, in a friendly way, for having the wedding so soon after the births of the two babies, but she's already lost most of her baby weight and looks incredible, standing next to me.

Megan is, quite rightly, the center of attention, in an ivory colored strapless gown, with a full tulle skirt and lace bodice. Down the back, are thirty tiny pearl buttons… I know this, because I did them up… and there are strings of pearls entwined in her loosely braided hair. While we were helping her dress earlier, we joked that Luke might not be so impressed with her choice of dress later, when he has to undo all those fiddly buttons, but judging from the look on his face, as he watched her walking toward him, I don't think he'll mind one bit. He's about as in love with Megan as it's possible to be.

I smile across at Will, who once again, looks spectacular in his tux, and he winks back, grinning, as Luke takes a half step closer to Megan and starts to say his vows:

"Megan… You're my life. I promise I will always be there for you. I will comfort you, honor you, respect you and believe in you. I will be your partner in parenthood, your friend, your confidant, your ally and your lover. I will worship and love you until the last breath leaves my body. I will spend every minute of every day of the rest of my life loving you, and only you. Today, always and forever, I am yours."

I blink back my tears as Luke wipes away Megan's with his thumbs, and she begins to speak:

"Luke… I give you my hand and my heart, my body and my love. I will care for you faithfully, and try to be worthy of you. I promise to be always kind and understanding, and a true friend to you. I will love you and cherish you for the rest of our lives and I thank you, with all my heart, for making me your wife."

Almost as soon as Megan finishes, there comes a cry from the crib which is set up just behind where Megan's standing and, within seconds, the cry becomes a howl.

"She's got perfect timing, I'll give her that," Luke says, smiling.

Megan turns. "I've got her," I say and I hand my flowers to Megan's friend Erin, the third bridesmaid, before bending over, pulling back the covers and picking up the tiny bundle out of the crib. She's all soft and sleepy still, even though she's crying.

Grace leans over to me, whispering, "Megan expressed some milk earlier. It's in the refrigerator… be sure to use the bottles in the left side of the door. The others are mine." She grins. "Nappies… sorry diapers, are upstairs in the nursery. Will you be okay?"

I nod. "I'll be fine." Megan looks at me a little wistfully as I start to walk back toward the house and I see Luke place his finger under her chin and turn her back to face him.

"We're not done here yet," he says, and everyone laughs. "Daisy will be just fine with Jamie."

I go up the steps and into the house, grabbing the milk from the left hand door of the refrigerator en route to the nursery upstairs. Once inside, I close the door and sit down in the rocking chair by the window overlooking the garden. I nestle Daisy into the crook in my arm and introduce the bottle into her mouth. She looks a little disgusted that it's not her mother's breast, but I guess hunger takes over and she settles quickly and starts suckling.

"You're a greedy girl," I whisper to her. She gazes up at me, her eyes fixed on mine. "And a beautiful one. You take after your mommy… well, and your daddy too." I kiss the top of her blonde head.

Once she's finished, I set her on my lap and rub her back. She doesn't take long to let out an enormous, loud belch. "Yep, definitely like your daddy," I tell her, and lift her into my arms. "Let's just change that diaper and we can get you back downstairs."

We get back out to the garden just as Luke and Megan are having their first kiss as husband and wife. I hang back a little, until they break the kiss, then approach and hand Daisy to Luke. "She's fed and changed," I tell him.

"Thank you," Megan says, leaning over and kissing me on my cheek.

"You're welcome. She's adorable."

"She's like her mother," says Luke and he takes Megan's hand, holding Daisy in his other arm and they walk down the passageway between the sets of chairs laid out in their garden, toward the house. Erin comes over and gives me back my flowers and then Will takes my hand and we follow his brother and new sister-in-law, and Matt and Grace come along behind, with Todd and Erin after them.

Once the official photographs are done, and the champagne starts to flow, I take Daisy again for a little while, so Megan and Luke can mingle with their guests. We're sitting in the living room, in the corner of one of the two large couches.

"There's Erin," I whisper to Daisy. Megan's friend is leaning with her back against the door frame leading out into the garden. The man standing in front of her keeps taking a step closer every few minutes. "I don't know who the man is who's talking to her… I think he might be a client of your daddy's… and I think Erin's a little bored with him already." She looks it, anyway.

"It suits you," Grace says, coming and sitting beside me, baby George in her arms. He was born two weeks early – so not that long after

Daisy in the end. He has a shock of dark hair and the most gorgeous chubby legs that really need squeezing… regularly.

"What does?" I ask her.

"Holding a baby. You're a natural."

"I don't know about a natural…"

"But you'd like to have children?"

"Yes, I would… one day."

"And Will?"

"I don't know." I turn to her. There's something about Grace that makes her easy to talk to, and share with. "We've never talked about it."

"You should," she says. "It's important."

It's not something I've thought about before. I suppose I've always just assumed that one day, I'd be a mother. But I'm not sure it's something Will wants. Given his childhood, I wouldn't blame him if he didn't.

"Are you okay, Jamie?" Grace asks and I realize I've kind of drifted off.

"Sorry? Oh, yes, I'm fine."

"I'd better go and find Matt. I think Erin needs rescuing." She gets up again. "Talk to Will," she adds and she smiles down at me and walks across the room and out into the garden.

I think for a moment about what Grace said. Would it be a deal-breaker for me if Will didn't want children? No. I want Will more than I want anything else, but I know I'd be sad… maybe a little unfulfilled if I never felt the joy of motherhood.

Since we got back together at New Year, everything has been a little crazy, which is maybe why we haven't had time to talk about anything important… To start with, Gavin decided he did want to use Will – unofficially, of course – so they met up at my house on the Monday evening after we travelled back from Boston, and got on really well, and Gavin briefed Will on what he needed him to do. Will worked on my kitchen table, setting everything up, and making it look real easy into the bargain. I still had to go into the office every day, so I missed him, but when I got home, we cooked dinner together and usually ate it in bed, watching old movies.

Scott and Mia moved in together… which has just meant I haven't really heard from him at all. I call every so often to make sure he's not neglecting his studies. He tells me he isn't… so I guess I have to trust him.

I resigned as soon as Jack was arrested, which was at the end of January, and Will handed in his resignation at the same time. I had to work out a month's notice, but Will didn't – Sean let him go on the spot, blissfully unaware that Will had played such a pivotal role in Jack's ultimate downfall. There was something kinda satisfying in that…

Will had to travel back to Boston a few times to meet with Todd, and also Matt about his investment, but that meant that by the time I finally left the department, at the end of February, the new business was all set up and I was able to move in with Will… and we started working together, all over again. Our first – and so far, biggest – client, was Gavin's department in Chicago. They've been using Will for all kinds of surveillance and investigative operations that Gavin wants kept under the official radar.

Since then, my house has been sold, to a lovely retired couple, and Will and I have been really busy… We had to spend a long weekend in Virginia, moving my furniture – Scott and Mia took most of it, I sold some and a few things came back to Boston with us. Then there's been the wedding to plan, which I became much more involved with once Megan asked me to be a bridesmaid… and of course, there's work. Other than that, we only really have time to eat, sleep and make love… and we do quite a lot of that, I'm pleased to say. I smile, remembering last night on the couch at home…

Talking about the future, and children… or even marriage, hasn't featured in our lives.

I guess it doesn't matter though. Not really. I'm happy as things are. Luke was right… Will really is an amazing guy and, whatever happens in the future, I'm truly blessed to have him in my life.

Will

She hasn't noticed me yet. I've been standing watching Jamie holding Daisy since Grace got up and moved away. I know she's thinking about something, I just wish I knew what. She was smiling a moment ago, but now she looks a little sad, a little far away… maybe even a little lost.

I don't like that idea. I walk over to her.

"Hey, you," I say.

She looks up. "Hello." She smiles up at me. That's better.

I sit beside her, putting my arm around her shoulder. "I like this dress," I tell her. "It shows off your skin."

"There's quite a lot of my skin on display."

"Hmm. That's what I like," I whisper, leaning over. "And the fact that I know what's underneath."

"How? You weren't here I got dressed."

"I'm using my imagination."

"Well, I hope it's up to the task. Megan – well, Luke really – provided us all with some very enticing lingerie to choose from."

"He did?" I can feel my cock stiffening at the thought.

"Yes." She nods at me.

"Fancy sneaking upstairs?" I ask.

"I've got my hands full…" She nods down at Daisy, who's looking up into Jamie's face.

"She seems very taken with you." I reach across and touch Daisy's hand with my finger and she grabs it tightly. "Her grip is something else, isn't it?"

"I know. It's like she doesn't want to let go."

I look at Jamie. "I know that feeling," I say and she turns to face me, gazing into my eyes.

"Me too."

I lean across and kiss her, just as Daisy starts to make 'cooing' noises. Jamie laughs.

"I'm not sure your niece approves of you kissing me," she says.

"Yeah, she does, don't you?" I take the baby from Jamie and cradle her in my arms. "You love your Uncle Will, don't you?" I say to her and she reaches out and grabs my nose.

"Well, she likes your nose, anyway." Jamie leans into me.

"I think she was aiming for the glasses… she's fascinated by them."

"Can we borrow our daughter back for a while?" Luke says from behind us, leaning over the back of the couch. "Megan wants Grace to take some photographs of the three of us."

"Sure," I tell him, looking down at Daisy, who's starting to nod off. "I think she's bored with me anyway. How's she gonna feel after a whole night in my company?"

"She'll be fine. It's real good of you two to offer to stay here and look after Daisy overnight." Luke says.

"I've got Grace on standby," I joke.

"You won't need Grace…" Luke replies. "Daisy's pretty good at night. And we'll be back by lunchtime tomorrow."

"The shortest honeymoon in history."

"That's not the honeymoon… and you know it." He nudges me.

"Yeah… but Megan doesn't."

Megan thinks their night in a luxury suite at the Boston Harbor Hotel is their honeymoon – at least until Daisy's a little older… But Luke always had other plans. He's taking Megan and Daisy to a private villa on the Amalfi coast in Italy for two weeks. Their bags are already packed. They've been stored in our guest bedroom for a couple of days, but they're now in the back of my Jeep, ready to transfer them into Luke's car before they leave for the airport tomorrow evening.

"Have lunch with us when we get back tomorrow?" he says, as I hand Daisy over to him.

"Surely you'll want to be on your own," Jamie replies.

"We're gonna have the rest of our lives to be on our own," Luke replies. "Besides, I think Daisy's rather taken with her Aunty Jamie."

"Please don't call me 'Aunty'," Jamie says. "It makes me feel like I'm fifty-something."

"You're not fifty-something," I tell her, leaning over to kiss her. "And you *are* Daisy's aunty."

"No I'm not… not really." The sadness returns to Jamie's eyes. I understand it now. Even I'm not that dumb.

Luke glances down at me, raising an eyebrow. "Come on," he says to Daisy. "Lets go find mommy, shall we?"

"You are," I say to Jamie once Luke's gone.

"You're her uncle," she says, turning to me.

"Which makes you her aunt."

"No, it doesn't."

"Yeah… it does."

"Will?" Matt comes into the room from the garden. "Can you spare a minute?"

I look up at him, then back at Jamie. "Of course he can," she says.

"We'll finish this later," I whisper to her. She nods and I get up off the couch and follow Matt outside, then through the other door, into the kitchen.

Todd's standing in one corner of the room and we go over to join him.

"What's wrong?" I ask.

"Nothing…"

"It's not nothing," says Matt. Todd glares at him. "Tell him," Matt continues.

"Tell me what?"

"If I do, you can't tell Luke. Not until later… after I've gone."

"Gone where?"

"London."

"*London?*" I'm stunned. I think it shows.

"Yes. Promise you won't tell him until after I've gone?"

"Okay. What's happening?"

He looks from me to Matt and back again. "Remember the case I've been working on?"

"The one you want to tie up before you join the business?"

"What case is this?" Matt asks.

"The double murder I told you about at Christmas."

"You're still on that?"

"Yes." He sighs. "We've kept it out of the media, but since Christmas, there have been four more identical homicides."

"What, double murders?"

"Yes."

"A serial killer?" I say the words under my breath.

"Yes. And the latest victims were killed in London. Everything fits; it's the same killer, we're sure of it. My boss, and the guy heading up the investigation over there, have decided that I should go there and work with them. I'm going undercover, so you might not hear from me for a while."

"This sounds dangerous," Matt says.

"If I get it right, it won't be."

"And if you get it wrong?" I ask.

He looks at me. "I'll try not to." He smiles. "I just wanted you guys to know where I'm gonna be. And to let you know I'll be going a bit quiet for a while."

"When do you leave?" I ask.

He looks at his watch. "I've got to get home, change and finish packing. I've ordered the cab to take me to the airport for just over an hour from now."

"What? But…"

"The London murders took place yesterday morning. They wanted me to fly out last night. I refused. I wasn't going to miss Luke's wedding. I told them either they accepted me flying out tonight, or I'd quit the force."

"Matt?" Grace calls from the doorway. "Can you come and see to George, just for a moment? I'm trying to take these photographs and every time I put him down, he screams blue murder…"

"I've gotta go," he says.

"Sure," Todd replies.

"Take care of yourself." Matt shakes his hand and pats him on the arm, then goes out into the garden, leaving us alone.

"When you talk to Luke," Todd says, turning to me, "tell him I'm sorry I had to duck out."

"Of course. He'll understand. He'll probably be pissed you didn't tell him yourself though."

"I didn't want to do anything to spoil his and Megan's day. It's been a great wedding, hasn't it?"

"Yeah."

"I never thought I'd say this, but he looks good married, and as a dad... It suits him."

"It does. You're not tempted?" I ask.

"Hell, no," he replies. "You're settled with Jamie," he says. "One of us has got to stay single."

"Why?" I ask him. "There's a lot to be said for finding the right woman."

He gives me a look that says he doesn't believe me. "I'll take your word for that."

About ten minutes later, I'm talking to Luke's secretary and her husband in the living room when I notice Todd going quietly out the front door. I watch as he climbs into his car and reverses out of the driveway and onto the street. He doesn't look back or wave, because he doesn't realize anyone's watching. Todd can be reserved, sometimes even more so than me, and I'm not sure he fully appreciates how much he means to the rest of us.

It's evening now and the garden is lit with fairy lights. It's very mild for late April, guests are still milling around outside while music plays and glasses are filled.

I'm in the kitchen with Grace, when Matt comes in. "Luke wants everyone out on the deck," he says.

"Oh... okay." I'm surprised. He didn't mention this to me.

Matt goes around, gathering up other stray guests and we all go outside. Luke and Megan are standing there, leaning against the railing. Jamie is already there too, holding Daisy, who's had a short nap and is wide awake again.

"Um... Hi everyone," Luke says, raising his voice. "I'm sorry to interrupt your evening. I promise I won't talk for long. We deliberately kept today's celebrations very informal, and decided we wouldn't have speeches, because Megan and I didn't want that kind of wedding." He pauses. "But, there was something I wanted to say." Megan looks up at him. I glance over at Jamie and, although she's rocking Daisy from side to side, she's staring at me. Luke clears his throat, then carries on, "There were quite a few people who helped us on the road to today, and who I'd like to take this opportunity to thank." He looks over at Matt. "Matt and Todd..." He looks around. "Wherever Todd is... well, they helped me find Megan when she was in trouble, and brought her back into my life... so I owe them a huge debt." He kisses the top of Megan's head. "And Matt," he continues, "... he convinced Megan that the future shouldn't ever be sacrificed to the past... even when that past is as checkered as mine." Everyone laughs. "Grace..." He looks at her. "Grace used her unique talents to give us a whole new way of looking at each other. She gave us a new, and very special perspective." He smiles and winks at her, and she smiles back. "But..." He turns. "We owe the fact that we're even together in the first place... to someone who's very special to us... and very, very special to me... My brother, Will," Luke says, and I flip my head around to him, "is my best man today, but he's the best man I know *every* day. He had the gargantuan mission of convincing me I could change... that I could be a better man than I was. And he even managed to persuade Megan of that... And anyone who knows me, will know what an enormous challenge that was." There's another ripple of laughter. Once it's gone quiet again, Luke continues, "Will is the most loyal, honest and decent guy I know." He looks at me. "And Megan and I want to thank you for everything you did to bring us together and for everything you've done to make today so special. And... we want to say happy birthday." He reaches behind him and pulls out a small black box, then comes over to me. "Happy birthday, Will," he says quietly and hands it to me.

Everyone is staring at us and Jamie comes across to stand beside me. She knows how much I hate being the center of attention.

"Shall I open it now?" I ask Luke.

He nods his head. I open the box. Inside is what looks like a solid silver dog tag, on a leather cord. It's engraved with the word '*Brother*'. "Flip it over," Luke whispers. I glance up at him, then back at the box. I feel

312

Jamie's hand touching my arm as I turn over the dog tag, and a lump rises in my throat as I read:

'The best gift our mom ever gave me, was you.'

"Thank you," I manage to say, and he grabs my shoulders and pulls me in for a hug.

"Anytime," he replies. From behind us, I hear a noise and we turn in time to see an enormous cake, topped with candles, being brought out by one of the caterers. Everyone starts singing 'Happy Birthday', and the cake is put down on the table in front of me.

"Make a wish," Luke says, then leans in closer and whispers, "and make it count."

I hold Jamie's hand as I blow out the candles.

I hope she makes my wish come true.

"Did you know about that?" I ask Jamie when everyone's moved away.

"He told me he had something planned, yes."

"Sneak." I kiss her gently, careful not to crush Daisy, who's staring up at us. "Do you think Megan wants her back after tomorrow?" I ask. "Or shall we keep her?"

"It's tempting," she replies.

"Do you want one, then?" I ask.

"A baby?"

I nod at her.

"I guess so... maybe, one day." That sad look re-appears in her eyes.

"Give her to me," I say to Jamie and she looks at me for a second before handing Daisy over. "You're gorgeous," I say to Daisy, running my finger down her cheek, "but you're going back to your daddy." I look at Jamie. "Stay here," I tell her. "Don't move. I'll be back in a minute." I turn and search among the guests until I spot Luke, talking to a man with a receding hairline and glasses. I go over to them. "Excuse me?" I say, cutting in. "I'm really sorry to interrupt."

"That's okay," Luke says, "is something wrong?" The man he was talking to excuses himself.

"No. But can you take Daisy for a while?"

"Sure. She is my daughter, after all." I pass Daisy over and Luke smiles down at her. "Is it diaper change time, or something? Is that why I'm getting her back?"

I laugh. "No, as far as I know, she's fine."

"Oh, she's more than fine." He kisses the top of her head. "She's incredible." He moves us to one side of the deck, away from everyone else. "I've never told anyone else this, although I'm fairly sure I wouldn't need to explain it to Matt, but having Daisy… it's made me love Megan even more."

"Is that possible?"

"You wouldn't have thought so, but it has." He kisses her again.

"Do you think you'll have more?" I ask him.

"I hope so, yeah." He grins. "But it's Megan's decision. Seeing what she had to go through, giving birth, there's no way a guy should ever get to call the shots on that one."

"But you'd recommend it?"

He looks at me. "Yes, Will, I would," he says. "Jamie's done an amazing job of looking after her today. It's been a weight off Megan's mind, knowing Daisy's been in such good hands."

"Jamie's loved every minute of it."

"And?" He grins.

"And that's why I'm giving you back your daughter. So I can have a quiet conversation with my girlfriend."

"Oh." He catches my eye. "*Oh*," he says again. "Are we talking kids, or kids and something else?"

"Something else and kids… ideally in that order."

He can't keep the smile off his face. He pats my shoulder. "Good luck."

"Do you think I'll need it?" I ask.

"Hell, no. Jamie loves you, that much is obvious."

"And the kids bit? You think she's…?"

"Yep… That's pretty damn obvious too," he laughs.

"I meant to say to you… that little speech you gave, about me being responsible for you and Megan being together…"

"Yeah, what about it?"

"I didn't do that much…"

"Yeah, you did. I know you don't find it easy to talk to people, Will. But you met with Megan, when you didn't really know her; you talked to her and told her how you felt about me. And she's told me you talked about mom too… I know you'd have found that hard. I also know there's a big chance we wouldn't be here if you hadn't done that…"

"And how about what you did to bring me and Jamie together?"

"What about it? All I did was have a glass of wine with Jamie, pick her up at the airport and bring her to your place. The rest of it was Jamie… and you… not me. I really didn't do that much, Will."

"Hmm… Somehow I don't believe you. And I still think I owe you."

"You'll never owe me," he says, and he puts his hand on my shoulder. "Never."

Just as I turn to go, he calls me back. "Sorry to hold you up when you've got something so important to do," he says, "but where's Todd got to? He wasn't around when I was making my speech and now I come to think about it, I haven't seen him for a couple of hours."

"He's had to go to London."

"London? What on earth for?"

"It's the case he's working on," I explain.

"Why didn't he tell me?"

"He didn't want to worry you. The job he's going to do… it could be pretty dangerous, and he's going to be working undercover and out of contact for a while," I say. "Look, would it be okay if I fill you in later?"

He glances over my shoulder to where Jamie's standing. "Sure," he says, and smiles.

I go back to Jamie and, without saying a word, I take her hand and lead her down the steps and across the lawn. It's magical out here, surrounded by fairy lights, and I take her to the furthest end of the garden, beneath a cherry tree that's got lights wrapped around its trunk and into its blossom filled branches. Jamie shivers and I take off my jacket and wrap it around her shoulders.

"It's good to have you alone," I tell her and I pull her closer, leaning down and kissing her.

"You've been busy today," she says.

"So have you. Luke said you've done a fantastic job looking after Daisy for Megan."

"Daisy's adorable. It's been no trouble."

"And you'd like us to have a baby too?"

"Not if you don't want to," she says, her shoulders dropping. She swallows hard and I know she's holding back her tears.

"And if I do want to?" She looks up at me.

"Do you?" she asks, her eyes sparkling.

"Yes. But I'm not ready yet."

"Okay," she says, taking a deep breath. "I understand. It's best to wait anyway. I mean, we've got the business to think about. It's early days yet and, without Todd, it's just the two of us. We can't—"

"Forget the damn business. It's got nothing to do with that."

"Is it because of your mom… Luke's dad? Do you need more time…?"

"No." She looks confused. "I'm not ready yet, because I want you to be Mrs Myers before we have babies. I want you to be my wife as well as my friend and my lover… and the mother of our children." I hold her face in my hands, staring into her eyes. "Marry me?" I say as the first tear falls.

She nods her head and whispers, "Yes… oh, Will yes," and I lean down and kiss her lips, tasting her salty tears.

"Thank you," I murmur, holding her close and I feel my chest, my heart expanding with love for her. Then I look over her shoulder and see Luke standing on the deck, Daisy in one arm and Megan in the other. I know he's been watching us, in case I needed him… just like he's done for most of my life. I nod my head at him, he returns the gesture, a smile spreading across his face as he pulls Megan closer and whispers into her ear, before turning her toward the house to give us some privacy.

I hold Jamie in my arms for a long time. We're alone. We're together. It's perfect.

The End

Keep reading for an excerpt from book four in the Series...
Finding Todd.

Finding Todd

Escaping the Past: Book Four

by

Suzie Peters

Chapter One

Todd

The guy standing in the arrivals hall looks bored to death. I guess he's thirty, or thereabouts. He's probably just under six feet tall, well-built, with short reddish-brown hair and stubble. He's holding up a card with my name printed on it, but he's looking around and doesn't notice me until I'm right in front of him.

"You looking for me?" I ask him.

"If you're Todd Russell, then yes." I'd hardly be asking the question, if I wasn't... I just look at him until he nods, holds out his hand to me and says, "I'm Adam Harris." I shake his hand and he turns away. "Follow me," he says over his shoulder.

"Where are we going?" I ask.

"My car... the car park."

"I got that. I mean where are you taking me?"

"Oh. Paddington Green Police Station."

"Okay." I kind of wish he'd said a hotel, so I could freshen up, but I guess cops like us are aren't allowed such luxuries, no matter which side of the Atlantic we work on.

"Andy – that's my boss – wanted to brief you and Holly as soon as you arrived." He keeps talking as we get in the elevator.

"Who's Holly?"

"You'll be working with her."

"I will?" I know I'm going undercover, although I don't know in what capacity yet, but no-one's mentioned a second role... or a female officer taking it. I hate working with people I don't know, and I'd like a heads up. "What's she like?" I ask.

"No idea, mate." He turns to look at me, smiling. "Never even met her."

"Excuse me?"

"She only transferred to CID a week ago... and then promptly went on holiday."

"Great."

"Yeah." His smile becomes a grin. "Rather you than me."

We exit on the fourth floor and as we approach a black Volvo, he pops the trunk, and I load my case inside.

I've only just climbed into the passenger seat, when my phone rings. I check the display. It's Grace and I can't help but smile.

"Hey, Grace," I say, connecting the call.

"Hey yourself," she replies.

"You're up early."

"George woke me. I've just finished feeding him."

"Thanks. I needed that image in my head," I tell her and she laughs.

"Where are you?"

"Just leaving Heathrow, on my way into, um... Paddington?"

"Okay. And why didn't you tell me you were going to England? I could have given you all kinds of tips for places to visit."

"I'm working, Grace. I won't have time for sightseeing."

"You might."

"I doubt it."

"Then I could have helped you out with my useful guide on how not to annoy the British. Matt and Luke make use of it all the time."

"That's because they're both real annoying. I'm not." She really laughs this time. "Okay... you can calm down now. It wasn't that funny. How is that husband of yours?" I ask, and Adam coughs. I guess he thought I was talking to my girlfriend, or wife. Now he probably assumes I'm talking to my mistress... If I wasn't so tired, I'd be tempted to have some fun with this.

"Matt's fine. He's still asleep."

"And the wedding?" I can feel Adam's eyes on me as we exit the parking garage. He's really confused now.

"It was lovely." She yawns.

"Is George asleep again yet?"

"Yes."

"Then go back to bed. It's only just after six-thirty with you; and it's Sunday. You can get another couple of hours' sleep yet."

"But Matt said we won't hear from you for a while."

"No, you won't."

"Oh." She sounds upset.

"You'll live."

"We'll miss you."

"I'll be home soon." I keep my voice as reassuring as I can.

"Take care of yourself, won't you?" I guess it didn't work. She sounds upset, and concerned now.

"I'll do my best."

"And say hello to London for me." That's better. She sounds a little more optimistic.

"Of course."

We say our goodbyes and hang up. Adam keeps looking at me. "That was the wife of a friend of mine," I tell him, because I don't have the energy to play games with him. "She's British." To me, that's enough explanation. It's all he's getting, anyway. Matt's more like a brother than a friend, but Adam doesn't need to know that.

He steers us onto the freeway... or motorway, as the Brits call it. "Good, it's not too busy," he says. Looks busy enough to me, for a Sunday morning.

I'm just about to say so, when my phone rings again. This time, it's Luke. I pick up.

"Hey," I say to him.

"When were you gonna tell me?" he replies by way of greeting. He sounds a little pissed with me.

"I didn't want to take the edge off your day."

"So you just left?" He seems offended.

"No. I told Matt and Will. They did explain, didn't they?"

323

"Yeah, Will did. But you didn't say goodbye."

"No."

"And we won't hear from you while you're there?"

"No. I'll be turning my phone off later today… You won't be able to contact me."

"Will said this could be dangerous… the job you're doing." His voice softens at last.

"It's a possibility. I'm hoping it won't be though."

"Take care of yourself, man."

Everyone keeps saying that. It's kinda hard to know how to reply. "Sorry I missed the end of your wedding." It's a reasonable change of subject.

I can hear him smiling. "You missed the main event."

"I don't want to know about that. What you and Megan get up to in your own time—"

"Not that," he says. "Will and Jamie got engaged."

"You're kidding me." I didn't see that coming… not for a while yet, anyway.

"No, I'm not. This means you're the last single man standing."

"It's a badge I'll wear with honor and pride," I tell him.

"Until some beautiful brunette comes along and steals your heart…"

"It's never gonna happen… not to me."

"We all said that. And look where we all are now."

"Tied down?"

"Happy," he says. I know he's right. My three best friends are all happily married, or engaged – evidently – and settled with incredible women, who a lot of men would kill to be with. I'm not envious. It's not something I want. I made my decision about that years ago and I don't intend changing my mind now. Not for anyone.

"Speaking of you being happy," I say, "why are you calling me at this time of day? I thought you and Megan had a swanky suite at the Boston Harbor. Surely you've got better things to be doing the morning after your wedding than talking to me."

"Megan's still asleep… I kept her up late last night." I can hear him smirking.

"Once again… I really don't need to know that."

"I'll wake her in a while. We're due to leave in a couple of hours…"

"For Italy?" Luke's planned a surprise honeymoon trip for them. Matt, Will and I knew about it, but Megan had no idea… and still doesn't, if things have gone to plan. It was the best-kept secret of the whole wedding.

"No, just to go home and relieve Will and Jamie of babysitting duties. We leave for Italy this evening."

"And Megan still doesn't know?"

"No. I'm gonna tell her on the way to the airport."

"Well… have a great time."

"We will."

"And give Megan and Daisy a hug from me," I tell him.

"Okay."

"I'll be in touch when I can… And I'm sorry I didn't tell you."

"You're forgiven. But only if you get back here safe and sound… and soon."

"I'll do my best."

"You'd better…"

After I've hung up, I notice Adam's looking at me again. "That was a friend of mine," I explain. "He got married yesterday. I had to duck out of the end of his wedding to catch my flight."

"Oh… so that's why you couldn't come over on Friday?"

"Yeah. I wasn't missing the wedding."

"Good for you," he says. "But Andy wasn't too pleased about that."

I glance across at him. "Do I look like I give a fuck?"

He grins at me and changes lanes.

"I'm Andy Reed." The guy holds out his hand to me and we shake. He's a little taller than Adam, but a couple of inches shy of me. He has cropped brown hair, is clean-shaven and is wearing the smartest suit I've ever seen on a cop. "It's good to meet you," he adds. "Come into my office."

I follow him, dragging my suitcase along behind me, and he closes the door once we're both inside. "Leave that in the corner," he says, nodding to my case, and I do. "We just need to wait for Holly."

He sits behind his desk and indicates the two chairs in front of him.
I take the left hand one.

"She's not here yet?"

"No. She was due to land at about the same time as you. Her flight
was coming in from Pisa. She's been on holiday… or vacation, I suppose
you'd say."

I'm confused. "Then why didn't we wait and pick her up?"

"Because she left her car in the long-stay car park. It would have been
pointless."

"Oh, I see."

He glances at his watch. "I don't know where she is," he says. "She
wouldn't have had to go through immigration, just passport control,
and that shouldn't have taken too long." He huffs out a breath. "We'll
give her a little longer."

"She's new, isn't she?"

"Yes. Very."

"And you chose her for this assignment…?"

"Because she's the only female officer I've got who's suitable," he
says.

I find it hard to believe a woman who's only worked in criminal
investigation for a week, and has spent all of that on vacation is the most
suitable person he's got. I think my skepticism must show.

"I've only got two other women in this department," he explains.
"One is nearly forty. She's good at her job, but for what we need, she's
not right. The other is pregnant – very pregnant. She goes on maternity
leave at the end of the week." He leans forward, resting his chin on one
upturned hand, and he opens the file on his desk. "I've read through
your case notes," he says.

"And your killings match ours?" I ask. I guess it's a dumb question.
They wouldn't have bothered to fly me all the way over here if they
didn't.

"Yes." He doesn't look up. "In every way."

"There's been nothing in the press at home. We've deliberately kept
it quiet. So it can't be a copycat," I add.

"No. I discussed that with your captain." He raises his head and stares at me. "Interesting man."

"That's one word for him." We exchange a smile. Carpenter has been my boss for the last two years… He's the main reason I'll be resigning as soon as this case is over and done with. The man's an idiot. He's gonna get someone killed one day soon, and it's not gonna be me…

"How's this going to work?" I ask him. "The undercover element, I mean…"

"I think we'll wait for Holly to arrive, then—"

Before he can finish his sentence, there's a knock on his door.

Holly

I know I shouldn't complain. I've had a week away in Italy. I spent four days and nights in Florence, and the rest of my time in Pisa. It was stunning. I'd like to go back there one day, in happier circumstances. It wasn't the holiday I'd planned; not even remotely. But it was a holiday – and I needed it. What I hadn't expected was the text message I got on Friday afternoon from my new boss, Andy, asking me to cut short my holiday and fly home. I was just looking into changing my ticket, when I got a second message, telling me not to worry… that I could catch my scheduled flight, and if I could get into the office by twelve today, that would be great. Well, it would be a bloody miracle, considering I didn't land until eleven, had to get my baggage, get through customs, collect my car from the long stay car park, which was a fifteen minute bus ride away, and drive from Heathrow to Paddington – which even on a Sunday takes nearly an hour. So, not a chance, Andy.

This time yesterday, I was having a panini and a glass of chilled Pinot Grigio at the Tower House in the Via Santa Maria… and today I'm driving down the A40 behind a removals lorry. The comparison is almost enough to make me smile and I haven't done that in a long time – not even during my holiday.

It's when I'm parking that I remember why I bought such a small car… You can park it pretty much anywhere and I find a spot easily. I suppose it also helps that it's a Sunday and less busy than usual.

I check the time on my phone. It's nearly a quarter past one. I don't imagine Andy is going to be too happy that I'm over an hour late, but I haven't even stopped to go to the toilet, let alone to grab a coffee, which I desperately need.

Whatever's so important that I have to come in on my Sunday off, I'm sure it can wait another few minutes while I just visit the Ladies' on my way to Andy's office.

As if my day wasn't perfect enough, I discover that my period has just started. It's a day early, and I rummage in my bag for a sanitary towel. I've got one, thank goodness, but I know there are none at home. I'll have to go shopping anyway when I've finished here, so I can pick some up then. While I'm washing my hands, I check my appearance in the mirror. I've seen worse. Okay, I've also seen better – but not usually in my own reflection. I hope Andy doesn't mind that I'm wearing jeans and a casual blouse, and no make-up…

"Tough," I whisper to myself. "He's on my time today. He can take it or leave it."

Once I'm finished, I go along the corridor to his office and knock twice.

"Come in," he calls.

I open the door and a man, who's been sitting in one of the chairs in front of Andy's desk, gets to his feet and turns to face me. He's enormous. He must be at least six foot three, with short, light brown hair and eyes the colour of milk chocolate. He's got dark stubble on his square jaw and, as he takes a step towards me, his mouth opens into a wide smile of brilliant white teeth. His leather jacket fits tightly across his broad shoulders and muscular arms… and I need to stop staring at him and pay attention to what Andy's saying.

"Holly…" Andy also stands. "Nice of you to make it." I ignore the sarcasm. It's not worth biting. I'll only lose. "Holly King, this is Todd," he says by way of introduction. "Todd Russell." The giant offers his hand and I take it. His grip is strong.

"Hi," he says. "Pleasure to meet you." He has a deep, yet soft, velvety voice with a pronounced American accent.

"You're American." I state the blindingly obvious.

"Yes, ma'am." He smiles again. I can't help but giggle. That's odd… I've gone from not smiling in weeks, to giggling like a schoolgirl, just because a handsome, tall, muscular American smiled at me. Grow up, Holly.

"They pay us to notice things like that," I tell him.

"Well, if it's anything like back home, they don't pay you enough."

"Amen to that."

"Okay," Andy says. "Enough of the mutual self-pity society. Come and join us, Holly." Todd waits until I'm seated before sitting down again himself. "Todd's come over from Boston," Andy explains.

"Oh?" I look from one to the other of them. "Is this why you needed me to come back early?"

"Yes," Andy replies. "Sorry about the mix up. We were trying to get Todd over here on Friday evening, but he couldn't make it, so there seemed little point in getting you to cut short your holiday in the end."

"Sorry for messing you around," Todd says, looking at me.

"You didn't." I look up at Andy. "I still don't understand why I'm here…"

"You're going to be working together – on a murder case."

The room starts to spin, just a little. "I'm sorry," I say, "did you say 'murder'?" I thought I'd be making the coffee and pushing paper around for weeks… maybe months, and I'm about to be put on a murder case, on what is effectively my first day?

"Yes."

"But… Are you sure you've got the right person. You do remember I've only just started here, don't you?"

"Yes," Andy says. "And normally I wouldn't even consider giving you a case like this to work on, but I've got no choice." Well, I suppose at least he's being honest.

329

Todd turns in his seat to face me. "There have been three double homicides in Boston since Christmas," he explains. "They're all exactly the same in terms of the way in which they're carried out, the manner in which the bodies are left, and so on. There was one the day before Christmas Eve, one in the middle of January and one in late February. Then it went quiet. I've been working the case, but haven't been able to find any leads. I'd started to wonder if our guy had given up... lost interest."

"Right," I say. "But what's that got to do with us?"

"We had an identical murder here," says Andy. "The bodies were found in the early hours of Friday morning, although we think the killings took place on Wednesday night, or early Thursday morning."

Todd looks up. "I wasn't told that," he remarks. "I was told the murders happened on Friday morning... we've already lost four days, then..."

"I did inform your captain of the details," Andy replies.

"Yeah, well he didn't pass that on." Todd looks angry.

Andy turns back to me, shaking his head, then continues, "Because of the nature of the killings, and the fact that one of the deceased was an American, from Boston, it didn't take us long to put our murders together with the ones in Todd's precinct. And his captain and our Superintendent decided he should come over here..."

"Seems sensible," I say. "But I still don't see why I'm involved?"

Todd looks at Andy. "You haven't really explained it to me either," he says. "All I was told is I'm going undercover. I didn't know anyone else would be involved." He glances across at me and smiles apologetically. I shrug my shoulders. I don't blame him for being doubtful about me – I'm pretty doubtful about me too.

Andy takes a deep breath and stares down at the open file in front of him. He doesn't make eye contact with either of us. "All the people who've been murdered were couples. They all frequented a particular club which has branches all over the world, but for our purposes, we're only interested in the Boston and Mayfair branches... especially the Mayfair one, since that was where our couple had been on the evening they were killed… last Wednesday." He glances up at Todd as he says the last word, like he expects him to say something.

Todd ignores Andy's emphasis on the day and leans forward. "Each of the couples in Boston had also visited the club there on the night they were killed. We've interviewed all the other guests, the members, all the staff, visitors, even the suppliers… everyone. We couldn't find a damn thing."

"I know," Andy says. "I've read the files. Your case notes are very thorough."

"So?" Todd says, again ignoring Andy's compliment.

"So, we're going to have you two pose as guests… as a couple…"

Todd lets out a long sigh. "You're kidding me, right?" Andy shakes his head. "I'd assumed you were sending me in to work in the club, behind the bar, or something…"

"You couldn't find out anything when you interviewed everyone. What makes you think that going undercover as an employee would work any better? You'd have to establish who you think it is, and then earn their trust… it could take months, and in that time, they could kill again. And if it's a guest – a member – who's responsible, you might never even get to meet them."

"And you think this plan is better?"

"We've set you up as members. Whoever it is targeted an American in London. Out of all the members he could have chosen, he went for an American—"

"He?" I interrupt, picking up on what they've been saying. "How do you know it's a he?"

Todd and Andy exchange glances. "Tell her," Todd says. "You're asking her to do this. I'm not. She has a right to know."

"The women," Andy says, looking from Todd to me. "The women in each case… they were all raped."

"And?" Todd says. "Tell her everything."

Andy glares at him. "They were raped… and sodomised."

"Sodomised?" I say quietly.

"Yes… you know… anal sex."

"I know what it means, Andy. I'm not that stupid." I think about what he's said. "Before or after death?" I ask.

"Before," Todd replies.

I feel very cold all of a sudden, but my mind is racing. "I still don't see how that guarantees it's a man," I say.

Andy stares at me. "Want me to draw you a picture?" he says.

"No. But couldn't it be a woman, or more than one person, forcing the male partner in the couple to perform those acts on the female?"

"We thought of that," says Todd. "We did DNA tests on the semen. It didn't match the male partner... not in any of the cases."

I turn to him. "And nothing showed up on the DNA database?" I realise the ignorance of that statement just as the words are leaving my lips, but I can't stop myself from saying them in time.

"Do you think we'd all be sitting here if it had?" Andy says.

"Cut her some slack," Todd barks at him, then turns back to me. "No," he says calmly. "Nothing at all."

"And what does he do to the male partner?"

"Do you really want to know? Whatever happens, it won't affect you."

"Yes, I want to be fully aware of what I'm getting into."

"Okay. Show her the pictures," Todd says to Andy, leaning back in his seat.

Andy turns over a few pages, then pulls out some photographs and, without even glancing at them, hands them to me. I look down and it takes me a moment or two to realise what I'm seeing – or what I think I'm seeing – and then I can feel my stomach churning, the bile rising in my throat. I put my hand across my mouth.

"Sorry," I manage to say and I run from the room, bolt down the corridor and clatter through the door to the Ladies'. I just make it into a cubicle before I empty the meagre contents of my stomach.

My walk back to Andy's office is shaky, to say the least. When I get inside, Todd gets up and comes over to me.

"Sorry," he says.

"You did warn me." I look up at him. His eyes are filled with concern. "I'm fine," I tell him, lying through my teeth. I feel anything but fine, and I'd still be in the Ladies' if it wasn't for the fact that I know I've got nothing left to be sick with... I've been sitting on the floor of the toilet cubicle for the last ten minutes, retching.

"Come and sit back down," he says, stepping to one side.

I notice that the photographs have been put away again. I'm grateful for that. I've never seen so much blood, so much mutilation. I don't even want to think about it, let alone look at it again.

"Is this really the best idea you guys can come up with?" Todd asks, sitting down beside me. "Sending us in as bait?"

"It's not my idea," Andy replies. "Your captain agreed it with my boss. I've had very little say in the matter. But, on the whole, I do agree with them."

"I still don't see why I can't go into the club undercover on my own," Todd says.

"I've already explained. It'd take too long; it's too unreliable. Our man isn't looking for a single American barman, or waiter, or bouncer; he's looking for an American couple – clients of the club."

"Er... I'm not American," I manage to murmur.

"Todd is. Remember... I said only one of the victims in our case was American. The woman was British."

"But how do you know the killer's looking for an American at all? That could have just been random."

"We don't think so," says Todd, with some reluctance. "The members concerned had only just joined the London club the week before. There aren't many American members. It seems a bit contrived to single them out."

"I suppose so." I turn back to Andy. "Do I have a choice?" I ask.

"Yes. You can say no, if you want to."

"And what'll happen then?"

"We'll have to re-think things. I've got no-one else here who can do this, but I might be able to get another female officer from another station to come in and take your place. It'll take me a little while to find someone."

"And in the meantime, he could kill again?"

"It's a possibility."

I nod my head. "I just can't see how we're going to pull this off," I say, almost to myself.

"Why not?" Andy asks. "Todd knows the set-up of the clubs. He's got experience of working undercover. You'll really just have to turn up and watch; keep your eyes open and let him be heard and seen. Let him make himself obvious as an American."

"I understand that. What I mean is, won't the killer follow us at some point, check us out, and realise that Todd goes back to a hotel, and I go to my flat…"

I look at Andy. He's staring at me. "No," he replies. "You're going to have to act like a normal couple all the time. Well, at least when you're in public. Behind closed doors, you can do whatever you want… Todd won't be staying at a hotel, Holly. He'll be staying with you."

Oh, will he now? "Um—" I don't even get to start my sentence, let alone finish it.

"And how do you know that's convenient for Holly?" Todd interrupts, sitting forward in his chair again. "Does she have space for me? Does she have a husband, or boyfriend?" He turns to me. "Sorry," he says. "I'm talking about you like you're not here."

"Go right ahead," I say turning to Andy. "Have you considered that it might not be okay with me? Or are you just going to ride roughshod over my private life?"

"We both know you live alone now," he says, having the decency to look a little embarrassed. "And we also both know you've got a big enough flat."

"And what if Holly doesn't want me living at her place?" I like the fact that Todd's concerned about how I'll feel, although I doubt Andy's going to pay any attention.

"The budget won't stretch to renting you the kind of place that people who frequent this club would be living in," Andy says.

"And Holly's apartment fits the bill?" He turns to me. "Sorry, but I know what cops earn, at least back home. I can't imagine it's that different over here."

"Don't apologise," I say to him. "It's nice to have someone fighting my corner for a change." He keeps his eyes on mine for a moment, a furrow appearing on his brow, then turns back to Andy.

"Holly's place is just fine. When you get back there, you'll see what I mean," Andy says, smiling.

"Okay," Todd replies. "But what about if this guy decides to do his research and finds we're living in an apartment that belongs to a cop?"

"He won't," I say.

"He might," Todd argues. "He's thorough."

"No. You misunderstand. I mean he won't find that my flat is registered to me. According to the Land Registry, it belongs to my father's company. Unless he decides to really dig deep, he won't find out anything that way."

"See?" says Andy, with an annoyingly triumphant gleam in his eyes. "It's perfect."

to be continued...

Printed in Great Britain
by Amazon